II PY

Edward Evans

Book Guild Publishing
Sussex, England

First published in Great Britain in 2008 by
The Book Guild Ltd
Pavilion View
19 New Road
Brighton, BN1 1UF

Typesetting in Meridien by
SetSystems Ltd, Saffron Walden, Essex

Printed in Great Britain by
Good News Digital Books

A catalogue record for this book is
available from the British Library

ISBN 978 0 9565 1484 4

Chapter 1

As we sat in the grand hall of Grant & Bulldozer's, the auctioneers for the Drug Enforcement Agency, I wondered if we had made the right decision to come to America and bid for a car. A friend had telephoned me some eight days earlier to let me know that a Rolls-Royce Sedanca de Ville Continental was up for sale on March 15th. All my friends had known that this was the car of my dreams since childhood and now the opportunity was here.

It didn't take a genius to find out who the previous owner was; a quick look on the DEA website for the details of the car; and then a phone call to the Rolls-Royce Enthusiasts Club and back came the answer: John Maitland. He was a convicted drug dealer and suspected drug trafficker; his car had been confiscated as it had been used to conceal narcotics. Only a limited investigation showed he was a powerful and respected man, and a sixth sense told me he would not like the thought of someone else owning his car.

I should have known better than to persuade my wife, Francesca, and my youngest son, Henry, who was equally as enthusiastic about Rolls-Royce motor cars as I was, to accompany me to New York to try and buy the car. I now knew what Julius Caesar felt like, in Shakespeare's play of the same name, when the Soothsayer told him to beware of the 'Ides of March'. He ignored it to his peril and I, too, fell into the same trap. Everything seemed to be telling me not to bother.

We left the calm of our family business in the Brontë village of

Haworth (for those who are literary-minded) to take a flight to New York. It was delayed four hours; our luggage went missing for a short time and eventually followed us to our hotel.

At the airport, the taxi arrived, the driver alighting almost before the vehicle stopped, pushing into the next cab, with the obvious drama which followed.

'Where do you wanna go?' he asked.

'Waldorf=Astoria,' we all replied in unison, in a way that ensured he knew it was our first time.

'OK!' he replied and then tried to engage us in conversation. 'Is this the first time to New York?'

'Yes, first time to America,' I replied trying to sound enthusiastic.

'Is it business or pleasure?' he asked.

That's when Henry stepped in, with the full story of my life and dreams about the Rolls.

Fortunately we were now approaching Brooklyn Bridge, which put a stop to all conversation, as we could clearly see the skyscrapers of Manhattan, seeming like an impenetrable wall, protecting the island from invaders. It is only when you cross the bridge that they part to allow you in. Then you realize the wall is there to keep in the inhabitants; Manhattan is a madhouse and our taxi driver quickly became an integral part of it. He blasted his horn at every other motorist who changed lanes without signalling, even though he was doing the same.

It was becoming dark and the road now seemed to lead along a tunnel of madness and noise, then suddenly, or so it appeared, we were in Times Square. It was a sensational difference. The bright lights, with their huge hoardings advertising almost everything, dwarfed our Piccadilly Circus in London. It was that big we could only be in the United States.

'All first-timers like to see Times Square,' our driver proudly announced, before dropping us off at the Waldorf.

'Forty-five dollars,' our friendly driver demanded.

'What?' I demanded. 'I could have bought the cab for that!'

Francesca tugged on my sleeve to shut me up. I paid the driver, aggrieved at what I thought was an extortionate fare.

The following morning, Francesca – always the businesswoman – insisted we went to the view of the car early. 'Let's get the business over first, call at the auctioneers and find out what the format is and *then* relax.'

That's just what we did. We took another ride in a yellow cab, this time to Grant & Bulldozer's, the auctioneers in the north of Manhattan. We entered the building, introducing ourselves to the receptionist, a typical all-American blonde. The sort you see 'at the movies' and the sort which Henry could not stop ogling. The tight figure-clinging sweater may have had something to do with it. Mind you, anything blonde, with two legs and a short skirt seemed to attract Henry, apart from a Scotsman that is.

'Down, boy!' Francesca whispered, as she saw me taking a not-so-sly look.

The receptionist telephoned up to Dinsdale Grant, the proprietor, and explained we had come from England especially to bid for the old Roller. A second or two later, Dinsdale Grant came out to meet us. A salesman if ever there was one, full of himself, with a loud checked suit to match. He was a big man and, like many successful American businessmen, was somewhat overweight. He had obviously just finished his latest sales refresher course, because his smile was that big it was almost unnatural, but he had a lovely American accent and was obviously well educated.

'I've got some bad news for you. The DEA have just withdrawn the car from sale.' His smile had disappeared.

'What!' I exploded. We all looked devastated.

'Just kidding!' he said, his smile returning as he stretched out his hand.

'Do you want to give me bloody heart failure?' I replied. My hand went out to meet his and my heartbeat slowed to normal.

'By the way I'm Robert Conway and this is my wife, Francesca, and my youngest son, Henry. And don't do that to me again!' I joked.

'You need a coffee?' he said, nodding to the receptionist.

'I'd love a cup of tea, if that's possible,' I responded.

'I'd forgotten you English have to have your tea. Right then, how many for tea, three?'

'I'll have coffee,' Henry replied.

'Right, that's two for tea and one coffee please, Carole.'

Henry was pleased to get Carole's name; it saved him using his well-worn chat-up lines and opened the door for a new attempt in America.

Dinsdale took us into his office. What a sumptuous place! A library around the edges of the room, a desk and chair in beautiful wood and leather and two lovely leather chesterfields and chairs to match, which we were invited to sit on. The rest of the room was decorated with ornaments and pictures, all of which gave the impression of taste. Something his suit belied. Nothing in his office denoted what his business was, but as with most businesses in the USA it was totally computer-orientated; any information was at the touch of a button.

Carole brought the drinks, leaving with a big smile for Henry, knowing she had made a conquest. The cups of tea weren't bad and the coffee, we were informed by Henry, was the best he had ever had.

'You don't have to say that, she's left,' I said smiling. 'Mr Grant won't let you anywhere near.'

'Dinsdale, call me Dinsdale,' he responded. 'She has lots of boyfriends. Another one won't make much difference.

'You said your youngest son?' Dinsdale asked, not waiting for a response. 'How many other children have you?'

'We've got two others, a boy and a girl. Philip, the eldest, he's the family protector and yet he's the only person I know who would get a parking ticket on your freeway for driving too slow. He's so careful, but as hard as nails. He takes after his mother

4

here,' I said, squeezing Francesca's hand. 'This one's like a tigress defending her cubs when anyone comes within an ace of causing difficulties for the family. Philip has a wife and daughter.' Words which prompted Francesca to take out the usual family photographs.

'Victoria is the middle one, but she is the brains of the family. Studied at university and now runs the business; very well, I would add. It enables us to spend a little time away. She also is a tough cookie. You've met Henry; he loves cars as much as I do, but also he loves the ladies and they usually love him. Need I say more?'

We got down to business and discussed the various rules of the transaction. Should our bid be successful, we were to arrange immediate payment and remove the automobile within seven days following the auction; if not, one hundred dollars a day would be charged. He had no idea of what the estimated price would be because it depended on who turned up, which I suppose was obvious.

He was not allowed to discuss any of the car's history, or where it had come from. It was simply his job to sell it and get the best price for the 'American Tax Payer'. The sad part about it from our point of view was that there was a large buyer's premium. This really did get on my nerves; why should the auctioneer take money from the buyer, as well as the seller? It's immoral.

'I suppose you would like to see what you've travelled all this way to buy?' Dinsdale said with a grin.

'We sure would!' I said with a light-hearted attempt at American idiom. With that Dinsdale took us, via the foyer and Carole, to a large purpose-built hall or warehouse where there were dozens of cars and other vehicles waiting to be auctioned. He pointed, but I had already seen her. II PY. She was as beautiful as I had ever dreamed.

II PY stood out from all the other vehicles, not simply because she had pride of place at the auction, had been specially cleaned for the sale, and had several people already inspecting her, but because she was *big* – over seventeen feet long and over two tons of sheer engineering magnificence. The Rolls-Royce radiator, individually signed by the man who made it, looked spectacular, shining like a trophy.

We stood in silence for a few moments, which was only broken by Dinsdale.

'She's a beauty, isn't she?'

It didn't need an answer; she was indeed lovely.

Dinsdale continued: 'I'll leave you now. When you've seen enough, just come straight back in to my office, OK?'

'OK!' I replied, still looking in wonderment.

Henry's eyes, however, were already averted, distracted by the many other vehicles for sale, perhaps more to his taste – Ferraris, Porsches, a Ford Mustang, in mint condition and many other sports cars.

It was the last viewing day prior to the auction and we were just two of many there to check out and select our potential purchase. I walked over and joined a middle-aged couple who were admiring II PY.

'Good morning,' I said politely, trying to engage in conversation.

'Huhhhh. Morning,' the man replied, showing his reluctance to speak to me.

'Are you interested in the car?' I asked, more out of excitement on my part than in any real attempt to talk to them. He grunted again and both walked away.

'Ignorant bugger,' I whispered loudly to Francesca in the hope that they might have heard.

I walked over to the car and began taking a keen buyer's interest, quickly becoming engrossed in its refinements. I was interrupted when a well-dressed man in his thirties came up and joined me in my deliberations. We chatted in general terms for a few minutes before he finally cut to the chase.

'I see you're definitely interested in this car then?'

'Oh yes!' I replied somewhat proudly. 'I've come all the way from England to try and buy it.'

'It's sold,' he said firmly.

'No, no. I've already checked,' I replied, looking at him somewhat quizzically.

'Let me put it another way: it's not in your best interests to bid for it.'

He had put my back up. 'Are you threatening me? Because if you are, you have the wrong man. I've told you, I have come a long way and I won't be put off.'

'It wouldn't be in your interest to be here tomorrow,' he whispered.

'Henry!' I shouted. 'This bastard's threatening me.'

Henry immediately left his Ferrari and ran over to me, but not before the surprised young man had hurried out of the hall in the company of a tall thin man.

I explained to both Francesca and Henry what had happened, but strangely they were not in the least perturbed, assuring me that it was just the competition trying to get potential bidders out of the equation in order to get the car cheaper. It was yet another warning I chose to ignore.

We continued to look around and found there were only two other Rolls-Royces – a Silver Shadow and a Silver Spirit – and it was obvious from the look of some of the other vehicles that they were used for illegal purposes. Steel girders welded to the front and back, special panels and spaces made in doors and floors. There was obviously a lot of money to be made in the sale of drugs, if you didn't get caught. In fact, *all* the cars were on sale for the DEA . . . we began to wonder what II PY had done wrong.

We, or should I say I, spent the next half an hour sitting in the car, trying the gears, lifting the bonnet drooling over the engine, opening the boot box, generally having a good play, before returning to Dinsdale Grant's office. The car must have belonged to someone who had cared for it. It was immaculate. I was surprised to see it had California number plates. Here again, however, Dinsdale would not be drawn into the reasons why.

'I can see you enjoyed yourself,' Dinsdale bellowed as we entered.

'Yes, he's like a big soft kid,' Francesca said.

'I saw you coming and Carole is bringing another round of drinks,' he continued, as we sat down.

'Dinsdale, before we go, I feel I must tell you; a young man tried to intimidate me into not turning up tomorrow.'

'Oh don't worry, it happens all the time! We've got cameras all over the place. I'll report it to the police and give them a copy of the film.'

He made so little of it that I, too, ignored it and tried to put it out of my mind. However, that niggling feeling I had had from the beginning was still with me.

Dinsdale ordered a yellow cab for us and, after a quick 'See you tomorrow' from Henry to his new-found passion, we were on our way back to the Waldorf.

Henry had decided to explore New York on his own and arranged to meet us at the hotel in time for dinner. Francesca and I had the rest of the morning and all afternoon to do as we pleased, on our own. It was like a second honeymoon, even if it was only for a few hours.

I said earlier that we had never had any real ambitions to visit New York and I suppose that still goes, but you cannot take it away from the place, it does have a real exciting charm. We took a cab to Times Square and then walked everywhere. To Broadway, Wall Street, 5th Avenue, all the main shops, including Bloomingdale's, Macy's and Tiffany's, just to keep up appearances. We then had lunch in a lovely little restaurant near Central Park, followed by a trip to the top of the Empire State Building, before finally returning back to the Waldorf somewhat tired and bedraggled. We were hardly an example of the typical hotel clientele.

Henry had already returned and was waiting, anxious to tell us that we were eating out, as he had found a gorgeous restaurant with wonderful food. We knew there would be some other love in his life.

We had just an hour to freshen up and to be led by Henry to this wonderful abode. However, from the moment we entered you could see why. The proprietor's daughter, Lauren, was beautiful, tall and elegant, with a Mediterranean complexion and long thick dark hair. What's more, she was single and had taken a shine to Henry.

We had a splendid evening, the food was excellent and the proprietor, Josh, and his wife, Marianne, spent much of the evening talking to us. Of course, they had been told all about us and knew we were over to buy an old Rolls-Royce. We exchanged addresses, with the inevitable invitations to visit each other and having insisted that we would pay for our meal – business, after all, was business – we bade our farewells. Henry decided he was staying on; this one seemed to have captured his heart, at least until tomorrow.

March 15th had arrived. I had hardly slept a wink, or so it felt like. I got out of bed with butterflies in my stomach and we went down to breakfast. Henry was already there. The food looked sumptuous, but I couldn't face it. Francesca and Henry were tucking in.

'You might as well eat something, you've paid for it,' Francesca quipped. It was probably the most expensive plate of Kellogg's Cornflakes I had ever eaten.

An hour or so later, Martin, the doorman, ushered us out of the hotel. Francesca tipped him fifty cents, which he appeared to look at with some disdain, which caused Henry to shout out, 'She's the poor relation.' Much to our amusement but not his.

'Hello, I'm Joe,' our taxi driver said, introducing himself to start a conversation.

I don't think he really wanted to hear what we had to say, despite the numerous questions he asked about us. 'So you're from England?' he said, continuing in his strong New Yorker accent. How had he guessed? Was it my accent or was it because I was dressed top to bottom by Marks and Spencer. I went along with him.

'Yes, we are.'

'You're goin to the DEA sale, are you? What d'ya wanna get?'

'A Rolls-Royce,' I replied.

'Naa, too big and not so easy to drive. You wanna get a Cadillac turn on a dime,' he said proudly. We looked at each other, rolling our eyes to heaven.

He wasn't going to get the better of me, England or our Rolls-Royces.

'Oh! So you know about Rolls-Royce cars then?' I asked.

'Yeah, I used to drive one before I took the cab.'

I don't honestly know how he could have got into one, let alone drive one, as he filled the front of the taxi with his huge bulk. He must have weighed twenty stone.

'What sort was it?' I asked

'A cloud or something like that . . .'

'You're too young; they were built in the fifties . . .'

He interrupted me. 'My boss was an old wrinkly.'

Francesca gave me a nudge, as if to say 'don't argue with him'. But I finished by saying, 'No wonder it was heavy and clumsy to drive; it's a bloody antique compared with any modern-day car.'

Thank God we were near Grant & Bulldozer's and were able to change the topic of conversation.

We pulled into the parking area, the taxi spinning round to get out quickly.

'Thirty-five dollars!' Joe said.

'Come on!' Francesca said angrily. 'It was twenty dollars yesterday and that's all you're getting.'

He accepted the money with bad grace and left.

The car park was beginning to fill up quickly. There were the usual second-hand car dealers, and I don't know why, but they seemed to have the same air about them as their English counterparts. There were the little cliques, the odd tradesman looking for a bargain and then, of course, there was my type of potential buyer. You know the one, yes that's him, the one who deliberately keeps away from the object in order not to show too much interest, in the hope it will not attract too much competition.

There was considerable interest in II PY, with many people milling round her. Thank God the doors are locked, I thought. I don't want all and sundry getting in and out of my car. I must have been thinking aloud as Francesca whispered, 'It's not yours yet.'

I consoled myself by the thought that she was a beautiful car and of course people would like to see her. I was also comforted by the fact that many of those I had seen looking at her had drifted along to the glamour cars. Henry, too, had spent the time listening to the chat and admiring a couple of old Ferraris, which, he informed us on his return, were collector's items.

He had had the sense to pick up the sale list from the attendant. II PY was Lot 27 – not long to wait. It seemed like hours before Dinsdale Grant walked up the steps to his pulpit-like stage, joined by Carole, to the delight of the audience and Henry.

'Right, let's get the show on the road,' Dinsdale Grant said as he opened the proceedings. For the next few minutes he laid down the rules of the bidding and the sales and the procedures for removing the automobiles after the sale.

I didn't hear a word of what he said. My nerves had kicked in. I began to feel ice cold and yet seemed to be sweating at the same time.

'Come on, pull yourself together,' Francesca said, as she grabbed my arm and pulled me along. Henry, even, seemed a little concerned.

'Just nerves, it's the excitement. I'll be OK when the sale starts.'

With that, Dinsdale Grant's voice began to boom out over the speaker system. 'Lot 1: a 1999 Cherokee Jeep, many extras. Start me off, $3,000 . . .' And then he rattled up in hundreds to $6,500 at the fastest rate I had heard anyone speak.

' . . . Lot 14: a 2003 Cadillac convertible. Nothing more to say about this one. It's a perfect automobile. I'd have it myself, but I've already got one' he boomed, laughing at his own little joke, but at least he did raise a little titter in the hall.

'Halfway there,' Henry commented.

After Lot 20 Dinsdale stopped for a fifteen-minute break and all present trooped off to the café. We beat the rush and our usual two teas and a black coffee for Henry were very acceptable.

Diane, our waitress, was a short plump, dark-haired girl, with a hairstyle reminiscent of the sixties and in a way far too old for a youngster like her. She was wearing a short skirt, so short you could see the top of her legs – most unflattering.

She had a squeaky, high-pitched voice with a strong American accent and was intrigued we were from England.

'I've always wanted to go there. I just love your queen and we all loved Diana.' She leaned over the table. 'That's why I changed my name.' We looked up in amazement as she continued. 'My real name's Tracey, but I thought Diane was more, umm, well sophisticated.'

'Oh you are so right,' I said reassuringly.

'The sale restarts in two minutes,' the loudspeaker boomed and everyone immediately returned to the place from which they had come. Dinsdale returned to his rostrum.

'Lot 21 . . .' Dinsdale didn't bother to wait for everyone to settle before taking his bids, again at full throttle. Lot 26 . . . the next one was ours; we were all gripped with excitement. Francesca, normally the calm one, held my hand tightly and Henry just couldn't stop smiling. If we were supposed to be nonchalant, we had already failed miserably.

'Lot 27. Now this *is* something special,' Dinsdale said. 'It's a 1933 Rolls-Royce Phantom 11 Sedanca de Ville, Continental, with its all-important chassis number II PY. There's a lot of history with this one. It was the first car Rolls-Royce ever built in one month, especially for the 1933 Paris Motor Show number II PY. Now who's gonna start me off?' He asked, pausing for a moment. 'I have a table bid to start of $30,000.'

I had come to my senses. I whispered to Henry: 'Let me know who's bidding and where they are.'

'There's that rude bloke you spoke to yesterday. I heard them talking, I think they are English.'

'How on earth do you know that?' I asked.

'They were standing by that old Porsche when I went to have a look at it,' Henry replied.

Dinsdale was not rushing this one and at the moment no one else was bidding.

'Come on!' he encouraged, 'I'll take it in thousands.'

'Thirty-one!' I had thrown my hat in the ring, but as usual, when someone breaks the ice, several other bids followed. Henry pointed to two bidders at the front of the hall: one Mexican-looking businessman to the side of the crowd, and the other was the English couple.

I leaned over to Francesca and whispered. 'Look over there, just behind the Mexican man. It's him, the tall thin man, who went out with the young man yesterday. You remember, the one who threatened me.'

'Come on!' Dinsdale entreated.

Forty-four thousand dollars and the bidding had slowed. It was now between the other two as I had not yet made a second bid.

'Forty-five thousand,' Dinsdale shouted, as he acknowledged the couple's bid, which turned out to be their last.

'Forty-six thousand dollars.' It was now back with the Mexican.

'It's gonna be sold, forty-six once . . .' Dinsdale said, looking around.

I interrupted him with my second bid. 'Forty-seven thousand!' There was a little excitement around the room, as this was by far the highest price offered for any car sold so far. Then there was an uneasy silence. The Mexican was looking across at us. There was no sign of emotion on his face; he just looked at us coldly.

'It's with you at the moment,' Dinsdale said, pointing to me. He paused again. 'The bid is at forty-seven. I'll take it in five hundreds.'

He looked at the Mexican, who nodded. 'Forty-seven five.' He returned his attention to me.

'Fifty thousand,' I said confidently. It was well within our budget and I sensed the Mexican could be out of it, but no! Dinsdale turned to him and he again nodded another five hundred dollars.

I again paused for what seemed like minutes. There was total silence in the hall, waiting for our next move. We were playing cat and mouse, with Dinsdale Grant as the referee.

'Fifty-five thousand,' I said calmly. The Mexican looked across and once again stared coldly. This time he knew he was in difficulty. He asked for time to consult, which obviously annoyed Dinsdale. 'You know the score,' he boomed. 'Two minutes!'

The Mexican went out of the hall leaving the tall thin man just staring in our direction. It was unnerving and neither Francesca nor I could actually look at him. It was as though he was looking straight through us and it sent shivers down our spines. If it had not have been for the excitement of the occasion and the fact that the Mexican suddenly returned to the room, we may have well called it a day.

'Fifty-six,' the Mexican called.

'It's up to you again,' he said, looking at me.

'Sixty thousand.'

There was a hubbub in the hall and we felt we were close to winning. Francesca was squeezing my arm so much I thought the blood would stop flowing. Henry was standing fists clenched. His knuckles, I noticed, were white. 'It's with you at the moment,' Dinsdale commented. As if we didn't know.

Dinsdale turned to the Mexican, but he shook his head. 'It's ours!' I yelled, turning to Francesca, who was now quivering with excitement. The tall thin man was forgotten in a moment.

'Sixty thousand dollars once . . .' He paused. 'Twice . . .' He paused again and bang went the hammer. He then pointed to me. 'It's with you.'

There was clapping and a huge cheer in the hall and I think the biggest was made by Henry, who was whooping for joy. Francesca just kept kissing me and squeezing me. It really was a wonderful moment and even II PY seemed to have a smile on her face.

Dinsdale directed me to his table, in fact to Carole, to make the appropriate arrangements, whilst he carried on with Lot 28. But I didn't hear any more and even Henry had gone over to the car to remove the 'flying lady' before she was taken as bounty by souvenir hunters.

Francesca and I signed all the necessary papers and the confirmation for the finance to be transferred by telegraphic transfer. Carole confirmed that, subject to satisfactory payment, we could take the car that afternoon. What was more pleasing to me was that we were five thousand pounds under our budget and the car in its present condition was worth considerably more. The price, however, was not the most important criterion; I now had the car that I had always wanted.

Francesca and I walked over to Henry, who was giving a guided tour to a number of interested onlookers, several of whom came to shake my hand. Must be a custom in America, because in England no one would bother, but at least it added to the magic of the situation.

'That bloke, the one who wanted the car, won't stop staring at us, Dad,' Henry commented.

'Don't worry, he's obviously disappointed. Let's go and have a cup of tea and we can decide what we are going to do.' The same chubby little girl came to serve us.

'Back again!' she squealed.

'Yes,' I answered a little irritably. Of course we were back again, but I suppose she was just trying to be friendly. 'Henry here just loves your coffee.'

'I see you bought the Roller!'

'No!' I replied, 'I bought the old Rolls-Royce.' No enthusiast ever calls a Rolls-Royce a Roller.

'That's what I meant.' She sounded crestfallen, as if I was taking the mickey, which I was.

'What do you want?' she asked.

'Two teas, they were lovely last time,' I replied, trying to get back in her good books. 'Shall we get something to eat? The smell of it is making me feel hungry.'

We were interrupted by the couple from the auction, who as Henry had said were English.

'Well done, you have yourself a beautiful motor car,' the gentleman said in a most condescending manner. 'Here's my card.'

'Blessington-Smith,' I said, reading the name out loud.

'Yes and this is my wife,' he responded before asking in a somewhat supercilious way, 'I understand you're from England and that the car will be going over there shortly?'

'Yes to your first question and yes to your second,' I replied trying to be just as diffident.

'Well, when you get back give me a ring and I will make you an offer for the car you will not be able to refuse,' he continued in this regrettable manner.

Diane was becoming somewhat annoyed at Blessington-Smith's interruption. 'Shall I come back?'

'No,' Henry interrupted. 'I fancy some of Diane's cooking.' That did it, the bit of flattery by Henry and we were back in the good books.

'We'll order now. Mr Blessington-Smith is just leaving and he knows I am not even going to consider an offer. I've bought it for our pleasure and fortunately we don't need the money.' I hated saying that, as I had never been one to brag, but I thought he would take the hint and go. This was not to be the case as he continued, 'You haven't heard my offer yet.'

'No. Please, I don't want to be rude, but we are hungry and this young lady is waiting to take our order.'

At last he took the hint and made his goodbyes and a final, 'My number is on the card, give me a ring and at least find out what our offer will be.'

'I will. Thank you,' I replied as he turned and left.

'What an objectionable man,' Francesca said loudly.

We ordered the giant breakfast, mine with a small steak as I was now feeling very hungry. Henry had the same, but Francesca's was a little more conservative in her demands, insisting on smaller portions.

When they came, I didn't believe I could have eaten Francesca's let alone mine. They were enormous. You can really understand why some of their citizens are obese; you have to be big to eat this quantity. But it was a well cooked meal and nice trying to eat it.

We had been at the table for about ten minutes when we were joined by a very smart, casually dressed man, in a tweed jacket and cavalry twill trousers, late forties early fifties, tallish with dark but greying hair. From the feminine point of view one would say he was quite attractive. He introduced himself as David Mainwearing. His voice was soft and well educated, with just a hint of an American accent, much like Alistair Cooke's in *Letter from America*.

'Congratulations, you've bought a beautiful Rolls-Royce. I had a few bids, but they weren't too serious. I've got a 36, 20/25 in as good condition I like to think. Anyway, well done.' For those unfamiliar with the terminology, Mainwearing's car was a 1936, owner-driver model 20/25.

'Thank you,' I replied. 'Would you like to join us? There's one in the pot if you'd like a cup of tea. It's a very respectable cup!'

'Yes, I'd love to,' he replied and so started a friendship which continues today.

I signalled to Diane to bring another cup, but she brought a whole new pot for three. 'Do you mind?' I said, pointing to our meals as we continued eating our banquet.

'Not at all,' Mainwearing replied. 'I'll be mother.' He began to pour our cups of tea. 'Well, I suppose you'd like to know why I'm here and it's not just because I am a Rolls fanatic. There's a lot of recent history associated with this car and I wondered if you would like this bit of background.'

'Yes, of course,' we all said in unison.

'By the way,' I added, 'I'm Robert Conway. This is my wife, Francesca, and this is our son, Henry.' I held out my hand over the table. 'Call me Robert.'

Henry nodded towards another table. The Mexican-looking businessman had come into the café and was sitting a few tables away. He was giving a good impression of someone trying to hear what was going on.

I looked over casually, momentarily catching his eye and nodded to him, smiling, but he did not respond, returning his eyes to his coffee.

'Don't worry,' I whispered to the group. 'He lost the bid. But I think he'll probably come and make an offer, similar to that time at Nostell Priory.'

I went on to explain how several years before, we had purchased a 20/25 at a Christie's auction at Nostell Priory in Yorkshire. Shortly after buying the car, we were offered 25 per cent more from one of the other bidders. The car itself had been partially restored, by Frank Dale and Stepsons of London, a well-known Rolls-Royce dealer. It had a fascinating number plate: EGO 129.

'You're not going to believe it,' I said, 'but about six months after we had sold the car to another dealer, we had a telephone call from the Drug Enforcement Agency in California, wanting to know if I still owned the car and then about two weeks after that, we had another call, this time from the police, asking the same things. Quite fascinating . . . It was a lovely car. I always carry a photo of Francesca standing next to it.' I took my wallet out and showed him the picture.

'We were younger then,' Francesca interposed.

'You don't look any older now,' David said chivalrously.

'Flattery will get you everywhere!' she replied, all giggly.

'No it won't!' I said sharply, but in fun.

David was just about to start his little story about the car, when the Mexican came over to our table and very politely introduced himself, handing me his card. Federico Morales. He was a partner in a firm of lawyers: Lambton, Freeston and Morales of Los Angeles.

'I was bidding on behalf of a client,' he explained, 'and I have been instructed to make you an offer in excess of what you paid.'

'How much?' I asked

'Five thousand dollars.'

'What, you must be joking! It's cost us much more than that to come here. No, no thanks.'

'Ten thousand dollars.'

That upset me. 'Why on earth did you offer me a measly $5,000 when your client would have been prepared to pay double? No, I'm not interested, thank you.'

'This is my final offer: fifteen thousand dollars!'

'No,' I insisted. 'I would have paid a lot more than I did and I'm certainly not going to sell it now. Thank you for your very kind offer.'

'OK, but where can you be contacted, just in case my client wishes to increase his offer?' Morales continued.

Henry was just about to utter the words 'Waldorf=Astoria', when David chipped in.

'They are guests of the *New York Times*.'

There was an unreal situation for a few seconds, before I broke the silence,

'Look, I'm sorry, but really I'm not going to sell it at any price, so there's really no point in any further discussions, is there?'

'No,' he replied and thanked me for my time.

We were astonished at David's interjection. Why on earth would he have involved himself in our conversation and come out with something like that? We all felt a little embarrassed.

Morales left and was followed out by the tall thin man. I pointed him out to David. 'No matter where we are, that man is always in the background watching.'

David waited for Morales to go out of earshot. 'We seem to have a very odd situation here and at the moment I don't have all the answers. But I think if I fill you in with the background, you'll get a better picture . . .' He paused for a moment, as we had all stopped eating, 'Finish your meal, and I'll order some more drinks.'

We were filled with anticipation. What was coming next? All his little interruptions in his story were making our anxiety much worse. If you have ever felt like saying to someone 'Come on, get on with it', you will know what I mean. The drinks arrived and David began a most fascinating story. He started by telling us a little about himself, how he was a freelance journalist, working for many newspapers and magazines, but I think it would be better if you read what he said, in his own words, just as he told us.

Chapter 2

'I'll introduce myself properly. I have no secrets; you know my real name, it's David Mainwearing and I'm a freelance journalist. However, I do have many *noms de plume*, as the French so aptly put it. If I work for the *Boston Herald*, I use one, and for the *New York Times*, I have several. I mainly work for the *Times* these days.

'You appear to have prospered and, like you, I have been somewhat successful. Otherwise neither of us could entertain a passion for owning a Rolls-Royce. Where I have scored in the main is with my investigative journalism and that's where this story begins.

'I have been a member of the New York Rolls-Royce Enthusiasts Club and have been on many rallies and made many friends. One of them was John Maitland. He was a much-respected member of the club and once owned your Rolls-Royce. He was a property tycoon. He was also involved in Wall Street and was a director of many companies. He had everything going for him. He was good looking, very tall and well built, dark hair growing grey at the temples. Everyone wanted to know John Maitland. He was always on the invitation list for parties, and was always the proverbial life and soul.

'He was very generous and over the years gave away millions of dollars to charities, political parties, police retirement funds . . . His influence could be felt every where.

'His home was in Greenwich Village, a fashionable part of New York. The house itself was set in beautiful, well-maintained gardens and was approached by the main gate. It was impossible to enter without someone exiting from the car and speaking on an intercom, which was deliberately placed about 3 yards away and could not be approached without getting out of the car. There were security cameras all round the garden and all up the drive. When I asked about the need for all the security, he explained that a neighbour's daughter had been kidnapped a few years earlier and this was a precaution.

'This was confirmed by Amelia, his third wife. She was a lovely woman and very generous, not only with her money but her time. She, however, was also very wealthy in her own right, having inherited the Battenburg cake empire. She took obvious pride in telling us how her husband John had been very brave and had helped to get the daughter back. I had asked why it had not been reported and he simply said it was a condition set by the kidnappers.

'They also had several other properties, one of which was in California, hence the car having Californian plates. He even had a driver specially trained by Rolls-Royce to drive the car whenever it was taken out, but it was never driven on the road unless he was taking part in a rally, when it was always transported on a specially built trailer. He spent thousands on that car; the slightest scratch would necessitate a respray.

'I often used to think that Gerry Rider, his chauffeur, was also his bodyguard, because he was almost always there, not only to drive him around. Gerry lived with his wife, Aprilla, and had a flat in the grounds. She acted like a housekeeper, doing most, if not all, the work around the house for Amelia.

'Gerry and Aprilla had a wonderful relationship. It was obvious to everyone that he was madly in love with her and hated being apart from her. There are few people in this life you can call soul mates, but in this case you could.

'Aprilla was not an attractive woman. In fact, one would think she was quite plain, but the moment she smiled, real beauty was exposed; everything lit up. I often thought of telling her to smile more often, but that would not have done.

'When they were out they always hand in hand, hers in his, and gripped so tightly, as if to send a message out to the rest of the male population, "Stay away, she's mine." I'll always remember when we were first introduced. He proudly took her hand and gently held it out for me to take. It was extraordinary, especially when you consider the circumstances which we were to find out later.

'Anyway, as a result of our membership of the club, we became friends with John and Amelia and, quite honestly, that's why I feel bad about the whole situation . . . but I'll come on to that in a minute.

'My wife, Eleanor, and I had been invited many times to his house, as they had been invited to ours, but it was never in the same style or as pleasant. They lived in a different world to us. However, our wives had become good friends, although their interests did not run to drooling over old Rolls-Royce cars. I remember one occasion when we were at his home. Maitland was invited, as he had been on several previous occasions, to take part in a rally in Europe, which he naturally accepted. He loved to tour in Europe and this one seemed just what he wanted – about two weeks away in France, Belgium, Holland, a little of Germany and Switzerland.

' "Why don't you come, you would have a wonderful time," he said, emphasizing the wonderful.

' "What about your business? Can you afford to go away, just like that?" I asked. "Oh, I don't mean that financially!"

'He interrupted me. "I know what you mean. We – and that means you as well – are only a phone call away and at worst twenty-four hours away by 747. Nothing can go wrong in twenty-four hours, can it?"

' "I suppose not, but aren't you worried about the car breaking down? I would be." John then spent the next few minutes trying to persuade the pair of us to join him on the rally. He succeeded.

'It wasn't difficult for me to say yes. It was something deep down I had wanted to do and it gave me the chance to see some of the places I hadn't seen for many years.

'We made all the arrangements there and then. John made all the air-freight arrangements for the two cars and for our flight to Charles de Gaulle Airport, Paris. What was most embarrassing was that he would not accept a dime in payment, despite my strongest of representations. I would not have gone had I known this would happen. The cars would be arriving some six days later, again at Charles de Gaulle, and would be accompanied by his driver. I felt a real sponger, particularly when his wife did not come along.

'He was a well-known person over here and even on the aircraft he was fussed over by the cabin crew. However, from the moment we landed, he appeared to want anonymity, booking us, for example, into the Novotel at the airport. He wanted to be Mr Ordinary.

'The next day he did, however, take us into Paris to see the sights and sample the delights of French cuisine, and then he left us on our own for the four remaining days to enjoy Paris, while he had some business to tidy up. "I told you it could be done on the phone," he said jokingly.

'For Eleanor and I it was a wonderful few days. It was spring. The weather was beautiful, warming up enough so your overcoat was not necessary, but not hot enough to give you that stuffy tired feeling. The Champs-Élysées was wonderful; the new leaves on the plane trees gave freshness to the place. The street cafés were now full of customers, and the waiters, their white shirts and black trousers partially hidden by their white aprons, rushed around in that efficient way only the French can do.

'We found a beautiful little restaurant in one of the side streets, typical French, with a wonderful menu and cuisine, but I think the most enchanting thing about these four days were our after-dinner walks on the Left Bank of the Seine. The trees, as I've said, were coming into full leaf, and the lights of the evening made them seem even fresher and brighter as they were reflected in the waters of the river.

'On the last evening, we arrived back at our hotel about ten o'clock, to be greeted by John, who had obviously been waiting for us. "Did you have a good day?" he asked.

'"John, not only a good day, but we really have had a wonderful time. I can't thank you enough," I replied.

'"The real good time begins tomorrow. We pick the cars up at the airport about eleven and make our way to the Bois de Boulogne, where we are all meeting for lunch. We then drive to the Champs-Élysées, round place d'Étoile, and make our way north to Arras and tomorrow we sleep in Belgium."

'We had a few late-night drinks in the bar, which I was pleased to say was on my tab, and to John's disgust I had arranged to pay all the hotel accounts, regardless of what other arrangements had been made. Whilst I know John wanted to pay, I felt he was delighted I had made the effort and this cemented our friendship and trust a little more.

'A good night's sleep was had by all. Over breakfast, John arrived to tell us our lift to the airport would be arriving in about twenty minutes. He delighted in telling me he had been up since six and had been taking the air. It certainly was another lovely spring day.

'The lift arrived. It was a private taxi firm and I got the distinct impression the driver knew John, who seeing my surprise immediately put my curiosity to rest. "I always use the same company when I come to Paris," he said, "*C'est vrai, n'est-ce pas, Henri?*"

'"*Quoi?*" Henri responded. John then went on to explain in French what he had just said to me.

'"I never asked", John went on to say, "but do you speak French?"

'"Not very well and certainly not as good as you appear to," I replied. But in reality, I did speak excellent French. I don't why I said that, but I thought it better that way.

'We arrived at the cargo area in Charles de Gaulle, where Gerry was waiting with Aprilla and both cars. His Phantom, I mean yours, was simply magnificent; it gleamed as though it had just come out of the factory, putting my 20/25 to shame. The two cars in fairness did look special and had drawn a small crowd.

'"Come on," John commanded. "Load up, we've got a long way to go and I'd like to get there for lunch. *A bientôt, Henri.*" We then loaded our luggage and left Charles de Gaulle, Gerry leading the way. Oddly enough, John was sitting in the back and appeared to be working. I must admit he looked somewhat regal, but of course you always do in a Phantom.'

David had signalled to the waitress to bring some more drinks, which she duly did in her own inimitable style. 'Same again?' she said in her jaunty manner.

I was just too interested in David's story to be interrupted by something as unimportant as tea.

David continued: 'We travelled along the A1 for a few miles towards Paris before turning off to the right. It was a beautiful day and the two cars drew a lot of attention from pedestrians and the normally brusque and unchivalrous Paris traffic seemed to give way to the two beautiful ladies.

'We all arrived at the Bois de Boulogne, the start point of our rally. It was a wonderful setting for the thirty-seven cars that were taking part, a far cry from the late evenings when a different clientele take over the park. John seemed to know everyone and, of course, made the introductions. We had lunch and I must admit they were a very friendly bunch and we made some good new friends, but of course you will know all about that. The rally finally set off at about 13.30. The cars ranged from a modern-day Rolls-Royce to some early 40/50 open tourers and my 20/25. John's Phantom Sedanca de Ville, the undoubted queen of the parade, brought up the rear, with Gerry driving and his Aprilla beside him.

'We drove along the wonderful tree-lined avenue Foch, its magnificent houses befitting the cars that were passing their doors. The rich of Paris had opened their windows to see the procession slowly making its way to the place d'Étoile and the Arc de Triomphe and the Champs-Élysées.

'We turned into the Champs-Élysées and went down to the place de la Concorde, passing hundreds of visitors to the city, from day trippers, with their inevitable cameras, to businessmen and women anxious to get on with their day, but all stopped in amazement to see us pass slowly down to the bottom and then back up again to the Arc, with its tomb of the Unknown Soldier. Even here, where there is always an endless stream of visitors, they stopped to admire us.

'We went down the Champs-Élysées again for the last time, giving passers-by a second chance to see thirty-seven of the best cars ever made. Ironically, many motorists seemed to want to join in with the spirit of the procession, particularly the younger end. There must have been at least sixty cars in the line by the time we reached place de la Concorde. Even the manic traffic here stopped to allow us through and pass the Tuilleries in style. Then it was out of Paris to St-Denis and away. It was an exhilarating experience, one which I will never forget.'

'You've certainly made it sound fantastic,' I said, interrupting his flow. 'It's something I really would like to do.'

'Well you must. Needless to say your car got most of the attention,' David said, continuing his story.

'We left St-Denis and Paris, making our way to the beautiful Forest of Chantilly and its castle. Here, even the magnificent men in their fine cars had to give way to the horses of the Écurie de Chantilly. It was a wonderful sight. The pace quickened to a steady maximum of 40/50 mph as we approached Senlis with its cobbled streets a reminder of what it was like in the Middle Ages. Not even your car would survive that for long.

'We were now making excellent time. No one had had any difficulties passing through Compiègne, Beauvais, Amiens with its

27

beautiful cathedral, and on to Arras. We stopped for light refreshments and fuel and then made our way to Calais, where we were to stay the night. Every town and village had the same reaction. They were all pleased to see us and wanted us to stay a little, but we were well organized and it was important to arrive at around seven o'clock in time for us to have a freshen-up before dinner. It may be glamorous driving an old Rolls-Royce, but it certainly can be very tiring.

'We arrived in Calais and pulled into the car park near the railway station, at the rue du Rhin. The council had cordoned off a large section and actually arranged to have some security for the cars, although the organizers had taken care of that. The accommodation had been booked for us. We were at the Metropol Hotel, next to the car park; some others were in the Maurice. We were all responsible for getting our meal. We decided to go to the Fin Palais where there was a young but exciting chef. We sat next to John at the dinner table. "Where's Gerry and Aprilla?" I asked.

' "Oh, they hate mixing with members. Gerry prefers to make his own arrangements." The topic was never brought up again. He did, however, say he was having a few problems with the car at the moment. "It started just as we left Paris, a slight knocking. I don't know whether it's mechanical or not. I'll get Gerry to check it over later."

'It had been a wonderful day, one of the best we had ever enjoyed, and it was this friendship and ambience which gave me great concern later on. But I'll come to that later on.

'Eleanor and I had a walk round Calais with a couple of members and their wives, Anthony and Mrs Blessington-Smith (everyone called him Smithy) and another couple, Roger and Cynthia Partridge, We palled-up, as they put it, over the next few days.'

'Blessington-Smith?' I asked.

'Yes. Why?' David responded.

'I've just met a Blessington Smith. He's given me his card,' I answered showing my annoyance. 'He says he is going to make me an offer I can't refuse. We found him pompous and thoroughly objectionable.'

'I am sure it will be the same man, but I didn't get to know him that well.'

David continued his story. 'The following day we took the route out of France, via Dunkirk, crossing into Belgium at the border village of De Panne, a smugglers' paradise, I was told, as all you English go there for cheap cigarettes. Anyway, I remember it being full of English cars and every shop selling some form of tobacco. From there we drove along the canal towards a town called Verne, with John bringing up the rear and me second from the back.

'It's very strange, but when you are in procession, you tend not to look what's happening behind; you're concentrating on the car in front and the countryside where you are going. However, as we approached a steep corner I happened to look in my mirror and John wasn't there.

'It was impossible for me to stop and in fairness I thought he had perhaps just been held up. We made our way towards Brugge, stopping at a large café for lunch, but there was no sign of John and I was beginning to feel concerned enough to telephone him.

'"John, where are you? We are all worried."

'"Don't be. That little problem I told you about yesterday, well it's happened; I can't move."

'"I'll come and meet you, see if I can help."'

'"No, he said don't worry, David. Gerry is useful in these situations. He's called the breakdown truck and he is taking the car to a specialist. You enjoy the rest of your break. I'm going back to the States," he replied.

'We were devastated. Our "host" had paid for our rally but was now going home almost at the beginning. Fortunately, we'd been befriended by an English couple, the Blessington-Smiths, so at least we had some company.

'I spoke to Smithy, you remember, Blessington Smith; he was a regular traveller on these rallies. I told him John had broken down. He told me he already knew and that he was going to see if he could help him. I asked him what the problem was and he simply said it was a recurring problem and didn't elucidate further.

'"What a pity, it's a beautiful car, he's spent such a lot on the body. He'll have to start on the engine," I said naively. I had heard it was the second time it had happened in the last six months.

'I turned to Eleanor and said, "We're on our own now; come on, let's make the most of it."

'The rest of the rally is unimportant, save to say that we had a wonderful two weeks and visited Brussels, Strasbourg, Berne in Switzerland, finishing back in Le Touquet in France. All the arrangements had been made to ship the car back and all I had do was to take the car once again to Charles de Gaulle and leave the rest to the agent. To our surprise, however, John's automobile was also waiting to be shipped. It was actually being driven to a marked bay. Again, I didn't think much about it. After a further night at the Novotel, we returned back to the States the following day.

'On our return, I immediately contacted John to say we were back and to thank him for the wonderful time we'd had and to tell him we had seen his car at the airport. It was also an excuse to invite him and his wife to dinner, as a thank-you.

'"Excellent," he replied. "We would love to come, but thanks are not necessary. I'm glad the car is ready; I miss the old girl."

'We had a few local outings and several evenings out over the next few weeks and our two wives became friendlier than ever. It was all very pleasant.

'In June, John again asked us if we would like to go on another European rally, this time, however, only to France and mainly in the South. This was too good to miss. I can remember visiting Cannes for the film festival and I even covered the Grand Prix at Monte Carlo when I was a young journalist. I had always wanted to return.

' "Yes, we would love to come but this time I'm paying," I said.

' "Of course, who's going to quarrel with that?" he replied, delighted we were going. "Let me do the bookings, it's far easier." I looked at him quizzically, but he continued: "All right, you can pay. I'll give you the bill when I know how much it is."

'That was settled, and all that was left to do was to make the appropriate arrangements to take the car to Kennedy and on to Nice.

'We arrived two days before the cars and all we had to do was pick them up. And Gerry of course. The four of us were staying at the Atlantic Hotel in Nice, which is about 400 yards from the front. To my astonishment, John again gave the impression that he didn't want to draw too much attention to himself. It was a beautiful hotel inside, and whilst the parking left a little to be desired, it was at least under surveillance.

'The next day, the four of us spent a pleasant few hours shopping in Nice. This was followed by lunch and a walk from top to bottom of the promenade des Anglais, one of the most beautiful walks you can imagine. It is flat for about two miles. On one side is sea; on the other you have the tall, well-kept, French-style buildings. The walk was interrupted by the occasional drink at one or two of the beach cafés.

'Back at the hotel, we sat down in the restaurant at about seven-thirty and were enjoying the ambience and the company, when John was called out on business. He met two men in the foyer. One was a well-dressed ordinary fellow and the other, a thickset man in his late twenties, trying to look like a gangster by wearing dark glasses. I could see most of what was going on through the mirror on the wall. I was absolutely intrigued but tried not to be interested for the sake of the remaining diners.

'John appeared to be laying down the law to the two men and the older of the two seemed more than a little worried. He was without doubt being threatened. Gerry arrived on the scene and was introduced by John to the others. He first shook the hand of the older man and then that of the younger. This time, however,

31

Gerry did not let go his grip, until he had inflicted a little pain. It was possibly to show the youngster he was a little out of his depth. I now realized for certain that Gerry was John's bodyguard.

'The rally was to begin at St-Tropez at 1400 hours on the car park at the port. The following day we began to make our way there; only this time, John didn't even make it to the start. He broke down outside Nice, heading toward Cannes. Gerry called for assistance. We suggested Amelia come with us, but she said she would stay with John and look around. We were once again on our own. For the first time I had real doubts about my good friend John Maitland.

'The rally was the best I had ever attended and I'm sure you could imagine the welcome sixty wonderful Rolls-Royces received everywhere they went. The scenery we saw – from St-Tropez to Toulon, Sanary-sur-Mer, Six-Fours, Marseille and Aix-en-Provence, then over the Alps to Grenoble, Gap, Sisteron, Corps and Grasse down into Cannes and finally Nice – was sensational. I quite quickly forgot my suspicions until we arrived back at Nice and the Atlantic. I again saw the two men I had seen previously, but this time everyone was friendly, shaking hands like long-lost brothers. John saw me looking

' "I had given them a warning that if the Rolls wasn't up to scratch they would be in trouble and fortunately it is," he said, trying to reassure me.

'But from now on, he couldn't. Whether it was my journalistic training or morbid curiosity, I wanted to find out more about my friend.

'We left for home the following day and, to my sheer annoyance, John had already paid the bill. I was furious, particularly as I had made a conscious decision to look into his affairs.

'On our return, whether or not it was to reassure me further, he asked me to take him to his garage to have the Phantom checked over and here he made his first unintentional mistake. I followed him to downtown New York, where he called at his garage. It was a normal run-of-the-mill place, double-fronted, almost triple, with a large showroom. There was a window to the left, with a few well-known make of cars on display, all second-hand.

'I did, however see a Ford GT, a beautiful automobile, way ahead of its time. To the right there were two Roller Shutter doors, which were more reinforced than usual, perhaps because of the quality of the cars they had for sale, or in for repair. Once the shutters were open, you could see all the way down to the rear of the building, which was quite extensive. They had some wonderful equipment installed and could carry out all forms of repairs, even down to complete body repairs and painting. What was so unusual was how clean the place was. You could eat your lunch off the floor and everything had its place. It seemed harmless enough, but really the area was not the sort of place a well-connected city gent, as you would put it, would go to, albeit with Gerry. I stopped outside and waited for John and Gerry to return as they had driven in.

' "I won't be a minute," John shouted across, "but this really is the best Rolls-Royce mechanic in the whole of the USA."

'They began having a conversation with the boss, when a large white Dodge Rough Track, complete with dark glass, pulled up at the entrance, three somewhat villainous-looking men got out and walked over to them. Gerry seemed to step forward and the three retreated backwards. No doubt about it, John was embarrassed and very angry. I couldn't make out any conversation, but I think I judged the situation correctly.

'They returned to my car and I in turn drove John back to his office, leaving Gerry at the garage. He spent the whole time saying how annoyed he was at those three idiots trying to push in. There an old saying in England, you know "He that protests too much . . ." but I'm sure you know it as well as me.

'I was now very suspicious that "something was rotten in the state of Denmark" to quote Shakespeare and I decided to discuss matters with my editor of the *New York Times*, Jason Sweeney. He had been one of my best friends for years. No interest in cars, but a real good friend to whom I could trust my life and vise versa. We decided that it could be very hot news, but all articles, if any, were to be written under an alias and all contact would go through Jason. In view of my friendship with Maitland, this action was essential.

'My first job was to trace the number plate of that car, the Dodge I had seen at the garage. This was not difficult as it belonged to Isis Imports. However, what was strange was that I found out it was a Cayman Island–registered company, with its directors registered as living in Bermuda. Just for completeness, I ran a check on the garage. To my utter astonishment, this too was registered to the same business.

'It was too much of a coincidence. There was, however, another interesting feature of the Isis company's New York operation. It was the owner of a large waterfront warehouse. Jason and I discussed our options and he decided to send Ed Fisher, an experienced reporter, to Bermuda to check out the directors.

'Ed left on the Monday. On Tuesday he telephoned to say he had found one of the directors, a Winston Gabriel, who turned out to be a very simple soul, who lived a simple life and received a wage of £100 sterling every month – his director's salary. He knew nothing about the company's activities. He had also shown him a series of pre-valued and pre-signed cheques, which he posted at a pre-arranged date every month to various addresses. He met someone every few months, but he couldn't give me any names because it was always someone different. He had no idea when the next visit would be.

'On Thursday, Ed's half-eaten body was washed up on a beach. It would appear he was thrown into the sea, to be eaten by sharks, but a storm had washed his body ashore before they finished the job.

'This was the second mistake. Had they done the job properly, it would have taken many weeks to find out what had happened. Instead we knew immediately he had been murdered, and in spite of explanations that he had been drunk and possibly fallen off a boat, we all knew he was too much of a professional to mix business with pleasure when on an assignment.

'There was nothing at this moment in time to connect John with any of this, regardless of personal misgivings. It was, however, extremely difficult to continue our personal friendship.

'The death of Ed Fisher cast a nasty shadow over the *New York Times* and my next meeting with Jason Sweeney confirmed they had made a big mistake killing him. They had now taken on the press and, in particular, the *New York Times*.

' "We'll get the bastards," Sweeney said, opening the conversation. "Let's shake the tree a little." He didn't mince his words: the following day's front-page headline was "Ed Fisher murdered investigating Isis Imports". There was a little about Isis, but it was mostly about Ed, what a first-rate man he was, excellent reporter, you know the sort of thing. But what was important was the fact that the television stations took up the story and Ed became a posthumous hero and Isis was in the public eye. The story could only run a couple of days because at the moment there was no more news.

'I think the story would have died had they not at this point made their third mistake. The headline had certainly shaken the tree because Sweeney received a telephone call and a subsequent visit from a Captain Frank Bellano, of the NYPD, the New York police. I just happened to be in the office when he arrived.

'Frank Bellano introduced himself as though he was a long-lost friend. "I've gotta ask ya a favour," he said with a gratingly strong New York accent. "I'll come straight to the point: this Isis business is causing us some problems."

' "What's that?" Jason asked

' "I'm coming to it. Look I'm hoping that this press talk is not going to wreck weeks of work. We've been looking into this Isis bunch and now it could be all go down the pan. We want you to lay off. Let it cool off for a while and we can pick up the pieces again and I promise you personally, when the story breaks, I will give you the first opportunity. OK?" he said, believing that was the end of that.

'Jason Sweeney didn't take kindly to being told to lay off, not even by a police captain, and responded accordingly. "I am not going to lay off," he shouted out, drawing the attention of all the staff in the main office. "When one of my staff who I send to Bermuda gets murdered, I will not lay off," he shouted again.

' "We don't know he's been murdered. We're still looking into it, but you've got to realize it will take time; it's in British jurisdiction," Bellano stuttered somewhat nervously.

'Jason continued bawling at Bellano: "You don't know it's murder! We do, and we're not going to let it go, not for a minute. Is that clear?" Bellano was taken aback and made the fourth mistake, by warning Sweeney to let go.

' "Now I've been reasonable and asked properly and now I'm telling ya. You will lay off or you'll have the entire Police Department and the Mayor on your back. Do ya get my drift?"

' "Watch this space . . ." Jason said, pausing. "Do ya get *my* drift"? End of conversation.

' "Lucy!" he shouted. "Show the officer the way out."

'Sweeney was never one to be bullied, so you can imagine the headline the next day: "Ed Fisher Murder: Police try to stop investigation. What's going on?" Sweeney had detailed his meeting with Bellano and had reiterated his eulogy of Ed Fisher and that was that.

'The story was continuing to run, with nothing concrete to write about and yet it was gaining a momentum of its own volition. One thing I have learned during my time as a journalist and in fact simply with my age and life experience is that when there is wrong-doing in the air and the sands of time begin to run out, people start making mistakes. They are so frightened of the consequences, they do not stop to think of the realities and how they can use the situation to fit their own circumstances. Desperate men do desperate things, or so the old saying goes.

'Sweeney was not going to lie down. In fact, he put Anne Peters and Walter Tynburg, two good solid reporters, on the case, with the instructions they must work together. Their first job was to see what was going on at the warehouse. What ships were docking, what was on the ship manifests and any matters of interest. They were diligent in their work and reported there was nothing untoward. However, they noted on certain days there was different activity, which to them was puzzling. For example, when unloading cargoes, particularly those from the Caribbean, they found there were always extra men involved. Also there was always two or three "hoods", which is the best way of putting it, standing around, as if on guard.

'The investigation now had a life of its own. Sweeney had been called into the office of the proprietors, Winston New Incorp., and was asked what the hell was going on. He had had a call from the Mayor's Office, too, decrying our vendetta against the New York police and asking for explanations. Sweeney, as only Sweeney would, pulled no punches, telling them it was only the beginning and that, in the near future, someone at the top was going to take a fall. He hadn't any clue of what were the real stakes at this time, only my hunches.

'Other media became interested, the *Herald*, *Washington Post*, all were sniffing around and like us couldn't find anything concrete. However, as I said, desperate men do desperate things and that is why John made his big mistake.

'One lovely sunny Sunday afternoon, the club held a rally in and around Central Park. It was a gentle affair, with all the automobiles looking very good, particularly yours. I'm getting used to saying that. It was, without doubt, the belle of the ball. Before we started, I could not help but to congratulate him on it.

'"That's the most wonderful Rolls-Royce I've ever seen," I said, sincere admiration in my voice.

'"Thanks, I must admit I'm a little proud of her today; it's a joy to be in it when it looks so good. But of course it's down to Gerry; he's done all the work," John said in reply. "Look, David," he continued, "I've wanted a word with you. Would you like to come over to the house later? Let's have a drink. Bring Eleanor, we'll make an evening of it."

' "That would be lovely," I replied. Somehow I wanted to refuse, but morbid curiosity drove me there.

' "OK, about eight, see you then."

'The rally was wonderful, but I felt like the poor relation. I hadn't had a chance to do the work on my Rolls, but I suppose it didn't really matter as they are always very friendly occasions and no one made any comment about its condition. I suppose I didn't care too much as I was wondering what John wanted to talk about.

'I picked up Eleanor and went to John's house, arriving on time. To my surprise, the gate was open. However, Gerry was en route to ensure no other stranger passed through those gates uninvited. They were soon closed after we had passed and the first time Eleanor made some comment about the security. "You would think he had something to hide." My pretence of laughter didn't go down very well with her.

'The evening was still very pleasant. John and Amelia met us and for the first part we sat on the terrace and drank a little champagne.

' "I can't fall out with them," he said, meaning the French, "regardless of what our government want us to do."

'The "little Champagne" turned out to be three lovely bottles of Jacquart. "They are not the most expensive, but it's our favourite," John said, turning to Amelia.

' "Yes and I have them brought in specially," she responded. "It's one of the few things I do well."

' "Darling, you do many things well, and I would miss you if you weren't here."

' "Oh how lovely!" Amelia said fondly.

'It was the first time we had seen any affection from John toward Amelia during the months we had been friends. But call it sixth sense, I detected from his voice and demeanour that he was worried about loosing it.

' "David and I are just going to the garage. I want to show him the car. We'll be back in a minute or two."

' "You and your car!" Amelia replied. "Don't bore David to death."

' "How could he, with a car like that?" I said.

' "Well, I thought he loved that big old automobile more than he loved me, but now I'm not so sure. Go on, don't be long; the food will be ready soon."

'John and I took a slow walk around the garden towards the garage, and it seemed he had changed his mind because nothing was said or intimated that he wanted a word with me.

'I could not hold out any longer and simply asked. "John, you said you wanted a word with me. Is it important?"

' "I've been trying to find the words and the courage to ask you to do a favour for me."

'I was more than surprised, perhaps a little flabbergasted, that he could ask a favour from me, especially when *he* was the one with all the contacts. That is, until he asked the question and I knew why it was me.

' "David . . ." He paused for a moment. "I find myself in an embarrassing situation. You're a journalist and you will have read in the news about the Isis company . . ." He stopped, wondering what to say next and then the bombshell came as he continued: "One of my associated companies has dealings with Isis."

'I've said that this was his biggest mistake because, in spite of all our suspicions, we had not found any evidence of any link back to John Maitland and here it was out of his own mouth.

' "I know you have worked with the *New York Times*. Would you find out what they've got and let me know. I don't want to face any difficult situations without being forewarned," he said somewhat dejectedly. ". . . And anyway I don't want to create problems for Amelia."

'I felt an absolute dirty turncoat. My friend was asking for help in a situation which I had created.

' "Of course, I'll do that for you. In fact, I'll go see Jason Sweeney tomorrow; I've known him for years," I replied, trying to be nonchalant, but knowing deep down this request had made John the architect of his own downfall.

'The following day I met with Sweeney and told him of what was now my embarrassing problem and that I wished I hadn't started it.

' "What?" Jason bawled, with his usual editor's hat on, kicking the door to, as he went through it, so that the office wouldn't hear his next outburst. "I thought better of you!" he said, deliberately pausing. ". . . You just think about what you've just said!" He paused and allowed his anger to subside a little, as he remembered he was talking to his friend.

'He continued: "Here's a man and forget the friend bit . . . here's a man we believe is heading up a multi-million-dollar criminal empire, one that's quite obviously involved in drugs and prepared to murder to protect it. David! David! My friend," he sighed.

'Sweeney was becoming excited, raising his voice a little. "David, we must bring him down. How many more kids need to die before we realize all drug dealers are evil. How many more will be murdered like Ed before you realize you need to help to bring him down. Forget him! If he's involved he's scum and not worth your friendship."

'We talked for a couple of hours, planning what the best way forward would be. I had decided that Sweeney was right. I was going all the way. We thought it better not to give him all the information we had and I would not mention the warehouse, or for that matter the garage. But I would confirm that we had the proof that Ed was murdered and that Maitland's name was mentioned. I wasn't to divulge the sources at the moment, although I would say I believed it was held on Sweeney's computer in his office.'

' "We'll see where the hare runs!" Sweeney said with delighted glee. "David, I'm glad you are back in the real world."

'I turned and left his office, with these words ringing in my ears.

'I thought it better to wait a few days before seeing John again. I did not want to appear too anxious, but he was the anxious one. It was only a couple of days later that he telephoned me to see if I had seen Sweeney, and as I confirmed I had, we met for lunch.

'John was already waiting for me as I walked into the restaurant.

' "Hi, David," he said, attracting my attention. "Come and join me. I've ordered a bottle of Valpolicello, as we're dining Italian."

'I could sense his unease. His brightness and *joie de vivre* was just a little over the top for him.

'It was a lovely little restaurant, typical of those you find in the area. It had a bar on the left, where you enter and the dining tables were all facing the bar area but set back on the right. Nicely decorated and very clean, but a little bit dark. Perhaps it was why we met there; it was very discreet.

'Gina was our charming waitress, the proprietor's daughter, and surprise, surprise she knew John very well, as he often dined there, which he cleverly confirmed. I was becoming very suspicious and now I was looking for the worst interpretation of everything he did.

' "This is a lovely place," I said breaking the ice. "You've been here before?" It was really a rhetorical question as I already knew the answer.

' "Many times!" he answered breezily. "The food's good and I can meet clients in peace."

' "I'll come to the point. I saw Sweeney on Tuesday and had a long chat about the Isis situation and I think if it hadn't been for Ed Fisher's murder, it would have gone away."

' "Was it murder?" John asked.

' "Oh yes! Sweeney has proof and, as a result, they've looked deeper into the financial aspects of everything and anything

associated with it and your name was unfortunately mentioned,"
I said, trying to sound a little embarrassed.

' "In what connection?"

' "Sweeney wouldn't tell me because he knows I'm friendly
with you, but I know he has something. He won't even tell me
his source and it looks like there's going to be a lot of trouble for
the NYPD and a police captain named Bellano. I think that was
his name. Apparently he tried to throw his weight around in
Sweeney's office, threatening what he would do if they didn't
stop the investigation. He had told Sweeney that they were
already investigating Isis, which was not true. Now he's going to
be suspended pending an investigation into corruption.

'I paused. I could see he was uncomfortable, but I pressed on
trying to make a little sound like a lot. "Sweeney keeps all his
information on his PC. I'll try and have a look the next time. I
often use it when I'm in that office, especially when he's not
there. He won't mind, I'm sure." I said, trying to be casual.

'I enjoyed the rest of the lunch, but John was not himself and,
in fact, this lunch was the last time I saw him socially and you
will hear why.

'The following weekend there was a vicious robbery at the *New
York Times* offices. The weekend staff were attacked by eight
armed men, all wearing ski masks. The receptionists and janitor
were seriously injured and the duty news team were subjected to
a terrifying five to ten minutes before all the PCs were taken from
the editorial office.

'For this reason and this reason alone, John and I never met
socially again. I knew and he knew that I would know who was
behind it. I did not need to put two and two together to make
five. He was a vicious criminal who would stop at nothing.

'He no longer attended the club meetings and we missed his
lovely car. Although we personally did not meet, our wives
continued to see each other, which made things very difficult,
particularly when questions were asked by Eleanor.

' "Have you two fallen out?" she would say quite often.

'"No not at all. He's very busy at the moment; we haven't even seen him at the club."

'Sweeney was relentless in his pursuit of Isis and after the robbery he headlined with: "What are they afraid of?" The story was basically about Isis trying to prevent investigation into illegal activities.

'"Let them get an injunction if they dare!" Sweeney yelled down the office.

'The NYPD started to take matters more seriously and as Captain Bellano could not give a satisfactory answer about his actions at the *Times*, he was suspended ... with tragic consequences.'

Chapter 3

'The *Times'* next headline was "New York cop murdered". Bellano had been beaten up and then shot. His body was dumped in a bin. It was obvious to Sweeney and me that this was done to shut him up. I am sure that they had hoped it had closed another avenue of enquiry, but in fact it had the opposite effect because it put the media spotlight well and truly on Isis and proved to everyone that something was wrong and that it should be investigated.

'Sweeney called Janice Fink of the Drug Enforcement Agency. She was the head of the outfit in the New York area. She was a fearless woman, small and dark-haired, whose name belied her strength and tenacity. She hated all drug pushers and users, spending her every minute bringing them to justice. The reason for this crusade was that her son was knocked down by a dealer under the influence.

'Sweeney had been a friend for many years and in some way had helped her in her career. Not that she didn't deserve promotion in her own right; she did. He told her of our suspicions, holding nothing back, including the name of John Maitland.

'Sweeney knew he could not compete with the DEA. They had enormous resources to search Maitland's personal accounts and those of his businesses, looking for the alleged dealings he had admitted to with Isis. However, they found no formal contact between Isis and Maitland's businesses, with the exception of one matter. They found he had an enormous bill from the garage for repairs, but this was really superficial contact and did not signify any misdemeanour.

'These days, with all the powers held by the revenue departments and international cooperation between banks and governments with regard to money laundering, the criminal does have to be, or have the facilities of, a financial whiz kid. Without doubt Maitland had that facility. What was also noticed was that, over the last few weeks, he had been gently moving some of his money to other banks and other countries, namely the Cayman Islands. The media publicity and the pushing from the DEA had forced the Internal Revenue to take action, putting a stop on all transactions from Maitland's known companies.

'He was now in a dilemma. He could go to court and fight for the release of the monies, or he could sit back and do nothing to keep things quiet. In fact, he chose a very clever route: he offered to help "clear his name" and threw his books open to them. Of course, no one gives up any information that they don't want to be found and it gave him valuable time to sort matters out.

'The IRS found that some small insignificant amounts of money had disappeared from some foreign accounts, but they could not at that moment trace any that had been transferred from the Caymans. The USA does not have any control in that area, which made matters doubly difficult for the Revenue. They had many questions to resolve, all of which, of course, gave Maitland more time, but the net was drawing in.

'He knew that although he had successfully hidden much of the money, he hadn't sufficient liquid funds available to keep his organization going. He couldn't go to banks and he knew he was being watched 24/7 by the various agencies. He needed ready cash to protect himself and the only way he could achieve that was to deal hands on, with the next delivery of drugs.

'In the meantime, Anne Peters and Walt Tynburg were continuing their investigations on the wharf and, as I told you, every now and then a shipment arrived, the unloading of which would be watched over by security guards, to give them a title. Sweeney had given them instructions to stick around when the next one came in and try to keep tabs on where all the characters went to, in particular the guards. It was, however, impossible to predict when the next shipment would arise, so it meant Anne and Walt were hanging around. Janice Fink of the DEA was in many ways trying to support Sweeney, but as the evidence against Maitland was somewhat tenuous she could not put her full resources behind him, so it was left to Sweeney to do the dirty work.

'Anne and Walt were parked some distance away and were using long-range lenses, trying to be as discreet as possible. They didn't take much notice of the giant forklift truck which came trundling along the road or when it passed them turning right between two warehouses. It disappeared for a few moments and then came trundling back toward them, signalling left. Again nothing suspicious. But suddenly it turned toward their car and began hoisting them into the air and then, in one movement, dropped them into the river.

'They were very, very lucky. The automobile floated for some distance. They had tried to attract anyone's and everyone's attention without success, but eventually some thirty minutes later the car wedged itself on the opposite bank and they were eventually rescued by passers-by. The forklift was dumped in the river and the driver never found. You can imagine Walt's favourite expression from that moment on, "Never buy a boat, buy a Toyota Corolla", and swore he would only buy Japanese cars.

'It was wonderful that their lives were saved, but what was equally wonderful was that it gave the *New York Times* yet another wonderful headline: "Attempted Murder". The article below then went on to talk about the way it was done and the possible motives. As I said, the story had a life of its own.

'We were not aware that the NYPD were carrying out an undercover operation in the same area. But we found out that yet another internal investigation was put in action because the cops were somehow pulled off, just before the attempt on Anne's and Walt's lives took place.

'Walt volunteered to go back to the warehouse and continue his investigation. However, Sweeney, now fully informed by the police, was told that the NYPD were also continuing their operations. In doing this, they might just as well have held a flag up to say they were there. Someone had tipped them off and their activities were strictly legitimate. Walt, however, had noticed the usual automobiles and several of the same faces carrying out various activities further up the river.

'Sweeney had agreed that Walt should investigate this, but at the same time decided not to inform the NYPD at this stage because they were leaking like a colander with every move. Walt therefore decided to concentrate on one of the cars in the hope that it would open up another opportunity.

'The one thing I have learned in the newspaper business is that drug dealers do not give up until they are caught and that there are always dozens ready to take their place. They try to think one step ahead because they cannot stop the drugs from coming in. They have regular customers and if the supply chain is broken, their customers quickly go somewhere else. It's obvious when you think about it: the drug trade is driven by a dreadful need and that need is immediate.

'The NYPD decided to raid the warehouse when the next shipment arrived. It was a massive operation and they had invited members of the press to be there, including the *Times*. We knew it would be a fruitless operation and the smiling faces of the dockyard and warehousemen said it all.

'It was a very foggy day. The normal sounds of the docks were dulled by this blanket which was over everything. The only real noise was that of the foghorns from the boats passing up and down. The calm of the morning was suddenly disturbed by the sirens sounding, guns blazing and the police chief's loudspeaker hailing for all to come out, hands in the air. It's not often you see criminals waving to the press and TV cameras. They made the most of it.

'The lieutenant shouted, "We are wasting our fucking time.

They knew we were fucking coming and someone's going to regret this." His anger was palpable. Several days of planning wasted and the whole thing being televised. They made a moderate search of the place, but of course everything was in order.

'The publicity gave Isis the opportunity to hit back and they too certainly made the most of it. Isis's lawyers started to talk of a witch-hunt and the vindictiveness of the *Times*, but they had no grounds for any of their claims. You know, some people will believe anything and they started a few stories in the competitive press, but we knew the truth.

'Walt unearthed the same scenario. The only difference was that some of the ships' cargo was being taken off board downriver. Again, it all looked legitimate, but he had made the connection with the garage. Unfortunately he had been seen for the second time and this time was one too many. Walt was killed by a hit-and-run driver outside the office. As per usual, the car was stolen, no one saw the driver, even though it was in broad daylight, and he or she has not been caught.

'Like any good reporter, of which Walt was one, he had filed his story immediately, so it was in the public domain. However, we thought it better to complete our enquiries before either informing NYPD or even the DEA. The latter was losing impetus at the moment. We also thought it better to cool off for a while to give them, "enough rope to hang themselves with".

'Maitland had been seen several times at the garage with his Rolls. It was in pristine condition and now to our surprise he was given permission to travel to Europe with it, I suppose for a rally, but I didn't know. However, what I did know was that the car and his entire luggage were given a clean bill of health before he was allowed out of the States. I'm sure he would have known that anyway, but it was good to know they were still quietly investigating him.

'We now believed that the trail of the drugs led directly to the garage. But we could not find any clue to where it went from there, without stopping every automobile, or every person to find out. A pattern was emerging, however, and that pattern resumed when Maitland returned from Europe. He and the Rolls were always seen at the garage several days after a suspected delivery. He was now taking chances and I believe it was because he felt his days were numbered and was going to maximize his returns before he was caught. I believed this was a correct assumption because, prior to the troubles, he was rarely seen in the area. He was too well-to-do and it may not have been good for business, but now, as I said, he was a regular.

'Sweeney contacted Janice at the Drug Enforcement Agency without giving too much away, fearing the same results as the NYPD achieved. Government employees are always vulnerable to the temptation of receiving bribes. They would never see large amounts of cash in the normal run of things.

'We did have further discussions, however, in which I was now being fully included. It led to the comparing of the two sets of information that we, the *Times* and the DEA, had collected, with surprising results. We had made the same connections, from different perspectives. Walt had reported that the drugs were now arriving further along the river. The DEA source was from another angle. They had an operative working on the boat smuggling the goods in. Surprisingly, they did not agree that the garage had any connection with the affair, but would keep their eye on it, all the same. It was, in real terms, up to us to make the connections stick.

'I was invited to go along with the DEA on the raid. This time there was no fanfare, just plain old-fashioned policing. It was a hot humid evening, not even a breeze to take away the traffic fumes of the day which seemed to hang over the area. There were about fifteen agents employed that night, all heavily armed and all well concealed, waiting for the signal to move, on what was a well-prepared raid. Nothing goes to plan when ships are involved, because so much depends on tides, winds and the like, so although they had an uncomfortable wait, eventually the Panamanian-registered ship *Clear Star* docked.

'The usual port and customs formalities cleared, the unloading started in earnest. After a few boxes had been unloaded, one crate suddenly attracted some extra attention from the crew; this was what we were waiting for.

'I was standing next to the captain, when he gave the order, "Go get 'em, boys" with his chest sticking out. I know these sorts of expressions aggravate people, particularly you Brits and I must admit it made me cringe a bit. However, go get 'em they did. It was a fearsome firefight for a few minutes; no one on our side was hurt. The villains gave up quickly, as they soon ran out of ammunition. They took one casualty, but I do not think even that was too serious.

'The prize of the evening, after an extensive search of the warehouse, was a find and seizure of one million dollars' worth of pure cocaine, with a street value twenty times that. You can imagine the excitement of the team, with a result like that, and my excitement when they gave me and the *Times* exclusivity for the first twenty-four hours.

'The prisoners were taken into custody and of course they now had nothing to lose and were singing like canaries, but not on the tune we wanted to hear. They were just bit players, pieces of a jigsaw, who had been cleverly put into the puzzle, not knowing who or where the other pieces were. They were like the Caribbean director who never saw the same person twice. They received excellent rewards for their services, which retained their loyalty, but also once in the web, there was no turning back and the fear of the consequences of trying to leave also retained their loyalty, 120 per cent.

'There was absolutely no lead to John Maitland because of the cell structure that was in place. For the bosses, whoever they were, it was possible to simply replace the group lost and go back in business quickly.

'I think you may know from the films and TV you have seen, that cocaine suppliers still want paying for the goods. It's not their fault that you have lost one million dollars' worth of coke. They will put it down to your carelessness and that's what I believed happened to Maitland. Without doubt he had millions of dollars, but I believe that at this moment in time he couldn't put his hands on any of it.

'It was obvious he had been dealing for many years. Had that not been the case, he wouldn't have been able to have such a sophisticated organization, and as a result of this he would be trusted enough by his suppliers to get a further delivery on credit. But there would be no second chance. One mistake is unfortunate, two looks deliberate as Maitland was about to find out. He knew the score, but he was being pushed from all sides, by the good guys and the bad guys, if you will forgive the expression.

'Sweeney called a meeting with the DEA at which I was present and they in turn brought a member of the Treasury Department. The object Sweeney was trying to achieve was a sharing of information, but the government agencies were being very cautious because of his high profile. They were also beginning to think that he, Sweeney, was taking the matters too personally, as a result of Ed's death.

'To humour Sweeney the DEA agreed to continue with the operation and Maitland was to be covered 24/7, but the DEA no longer had an agent working undercover on likely ships entering New York. So it was going to be more difficult to maintain effective surveillance. But everyone needs a little luck and Sweeney got his.

'Walt had entered on his computer all the information he had obtained, from people he had seen to numbers and makes of cars, and a casual check revealed that the same auto, a Chrysler Neon, had been seen at a different warehouse. Together with this information was the fact that Gerry – you remember, Maitland's chauffeur – had taken the Rolls-Royce to the garage. We knew that in recent weeks Maitland had been seen at the garage shortly after possible deliveries had been made and this time Sweeney convinced the DEA to raid the garage.

'The coincidences became too good to be true. Maitland

51

requested permission to take the Rolls and himself to Europe for yet another Rally and this was granted. Gerry had taken the Rolls into the garage for what I presume were his normal rally checks. Now, it was just a question of waiting to see whether Maitland would come.

'All of us were on tenterhooks. A day turned into two, three and then a week, but on the eighth day it started. The surveillance on the other warehouse had borne fruit. A ship had docked and was unloading its cargo of engine parts. One or two crates in particular were again attracting more attention than the others. They were offloaded and taken into the warehouse accompanied by the "hoods".

'Everyone had agreed that the rule this time was to follow Sweeney's hunch. This decision had been taken on the understanding that, should things go wrong, the *Times* would take all the responsibility and would print as much in the paper. At the moment, neither the DEA nor the New York police could risk taking responsibility because of the increasing behind-the-scenes pressure being brought to bear by Maitland's lawyers, but nonetheless they agreed to support us.

'The surveillance continued and after a further forty-eight hours, with no heat on them, several boxes were taken out of the warehouse, accompanied by their protectors and taken to the garage. The suspense was absolutely unbelievable. Were there drugs on the premises and, if so, would Maitland have the confidence to come? Were the drugs being taken by others during the garage's normal daily business routine?

'The DEA, seeing that Sweeney's hunch was working, gave full support and quickly set up a network of surveillance. All roads leading to the area were monitored from the buildings. The garage itself was covered from every angle. All phones had been tapped and cars entering and leaving on more than one occasion were followed to their destinations.

'A further three days gave us the answer. I did not want to be part of it and stayed out of the way, overseeing events from a distance with my binoculars and a video link. We suddenly got the signal that in my heart I didn't want to receive: "Roller's on his way." It was the code name given for Maitland. He had been seen with Gerry in the area.

'We were all tingling with excitement and expectation. No one spoke. All had their fingers crossed that he would make his way to the garage. It seemed to take for ever; we then received the next signal. "Rollers arrived" and finally "Rollers inside". It was the signal everyone had been waiting for. Now we would know the truth.

A well-conceived plan was put into operation They were to wait until Maitland was in one or other of the cars and then one of the NYPD pre-arranged autos would pull past slowly and stop. This would be followed by a New York trash lorry that would break in front of the garage blasting its horn, as if to complain about the driver stopping. One of the passengers would get out of the car and look at the cars in the window, in fact go into the showroom.

'The entrance was now blocked and the showroom route of escape effectively cut off. The rear of the building could only be accessed on foot. That, too, had been blocked.

'The signal was given and many well-armed men charged into the building, as though it was the Normandy beaches. They met no resistance; well, quite frankly, the DEA were too quick. Ten minutes passed before we received the final message. "Roller secured", which meant all in the building were in custody, including John Maitland, who had been sitting in the rear of his Phantom. I keep forgetting: it's your lovely automobile.

'The forensic team were called in and went to work to find the drugs. Six thousand dollars' worth of pure cocaine were found, hidden in the Rolls-Royce, under the back seat, but otherwise there was nothing. All the cars were impounded and stripped down, but not a trace. We assumed that they had successfully taken the drugs out of the area over the few days before the raid.

'The only person who could be charged was John Maitland, in

spite of Gerry's attempt to say that he was the one who put it there. Maitland's fingerprints and DNA were on the packet. It was conclusive. He was arrested, charged and given bail of one million dollars, which was paid within the hour of it being granted.

'Sweeney, however, was not going to let him get off lightly and portrayed him in the *Times* as a vicious drug dealer, a far cry from the sophisticated philanthropist he was otherwise commonly known as. If Sweeney could not ruin him financially, he certainly would socially.'

Chapter 4

'Maitland could afford the best lawyers and certainly got them. He was caught red-handed and was hoping to plead guilty on a plea bargain that the cocaine was bought for a couple of friends who were desperate. A feeble excuse, but together with his twenty million dollars of charitable donations, in particular to children's medical research, and the fact that he had never been in trouble before, led to rumours that he would get a hefty fine or have to work in the community.

'It took six months to get to court, but when Maitland walked up the steps to the courthouse he looked decidedly confident. Naturally, as he was a very well-known figure, there was considerable media interest. There were cameras flashing and microphones being pushed into his face. He stopped at the top of the steps and turned, directing his attention directly the television cameras. "This is a terrible misunderstanding and I'm going to throw myself on the mercy of the court. I believe in the justice of the American legal system and I know it will give me a fair hearing."

'I was standing next to Sweeney when Maitland passed and he caught my eye, but in doing so, turned away sharply; he couldn't face me. I know he was embarrassed at seeing me. Sweeney, who was busily noting everything, turned to me and whispered, "He knows something and he's going to get away with it. He's done a deal."

Everyone was trying to push into the court building. There

was pandemonium and the police had to be called, before even Maitland could enter the courtroom. The proceedings were due to start at about ten o'clock, but it was now nearer to twelve-thirty and the court hit another problem. The judge booked to take the hearing was taken ill and a new one had to be found quickly. The new judge, none other than Wilkins Thornber, a very tough old man who had been around since the beginning of time and who would stand no nonsense at all, entered the courtroom and simply told all present to return at two o'clock; proceedings would begin then. I detected some concern on the faces of the Maitland's team. All of a sudden, none of them wanted to talk to the press, they were clearly somewhat uncomfortable.

'Sweeney and I called in at the local bar for lunch and found many from the press corps already dining. It seemed that there was a consensus of opinion that his team didn't like the new judge, but I was more surprised by comments made in the bar. It was apparent that Maitland was not as popular with everyone as I had thought. Perhaps I had been blinded by our mutual love of Rolls-Royce motor cars and the glamour of the friendship we had had. Several reporters were openly saying he was a shady character, and that it had only been a matter of time before he got caught. Some were even hoping he would get "what was coming to him". I thought to myself: Where the hell had I been when everyone but me could see Maitland for what he really was.

'We arrived at the courtroom and waited for things to begin. There was a general hubbub. Maitland sat stony-faced and motionless. His team were busy discussing their approach when the noise was broken by the sound of the usher: "Silence in court! All stand! Judge Thornber presiding.' Silence was immediate; you could hear a pin drop. The judge walked slowly to his place and sat down with the gravitas that only comes from the experience of years in the job.

' "The court is now in session," he said in his commanding sort of way. I can't really explain it, but you *felt* his presence.

' "May we approach the bench?" Jason Wendlesmit, Maitland's attorney, asked.

'Thornber nodded.

' "We request a short adjournment, say fourteen days," Wendlesmit asked.

"You better come up with something good; you've had six months to get this together," Thornber said sternly.

'We could all see Wendlesmit was in difficulty, regardless of the fact that he was one of the best criminal lawyers in New York.

' "We have further mitigation to put to the court which we would hope would materially affect possible sentence," Wendlesmit almost stammered.

'The wily old bird Thornber looked at him sternly and said, "You've got *me* now, Mr Wendlesmit, and there's nothing you can do about it. I'm going to see this through to the end." He paused, staring at Wendlesmit, before continuing. "Have *you* any comments to make, Mr Wiseman?" he asked the prosecutor.

'Wiseman just shrugged.

' "Exactly! My thoughts entirely," Thornber remarked. "Let's get on with it and please, Mr Wendlesmit, don't waste any more of the court's time. I want to try and resolve matters today."

Wiseman the prosecutor, not the most experienced lawyer to have in a trial in the public eye like this one, outlined the case against Maitland, describing how he had been caught red-handed with the pure cocaine hidden in his Rolls-Royce. He made a big play on the words "Rolls-Royce", and then went on to suggest that there were a lot more drugs that *hadn't* been found.

' "Objection!" Wendlesmit shouted

' "Sustained!" Thornber said, scowling. "I will put that sort of behaviour down to your inexperience, but do not let that happen again." Then, turning to the media circus in the courtroom, he said, "And I don't want to see or hear any reports in the media about what you've just heard. Is that understood?" He paused for a moment. "What you believe and what you know are two distinct different things. Remember that!"

'The prosecution finished laying its case, but there was nothing new stated. We and the rest of America had already read and heard what the case was against Maitland and all we were waiting for was the result.

'Wendlesmit began the defence mitigation. "Mr Maitland, my client pleaded guilty to the charge on the basis that a certain course of action would take place and that the . . ."

' "Stop a moment!" Thornber said, interrupting Wendlesmit in full flow and speaking somewhat loudly as if he wanted to make sure everyone heard. "No deals have been struck with this court and remember it is my court that you are in now, Mr Wendlesmit."

' "Yes, I know that, Sir, but I thought it right to appraise the court of our discussions with your colleague, which the prosecution are fully aware of."

' "The court and myself are also *fully* aware of the facts and of all the pre-hearing arrangements and will take that into account when the time comes," Thornber responded somewhat annoyed. "Continue, Mr Wendlesmit."

'There was deep concern in the Maitland camp and Maitland himself began shuffling uncomfortably in his chair. They were not having any of their own way. Wendlesmit had to continue in what was now a very delicate situation. The rumours we had heard before the hearing were right.

'Wendlesmitt continued: "John Maitland bought these drugs for two friends and like any loyal friend he will not name them and destroy their position in the community, whatever the cost to himself. How many men would be brave enough to do something like that?'

'I had to give Wendlesmit his due; he really did put up a good fight. Everything that Maitland had done for the community was mentioned. Almost every penny he had given away was alluded to and praised.

'One could almost have felt very sorry for Maitland had it not been for the fact he was a drug dealer. Where had he got his money from to give away? If you had asked that question of

Sweeney, he would have told you: "From all of the poor devils he hooked into his filthy trade."

'Wendlesmit finished his mitigation and sat down. The court-house fell absolutely silent, which was broken only by Thornber. "There isn't enough time for me to consider matters. I will give my decision tomorrow morning." He banged his gavel on the table and announced, "This court is adjourned until ten o'clock tomorrow." With that, he got up as the usher called out "All stand", and left the room.

Maitland, visibly shaken, was being consoled by his lawyers, who in turn were trying to reassure him that all was not lost. We on our side felt much better. He was not able to manipulate the court. We were also very surprised that he did not speak up on his own behalf because he was a good speaker, eloquent even, but I suppose he couldn't take the risk of being cross-examined, just in case there was a slip.

'The following morning Maitland was hustled into the court without any fanfares. The media circus was still there, anxious for a story, and still creating the same chaos in and outside the court.

'"All stand!" the usher yelled, trying to be heard above the noise. "Judge Thornber presiding." The same quiet routine took place as the judge sat down to begin his sentence. I can't remember it word for word, but what I can remember is that there was a deathly silence.

'Thornber began outlining the case against Maitland. "The fact is . . ." He paused. ". . . In my opinion it was a large quantity of drugs. John Maitland has already admitted he had obtained them for friends, though it's an excuse often used by those wishing to escape a severe sentence . . ." He paused again. "On the other hand, it is obvious to all that the defendant is a man of some substance and would not need to sell this quantity of drugs to make money. I have not taken into account the possibility of further drugs not recovered and have noted in the record that the reference to such by the prosecution was ill-judged." Thornber paused for a moment and took a drink.

'Sweeney leaned over to me and whispered, "I told you he going to get away with it."

'The judge continued: "I have listened intently to the wonderful gifts the accused has made to various charities, and without doubt he must be congratulated for this work." There was a little noise coming from the back of the courtroom, to which Thornber addressed a few choice remarks about what he would do to them if they continued.

'I noticed that Maitland and his lawyer were looking decidedly confident. Sweeney was almost coughing with anger.

'He whispered to me. "Congratulated! For what? Killing young kids! I would have thought more of Thornber than that!" He almost spat out the last words.

'Thornber returned to his business, with a final warning look to the rear of the court.

' "*However*, this is a serious crime, and the defendant deliberately concealed the cocaine in the back of his Rolls-Royce. As is the custom in this sort of case, any asset which has been used in the perpetration of a crime will be confiscated and I make that order now.

'The look of bitter disappointment on Maitland's face was clear; he always said he loved the car. But there was worse to come and I watched as the colour drained slowly from his face as he listened to the rest of Thornber's judgement.

' "You were a man who had considerable respect amongst your peers and were looked up to by many. People admired what you had achieved and what you have given to the community. Yet you involved yourself in the grubby trade of drugs. You knew where to go to get these drugs and the drugs you obtained were of the highest purity. What example is this to set to others, especially as one of your charities was set up to help youngsters who succumb to drugs?

' "I do bear in mind that this is the first time that you have been before the court, but I would point out that anyone who is caught with this quantity and quality of cocaine could reasonably expect a period of incarceration of up to ten years. Had the quantity been more, it would have been much different. However, in view of the comments I made earlier I am taking a more lenient view." He paused. "You will spend two years in the state penitentiary."

'There was a gasp in the court. No one had believed that this could happen, not even Maitland, who was now leaning forward with his head in his hands.

'"My client will appeal this decision," Wendlesmit said, addressing the judge. "May he please have bail."

'"No, bail is refused. Take him away." With that, the sheriff's men walked over to remove Maitland. There were hurried discussions between the defence team and Maitland, which I didn't hear because of the uproar in the court, Even Thornber's gavel couldn't quell the noise. A handcuff was placed on Maitland's wrist and he was led away, a totally broken man.

'The judge called us to order and closed the proceedings, with us all standing, still in uproar, as he left.

'Sweeney was disgusted with the result. "He should have got ten!" he stammered. "It's money talking again."

'"Look, he got two years. It won't be pleasant for him in prison, particularly if any of the people he has crossed are in there as well," I said, trying to calm him down.

'"You know as well as I do this was just the tip of the iceberg. Where did those drugs go, and what happened to all the money he's made? The Treasury have found zilch. Where the hell is it then?"

'We went back to the office to formulate the following day's story, with the headline "Only two years!" and with Sweeney's personal slant on the case.

'"He's a bloody murderer!" Sweeney shouted down the office. "But we'll be lenient because he's given us the bloody money to bury them!"

'Worse was to come. It was obvious he would appeal, but despite Thornber's judgement he was granted bail, for the sum of five million dollars and surprise, surprise, it was paid immediately. "So he's free!" Sweeney exclaimed, again letting everyone know how he felt.

'Janice Fink at the DEA promised to keep her eye on Maitland, but after conviction, even knowing that they had missed a possible large quantity of drugs, it would look like persecution to pursue him openly. They would be ordered to pull off.

'So there we are! You've bought a beautiful car with a story behind it.'

Chapter 5

We were all spellbound as David Mainwearing finished his tale. From what he had said and the way he had said it, you could tell he was a journalist. Our thoughts were interrupted by the loud-speaker announcing Dinsdale Grant was taking a twenty-minute afternoon break.

'What time is it?' I asked

'Three o'clock!' David replied.

I couldn't believe it. He had kept us captivated for over three hours; we had missed lunch and were now well into the after-noon. It was time for further refreshments from our lovely Diane.

'You've been here a long time,' she chirped.

'Yes,' I replied, trying to imagine how sophisticated she would be with the name of Tracy instead of Diane. 'We are only staying to keep you coming over.'

'What can I get you this time then?' she said, pushing out her somewhat large chest with pride, particularly in the direction of Henry.

'Same again, please.' With that she went bouncing off, with something more in her step than before.

'What happened after that?' I asked, turning my attention once again to David.

'Not a lot. Maitland appealed and was granted bail on a recon of five million dollars, which was soon paid. However, his pass-port was taken and his movements closely monitored. He applied to retain the car, but at his hearing, which was only six weeks ago, his appeal was partially refused. He was to serve his sentence in what you term an open prison and, as you can see, you now own the car.'

'What happened to Amelia?' Francesca asked.

'She was devastated. She wanted to attend the trial, but at least he had the decency not to allow her there. Ironically, our wives are still friendly, but I thought it best to keep out of the way, at least for a little while . . .' David paused while Diane gave us our refreshments. 'When he comes out, I think he's going to want to buy the car back. He loved that Rolls.'

'Tough!' Henry said firmly.

'Did they ever find the other drugs? Or do you think they found all that there was?' I asked.

'Oh there were more drugs all right, much, much more. We know it and I think the DEA know it, and that's why Wiseman tried that stunt in court, but they were never found. When the DEA had everyone in for questioning, there was apparently a climate of fear and no one really gave them anything. In fact, Sweeney now believes Maitland deliberately got caught with the drugs, so that he could clear the air and wipe his slate clean, but things backfired when the judge became ill. I just wish we could have found them. Without a doubt he would have got ten to twenty for that crime.'

We spent the next half an hour or so socializing, exchanging names and addresses and telephone numbers, and promising to keep in touch. After a few more reminiscences about II PY, David took his leave, with me promising to contact him the moment the car arrived back home.

We returned to the office just as the sale was ending. Henry had taken an interest in a couple of Ferraris. Personally, I think it was purely to impress Carole, but it didn't, especially as he thankfully dropped out of the bidding just after it started.

We were to be given authorization to take the car as and when confirmation was received that the monies had been paid into Grant & Bulldozer's account, which was to be 9.00 a.m. local time the following day. This gave us some time to contact Andante, the local shipping agent in Bradford, Yorkshire. It was a firm I'd used several times before, so we knew we could rely on them to bring the car home in good order.

I eventually got through to Andante and spoke directly to the boss, Jazz Murphy, who confirmed that he could arrange the shipment on the MV *Cormorant*, which was currently in the New York docks. The ship had been to Fiji, then made a special trip to New York. We could travel on the boat, which was like manna from heaven; it saved me flying back in misery and I could travel with the car.

The plan was for Francesca and me to travel back to the UK by boat along with the Rolls while Henry returned, as arranged, by Virgin Airways. Then he and Philip, our oldest son, would come and pick us up at Liverpool docks with the trailer.

As we left Grant & Bulldozer's, Henry spotted Morales again. This time he was talking to a group of men at the entrance and as we passed I caught his eye and nodded. He gave me a scowl that would have turned Lot's wife.

'He's a bad loser!' I remarked as we got into the taxi.

'That's because they don't lose very often!' the taxi driver commented.

'Who doesn't?' I asked.

'That type, the bad guys. Don't do business with them.'

'I won't!' A shiver ran down my back. Francesca could feel my discomfort and gripped my hand tightly.

'The sooner we are out of this place the better,' she said.

Henry continued to look casually out of the window and noticed that Morales had signalled to another car, which began to follow us. 'I think we're being followed.'

'You certainly are,' the driver inteerrupted with barely concealed excitement. 'It's only an old Chevy. Do you want me to try and lose him?'

'Umm, nohhh,' I said, shrugging my shoulders. 'What's the point? We're only going back to the hotel.'

'What do they want?' asked the taxi driver, a little crestfallen.

'I've bought a wonderful car which belonged to their boss and I think he may want it back.'

The taxi pulled in at the Waldorf, with the old grey Chevy stopping some distance away, its occupants watching our every move as we got out. I paid the driver and he departed, saying, 'Be careful with them!'

I went into the hotel. Henry had taken the Chevy's number for reference, but the driver and his passengers were too far away for us to be able to identify them. The moment we arrived at reception, we notified the hotel, who in turn notified the police. It wasn't long before the police arrived, questioned the occupants of the Chevy and moved them on. Round one to us, I thought.

Both Francesca and I were somewhat concerned at these developments. It had now become obvious that John Maitland did not want to part with II PY and we were beginning to think that he would do anything to get it back. It was with this in mind that I decided to phone Jazz Murphy, the boss at Andante, to ask if a. he could pick the car up at 9 a.m. the next day and take it to the port and onto the boat quickly, and b., if he could get us on the boat as soon as possible, even if it meant paying extra.

Have you ever tried to phone the UK from the States? If you have, you will know what I mean. Jazz had gone, it was now eight o'clock back home and it was only by luck that someone was left in the office, who kindly gave me his home phone number. I explained fully our dilemma and he agreed to see what he could do and would ring me back as soon as possible. Now it was just a question of waiting for Jazz to call.

None of us could eat a thing. It was simply a question of pacing around and going over the same things, time and time again, for the next two hours.

At last Jazz phoned. 'It's going to cost you. Pickfords are going to collect the car. It will be containerized at the auction house and taken to the docks before eleven o'clock your time. My only problem is I cannot get in touch until tomorrow morning, late on, to confirm when you can board. The boat sails on the 18th, so you would board on the 17th anyway.'

'No, Jazz. I want us to board before then, if possible, it's very important,' I said almost pleading.

'Look, you know I'll do my best. I'll ring you as soon as I can, but as I said it will be late on.'

'OK thanks for what you have done, I do appreciate it. Oh by the way, could you confirm when the car is actually on board and leave a message with the hotel?'

'As I said, it will cost you. Ring you tomorrow. Bye!' Jazz put the phone down.

The three of us ate in the hotel restaurant, not wanting to risk going out. None of us would admit it, but we were a bit scared. Strangers in a foreign land and all that.

We had initially arranged to fly home on the evening of the 16th, but Henry wanted to stay until we were safely on the boat. We compromised. He would fly home first thing on the 17th. So the following day, it was a question of waiting until Jazz phoned and then the remainder of the day we would spend sightseeing. Just before lunch local time, Jazz phoned and confirmed we could board after 10 a.m. tomorrow. All we would need to take with us was our passports.

After all the excitement, we decided to take a walk in Central Park. It really is a beautiful place and reminded me of Hyde Park, Regent's Park and St James's in London. It was a lovely afternoon. The first buds of spring were pushing through, and there were the inevitable joggers wending their way along the paths and office workers taking their lunch. Just like in the movies.

We made our way to one of the many restaurants which border the park. The sight of all that food had made us feel hungry. We entered, sat down and I ate one of the biggest and best rump steaks I have ever eaten. I really don't know how the Americans can prepare, cook and serve a meal like this, in the centre of a city, for less than half the price we would pay back home.

We all needed to walk off the meal, especially me, as I felt at least a stone overweight, so we did the typical tourist route through the city – Broadway, Madison Avenue, Times Square . . . you get the picture. It did the trick and helped the lunch down. The only thing that spoiled the experience was that all of us kept looking over our shoulders, just in case.

The following morning, we had to be at JFK for ten o'clock for Henry's flight. Virgin Flight Desk. Within a couple of hours he was away, although he was feeling very concerned about our welfare. We did our best to reassure him; we would be on the boat within an hour of him leaving.

We returned to the Waldorf to pay the bill, check out and go to the docks. On the receptionist's desk I saw a copy of the day's *New York Times*. Grant & Bulldozer's had been attacked. Dinsdale had been injured and was in hospital and his offices had been robbed of all their records, including the computers. They had tried to set fire to the place, but had failed due to the prompt action of the New York fire brigade and a rather expensive sprinkler system. Both Francesca and I immediately felt that this had something to do with II PY. Perhaps they were trying to find out who had bought it and where it was going. The only person who would know was Dinsdale Grant.

I had had a sneaking suspicion that the 'Old Grey Chevy' was around when we went to the airport, but I hadn't liked to say for obvious reasons. So when we checked out of the hotel, after paying the account, we ordered a cab and asked the driver to drive around until he knew we weren't being followed. It only took a few minutes for the driver to confirm that was the case. We then gave him the instructions to go to the docks.

'Have you got problems?' he asked.

'You might say . . .' I mumbled. I didn't want to talk about the affair, but New York cabbies seem to have the happy knack of making their passengers talk. I briefly told him about our situation, which made him ask, 'Where are you going?'

'That doesn't matter. Just take us to the docks,' I replied and spent the rest of the journey lost in thought, with Francesca holding on to me.

We arrived at the port, checked in at the offices, passed through Customs and walked across the quay to the boat.

The *Cormorant* was basically a cargo vessel. The top deck had two large cranes which were obviously used for the loading and unloading of containers. The bridge, the crew's quarters, together with the passengers' cabins and restaurant, were situated at the rear of the ship in a large block, which seemed to tower over everything, particularly when you happen to be looking up from the ground.

Had I known I would have to walk up a gangway at the side of the boat to enter it, I might have changed my mind and travelled Virgin. It never looks very high when you see these situations in pictures or at the cinema, but when you have to face it in real life and you suffer a little from vertigo, it can seem a lot more daunting. As I gingerly climbed the narrow steps, I felt the gangway moving beneath my feet. I was absolutely terrified. It took all of Francesca's skills of persuasion, and some of the crew cheering, or should that be jeering?, to help me conquer the last half.

At the top, I was thankful to be met by the purser, Bill Edwards, a New Zealander, ex-Royal New Zealand Navy, a big tough bloke. He was possibly in his late forties, of medium height, but built like a 'brick shithouse'. He had another striking feature, a thick shock of black hair, not a sign of grey. Not surprisingly, everyone referred to him as 'Blackie'.

'You'll be pleased to know, your car came on board early this morning. It's in that container over there,' he said in a distinctive Australasian accent, pointing to a large rusty, old-looking container situated on the deck itself. 'Don't worry, it'll be OK,' he added, seeing the look of concern on my face. 'That is, unless it's rough, then it might just slip off!' He was still laughing to himself as he took us to our cabin.

We entered the *Cormorant*'s aft section where the bridge, crew and passenger facilities were. We took the lift to the third floor and walked along a short corridor to Cabin No. 6, which was at the end. He opened the door for us and allowed us to enter. It was magnificent, so clean, so well appointed, spacious and with a lovely comfortable bed.

'Wow, I didn't expect this!' Francesca said in amazement. 'It's almost the same as the Waldorf.'

'Better!' Blackie replied, as he began to show us where everything was and how it worked.

It's usual when you arrive on board a ship to spend the first hour or so exploring for yourself and that's just what we did. We walked every little nook and cranny, possibly because there was nothing much to do and the fact that the last few days had been so full of activity and excitement that there was a sense of anticlimax. That was, until we ventured out on to the cargo deck to watch the activity.

I was being somewhat daring and began looking over the port side of the boat, at almost the point where we had come up the stairs.

'Isn't that the car that's been following us?' Francesca suddenly asked, pointing out the Old Grey Chevy, as it pulled up at the side of the ship.

There was no mistake. I recognized the driver as he got out and was joined by two others at the rear of the car. They talked for several minutes, before the driver reached into the boot and brought out a large holdall, which he gave to one of the men. Another last-minute conversation and the man gave a casual wave and began walking up the steps. All this time we were standing back, hoping that they would not see us and thankfully none of them looked up.

'What's so important about this bloody car?' I cursed. 'We know it was Maitland's pride and joy but this is unbelievable!'

'He probably resents having it taken from him by the DEA,' Francesca replied.

'You're probably right, but he's going to a lot of trouble to try and buy it back.'

We walked down to the entrance, just as the man arrived at the top of the steps.

He was a thin wiry individual and looked Vietnamese. He had the same sort of complexion and the dark hair to match. He was not very tall, so I thought I would be able to manage him if there was any trouble. He showed no sign of recognition, neither of me nor Francesca, even when he asked if I could tell him where the crew office was. There was no need, however, as Blackie arrived and took him to the crew's quarters.

'He doesn't know who we are,' I said thankfully.

'Either that, or he's a bloody good actor,' Francesca retorted.

'No, but I think you're right; there would have been some glimmer, some sign?'

'We should keep an eye on the container, all the same. It's obvious he's been sent to keep tabs on the car, to see where it's going.'

We decided to tell Blackie about the situation, but understandably he was more concerned about getting the ship away on time the next day.

'Don't worry!' he said somewhat condescendingly. 'I'll keep my eyes open for you,' he continued as he walked over to check on some other problem which had just arisen.

'He's some bloody use!' I whispered angrily to Francesca.

At last we were setting sail. The ship slipped its New York harbour berth at 3 p.m., bang on time. As we slowly drifted into the main channel, it was a beautiful sunny afternoon. There was a magic about the movement, the slow rhythmic beat of the

71

engines, as the *Cormorant* gently passed other boats tied up to their berths.

Everyone on board, passengers and crew alike, came out to see New York disappearing into the distance. The skyscrapers of Manhattan were becoming little bumps on the horizon, before finally vanishing and leaving us with nothing but a calm grey–green Atlantic Ocean. Apart from the odd ship passing in the day or night, this was all we were going to see for the next six days.

The first night at sea was very pleasant. Captain Edward James, a dyed-in-the-wool merchant seaman and his officers introduced themselves to all twelve passengers on board. Each night each of the higher-ranking crew took it in turns to dine with a table of passengers. It was our turn, on this occasion, to have the captain and an engineering officer, William (Bill) Beddowes, sitting at our table.

Captain James was an interesting character, though somewhat smaller than one would imagine a captain to be. He had been a ship's captain for over twenty years and, of course, had sailed all over the world. Bill Beddowes, however, was a young officer and, or so we were told, a genius with diesel engines and anything electrical.

The captain told us that the ship was one of the few built on the Tyne. It one of the best he had commanded and would weather the worst of the seas. This was said as a precursor to warning us that we would be running into rough weather the following day. That proved to be an understatement. As it turned out, we had almost twenty hours of the most mountainous seas I had ever seen.

The ship had no stabilizers as such, or at least not compared with those on cruise liners, so you were totally in the hands of the captain, who would endeavour to take the smoothest course. Not surprisingly, we were not allowed out on deck, so we were left to our own devices, watching videos and attempting to eat or drink in the restaurant. Needless to say it was very difficult to eat anything, and if you did, it was difficult to keep it down.

Blackie's constant jibes about the safety of the car, although perhaps meant in fun, made me extremely concerned about it. The mountainous waves had, on the many occasions we had been watching, completely washed over the decks. I was filled with anxiety, not only because of the possibility of the container being swamped by the water entering, but because of the damage the car might be sustaining from being rocked about.

On the third day the tempest subsided and some form of normality returned. It was now possible to eat and at least walk in the fresh air. We had enjoyed our first dinner, this time in the company of Blackie, the purser, and the senior engineer, Jim Percival. Following dinner, as it was such a lovely evening, we decided to walk round the ship and inspect the container. We felt somewhat rude as the other table guests were remaining to chat to the officers, but after being cooped up all day, we were desperate for some air before 'turning in'.

It was getting dark, but naturally our first port of call was the container, to make sure it was still there, or not damaged in any way. To our utter amazement, the door was slightly open and we could hear some thing or someone inside. I whispered to Francesca to go and get an officer, whilst I kept watch, promising at the same time I wouldn't do anything on my own. Very quickly, she returned with Blackie, which gave me the courage to shout into the container. 'What the hell do think you're doing?'

My shout stopped whatever was going on, as all went deathly quiet. We waited, but nothing happened. Blackie took control and walked over to the container door and shouted. 'Come out, yer bastard, before I come in and get ya.'

Again we waited, in absolute silence, for him or her to come out. But somehow I knew it would be our Vietnamese friend. We heard a movement in the container and it was obvious that the person was on his way out. Blackie stood back a little behind the container door.

A shadowy figure came out, armed with a knife. It was as I suspected, the Vietnamese. He came out cautiously, not seeing the others, only me. He pointed his knife at me, waving it about in an aggressive manner with a sneer on his face which matched his determination. He looked an evil man.

I backed off, absolutely terrified, with him following me, menacingly, still pointing and waving the blade in the direction of my chest. Everything seemed to be happening in slow motion but I knew if I took my eye off him for one second, I could be attacked.

I could see he was nervous, as he began looking quickly all around him. He could now see Blackie and Francesca, together with the other members of the crew who had heard Francesca's pleas and were now running towards him. I backed off further still, in case he panicked and went for me. It was a tense situation for a few moments as we simply stared at each other.

Blackie now took control of the situation in his inimitable way. 'Put the fucking knife down, before I break yer fucking arm,' he yelled as he walked cautiously toward him.

The Vietnamese was effectively surrounded, and when the realization dawned on him that he had nowhere to go, the poor sod began visibly shaking, his fear so intense, you could actually see the sweat pouring off him. He looked straight at me, staring with eyes that now seemed hollow. Was I that terrifying?

The massive frame of Blackie was now only within a couple of yards of him, but even this did not create the fear that he saw in me. He now seemed hypnotized by his fear, so Blackie leaned forward to take the knife, which brought him back to reality. It was enough. With one last terrified stare in my direction he turned round, ran to the side of the boat and jumped over.

'Oh God, no!' Francesca screamed.

'Man overboard! Man overboard!' Blackie shouted.

74

I looked round to see who else was with us and saw a tall thin man walking back to the passengers' quarters.

Suddenly the ship's alarm sounded and the engines stopped, but as with all ships at sea it's impossible to stop dead. The way carried us on at least a quarter of a mile before the captain ordered the ship to turn around to look for him.

'Poor bastard!' Blackie said dolefully. 'He'll be dead in twenty minutes if we don't, if he isn't already.'

Everyone, passengers and crew alike, was leaning over the rails in an effort to see him. The ship's searchlights were directed into the sea and followed every shout and every possible sighting, but light and waves play funny tricks, with the result there were several false dawns.

Some of the passengers were somewhat excited with all the activity, not knowing the reason behind it. The crew, however, were glum; after all, he was one of them, even if he was a scoundrel. Everything was to no avail and after an hour the engines were restarted and once again we were on our way.

The crew were in a sombre mood as we all made our way back into the accommodation. Only the passengers were chattering as they passed on the gossip, as bit by bit the real story filtered out.

'It wasn't *me* he was scared of. It was that tall man. I'm sure he was at the auction,' I commented, turning to Francesca.

'Darling, it's your imagination getting the better of you. But tell Blackie all the same.'

A little later the captain asked us to join him in his cabin, along with Blackie. It was a sumptuous room with a beautiful large table as the centrepiece and chairs to match. There was polished wood everywhere, including the captain's desk in the corner, complete with computer. Tasteful curtains covered the brightly polished brass portholes.

Captain Edwards stretched out his hand to welcome us in. 'Mr and Mrs Conway, thank you for coming, I do appreciate it. Please sit down,' he said, directing us to the chairs round the table.

The formalities over, Captain Edwards began outlining the reason for the meeting. 'This is a very tragic situation. To lose a man at sea is not only very sad, but also very difficult from the maritime law point of view. I have naturally to make a full report, which has to include the possible reasons why the man jumped overboard and what we did to search for him. I am personally responsible for every member of my crew.

'Firstly, do you know this man?' he asked looking directly at me.

'No,' I replied. 'But I do know the people who gave him a lift to the boat. To be precise, I have seen the driver of the car before; he's been following us since we bought the Rolls-Royce that's in the container, a couple of days ago. I think they were employed by a man called Morales. He gave me his card. He's a lawyer.'

I told him the circumstances of how we had met at the Drug Enforcement Agency's auction at Grant & Bulldozer's, about Morales' offer to buy the car, and finally the story told to us by David Mainwearing. They were almost as enthralled as we had been and remained totally silent until I had finished.

'It's probably nothing, but I think the tall dark-haired man has something to do with it. I can't be one hundred per cent sure, but I think he was at the auction.'

'I can't take any action against him unless you can give me further evidence, but what I will do is keep an eye on him and on the woman he's with.' Captain Edwards turned to Blackie. 'How did this man become a member of the crew?'

'That's down to me, I'm afraid,' Blackie replied. 'Diaz went AWOL and we were already two short. I had to replace him quickly.'

'That's not what I asked,' Edwards said impatiently. 'I want to know how this man came to be aboard. Who recommended him to you in the first place and when?' He paused. 'We'll deal with this matter later; it doesn't concern the Conways.'

He turned to us again. 'Why didn't you mention you had seen him come aboard?'

Blackie interjected. 'They did! They mentioned it to me as

he came on board. I now realize I should have given it a greater priority, but I thought the car would be safe at sea. The Conways assured me they had not seen him before, and when he passed them he definitely showed no signs of knowing them.'

'Blackie, I want your full report by tomorrow, detailing: one, how he came to be on board; two, who were his referees; three, who knew what was in the container; four, what you are going to do to secure it and prevent a reoccurrence; and lastly, what damage was done to the cargo, if any, and what he was doing. Then I want you personally to make sure the container is sealed. From now on, you will take personal responsibility for its security.' Then, turning to me, he said, 'I want you to go with Blackie, check the car as early as possible in daylight to see what he has done from your point of view, if anything. I think we will leave it there tonight. Mr Conway, Mrs Conway, if you do think of anything you have left out or forgotten, please let me know as soon as possible.'

He stood up, held his hand out yet again and wished us goodnight.

The following morning, at breakfast, Blackie joined us and suggested we inspect the car as soon as possible because he wanted to seal the container doors quickly.

'I've already checked last night and again this morning to see whether or not there are explosives in it or under it and it's clear,' Blackie said reassuringly.

That brought it home to us: how dangerous the situation could have been. From what Mainwearing had told us, though, I didn't believe Maitland would do anything to damage the car.

Blackie continued. 'I'd like you to have a good look because you'll know what to look for.'

'What for instance?' I asked.

'I don't know. I don't know Rolls-Royce cars. You may just see something.'

'Of course I'll look, but to be fair I have only seen this car once and then only for a few minutes.'

We finished breakfast, in a fashion less leisurely than I would have liked, and went with Blackie to the container. We were met by several of the other passengers and crew, all anxious to see what all the fuss was about. Blackie opened the container. There she was, II PY in her full glory. She had been backed in and was firmly strapped down. She looked out of place, a lioness trapped, but still proud and defiant. She looked magnificent, impressing not only the passengers but also Blackie.

'She's a beauty!' he said. 'But not worth the life of a man.'

I just stopped and admired her for what seemed liked minutes, and yet I'm sure it was only seconds before Blackie told me to hurry up. I went in. My search took about half an hour. I checked every detail that I could think of, but I really had not the experience to look properly. However, I reported to Blackie that I couldn't see anything untoward and left it at that.

By this time several of the passengers were becoming a little impatient and asked if they could have a quick look at her. But Blackie refused and said, almost repeating himself, 'This car has already cost the life of one man. I don't want to see it happen to another.'

Chapter 6

The harbour bar at the Port of Liverpool was a welcome sight, even at the ungodly hour of seven in the morning. The Liver Building was standing out proudly in the early-morning sunshine. The Albert Dock and its huge regeneration area was waking up as the ship slowly passed on its way to its berth in the container section of the port. There was a lot of activity on board and on the dock side as the *Cormorant* came to a stop and was secured.

As we packed our case and prepared for disembarkation we felt our excitement rising. The thought of Henry waiting with the trailer on the dockside for the car and then driving it home was running through my mind. Just to look at it in the garage for me would have been enough! It would be like some wonderful painting hanging on the wall.

We were disturbed by the steward who requested we join the captain in his cabin.

'You'll be glad to leave all this behind,' he said as we entered. He gestured for us to sit down. 'I presumed you would like a drink,' he continued, 'so I have taken the liberty to order you a pot of tea.'

The steward duly brought a pot tea for us and an enormous cup of black coffee for the captain. His cup was beautifully decorated in the Breton style and my admiration for it brought forth a story from the captain how it had been given to him by the then love of his life, when he was a young sailor at La Rochelle.

'I take it everywhere,' he said fondly. 'It brings me luck!' He paused for a moment lost in thought, leaving Francesca to give me a knowing smile.

We were soon brought back to earth when the captain announced, 'I have got some bad news for you. No! Nothing serious!' he added, as he saw the look on our faces. 'I'm afraid you're not going to be able to leave the ship until you have been interviewed by the police. It's normal in circumstances such as these, a body lost at sea, a crime committed and so on.'

'How long do you . . .'

He interrupted me. 'We will be docked and secure in about an hour and they, the police that is, will come aboard and interview both of you and the crew. I have asked them to deal with you first to prevent you being too delayed.'

'Did you find out how that man got a job on board?' Francesca asked.

'Two stories so far . . .' He stopped to think for a moment before continuing. 'The first is that the normal crew member was bribed to leave the ship and this chap came and presented himself, offering his services. The other is that one of our officers took a bribe. I think the latter is probably the most likely, as we found new seals in the container which could only been obtained from certain people. I think there are more than one or two people involved in this.'

'What about the car?' I asked. 'When will that be unloaded?'

He went over to his phone. 'Get me the purser, will you,' he asked the person answering.

'Blackie, I've got Mr and Mrs Conway with me. Have you any idea when their cargo will be unloaded? . . .' The conversation continued for a moment. 'Yes I do, right thanks, Blackie.'

The captain returned to the table. 'Yes, I'm afraid it may be a good five hours before it's unloaded, and then the police want to take a look at it. But I will try to expedite matters for you as quickly as I can.'

'My son Henry is waiting at the dockyard to trans-ship the car to our trailer. Is it possible for him to come aboard and wait with us?' I asked.

'That's normally not allowed, but I suppose as the circumstances are not normal, I do not see any problem. Once aboard, he will not be allowed to leave without permission, or without passing through Customs. I'll give him a letter if necessary, or the police will I'm sure. As soon as we dock, tell him to go to the container dock and ask to be directed to the *Cormorant*. You're free to either stay here or wander round the passenger areas, but you must stay away from the cargo decks while we are unloading.'

'Thanks!' I replied. 'Will the restaurant still be open?'

'Of course, though I don't know what the menu will be like. I'm sure it will be adequate.'

With that, he apologized for the inconvenience and left us to finish our tea, contact Henry and wait for the police. 'I'll contact you as and when,' he commented as he walked out.

It was an absolute nightmare for Henry to come aboard. Firstly he had to persuade anyone and everyone to allow the Land-Rover and the trailer through into the security area. Secondly, after being allowed through, he was not allowed to park or leave the vehicle unattended. However, in the end he managed to persuade someone that he was picking up important cargo and that the trailer was required urgently. That seemed to be sufficient and they released him.

It was a least an hour after the ship had formally docked that we saw him walking across the dockyard toward the ship and up the gangway to meet us.

'What a performance I've had to get here!' were his first words.

'Oh hi, Henry, nice to see you too,' I said sarcastically.

'Sorry! Good morning, Mother, Dad . . . but it has been a bloody nightmare. So tell me, what's been going on?'

I detailed everything from start to finish, as we walked to the restaurant. Hours seemed to pass. Things were becoming a little irritating just hanging around waiting. It was already one-thirty, and although we knew the police were on board no one had made any attempt to see us or to offload our container. It was sod's law: the moment we ordered lunch in the restaurant, we were summoned to the captain's cabin. By this time, however, I was somewhat annoyed and advised the steward to tell them that we would see them after lunch. I knew from experience it would have the desired effect.

When we finally arrived at the cabin, there were two police officers waiting to see us, a Detective Inspector Perrin and a Sergeant Wilkins, who were both very offhand in their manner, particularly when I gave them a 'rollicking' for keeping us waiting all this time. Wilkins had the gall to say they could keep us here as long as they liked.

'Try it!' I said angrily. 'I've got a cabin. Have you?' I replied.

'Look, Mr Conway,' Perrin said, at last trying to be conciliatory, 'all we need from you is your story from the beginning and you can go.'

'Is it the man's death you're interested in?'

'Yes.'

That was simple. I simply outlined events from the time when I saw the container open to when the poor sod jumped over the railings and was never seen again.

'What about buying the car and the trouble you had in New York?' Perrin asked.

I simply pointed out that the car had been certified clean by the DEA, that it had all its export papers, and that apart from checking the car for the captain the other morning, I hadn't touched the car in any way.

'Look, I and my family are very tired. We simply want to take the car and go home. If you want to come and see us and ask your questions there, we will, I promise, be pleased to help you. I'm really not in the mood to answer questions at the moment and you've got all the information about the man. Can we go?'

They were not overly happy with my attitude, but we were allowed to leave. Wilkins's parting shot was: 'We could impound the car.'

I went straight back at him. 'You could, *but* if you hadn't got a good reason, I would get it back within twenty-four hours *and* it would be transported at your expense *and* if you damaged it, I hate to think what it would cost the chief constable to put it right.' I turned to Perrin. 'Do you have to employ idiots like him? We would have got much further if he had used some common sense.'

We disembarked down a passenger gangway, which was much better for me as it took away much of the feeling of height. We could see the container on the dockside. It had been opened and unfortunately there was a small crowd in front of it. Henry suggested we fetch the Land-Rover and trailer, offload our luggage and then pick up II PY. One, it would save time and, two, it would give us an excuse not to talk to people as we would be too busy putting the car on the trailer.

'Sensible suggestion,' I said to Henry, commenting he was at last using his brains. But even this turned out to be another nightmare. To get out of the security area to the dockside took over half an hour. We eventually arrived at the container, pulled alongside, moving the few people out of the way at the same time. Henry then manoeuvred the trailer in order to have a straight run on to it.

Our intentions were then thwarted by three members of the press. We were greeted by a woman from the *Daily Mail* and two male reporters from the local papers. They were simply doing their job, but we were in no mood for questions.

Sergeant Wilkins joined the group and immediately began talking to the reporters, which gave us the opportunity to hitch the car up and hopefully get away.

'It looks fantastic!' Henry commented, as he saw II PY for the first time since the auction.

'Hitch it up and winch it on!' I ordered Henry.

'No, drive it out. Let's see her move on her own,' Henry countered.

I needed no persuasion. I went into the container, opened the front passenger door of the car and sat inside. It was like sitting on a cloud. I slid over to the driver's side. It's always easier to get in that way; otherwise you have to climb over the brake lever. I put my hands on the steering wheel and just dreamed. It was here. The something I had wanted since I was a young boy, I was now holding in my hands.

I put the key in, turned the battery on, switched on the ignition, adjusted the throttle control and turned the starter switch and immediately brought into being the power of this six-litre engine. The roar in the container made the small crowd lean forward and watch II PY as she glided out. The look on their faces told me she must be a wonderful sight. The press cameras whirred and clicked. We felt a little absurd, a bit like celebrities, and would be shocked the following day to see the car featured on the front page of the *Mail*, with the three of us inset. 'Beauty comes home,' read the caption. 'But what mysteries surround it and why did one frightened man kill himself when he saw the car?'

We finished loading the car. I removed the 'flying lady' for safe-keeping. Henry then produced a new lightweight cover he had treated the car to. Within ten minutes we had cleared the port authorities and were looking for directions to the M62. We were strangers to Liverpool and we soon became hopelessly lost, driving through the city centre at the height of the rush hour at 10 mph, not just once but twice.

With all the publicity that we would receive and the inevitable press comments the next day or so, we all felt it would be better not to take the car to our place and decided to ask our friend John Knighton of Royce Motors to keep the car hidden in his workshop. He has a fine reputation as one of the best Rolls-Royce mechanics in the business.

We arrived at John's garage about an hour and a half later. The garage itself is an old wool warehouse, hidden away in one of the side streets in Bradford's town centre. It's roomy enough to house some twenty or more Bentleys and Rolls-Royces at any one time in various states of repair.

'Come on, let's see it!' John demanded as soon as we drove in.

Henry removed the cover.

'Bloody hell! What a car!' he exclaimed. 'No wonder he wants it back!' He was referring, of course, to Maitland whose antics we had explained. 'Look at the finish; it cost a fortune to get it like this. Go on, how much did it set you back?' he asked, as he still looked on in amazement at one of the nicest cars he had ever seen. 'This will win everything. Go on, how much?'

'Forty-seven thousand pounds, or thereabouts,' I proudly replied.

'Never!'

'No, I promise, *that* was the price.'

'Well, you've got a wonderful car for next to nothing.' With that John himself put the cover back on. 'We've got to keep this beauty clean.'

We arrived home to a disappointed family, who had been waiting all day to see the car. They saw the point, however, when we were besieged by the press and friends the following day as the story broke in the *Daily Mail*. We all agreed that no one would make any comment to anyone except on my say-so. This way we felt we would get rid of the 'circus' quicker and we were right. Through the day the interest waned and everyone went their way, except for one man who had waited patiently all afternoon, sitting in his car outside the house. I went over to him and asked if I could help him.

He introduced himself as Clive White. He was an investigative reporter with the *Daily Mail* and would like a follow-up story on the car and its history.

'I've discovered it belonged to a well-known American businessman, a chap called John Maitland. Is that right?' he asked.

'Yes,' I replied.

'Is it true he was convicted of smuggling drugs and that the car was confiscated?'

'No, not quite,' I replied. 'Tell you what, would you like a cup of tea and I'll get you the phone number of a friend. He's David Mainwearing of the *New York Times*. I'll introduce you to him over the phone and you can take it from there.'

'That would be great!' Clive followed me down our drive to the front door. 'Did you buy it from the Drug Enforcement Agency?' he quizzed.

'Yes, it was at one of their auctions in New York,' I replied.

Francesca met us at the door and I explained the situation.

'He's been waiting in his car very patiently half the day,' I said breaking the ice and drawing a smile from him.

Clive was probably in his mid-fifties. He was tallish, with very grey hair, which made him look a little older than he was. His questioning suggested both his experience and intelligence. It was all too easy, I found, to prattle away without thinking – he was the perfect journalist.

By the time tea arrived I was in full flight, giving him a potted version of what Mainwearing had told us at the auction. He stayed about an hour and confirmed that nothing would be printed until he had confirmed matters with the American journalist. I couldn't contact David, so I gave him his phone number and left it at that. I promised I would contact him should anything else crop up and Clive took his leave.

*

Two or three days later, about ten o'clock, Francesca was disturbed by the two dogs barking at someone attempting to enter the front gate. She looked out and to her utter astonishment saw Morales standing at the gate.

She yelled to me, 'Darling, it's that Morales fellow from America! Don't let him in. Please!'

I went outside and walked slowly up to the gate. 'Don't try and come in! The dogs will bite you. What do you want?'

'I would like to talk to you . . . I'd like to make you another offer.' I didn't respond, waiting for him. 'Can I come in? It would be easier to discuss our business inside, rather than out here . . .'

'There's nothing to discuss. I will not accept any offer from your client. Please just go away and don't come back.'

'Mr Conway . . .' He paused for a moment. ' . . . You don't know who you're dealing with and I think . . . No, I *know* you are making a big mistake . . .'

He was interrupted by Francesca, who had been listening by the door and had heard the veiled threat. She came out shouting: 'Go away! You heard what my husband said. We're not intimidated by your grubby little threats and insinuations. Now go away, you horrid little man.'

'You heard! Now go away or I will call the police.'

Morales shrugged and turned away to a newish Mercedes car parked along the road. The car had tinted windows (don't all drug dealers' cars have tinted windows?), but as Morales opened the rear passenger door I could see there was another person in the back seat, though I could only make out a shape.

The Mercedes slowly drove towards me and then stopped. The electric window stopped halfway down, enough for the mystery back-seat passenger to be able to lean over and talk to me. I noted the man's dark sleeked-back hair and his tanned complexion. 'You will sell the car, Mr Conway; I can promise you. Not only that, you will be glad to. No! You will be *asking* us to buy the car from you,' he sneered.

I was at the end of my tether and suddenly I snapped. 'You

don't know me, you pathetic lump of shit. You come round here again and we will see.'

'Stop the fuckin' car,' he shouted to the driver. 'I'll get this bastard now.'

'Leave it! There's plenty of time,' one of the other passengers said to him.

The Mercedes pulled away slowly, only to be met by our son Philip's lorry, which had turned round the corner and was face on with our visitors.

'Everything all right, Dad,' he shouted, leaning out the window.

'Yessss,' I replied, 'but these bastards have just threatened me.'

'What?' he yelled and began driving the lorry towards the car.

The Mercedes stood its ground until Philip drove slowly into the front, pushing a large dent into the bonnet. The driver reversed sharply for a few yards and started to get out, but quickly retreated back in as Philip again drove into the front adding further damage. He pulled the lorry level with the offside passenger door and shouted, 'Don't you fucking threaten me or my family ever again!'

The window went down and the dark-haired passenger slowly but quite deliberately snarled. 'You're dead.'

'And you'll need your car repaired, dickhead!' With that, Philip reversed his lorry, ensuring the bumper gouged the side of the car.

The Mercedes now had sufficient room to pass and rapidly accelerated to the end of the road and away.

Two weeks passed and we thought the whole affair had blown over. We were even considering bringing II PY to Haworth. It was a Monday morning and Henry and I were going into Bradford to the bank and to see John at Royce Motors; Philip had other things to do and asked for a lift in.

Francesca remained at home and it was normal for us to leave our dogs patrolling the grounds. They act as a warning to anyone left at home that someone is at the gate. For the first time in a long time, I forgot to release them into the garden.

This was a terrible mistake, as Francesca did not see the black, sinister-looking twin-cab Toyota pickup drive slowly past the gate. Neither did she hear the five men get out and walk slowly to the gate, nor did she hear them walk down the path to the front door and start to check the house, all of whose windows faced on to the road. What happened next Francesca told me later, when it was over. She told her story, half crying and half laughing, although in reality it was a terrible and traumatic event.

The men were led by a swarthy Mediterranean-looking man with longish dark swept-back hair. He was smartly dressed in a light-grey silk suit with a red shirt and black tie, but the whole effect was ruined by a pair of brown winkle-picker boots. He checked all the rooms before arriving at the kitchen porch door. Seeing Francesca there alone and facing away from the door, he signalled the others to stay out of sight whilst he knocked on the door. Francesca walked over to see who it was.

'Mrs Conway?' he asked, through two doors.

'Yes?' Francesca replied. 'Can I help you?'

'I wanted a word with your husband, if that's possible.' His voice was polite, obviously trying not to arouse suspicions at this stage.

'He's not in.'

'When will he be back?'

'Oh any time now, but I cannot be sure,' she replied a little hesitantly now, hoping her answer would put an element of uncertainty into the visitor's mind.

'Well, I won't wait. Can I leave you my card and ask him to give me a ring?' He felt in his pocket as if to retrieve a business card, which made Francesca start to open the door. As she did so, she saw one of the other men at the side of the porch. She tried desperately to close the door again, but it was too late.

The visitor viciously kicked the door, which sent Francesca

flying backward across the floor and careering into the table in the centre of the room. She fell to the floor in some pain. Before she had the chance to recover her senses, the five men, four of them now wearing ski masks, burst into the room. The swarthy man in the suit immediately began barking orders to the others.

'You!' he yelled, pointing to the tallest. 'Go and check the rest of the house. Quick!'

Francesca was beginning to come round and was trying to get up when a swift kick in the stomach took her back to the floor, prostrate.

'Get something to tie her up,' he said, pointing to another. 'And you, go back and look after the car. If you see anyone come near blast the horn. Got it?' he commanded, almost spitting out the words.

'Take yer bloody mask off first!' he shouted as the idiot started walking out with it on.

One of the men had found several rolls of post-office parcel tape and came back to give it to the swarthy man. 'No!' he exclaimed. 'You,' pointing to another. 'You help lift her into that chair and tie her up.'

The tall one came back into the room. 'No one in the house, but I found another door which I can't open. I think there's a room the other side.'

'Well, break it down,' he snapped.

'I can't, it opens the wrong way and it's a bloody thick door.'

'Fuckin' hell, do I have to do everything me fuckin' self? Come with me!' he shouted. 'And you two, fuckin' hurry up with her, it's not a fuckin' picnic. And keep yer fuckin' eyes open while I go with him. Right?'

Francesca was looking somewhat worse for wear, as roll after roll of BT tape was tightly wrapped round her, tying her firmly to the chair. She couldn't move, her arms were solid to her side; only her legs were free, but she was unable to stand. They then wrapped two or three strands around her mouth to prevent her speaking, leaving just enough space for her to breathe through the nose. A large bruise was beginning to show on the side of her face where she had fallen.

The Boss, we'll call him that, because at no time did any of the men speak, giving any clue to their names or identity, came back in. 'Where's your husband?' he asked, ripping the tape from her mouth with gusto. She screamed as the tape nearly pulled some of the skin off her face.

'Pig!' she yelled.

'Where's your husband?' the Boss asked again.

'I don't know. I presume he went into Bradford.'

'When's he back?' he asked.

'I don't know, anytime before lunch, I don't know.'

'You must know!' he said firmly.

'Why? I'm not expecting him. I was supposed to be going out with a friend at half past eleven. I can assure you I haven't been waiting in just for you.'

Francesca's sarcasm caused a little titter of amusement from the others and riled the Boss. Fortunately the phone rang which prevented matters becoming worse.

'I'm going to pick up this phone,' the Boss told her, 'and you are going to answer it and you are going to behave as though things are normal.' He pulled a flick knife out and ran the blade over her face. 'Do you understand?'

'Yes!' she stammered.

He put the phone to her ear. She was quivering with fear and emotion. 'Stockton House,' she answered.

It was me. I was phoning to tell her I'd be home a bit early.

'Darling, it's me. I rang to tell you I'd be home early to see you before you went out.' I could tell something was wrong and I asked, 'Is everything OK, darling?'

Oddly, Francesca answered in French, which she never did ordinarily. She had an appalling accent. 'Pas de problème, mon chéri.' The boss put the blade to Francesca's head and covered the mouthpiece.

'What the fuck are you doing?' he asked.

'My husband's French, or didn't your boss tell you that,' she said quickly.

It was fortunate that none of the parties there knew any different. The Boss, however, had the sense to say that he could speak French and that she should be careful.

Francesca took the chance that he didn't. 'Nous avons cinq hommes ici dans la maison. Il est très difficile de parler . . .'

'What did you say?' he demanded, covering the mouthpiece and then putting the phone down.

She was right; he didn't speak French.

'You know what I said. I asked him what time he would be home and he said just before lunch. Happy now?'

'He'll be here in about two hours,' he confirmed to the others. 'You think you're so fuckin' clever, don't you?' he said, turning his attention to Francesca. She simply ignored him, which made him annoyed. 'I said you think you're so fuckin' clever. Answer me when I talk to you, you fuckin' snotty-nosed bitch.'

Francesca again tried to ignore him, which again made matters worse. She was making him look small in the eyes of the others.

The Boss walked over to Francesca, stared at her momentarily and whispered, 'I'll give you something to be stuck up about!' He grabbed her head in his hand pulled it to his face and kissed her full on the mouth. He pulled away, leaving great strings of saliva from his mouth on hers. She hated it, spitting out everything that could have possible come from him.

'You dirty bastard!' Francesca shouted, spitting more out on the floor.

'Oh, she wants some more, does she?' he said, laughing as the others egged him on. He leaned over once again putting his lips on hers. This time she did not move away. She accepted his lips on hers and pushed gently on to his. He softened his movements and became less violent, holding his hand up in the air to show the others he was winning.

'I knew you wanted me,' he bragged and began kissing her again.

He was aroused, taking his jacket off without his mouth leaving hers. She sucked his bottom lip into her mouth and sucked again. Suddenly she held his lip in her teeth and bit, with the ferocity of a tigress.

The Boss screamed, trying to pull away, but Francesca did not let go. She bit deeper into the lip. The skin tore like perforated paper and the blood flowed as if from a fountain. Finally she let go, leaving almost the entire lip from the start of his chin hanging on by just a slither of skin. He fell back screaming in pain, but the tigress was not finished yet.

Moving the only part of her body she was able, she kicked out at the Boss's testicles. Now he was writhing in pain on the floor, watched by his men in total amazement. They were momentarily transfixed, unable to move themselves in sheer disbelief. Francesca bumped the chair across the floor in the direction of the unfortunate boss, intending to land another telling blow, but was caught with a thumping right cross to the face, as one of the men stopped her in her tracks. She was trapped in her chair still unable to move when a second blow sent her crashing to the floor. The chair was giving some protection against the kicks which were raining on her. She feigned unconsciousness and lay motionless on the floor, hoping they would stop. They did.

The Boss's blood was still pouring everywhere. He looked at himself in the kitchen mirror. He could see his bloodied teeth were where his lip should have been.

One of the men, the tall and skinny one, in sheer shock exclaimed, 'She's eaten Bas's fuckin' lip. Christ! I don't fuckin' believe it!'

Bas's face was swelling up fast and without his bottom lip he was unable to speak properly.

'Get me to a uckin oskittle kik!' he yelled, trying to make the tall one understand.

'What did he say?' the tall man said, turning round to talk to the others.

'I think he said he wants to go to the uckin oskittle kik,' one of them replied, trying not to laugh.

The tall man removed his mask and immediately took his boss outside. Francesca heard the pickup start up and screech down the road. She still lay motionless on the floor, listening to everything in the hope of learning more about her attackers.

The tall man returned to the kitchen. 'He's gone to the hospital,' he said. There was total silence for a few seconds, when suddenly in unison the three remaining men burst out laughing.

'I suckose oo inks hat unny!' one said, trying to mimic Bas.

'He was a fucking mess tho', wa'n't he? I wouldn't like to be in her shoes!'

Momentarily there was panic in his voice, as he realized Francesca hadn't moved for some time. It was blame time.

'You shouldn't have hit her that hard, you've fuckin' killed her!'

'No I didn't! No I didn't.'

They were all becoming a little worried about their situation. Suddenly they noticed a man walking up the drive carrying a ladder and a bucket.

'It's the fuckin' winda cleana!' said the tall one. 'Get shut of him. Tell him we don't want them done ... Take yer fuckin' mask off first, ya stupid prat.'

The 'stupid prat' took his mask off. He was a blond lad with a couple of days' growth on his chin. But it was too late to take evasive action. Philip, who was posing as the window cleaner, had arrived at the outer kitchen door. Henry, Philip and I had arrived at the house some five minutes before. I had also telephoned the police.

'Is yer missus in?' Philip asked. 'Coz she's asked me to do one of the bedroom windows; she wasn't happy with one we did.'

'Well, do 'em then!' the blond lad said.

'I don't know which one,' Philip replied.

'Do 'em all!'

'Look, mate, would you do anything you weren't getting paid for?' Philip asked.

The tall man in a loud whisper yelled. 'For fuck's sake, just show him one of the fuckin' windows and he'll go away.'

The blond lad opened the porch door and walked out. You could hear his leg break a hundred yards away as Henry, hiding behind the porch door, swung a pickaxe handle full force into the lad's shin. There was a frenetic scream as the lad fell to the floor in agony.

Philip jumped on him. 'Make any more noise and I'll break every bloody bone in your body!' He pulled the blond by his good leg and left him out of sight at the side of the porch.

Henry went in through the front door, locking it behind him, and walked through the dining room and into the kitchen armed with his pickaxe handle. At the same moment Philip flew through the kitchen door.

'Where's my mother, you bastards?' he yelled, not seeing Francesca on the floor, still tied to the chair.

The tall man looked in Francesca's direction. Philip saw his mother lying tied up and saw red. He lunged at the tall man, vaulting the table and planting two booted feet into his stomach, knocking him to the floor. He was about to get up when a well-timed strike with the pickaxe handle from Henry put him out of contention.

He screamed out in pain. 'You fucking bastards, I'll get you for this!'

'I don't think so,' Philip yelled, landing another blow on the tall man's chin, knocking him senseless.

The remaining man made to escape, but ran into the arms of the police who were arriving in force.

Philip and Henry went over to Francesca and lifted her up as the police were entering. I arrived a second or two later and helped the police release her. She was in a poor state, covered in blood and terribly bruised around the face.

'Where else are you hurt? You're bleeding badly,' I asked.

She began sobbing her heart out and shaking with delight at seeing us again. Suddenly she began to hold me tightly and stayed like that for well over five minutes before having the courage to do anything else.

Philip went over to the man on the floor and repeated what he had said, whispering in his ear, 'You'll get me for this, will you? Well think on, you lump of shit. I've got your photograph.' He paused and took the man's picture with his phone, the flash adding further torment to him.

'He's threatening me,' he shouted to the constable.

'I'd threaten you, if you'd done this to my family,' the officer replied. 'It's a wonder he didn't really hurt you.'

Philip, still whispering, added, 'Within twenty four hours, I'll know where you and your family live and what you had for breakfast and this is not a threat it's a promise, you bastard.'

'He's doin' it again!' the man yelled to the officer, to no avail.

The police had called for an ambulance in order to take Francesca to hospital, but in view of the injuries sustained by her assailants, it was decided that a police vehicle would take her to the hospital and that the other two would be taken under guard in the ambulance.

The chief inspector entered the kitchen, where Francesca was beginning to come to. He introduced himself as Chief Inspector Walker. 'I'm really sorry to trouble you and I know how you must be feeling, but I really do need to ask you a few questions.'

'Can't it wait until tomorrow?' I asked.

'No, not really,' he replied. 'We have been led to believe that there were five men and we only have three under arrest and I want to make sure.'

'There were five!' Francesca said. 'And I will answer your questions.'

'Can you describe them?' he asked.

'Yes . . . well, one of them. The other one was sent out to look after their car.'

'Did you see the car?' he interrupted.

'No.'

'Please continue,' he asked.

She gave a full description of Bas, from top to toe, leaving the *coup de grâce* until last. 'I believe he's been taken to hospital.' She looked a bit sheepish.

'Why's that?' he asked. We all stood waiting to know why.

'He was forcing his attentions on me, so I bit his bottom lip completely off!' she said, becoming more herself.

'Good old Mum!' and other such laudatory phrases came out of the two lads.

'Well done, love!' I said, cuddling her.

Walker immediately phoned the office to order a check on all emergency hospitals to find out whether Bas had been treated there. It wasn't long before the call was returned: yes, he had been taken to Airedale General Hospital and had been admitted and was undergoing emergency surgery. He had used the excuse that he had been playing with his dog and that it had accidentally bit him.

'Some bitch!' Francesca commented laughingly.

Chapter 7

Inspector Walker had the common sense to have the hospital CCTV checked as soon as he realized Bas had been taken there and sure enough the driver had been seen walking him into the Accident and Emergency entrance. He was known to the police and they were sure he would soon be picked up. We had tried to make a connection with matters concerning the Rolls-Royce and of course implied that in our statements, but in fairness none of the villains had made any reference to the car or to any person. The police felt it might be just an attempt to extort money or simply to rob the place. They did say, however, that they would keep an open mind.

We passed the story on to Clive White, the journalist at the *Mail*, who, of course, made the most of it, using a great deal of press licence. He made reference to the car, despite us clearly telling him it was never mentioned. His story referred to Francesca's bravery but the only picture was another one of the car. Even if the police didn't see the connection, *he* clearly did.

We had had enough of hiding the Rolls and decided there and then to bring her home.

'If we are getting all the grief, then we might as well get some of the pleasure,' I said defiantly. And to my astonishment they all agreed.

We made arrangements straight away to collect the car from John's the following day. We arrived about eleven o'clock. John had already put the car outside; he had even cleaned it.

'I shall be sorry to see it go,' he said as he came out to meet us. 'It's been good for business!'

'John, how much do you want for storage?' I asked.

'Nothing! I told you it's been good for business.'

'Thanks, I'll see you right.'

I put the 'flying lady' on the car and drove slowly out of the yard. You cannot believe the thrill it gave us just to sit in this magnificent car, over seventy years of age, and purr through the city. We slowly drove on through Saltaire, Bingley, Keighley and on to Haworth. We had a few trips around the village and then to our house and into the garage. We had an hour's cleaning to do before we removed the 'flying lady' once again and put the cover on.

The following day we received a visit from Inspector Walker. 'You look a lot better, Mrs Conway,' he said on entering. 'I hope what I have got to say will not cause you too much worry, but Basil Waites escaped from custody early this morning.' He paused for a second or so before continuing.

'I might as well tell you the whole sorry story. He was being treated in a side ward, not only because of his condition but also because we needed him to be segregated from the other patients. We posted a full-time officer outside his door to keep an eye on him.

'This morning, he managed to persuade a nurse to let him have a bath. Whilst supposedly taking it, Waites somehow managed to take his clothes with him. He dressed and walked out, unnoticed by anyone, until he reached the ward exit door. A nurse shouted for him to stop, and he ran down the corridor.

'Several people tried to stop him but to no avail. He pushed one old dear lying on a trolley into two men; wheelchairs were pushed in the way of others, before he managed to escape outside. Seeing a man parking his car on a visit to the hospital, he ran across to him, opened his door, pulled the man out and physically threw him out of the way. He then got into the car and in his haste damaged the car next to him and another as he was leaving.

There was pandemonium, with sightings of him everywhere, not only within the hospital, but in the grounds as well. No one knew where to start.'

'So where was the policeman?' Francesca asked.

'You may well ask!' Walker replied. 'It would appear that one of the nurses had persuaded the officer to have a cup of tea in their retiring room, whilst Waites was having a bath. They shut the door behind them and, of course, didn't hear or see anything.' I'll tell you now, I've been in this game a long time and I have become somewhat cynical. I think there's more in it than meets the eye. I think our little nurse has a lot to answer for.'

'Where does that leave me?' Francesca asked.

'I really don't think he'll stay in the area. He's not stupid. He'll know we'll be looking after this place. He also needs medical attention. He's had laser surgery. They had to weld his lip back on and he needs to rest for at least ten days. It was quite a serious wound you gave him, Mrs Conway.

'We're going to keep an eye on you all, particularly the house. There will be regular patrols past the house and the local bobby will also be instructed to make regular visits. Anything you see or hear, anything out of the ordinary, you report it to us immediately. No matter how insignificant you may feel it is. Let us be the judge and we'll assess its significance.'

The next few weeks were wonderful. Francesca had recovered from her ordeal and we had had many lovely trips attending rallies and shows, picking up a couple of 'best in show' awards.

I had kept in touch with David Mainwearing and over the weeks we had built up a rapport. I told him everything that had happened in relation to II PY, and he would always remark: 'I can see Maitland's hand all over this.'

On the more pleasing side, he had decided to come over for the annual Rolls-Royce Enthusiasts Rally, which this year was being held at Kelmarsh Hall in mid-June. This is the big one from the owner's point of view. It's the one evereyone likes to take part in and the one I was determined to show II PY at its best. David and his wife Eleanor were to stay with us and he was of course shipping his 20/25 over with him.

The following weekend was free, a wonderful opportunity for just the two of us to enjoy a day out with II PY in the sunshine. We thought a visit to the Dales via Skipton and Grassington would be ideal.

I drove out of the drive and took the road to Keighley. I noticed a blue BMW behind us but didn't think much of it at the time. So many visitors use our road to park when visiting the village. Still, it was a bit odd it kept behind us, considering we were only travelling at fifteen to twenty miles per hour and other cars were passing us.

I panicked a little, and was so busy looking in my mirrors to see where the BMW went next that I almost hit a stationary car, which caused Francesca to cry out. The relief was unbelievable when the BMW turned the other way.

'What's the matter, darling? You nearly hit that car,' Francesca asked.

'I thought we were being followed, but it's turned off' I replied. 'Just getting a bit worried, love.'

We were now on the Skipton road leaving Keighley, intending to take what was now the fast bypass to Skipton. Round the roundabout and we were on the dual carriageway.

I had driven about a quarter of a mile at the amazing speed of fifty miles per hour when my heart skipped a beat. The BMW was about one hundred yards behind. Instinctively I knew something was wrong. I put my foot down, my heart pounding.

'That BMW is behind us again,' I told Francesca, 'Keep your eye on your mirror and ring the police.'

'I didn't bring my phone.'

'Oh Christ! Nor did I.'

Francesca gripped my hand in sheer fear, but the car was now touching eighty and control of the car was more important. We were almost at a roundabout. I pulled my hand away, grabbed the steering wheel and braked sharply. The BMW came along side, and the front-seat passenger put his window down and put his thumbs up, pointing to the car as if to say what a beautiful machine. The BMW sped off and we rounded the roundabout far too fast.

Our relief was short-lived. The BMW was waiting a little further on. The driver's window was down this time and he made the same sort of gestures, but somehow, this time they seemed empty, play-acted. I put my foot to the floor. The roar of II PY was tremendous as she took us up to eighty again. We now had a few cars between us, as I began slowing down for the next roundabout. We kept on the busy Skipton road, rather than turning off and going along quieter roads.

'They're behind us again,' Francesca yelled.

There was nothing I could do except play cat and mouse. Every time he started to pull out to overtake, I pulled over a little, until a vehicle approached the other way. I knew it was irritating the other motorists, but I felt there was little else I could do. In my mirror I could clearly see the driver running his finger across his throat signifying, 'You're dead.'

Sweat began to run down my back like an icy stream, sending shivers through my body. I couldn't speak; my lips were totally dry and almost stuck to my teeth. Francesca had gripped my arm so tight it seemed the blood would stop flowing.

The road was now clear. I put my foot down again as hard as I could. II PY must have known we were in trouble and responded like a bull elephant in full charge. I was now driving on instinct, spending more time looking behind me than where we were going. The road seemed to be flashing by, and the hills and fields seemed a mixed-up haze. I could see a lorry in the distance coming towards me. We're safe! I thought, I can beat him to that.

'He's coming!' Francesca screamed. 'He's coming, he's coming!'

There was nothing I could do. The acceleration of the modern car far outweighs II PY and sure enough the BMW drew level. I braked sharply as hard as I could, but again the modern car was able to brake easier than me. I was now only a few feet in front of him and I could see the rear passenger window starting to lower with sinister slowness. It was drawing level. The rear passenger had a gun!

'Get down, Francesca!' I pleaded with II PY to go faster. 'Come on, *come on*!' I shouted to her as the lorry approached ever nearer.

He was now almost level. I took my foot off the accelerator and II PY turned into the BMW, clipping the front passenger door. Her two-ton weight charging at sixty miles per hour was enough for the driver of the BMW to lose control. He was braking sharply, fighting his car, trying desperately to avoid the lorry which was now too close for that driver to miss. The inevitable collision was unbelievable. The BMW careered into the air and flew across the road landing with its roof on a stone wall just behind us. I braked hard and stopped over a hundred yards further on. We were both too shocked to move for a few minutes. But our peace was shattered by the drivers of both the lorry and another car, who came running over to us shouting what seemed like abuse.

'You fucking maniac. Look what you've done!'

I got out of the car. 'Are they all right?' I asked stupidly. It was unlikely anyone could have survived a crash like that.

'No, you stupid bastard. You've seen to that. You and yer fancy fucking Rolls!' the lorry driver shouted venomously.

'Would you please ring Keighley police and ask for Inspector Walker?' I asked.

'Don't you worry, matey,' he sneered, 'I've already called the police.'

I went back to my car to check on Francesca. She too was coming round and realized that everyone was blaming us. That's when the doubts started to come into my mind. Had I really seen a gun? Oh God! What had I done?

103

'Darling, I did see a gun . . . I promise I did see a gun . . . I did, I know I did . . .' I was totally distraught, my voice trembling. 'Oh Christ, they must find a gun, they've got to.'

'We'll be all right, darling!' she said, trying to comfort me, but I could see from her face that she too was having doubts.

We could hear the sounds of police vehicles racing ever nearer, and then an ambulance and finally a fire engine joined in. We both sat in silence, listening to the wailing getting closer. My stomach was in knots. The doubts created in my mind had overtaken the belief in what I had seen and I was now awaiting my fate.

I could see the cars moving over to allow the first of the police cars to pass quickly. It came thundering along the middle of the road and screeched to a halt. The two officers got out to inspect the carnage and were greeted by the lorry driver, who had seen everything and was immediately putting the blame where it belonged. They must have told him to wait, as he was left standing, still remonstrating with others. The officers went over to the remains of the BMW to check the car over for survivors. The second and then the third police car now arrived, followed by the ambulance.

A few minutes later the fire engine arrived. They soon ascertained there were no survivors and began the cutting out of the bodies.

In the meantime the lorry driver had had a field day. More expletives were used by him, about me, in the following half-hour, than I have heard in years. Several other witnesses were also interviewed before the police came to me.

An officer walked slowly to the car. I saw him in the mirror stop and make a note of the number, before coming to my door.

'Would you get out of the car please, sir?'

'Yes, sure!'

'May I come?' Francesca asked.

'No, ma'am. But we'll need a statement from you later.'

I followed the officer back to his car, amidst a torrent of verbal abuse from two or three people whom the lorry driver had 'enlightened'. 'He wants bloody locking up,' one shouted. 'Yeah and throw the key away!' said another.

I got into the police car, anxious to put my point over quickly, but I was quite properly stopped and put through the roadside breath test to see if I had been drinking.

'I haven't been drinking at all,' I said.

'We shall see,' the officer said, with a note of animosity in his voice. 'One continuous blow into the bag, please, sir.' The result was negative.

'You looked surprised,' I said to the officer.

'I'm neither one nor the other. I'm just here to do my job, sir.'

'Could you ring Inspector Walker from Keighley Police? He knows our circumstances.' I asked.

'No, I'm dealing with this matter, and when I have I'll decide when and who you will speak to.'

This got me annoyed. 'Please don't adopt this attitude with me before you know all the circumstances, because . . .' I stopped and left it at that.

'Are you threatening me?' he asked.

'Don't be silly! Of course not.'

'Well, let's see if we can make some progress then, shall we?' he said superciliously. 'Now let's hear your side of the story.'

I started from the beginning, telling him the story of the trouble at the house and the threats made and all about the BMW following us, exactly as it had happened. I had definitely seen the man point a gun at me through the passenger door window. 'I had no alternative!' I exclaimed as I finished my story.

For a moment the officer was lost for words, before coming back at me with 'Let's hope we find a weapon then, eh?'

'May I go and see my wife, please?' I asked.

'Yes, go on,' he said as he walked over to the other police officers and in turn to the firemen working on the car.

We sat in II PY awaiting our fate but were able to listen to the conversations going on all around us, including those of the local press who had arrived to photograph the accident and the Rolls-Royce. The lorry driver had to get in on the act by having his photograph taken as well and of course telling his side of the story.

We had our first crumb of comfort when we heard one of the firemen call over to the police. 'Sergeant, would you come over here, please?'

The sergeant duly walked over, followed by the lorry driver, who simply wanted 'to nose' but was duly told to go and wait by his lorry. He quickly studied the situation and asked the firemen to stop work. He immediately phoned his inspector back at Skipton Police Station and very quietly apprised him of the situation. We were unable to hear what was said apart from the fact that a scenes of crime officer was being sent out and that they were to clear the site of everyone immediately. This included us and the other immediate witnesses. We were all instructed to sit in our vehicles and stay put.

From this moment on, I knew we would be vindicated. The area around the car was taped off and about half an hour later the police screened everything off.

The young officer who had interviewed me earlier came over to us. 'Was it Inspector Walker at Keighley Station you wanted me to speak to?' he asked.

I nodded. 'So you've found the gun?'

'All I can say at this stage is that some things you said have been confirmed. I've got all your details; you're free to go now. I'll contact you shortly.' With that he rejoined the others.

I was so relieved with the news that I got out of my car, walked over to the lorry driver, and began shouting at him. 'Do you think I would have done that deliberately, you jealous bastard?'

The young officer came running back over and asked me to calm down and to go home. I left leaving the lorry driver looking somewhat perplexed at my outburst.

For the first time I had the nerve to look at the damage on

106

II PY and genuinely I couldn't find anything, save two scratches on the bumper.

The following day, a Monday, I contacted Clive White and gave him all the facts, without missing a thing. We all thought that the more publicity we received the more people would be aware and the better protection we'd gain for ourselves. The *Mail*'s Tuesday headline was 'Mystery Rolls Claims Four More', and once again featured a photo of II PY in all her glory. The names of the victims were announced the following day, and Basil Waites and the driver of the car who had been involved with the attack on the house were amongst them. It sounds rather cruel to say, but I was rather relieved that Waites was one of the victims. I felt somewhat guilty about feeling relieved that we would be getting no more trouble from that quarter, but I consoled myself with the thought that it had boiled down to a question of his life or mine.

Chapter 8

June continued May's fine spell. Temperatures were running into the seventies and we made the most of it. The car had become something of a celebrity and was easily recognized, not only from the *Daily Mail* but also from the BBC's *Look North* and Yorkshire TV's *Calendar* programmes. We basked in the reflected glory. We were now only fourteen days away from the Kelmarsh Rally. David Mainwering was arriving in Manchester in two days, his 20/25 four days later. II PY was in excellent condition; even the slight scratch on the bumper had been removed.

We were a little late leaving for Manchester Airport the day David and Eleanor were due to arrive. So much so, I forgot to release the dogs from the pen in our rush not to be late for them. David hadn't changed in any way from the day we first met him at the Grant & Bulldozer's auction. We went through the introductions.

'I've heard so much about you,' said Eleanor. 'It's lovely to meet after all this time. In fact, I feel as though I have known you for years; David has talked so much about you and your ... adventures!'

'They weren't adventures, at least not the kind I like!' Francesca replied. 'But at least it's over now and we've had some lovely days in the car.'

From Manchester we went via Colne, Laneshawbridge and then over the moors to Haworth. The pretty way, Francesca calls it, and sure enough our guests wanted us to stop and have our photographs taken with the moors in the background. We arrived at the bottom of the hill in Haworth, turning left into our road, when we were met by a neighbour. It was Brian Uttley, a former middleweight boxer, with a shock of black hair and a face showing the amount of bouts he had fought, but still somewhat fit and active for a man of seventy.

'I've been trying to get your kids for hours!' he said excitedly. 'I heard the dogs going mad and I knew they were locked away. I went across to see what was going on and saw this fella walking down the drive. He was having a good look round.'

Francesca and I glanced at each other.

'Did you give the OK for Willy Betz the transport firm to take your Rolls?' Brian asked.

'What!' I yelled. 'No, I bloody didn't! What's happened?' I asked.

'Well. about an hour ago, I saw these men walking down the drive. One of them was the bloke who came earlier. I thought there was something funny, so I went down to ask 'em what was going on. They told me that you had asked them to take the car to Coventry for a show. I had no reason to disbelieve them until a few minutes ago I notifed the broken lock on your garage door. I'm so sorry, Robert.'

'Don't worry, Brian. It's not your fault. Have you phoned the police?'

'No. I was just about to. Perhaps there's one thing you could tell them. When the lorry was leaving, the driver knocked the top off the wall. It's bound to have left a mark.'

'Thanks, Brian. I'll ring the police.'

I dialled 999 and gave a full description of the lorry and the men, exactly as Brian had told us.

I took David and Eleanor into the house and managed to contact both Philip and Henry. The latter was in Keighley with Philip at the builders merchant in Bradford. I explained what had happened and asked them to patrol all the main roads to and from Keighley and Bradford, including all the roads to Leeds and the motorways. I was going to stay in Haworth to coordinate the action. I told the lads to get as many of their friends as they could to search the area; I would see them OK for their costs. David also suggested we contact Clive, in view of the fact the *Mail* had been reporting on the car.

Henry has many friends, all of whom wanted to help, and among those he roped in was Faisal, the Pakistani owner of the local Keighley Taxi firm. Henry told us he was only two minutes away from the taxi office and thought it would be an excellent idea if he could get the taxis to help him. He went to the taxi rank by the station and ran in.

'Faisal, I need your help urgently. My dad's just rang me. His Rolls-Royce has been stolen about half an hour ago.'

'Is that the one that's been on the telly?' he asked, in his strong Yorkshire accent but still flavoured with his retained Pakistani accent.

'Yeah,' Henry replied, explaining exactly what Brian had seen.

Faisal suddenly became excited, he took the microphone off Ali, the young man who controlled the taxi movements, switched over to loudspeaker so that he was sure all of Keighley would hear, and shouted excitedly: 'Listen all drivers. Have any of you seen a big yellow Artic with Willy Betz on the sides driving away from the area? It's urgent – they've just nicked that Rolls-Royce from Haworth and it's around 'ere sumwere. Cum on, think,' he said, 'sumon must 'ave sin it,' he jabbered.

Henry could hear a succession of crackly voices as the cabbies chattered excitedly amongst themselves. Then suddenly Wasim, one of the drivers, shouted, 'I've sin it.'

'Where abouts ar ya?' Faisal asked.

'Long Lea,' he shouted over the intercom.

'Don't be sa bluddy daft! How the fuck could ya get a twenty bluddy ton artic on Long Lea?'

'It ain't an artic, it's a yellow transit.'

''Ow the fuck can ya get a bluddy Roller in a soddin' transit?' Faisal shouted back. ''As anyone sin it?' he asked again, more insistently this time.

There was no reply. 'Right,' Faisal shouted, 'Drop everythin' and start searchin'. It can't hav got to Bradford yet!' He gave instructions for some to go Bingley, others to Shipley, Saltaire and the outer areas of Bradford, covering all the major roads, including the road to Leeds.

Henry was just to leave when Wasim called in again.

'What's it on this time? A fuckin' motorbike?' Faisal replied, to roars of laughter from all present in the office.

There was a crackle.

'Where the fuck's Walls' Place?' Faisal asked.

Henry seized a secondary microphone.

'I know!' he interrupted. 'Carry on! This is Henry, Henry Conway.'

'Well, we got held up by this lorry backin' in . . .' Wassim said. 'I'm sure it was yella.'

Henry ran out of the office followed by two of the drivers and made his way quickly to T & M Walls, shipping agents, telephoning me as he went. Their warehouse was only a couple of blocks away and they arrived within three or four minutes.

'Check it out, but be careful,' I told Henry when he rang. 'Ring me back as soon as possible.' I then rang the police to advise them that II PY might be in Walls' warehouse and they agreed to get there as soon as possible.

Henry, together with Rajid and Aftab the drivers, carefully checked around the building, but it seemed deserted. They walked back to the rear of the building and found a door and within ten minutes they were in. The building was empty apart from a few sealed boxes, which seemed as if they were empty, two large yellow tarpaulins with Willy Betz written on, and a couple of large cans of black cellulose paint which had recently been used.

Henry and his friends were interrupted by the police, who came in force to catch the villains, but only managed to catch Henry. Thankfully I had warned the police about Henry's presence and they were released immediately.

It was obvious that the operation had been well planned: the thieves had changed the appearance of the vehicle and now had a free run to wherever. Henry and the others went to all the properties nearby to see if any one had seen a large lorry leaving Walls and at what time and what colour. The local shopkeepers had all thought something was going on. Walls were no longer in business, so it was somewhat unusual for the building to be used. One even commented that the drivers were clearly not used to the manoeuvres and had blocked the road for several minutes. He also said the lorry was red and that he knew it belonged to a firm called 'Norbert something – a foreign-sounding name'.

Henry ran back to the warehouse and informed the police of what they had found out and they in turn promised to chase it up. He thanked the two taxi drivers and raced back home. In the meantime Philip had also arrived and everyone sat in the lounge to think things out. David started using his deductive powers.

'Let's look at what we've got. One, they've changed the truck's appearance; it's now red. Two, it possibly belongs to a firm named Norbert.'

'Dentressangle!' Francesca interrupted. 'It's a French company and the livery's red. I've seen them somewhere before.'

'Excellent!' David commented. 'Three. Why were the sealed cartons lightweight? It's obvious; it was simply packing to conceal the car amidst the cargo. We know Maitland has many contacts in Europe and I believe he is trying to take it there.

'Four. Why the black paint? It's obvious the trailer was damaged by the wall and on close inspection would be seen. Therefore new black paint, perhaps all round the edge of the trailer, would fool all but the most experienced eye. The damage would be visible if you were specifically looking for it.'

Philip interrupted. 'Are you sure your name's David and not Sherlock?' There was a ripple of laughter.

'We've got to put ourselves in their position,' David continued, 'we need to think what they would do. Where would they go and how quickly? Now, I don't remember all the names, but we've looked in Bingley, I think you said, Shipley, on the Leeds road and elsewhere. I presume these are all in the same direction.'

'Yes they are,' I replied. 'They're the quickest routes to the motorways and to Hull docks.'

'Well, there you are, that's exactly what the thieves would have worked out. So it's my contention they would go in the opposite direction. What have we got that way?' he asked.

Philip and Henry then detailed the routes they could take, one way via Skipton to the M6 the other via Cowling and Colne to the M66, which would lead to the M6 and Manchester.

'Almost the way we came,' I interjected. 'The other would be to go down the M66 via Blackburn down to Manchester.'

'We have to assume they would want to leave the country quickly, probably to Europe.' David said, taking up his argument again.

'What about Liverpool docks then?' Henry asked'. That's the nearest.'

'My English geography isn't that good, but I wouldn't think a lorry would take a ship from Liverpool to Europe. It would take far too long. That means Dover or Folkestone.'

'He *is* Sherlock Holmes, no question,' Philip quipped again.

I interrupted with one little gem of information. 'The driver wouldn't want to draw attention to himself by driving too long and too far. He's not going to do the trip down south in a day, so he's going to stop.'

'Good thinking, Dad,' Henry said cheerfully.

'Can't leave it all to the Americans, can we?' I replied jokingly.

David continued. 'When he stops he will want the lorry to be inconspicuous, say at a truck stop, and he will stay there until he can safely drive again. Now how many hours do they need to reach Dover, say?'

'I think it's about eleven, but they have to have had a break of about an hour. I'm not too sure,' I answered.

'OK, let's look at that. Say two hours to pick the car up, two hours to change the lorry, one hour rest. Two and a half hours to the M6. So the maximum he has is three and a half hours. Where could he get in that time? And where are the rest places?'

It was an excellent piece of deduction. I went to the office and brought back a motorway map. We decided that we would take three cars. It was at about this time that Victoria arrived with her young man, Andy. He was a giant of a lad. He played rugby and was strong as an ox. He spent many weeks a year out of the country, in Russia and other European countries. We quickly briefed them on the day's events and our intended actions and he agreed to join us in the search. We could now take four cars. Philip in the XK Jaguar; Henry in his Lotus; Andy in the 'souped-up' Peugeot, with David and myself in the XJ Jaguar.

We would work in two teams: Philip and Henry in one, with Andy, David and me in the other. Each team would stop at every alternate services on the M6 and M1 as far as Toddington on the M1. We agreed that if any of us passed a Norbert Dentressangle truck, we were to notify the others immediately, slow down, allow him to pass and check for damage on the near side. If it fitted the description, we were to follow it until it stopped. Victoria was to coordinate all movements from base. It was a well conceived plan based on some well-founded assumptions. All we needed was a plan of action if we did find the truck.

It was my turn to have some serious input into the strategy. A friend of ours, Bruce Wilson, a gentle giant of a man, a former wrestler known as 'Gentleman Jim', was now a long-distance lorry driver. There was a chance he was at home as his work days were somewhat erratic. A quick phone call revealed he was free and not working for a further two days. This was wonderful. Not only was he experienced with all heavy vehicles; he was a useful bloke to have on your side, especially if things became too heavy. Bruce arrived in his car, with the boot loaded with tools, winding handles and wooden blocks. 'These, I promise you, will be useful if we see the truck,' he said as we were loading them into the XJ.

We were ready. The lads set off; they were going via Blackburn and would be in the Knutsford Services, Manchester, within ninety minutes. Andy took Bruce for company and would go via the M62 to the M6. David and I were following on, taking the ring road round Manchester. We, too, would meet at the Knutsford Services in ninety minutes. Francesca and Victoria were to put the police in the picture, though Inspector Walker warned us not to take the law into our own hands.

We were on our way, over the moors through Laneshawbridge for the second time that day. We reached the Manchester ring road in forty minutes. By this time, according to Victoria, Philip and Henry had already passed two Norbert Dentressangle trucks and checked them out, but to no avail. Neither Andy nor I had even seen one on the journey to Knutsford. We all arrived well within the ninety minutes agreed. A quick check of the details and we were away again. Bruce gave his experienced input. 'Check the trucks parked on the exit road first, then around the edges, before you check the interior. If the driver sees the trucks being checked, he may get nervous and set off.'

'What do you mean?' David asked.

'A lot of drivers have driven over their hours and don't want to be caught. If they see someone checking, they will drive off, rather than risk it. This driver, *if* we see him and it's a big *if*, will already be nervous. He'll move out at the first sign of trouble.'

'Good thinking!' David commented.

'Don't be that surprised,' Bruce said laughingly, 'I did go to school!'

'I didn't mean any offence,' David replied, somewhat embarrassed.

'None taken.'

We set off again, the lads heading for the Keele Services, whilst we would check all other stops on the way down. 'It's a waste of time,' Bruce said as we were walking round the Road Chef services, the first after Manchester. 'He will have got much, much further than this. At least as far as Watford Gap on the M1 or even further. We don't mess about once we've got going,' he said proudly, sticking out his enormous chest.

'It's safer to check everywhere, just in case they try to swap trucks,' David commented, with his usual logic.

'It would be very difficult to alter or change loads without drawing attention, especially as the Rolls-Royce has been splashed all over the newspapers and the TV,' Bruce added.

'Good point!' I said. 'Let's get on.'

We all met up at Keele for a quick break, reassured by Bruce's comment that if the lorry driver had parked up he would not be able to move for several hours. In view of this, we decided to travel in convoy and check each service area together.

We had passed Stafford. Wolverhampton and Birmingham and were now following the signs to the M1. Night had fallen, making it very difficult to check the nearside of any Dentressangle lorries we might see. Toddington was the last services we were prepared to go to.

'He wouldn't travel any further than this because, even if his hours hadn't run out, he wouldn't risk going through London over his time. He would definitely draw attention to himself,' Bruce said, taking control. 'He'd be mad to go on.'

Toddington Services was quite busy. In fact, we had a little difficulty in finding a place to park. We carried out what had become our normal routine: I would check the interior areas with David, while Philip and Henry did the far reaches. So far Andy and Bruce had been unable to find a space to park. This suited Bruce as he had seen a Dentressangle lorry parked on the exit road, just where he had predicted. He parked up about twenty-five metres to the rear of the lorry and they both walked back to meet us. In the meantime Philip had his eye on two more lorries, at the far left, almost at the entrance. 'I bet that's him,' Bruce said, pointing to the exit road. 'It's where I would be in the same situation.'

'What shall we do?' I asked, my heart beginning to race.

David's logic once again came into play.

'We can't go about in a group; it will draw attention. So I propose that three of us go and each check a truck as quick as possible.'

A little later Andy rushed back to the group.

'I think it's that one over there . . . The driver's not in the cab,' he said excitedly. 'There's a very long, deep groove covered with new paint.'

'I think we've got it,' I exclaimed, feeling my temples thump with the adrenalin. 'Bruce, have you any ideas how we can check?'

Bruce left us without a word and looked casually over the vehicle, returning with a few pearls of wisdom.

'I don't think there's much weight on the trailer; the tyres are not under pressure. We will have to get in at the far side. We'll have to undo the first four or five clips and the draw wire, which seems to be on the trailer as well. It'll take a few minutes and whoever goes in will need time, cover and protection. The car may be hidden in the cargo . . . We don't know.'

David interrupted. 'Perhaps one of the cars should fake a break-down at the side of the truck to provide cover. Bruce, you look the most useful, you stay back! Henry you go in! OK?'

I took the Jaguar over to the side of the lorry and lifted the bonnet. While Philip helped Henry get into the lorry, the rest of us pretended to be looking at the engine.

We were disturbed by a man walking over to us. 'It's the driver!' Bruce exclaimed quietly. He was not in the least concerned until Henry in his excitement shouted, 'It's in here.' The driver immediately drew a knife, which was like a red rag to a bull as far as Bruce was concerned. I don't think I've ever seen a man disarmed so quickly in my life, followed as quick as a flash by a forearm smash, which knocked him out.

'Open the boot quick,' Bruce shouted. 'He may have friends.'

I opened the boot and Bruce immediately took out a winding handle and started lowering the trailer legs. Soon the driving wheels were almost off the floor. In the meantime I phoned the police.

Bruce was right; he did have friends and they came skidding to a halt in a black twin-cab pickup.

Four men got out. 'What the fuck's going on?' one of them shouted. Then after seeing the driver on the floor out cold, he took out an automatic pistol and told us to stand back. We had no option and did just that, with the exception of Henry, who was still in the lorry, and Philip, who was hiding at the other side. It was difficult to get a good look at the men because it was very dark, but the gunman's face, I noted, was badly marked, possibly by boyhood acne.

The driver began to come round and was helped to his feet by the other two. The third got back into the driving seat of the pickup and waited whilst we were held at bay by the gun.

'There's only three now,' Bruce whispered, as he saw the man getting back into the pickup.

'Shut your fucking mouth, Grandad, unless you want this shoved down it!'

Bruce fell silent but continued to look directly into the gunman's face. He was fearless.

The men started to become agitated. We could all hear the wail of police sirens in the distance.

'Get this fucking thing out of here, quick!' he yelled to the truck driver. 'Get in!'

The driver of the lorry struggled into his cab and started the engine, whilst the others jumped into the twin-cab and waited for the lorry to move. The driver put the lorry into gear and the engine began to race. The drive wheels were spinning like mad.

The noise caused Scarface as I'd dubbed him, to become confused. He started waving the gun around and yelling at the top of his voice to the one of the others to let the trailer down, as he could now see what Bruce had done. 'Hurry, you stupid bastard.'

The unfortunate fellow's face met the raw steel of a turning handle. There was a dull thud as he almost simultaneously hit the floor. Philip had been hiding behind the wheels of the trailer and waiting with the turning handle ready in his hands.

The other guy quickly came round to help but was now faced

with the two lads. Henry jumped on to him from the trailer, whilst one well-timed kick from Philip to the lower regions of the man's anatomy put him out of contention.

The lorry driver, who could now see it was a hopeless cause, jumped down from his cab, and both he and Scarface scarpered back to the twin-cab.

This was too much for Bruce, who charged over to them shouting, 'I'll give you bloody Grandad!' and he grabbed the lorry driver's leg before he could fully get into the vehicle. It moved off with Bruce still holding on and being dragged along. The car braked sharply in the hope of shaking him off, but it had the reverse effect: the lorry driver was shaken out of the back and, with Bruce still holding on, he fell out on to the road.

'Never mind him! Just get out of here quick,' Scarface was yelling, as the the black twin-cab sped away. Within a few minutes two high-speed police cars stormed into the services. The three crooks, looking dazed and more than slightly worse for wear, were rounded up and led away. Bruce was grazed, but really none the worse for his moment of bravery.

I quickly phoned Francesca with the good news. 'We've got it!' There were shrieks of joy and amazement from Victoria and Eleanor, as she passed on the news. I handed the phone to David, who by now was totally exhausted. 'Hi, sweetheart. Everything's OK. We've found the car and the police are here. You told me this trip would give us a well-earned break, cos nothing happens in little old England.'

Chapter 9

We were taken into the cafeteria by the police so we could give them our side of the story. In the meantime they taped the area off as a crime scene and told us we would not be able to reclaim the car until it had been fully checked and dusted over. The Kelmarsh Rally was at the weekend and I had to plead with the police to release the car.

David whispered: 'Get your friend Clive to do a feature and let him know the police are holding things up. It's surprising how the police cooperate when they're under the spotlight!'

I telephoned Clive, who was not very happy at being woken up until he heard the bones of the story. He said he would meet us later on for the full facts, but he had enough for the early edition and would ring me.

We managed to get accommodation at the nearby Travelodge but we were too tired to even talk, and after a shortish night's sleep and a good breakfast, we were on our way home. There was a wonderful welcome from the family, only ruined a little by the press and TV reporters, camped out in the road, awaiting our return.

Clive was amazing. His stories in the press emphasized that the car would be in the Kelmarsh Rally and that the police were doing everything to ensure it would be. He even got the chief constable involved. It all worked a treat. Within two days the police phoned to let me know I could go and collect the car.

Henry and I drove down to Toddington and arrived about two o'clock. There was a little crowd of spectators around to see us load the car on to the trailer. Several wanted photographs, though it didn't look quite the same without the 'flying lady', which was at home for safe-keeping.

The journey home was uneventful, save for the hundreds of motorists who hooted their horns as they passed and we arrived in Haworth late evening. Fortunately, no one was around, other than the family and our guests. II PY was a little dirty, but it didn't stop David and Eleanor admiring the car, which they'd last seen in the possession of a now-convicted drug dealer.

'She's just beautiful,' David said with delight.

'I know and we've been married over thirty years.'

'I meant the car!' David responded with a laugh.

A couple of days later, David, Eleanor and Henry went to Manchester cargo terminal to collect their car. There were no unusual circumstances; no one had been chased by criminals.

'It was a bit of a let-down,' Henry commented on their return.

They arrived back in plenty of time and immediately started preparing for Kelmarsh. There was great excitement building up in all of us. I was thankful there was no rivalry between us, as the cars were in a different class. I was after the big one: 'best car in show'.

I had booked us all into the Blatchett Arms Hotel on the Friday before the rally was due to start on the Saturday. We arrived just after midday in time for lunch, enjoying an odd bevy or two in the Bonham's marquee where we admired the lots which were to be auctioned the next day.

It was a glorious day for any festival, but this was looking really good. We arrived just before lunch, having packed our picnic in the back of the two cars. We unloaded II PY from the trailer and set off for Kelmarsh Hall. It was like a scene from some old 1930s movie, the wonderful array of beautiful cars matched by the glamorous dresses and hats worn by many of the ladies. Everyone seemed to be drinking chilled champagne or tucking into fresh salmon and strawberries. We could all be millionaires for a day.

When judging began, we and II PY were lined up with several other Phantoms from the 1920s and 1930s. It soon became obvious, however, that we had something special. The clue came from the constant stream of visitors we were attracting and we soon had to stop the public and the enthusiasts from touching and opening the doors. We all stood round the car, Francesca in her 1920s-style sleeveless pleated dress and feathered hat and me in my boater, cream trousers and striped jacket. Henry, dressed as a young Oxford type straight out of *Brideshead Revisited* attracted many admirers.

Sunday was the results day, and when it came, it was still a most wonderful surprise. We had won the best Phantom and the 'best car in show'. Francesca and I simply hugged each other in excitement, something really not done at a Rolls-Royce rally, but who cared? It was exhilarating. There was a further surprise. An advertising agency asked if we would be prepared to take the car to Le Touquet and then on to St-Tropez to make an advertising film.

The agent's name was Ed Special. 'And I am,' he said, introducing himself. He was a long-serving American advertising man, with the charisma to match; a roly-poly sort of man, with a beard and loose-fitting bright clothes, that made him look like Burl Ives, the American singer and actor. He gave Francesca his card. I noticed how he could hardly keep his eyes off her. Who wouldn't the way she looked today? We spent about fifteen minutes negotiating fees and timings, then exchanged details and phone numbers. We were really very excited about the thought of an all-expenses-paid trip to our favourite area in France, a place we as a family had visited for almost forty years and where we have a house in a lovely village near St-Tropez.

We were about to resume our victory celebrations, when we were approached by David and a very smart-looking man and woman. They turned out to be Mr and Mrs Blessington-Smith, the couple who had become friendly with David and Eleanor during their European rallies. They were very complimentary about II PY's condition.

'I do hope you have better luck with the car than John had,' Mr Blessington-Smith said in a friendly but somewhat condescending manner. 'The body is absolutely super, but the gubbins has caused some problems in the past.'

David and I looked at each other, knowing what the truth really was. 'I think the problem has been sorted out now, don't you, Robert?' he said, answering for me, before dashing off to his car.

Blessington-Smith had waited around until I was on my own and immediately came to the point. 'As I said before, I would like to buy your car and I am going to surprise you with my offer.'

'Not interested,' I responded sharply.

He came back equally as determined, 'You haven't heard it yet.'

'I don't need to and I don't want to sell.'

'I'll give you a hundred thousand.'

'Dollars or pounds?' I asked.

'Pounds. I knew you had a price.'

'Yes I have, but yours is the third I have had today and nowhere near the other two,' I said triumphantly, knowing it wasn't true.

Blessington-Smith began to show his annoyance, when he asked, 'Who were they from?'

I was rescued by several other well-wishers who were simply admiring the car and wanting to chat and it gave me the opportunity to wish Blessington-Smith a polite goodbye.

'We'll leave at that then, shall we? Bye,' I said as he left scowling.

The next surprise was far less pleasant. Morales was among the people still milling round the car, and with him was the 'Tall Thin Man' yet again. They parted quickly the moment they saw me glancing in their direction. I was chatting to a group of people, and Morales began signalling to me, trying to attract my attention. He was clearly anxious to talk to me.

Having sent off Henry to go and find David, I sauntered over to Morales, stalling as long as I could.

'It certainly looks a great car,' Morales said in an ingratiating sort of way.

'Yes, it is. We've spent a lot of time on the car, especially for the show, but really it is down to John Maitland. He's the one who has really looked after the car,' I replied.

'That's what I want to see you about,' Morales continued. 'My client would like to make you another offer.'

I stopped him in mid-sentence. I could see Henry and David hurrying over to see me.

'Mr Morales, you've met my son, Henry, and I think you've met . . .'

David interrupted me, holding his hand out. 'I'm George Simpson, Mr Morales, of the *New York Times*. We met at the auction. I tried to buy this beauty.'

'Aaaah yes, I remember!' Morales replied. 'I would like to talk to Mr Conway in private, if that's possible?'

'I'd rather not,' I replied. 'I've had that much trouble since I bought this car.'

Morales interrupted me. 'That's none of my client's doing; he simply wants to buy the car.'

'No, I want George and my son with me. I think we should stop pretending. We all know you represent John Maitland . . . the drug dealer.'

Even David baulked at that comment.

Morales was momentarily lost for words. 'He was found with a very small amount of drugs in his possession and for that he went to prison and lost his automobile.'

'Please, I need to have some answers to one or two questions,' I asked. 'One, why is it so important to Mr Maitland to have the car. Two, why has he caused my family so much grief, and three, who is the thin tall man I keep seeing both with you and without you?'

'My client, Mr Maitland, has spent hundreds of thousands of dollars on this car. It's his relaxation, his hobby. He just wants it back. He has also asked me to assure you that he has had nothing to do with the . . . difficulties you and your family have encountered since returning to England . . .'

'That's hard to believe!' David said, interrupting him.

'And what about the man?' I asked, reminding him of the third point.

Morales seemed very reluctant to answer and simply changed the subject. 'My client is a very rich man and has asked me to offer you one hundred and fifty thousand pounds sterling for the car.'

There was a stunned silence for what seemed like minutes. 'I . . . I don't know what to say,' I finally said.

'Well?' Morales asked. 'Tempting enough?'

'Yes it is, I'm afraid to say.'

I saw the look of disappointment on David's face.

'Look, Mr Morales,' I continued, 'I cannot make my mind up here and now, and in any event I cannot do anything about it until the end of October. I've got three or four bookings for the car. Two photocalls in Calais and one in Le Touquet and St-Tropez, possibly at the beginning of November. We have also agreed to take part in the inaugural Rolls-Royce–Bentley Race from Charnay to London via Paris in the middle of November. I've promised and under no circumstances can I let these people down. I will consider it after then, but not before,' I said firmly.

Our conversation was curtailed by the arrival of the club president who wanted another photocall for the family and the car.

'I'm sorry, Mr Morales, we have to go. One thing I can promise you is I will not sell it to anyone else.'

'Thank you!' Morales said, still trying to ingratiate himself.

'He didn't answer the third question,' David remarked.

On the way back to Haworth that evening we decided to stop at the motorway services for a bite to eat. Henry stayed with the cars. We were nonchalantly drinking our beverages, when David suddenly announced, 'Robert, I believe him.'

'Who?' I said, somewhat bemused.

'Morales, I believe him,' David repeated.

'Believe what? I'm sorry I must be tired.'

'I don't believe Maitland had anything to do with the troubles.'

'Why?' I asked, my senses returning to normal.

'Why would he be prepared to pay a large amount like that for the car and at the same time try to steal it? It doesn't make sense.'

'Go on,' Francesca said, getting a little concerned at the prospect of more intrigue.

'Maybe not only Maitland wants the car but someone else, too . . . Maybe there's something about the car . . . *in* the car that Maitland's not telling us.'

'You're right,' I said, beginning to get into the swing of things. 'I was starting to think myself that the notion Maitland wants the car simply because he loves it is bullshit.'

'Exactly!' David said. 'But think on. What could possibly be in the car that the DEA could have missed? I know they had the car searched thoroughly, but they must have missed something. Oh God, I wish I wasn't going back so soon.' David was due to go back to the States in two days.

'It really needs experts to search the car and we couldn't do it properly, could we?' I proffered.

'We could try!' David responded.

I did not want the car taken apart and spent an hour debating all the various scenarios which could give us a clue as to what was really going on and who was really behind it. Was it Maitland and Morales or the Blessington-Smiths? The latter had been very pushy over the last few days and I felt his innocent blustering covered some underlying deception. Could Ed Special be behind things, as he wanted to borrow the car? At this point anything seemed possible.

'David, would you do me a favour?' I asked. 'Could you find out exactly how the car was searched and what was found? It would save a lot of work if I knew.'

'Of course I will,' David replied. 'I fully intend seeing Sweeney at the *New York Times*, the moment I get back to tell him about my suspicions. Come on, it's getting late.'

On his arrival back in New York, David was as good as his word. Sweeney's first reaction was to put something in print. However, Janice Fink at the DEA warned Sweeney that any action would be premature. If the car was found with drugs hidden inside, there would be no possible chance of convicting Maitland, for obvious reasons. After all, he was no longer the owner of the automobile, and he could claim the car had been tampered with. She suggested that things should be left as they were and that they should wait and see how things panned out.

This was all a bit of a relief to me, despite my desire to resolve the mystery. My car, for the moment at least, could remain untouched.

Chapter 10

The heady days of Kelmarsh were fast disappearing into memory when we were brought back to reality with a bump. Philip had, on several occasions, seen a black Toyota twin-cab pickup parked along our road. We had reported it to the police, but unfortunately we were treated as though we were being paranoid, probably because it seemed that all those who were after us had either been killed or were in custody. With Inspector Walker on holiday we couldn't make much headway. They did, however, promise to keep up patrols past the house.

One day Philip decided to take matters into his own hands and casually walked over to the car. As he approached, the passenger-side black-tinted window slowly slid down, revealing a really nasty-looking individual. He grunted, as if to say 'what do you want?'

'I just wondered if you were lost or wanted something,' Philip asked politely.

'Fuck off!' The black glass slowly returned to the closed position.

Normally, Philip would have opened the door, pulled the man out and flattened the man, but for some reason he restrained himself and casually walked away. He phoned Henry.

'What's up?' Henry asked.

'I think we've got a problem. Where are you?'

'I'm in town.'

'Get here as quickly as you can. Come down Butt Lane. When

you get to the bottom, you'll see a black pickup. Give me a ring when you're there. Don't turn into our road until you see me come round the corner from Bridgehouse.

'Now listen carefully. They're parked by the park entrance, facing Bridgehouse. I'll pull in front of them with the lorry; you pull behind them. You are in the Land-Rover, aren't you?'

'Yes, of course.'

'Pull within a couple of feet from the back and I'll do the same at the front. We'll then see what they want.' He paused for a second or two. 'Oh and bring *something* with you. OK?'

'Yes OK. See you in a minute.'

Philip drove out of the drive in his lorry, driving out in the opposite direction of the Toyota pickup, to give the impression he was leaving the area. When out of sight, he did a U-turn, parked up and waited for Henry's call. It came about five minutes later and Philip's plan was put into motion. Philip drove his vehicle around the corner into our road and quickly toward to pickup. Henry did the same. Within seconds the pickup was unable to get clear. Henry opened his door to get out, leaving the engine running. A fortunate action, as the passenger opened his window and leaned out waving a pistol.

Philip panicked momentarily, but he had the sense to close his door and duck down. Then the adrenalin kicked in. In one quick movement, he put the lorry into first gear, revved up hard, released the clutch and banged the lorry into the pickup. He rammed it so hard that it pushed the pickup back into the Land-Rover, which was just pulling up. Thank goodness for modern Japanese technology. The severe knock released the air bags at unbelievable speed, trapping both the driver and his passenger in their seats. In the confusion the gun went off several times, puncturing not only one of the air bags, but also shattering the passenger window and the windscreens of the pickup and the lorry.

Philip lost all control. He jumped out of the lorry and charged like a mad bull at the passenger pummelling the man's face and arms. 'You bastards, come here again and I'll kill you!' It was only the intervention of Henry that prevented him from doing it there and then.

Neither of the lads had seen the driver's air bag deflate and that he was beginning to come to. They only realized when the pickup started up and the tyres began screaming against the tarmac, causing a pall of black smoke and sparks to fly in the air. The driver was pushing the pickup against the Land-Rover to give himself room to manoeuvre. He succeeded. The pickup screamed out of its captivity, raced down Belle Isle Road and out on to the main road.

Suddenly the boys noticed the gun lying in the road. It must have been dropped during the struggle. Henry was about to retrieve it when Philip shouted, 'Don't touch it! Let the police have it; I'll give them a ring.'

The police arrived in force, all guns blazing and all sirens wailing. I think there were six cars involved. They sealed off the road, the Land-Rover and the lorry and began to search for any further evidence. Philip and Henry returned to the house to await questioning. It seemed like half the village had heard the sirens and were trying to get down the road to see what was going on.

Inspector Munro didn't seem convinced that this had anything to do with the Rolls-Royce, though he promised to keep an open mind. However, we were sure and sought the help of Clive White of the *Mail*, to whom we had promised to give any newsworthy information, for previous favours rendered. He was grateful and turned up about half an hour later, much to the chagrin of the police inspector in charge. Francesca detected a little hostility in his attitude toward me, but I shrugged it off. He was just doing his job. Clive White, at the *Mail*, came up trumps as usual, making full use of the story. However, nothing much came of it, though the patrols were finally stepped up outside our house.

It was the end of July, coming up to our birthdays. Mine was the 31st and Francesca's was the 6th August. We always had a joint birthday party and this year was no exception. We had decided to stay at the fabulous Midland Hotel, at Morecambe, which was constructed the same year as II PY in 1933.

We were a little late going to bed this night, as we had been having a drink or two with our friends. I had drifted off to sleep when I woke up sharply as I heard Bill, one of our Border collies, growling. There was the noise of a scuffle followed by a muffled crack and loud howling from Bill, and then an eerie silence. Meg, our other collie, also started to howl. She always did this when she heard an ambulance or police siren sounding in the distance. This time, however, she seemed to be howling because she was in trouble. She then started barking and there was another muffled crack; followed by a continuation of the howling and again silence.

Francesca thought I was imagining things, but we decided to take a look.

'You wait here and keep an eye out,' I said, as I left her getting dressed to follow me. 'If I'm not back in ten minutes, phone the police.'

'Wait for me!' she demanded, but I was gone.

I looked out of the dining room window and could see a flashlight. Foolishly I didn't phone the police; I phoned Philip and Henry instead. I phoned Philip first.

'I think we've got intruders in the garden. Can you get down here as fast as you can. Phone Henry and tell him likewise.'

Philip was concerned. 'Phone the police, Dad, and don't go out. I'll be there in a minute.'

'Come down Butt Lane with your lights off. They're in the garden, probably from the railway. If you go over the waterfall we might catch them.'

'There is no *we* in it, Dad. I mean it. Don't go out! I'll be there as quick as I can.' The phone went dead.

I went through to the back of the house and let myself out on to the drive, keeping close to the wall of the house to prevent the emergency lighting from coming on. The gates were still closed, with the locks intact, which confirmed that the intruders had come from the bottom of the garden over the river or from the railway and coalyard.

I crept slowly round the rear of the house and then on to the rear balcony, where I could get a better, if not perfect, view of the area. I could see two men in the garden across the river, making their way to join another one or two people who were trying to break into the garage.

Meanwhile Philip, who was waiting at the bottom of Butt Lane for Henry, had seen two men leaving a car in the railway yard and then cross into the bottom of our garden. Henry at last joined him and together they crossed into the railway yard. Two cars were parked there, their engines still warm.

'Have you got anything?' Philip whispered to Henry, pointing in the direction of the tyres. Henry signalled he had and took out a penknife and jabbed it into the front tyre of the Land-Rover causing it to lean over quickly. The interlopers had left a man inside; obviously to look after the vehicles and perhaps to facilitate a quick getaway. He was taken by surprise, but quickly jumped out of the vehicle and charged at Henry, but not before the latter had put his penknife to good use again, this time puncturing the back tyre.

Henry's attacker caught him in the arm with a flick knife, he had suddenly produced. 'What the fuck are . . .'

He didn't have chance to finish his question before Philip cracked him on the back of the head with a large lump of coal. He fell to the ground like a stone and lay motionless. Neither lad checked to see if he was alive or dead; they were more concerned with what was happening to us at the house.

'Are you OK?' Philip asked.

'Yeah!' Henry replied. He wasn't; he was bleeding profusely, but he did have the nous to puncture the front and back tyres of the Jaguar before continuing their mission.

They climbed into our garden and carefully moved their way towards the house, Philip on one side of the garden, near the path, and Henry on the other, totally hidden by the shrubs and trees. Henry was creeping toward the river bridge, when he was disturbed by Meg. She was shivering with fear. Henry saw Bill lying motionless on the path, near the bridge, covered in blood. He signalled to Philip. 'I think Bill's been shot,' he whispered loudly.

Philip was filled with rage at this stage. He loved the dogs madly; whoever had done this was going to pay. Philip could now see me up on the balcony and signalled he was going over the bridge. I tried to stop him but he was hell-bent on revenge. He was armed only with a garden hoe against possible guns and definitely knives. By now, we all knew, they must have broken into what we call the barn, the place where II PY is stored.

In the distance were the blue flashing lights of police vehicles. Francesca had obviously phoned them. It gave me a little courage to do something; I shouted to Philip at the top of my voice.

'Philip, the police are on the way.'

Four men immediately came running across the river, straight towards Henry and Philip, though they didn't know it. The first two simply ignored Henry, who was crouching down tending to Bill, who lay limp and apparently lifeless on the ground. Philip, on the other hand, was prepared for a fight.

'Now!' he shouted, as the first of them came within striking distance. He swung the hoe across with such force, meeting the runner full in the midriff. The hoe snapped in two, with a loud crack, as the runner fell to the floor in agony. This was followed by a loud scream as the second of the two, not seeing his accomplice's plight, tripped and fell headlong over his writhing body, again with a loud crack, as some part of him hit the stone footpath.

Philip jabbed the hoe, which had broken like a sharp greenstick fracture, into his body.

'Move a fucking inch and you're dead!' he said with such venom and hatred that even the air seemed poisoned. But his victim hadn't heard any of it; his body was motionless.

Two others with flashlights managed to see the mêlée and

escaped to the bottom of the garden. The last of the group was a different kettle of fish. He came out of the barn brandishing a gun and carrying what looked like a camera.

The police had arrived and, jumping out of their cars, ran toward the front gate. I ran to meet them shouting, 'They're armed. This way, quick! They're down there.'

The police stopped in their tracks and began a cautious approach down the drive to the garages.

In the meantime the last of the bunch came over the bridge towards Henry and Bill. He pointed his gun at Henry, who was now standing up, albeit somewhat shakily.

'Get out of the fucking way!' he snarled.

'Don't shoot! I've got nothing,' Henry pleaded, arms outstretched.

By this time the police had their flashlights trained on the man and one officer began shouting, 'Put the gun down. Don't do anything silly. Put the gun down.'

This did not get the reaction the police wanted. The man, who we could see now was in his late thirties, shouted back. 'Put those fucking lights out or I'll shoot the bastard. Put 'em out now!'

'All right, all right,' the officer replied. 'Just keep it calm.'

The light went out and for a few seconds it was pitch black until our eyes became accustomed to the darkness again. The man grabbed hold of Henry's clothes and pulled him close to him, still pointing the gun. This was too much for Meg. Summoning up the courage to attack the man she leapt at him and embedded her teeth into the arm holding the gun, which went off several times, fortunately missing Henry.

The man staggered backwards, his leg millimetres from Bill's head, but that was enough; Bill struggled, every bit of energy left in his body was used to lunge himself forward and bite into the leg. He let go quickly; he had nothing left to give. The man dropped the gun and toppled into the river, with Meg still holding on. He splashed backwards into the river, which at this point is about three feet deep.

The man panicked, shouting that he couldn't swim until he realised it was shallow enough to walk. Meg had also done her job and was able to swim out of the way. The man was able to get out and make his escape. Philip did not chase after him, thinking he was still armed. Instead he went to help Henry, who, despite having been injured, had picked up Bill and was carrying him up to the police. The dog was still breathing but only just.

The senior officer present, Inspector Walker, quickly dispatched officers to the railway yard, where they found the young driver in a sorry state, sitting on the floor next to the Jaguar. The others had not only abandoned him but also the two vehicles. Inspector Walker called for further assistance and a search of the area was ordered. However, they were unable to trace any more of the men. They had vanished.

Walker acted in an excellent and businesslike fashion. Not only did he arrange all the police work, he also had a police car take Bill to the vet. Henry went with him, absolutely distraught at the dog's condition. Bill was barely alive; you could tell he was desperately hanging on to life and glad that Henry was with him. The vet was already waiting as they arrived. The dog was taken in and operated on immediately to remove the bullet. The moment they took the dog into the surgery, Henry passed out. The loss of blood had been greater than he had thought. He was taken to the local hospital for treatment and had fifteen stitches in his arm. He remained in hospital for two days.

There were other consequences. The following day, when Inspector Vaughan Munro came on duty, he promptly arrested Philip for grievous bodily harm. He had taken a statement from the man in the railway yard, who simply stated he had been out drinking and wanted a pee; he had gone behind a steam engine and was attacked for no reason whatsoever. I was surprised he had been able to get any statement at all from the man, as he was supposed to be suffering from concussion. It was an incredible moment seeing Philip taken away in handcuffs, when we were supposed to be the victims.

We immediately contacted Keith Holden-Fitzpatrick, a local criminal lawyer, who had a very good reputation. I outlined Philip's plight to him and he immediately went to the police station to represent him. He also suggested off the record that I should contact the press and tell them the story. Clive of the *Mail*, of course, came back into the picture.

Munro's interviewing techniques were an utter disgrace, and as a result Keith would not allow Philip to answer any questions until he had seen what evidence they had against him. Munro cut the interview short and took pleasure in locking Philip up again. My son, of course, was distraught.

'Don't worry, Philip,' Keith said soothingly. 'This moron won't be able to keep you in long. I'll have you out before lunch!'

I decided it was time to make more use of Clive. It made a fantastic storyline: how the family had fought with the attackers and how the dogs had been injured saving our lives and how Inspector Vaughan Munro had arrested Philip for saving his brother.

Several other papers wanted to interview the family and the police. An impromptu press conference was organized, which Munro headed up for the police and where he showed his true colours. 'We only have his word that he saw the man attacking his brother with a knife. We found nothing at the scene and the victim's injuries are consistent with being attacked from behind.'

'What measures have you undertaken to search the area in daylight? After all, it's still reasonably early,' Clive demanded.

'We have taken and will take what action we feel is appropriate in this matter,' Munro responded somewhat aggressively.

'It doesn't seem like it!' Clive said sarcastically and walked away.

However, Munro made a fatal mistake. All police officers have their favourites when it comes to the press; it's only human nature. They will often confide in the reporter off the record and this unfortunate officer did just that. The rest of the reporters had dispersed. Clive, however, had popped into the toilet, leaving his bag in the waiting room, with his tape recorder still switched on.

Inspector Munro went into the waiting room, with his favourite reporter, none other than Western Flynn of the *Yorkshire Post*. Munro was a little shaken by the hostility of some of the questioning and at the same time frustrated with the attitude of some of the reporters.

'That fucking Conway family is driving us up the fucking wall. I can't see what the fucking fuss is about. Many people have old cars; I don't see why he's so special.' His jealous anger spilled out. 'His fucking son thinks he can take the law into his own hands; well not under my watch.'

'Vaughan, he's got a lot of support, some big guns from the nationals. For God's sake, don't leave yourself open,' Flynn interjected, trying to cool Munro's temper.

'I know what I'm doing. I'll see that pompous arsehole get what's coming to him.'

'Vaughan, let it go. It's . . .' He stopped in mid-sentence as Clive came back into the waiting room, picked up his bag and walked toward the exit.

'See you, Clive,' Flynn said, acknowledging a fellow reporter.

Clive turned and murmured, 'Flynn.' He then returned to base to write up the story.

It was only when he had finished writing that he noticed the tape was still playing. Of couse, he couldn't believe it when he heard Munro talking to Flynn and immediately telephoned his editor.

'Phone the chief constable. Tell him about the situation and what you will be including in your story. Let me have your copy before three o'clock. It's a good story, you lucky sod,' John Brooksbank, his editor said, before signing off.

Clive phoned the chief constable, gave him the full picture and even what the headline was likely to be the following morning: Inspector Envy: Vindictive Copper Bends the Rules'. Almost before Clive had signed off, the phones had been ringing from Police HQ to Keighley Division. The local superintendent called Munro in, suspended him and ordered Philip's release.

I went to the police station, accompanied by Keith, to collect Philip. Superintendent Wissard apologized but said that unfortunately the charges could not be dropped as the young man had made a statement stating that he had been attacked by two men with a knife whilst having a wee. He told the police that he had fought with the one of his attackers and turned the knife on him.

'It really does need to be investigated, despite the attack in your garden,' he said with some embarrassment. 'Unfortunately this matter with Inspector Munro has clouded matters, but I have put Inspector Allsop in charge of the case and arranged a fingertip search of the area in an effort to find the knife. I'm sorry to say we haven't taken a statement from your brother yet.'

We returned home sick to death of all the trouble and wondered when it would stop. I wanted to get rid of the Rolls there and then, and had it not been for the promises I had made for the photo shoot in St-Tropez and Le Touquet and to the organizers of the Beaujolais Race at Charnay, it would have been sold. The offer from Morales had been exceptional.

Late the following evening, the police found the knife. The young man had thrown it as far as he could, in the condition he was in, and it had landed in the undergrowth on the far side of the railway track. It wasn't going to take too long for them to decide whose fingerprints were on the knife. Henry's certainly weren't and also it would confirm that his was the only blood on the knife. Allsopp was good enough to telephone to say that all the charges would be dropped against Philip.

Quite by chance one of the officers looked over the side of the bridge and saw an object which looked like a camera lying at the bottom of the river. Five policemen set about trying to retrieve the little object from a small area of water.

I want you to imagine the situation. The water is approximately three feet deep and the height from the water to the

138

bridge is another five. One inventive officer found our grand-daughter's fishing net, which is approximately four feet long, and spent the next three or four minutes splashing about, trying to reach the camera from the bridge. Two further officers were called to assist him, which they did by holding his legs, allowing him to reach further down. It didn't take long for them to realize he still couldn't reach the bottom; but also that somehow they had become stuck. A fourth officer also came to assist and jokingly pretended to push one of the others into the water and quite accidentally succeeded, causing the one leaning over and one of his helpers to fall in!

The water was now so churned up with the mud from the bottom it was impossible to see anything. However, it soon cleared, and the fifth officer simply walked down to the river's edge and with a long stick dragged the camera to him without getting wet.

The police had found an expensive digital camera and, regardless of it having been in the water for several hours, their scientific department were able to recover the photographs on the computer disk in the camera. There were only three pictures, all of them of II PY. Proof, at last, that the criminals' interest was in the car and not in the family.

Inspector Allsopp had been convinced for some time that the troubles were about the Rolls-Royce and not the family and he now voiced them publicly. He could not, however, convince any of the hierarchy in the force that it would be worth taking a look at the car. He did add a few more patrols to the area and was delighted when I told him we were considering selling the car back to the previous owner in the States.

Clive as usual gave a good account of the happenings in Haworth and of course added a bit to keep the story running.

Bill, by the way, was released from the vets into our care a week later. He had lost a lot of weight and felt very sorry for himself, but you could tell from his demeanour that he was loving all the care and attention he was getting. It was good to have him back.

Chapter 11

Throughout August we were asked to inform the police every time we were taking the Rolls out, giving them a rough itinerary of where we were going. This was simply a precaution and gave us some assurance that they were now showing interest in our plight. We booked our weekend at the Midland and took II PY with us. It was a fitting setting for the car; the management even asked us if we would keep her parked in front of the hotel.

Saturday turned out to be sunny and we decided on a drive to Blackpool. We left the hotel, with me sporting my boater and Francesca looking fabulous, and arrived in Blackpool about lunchtime. The place was packed and the traffic on the Golden Mile was horrendous. We were moving at a snail's pace, which at least enabled us to admire the view and others to admire the car.

We were joined in the queue by an old pink Vauxhall Cresta. It followed us for a few minutes and then overtook. The passengers all waved as they passed and I thought no more of it; it was like just old ladies from a different age acknowledging each other. About fifty yards further along the Cresta stopped, and the passengers got out on to the pavement.

I naturally stopped the car waiting for the Vauxhall to move off, but it stayed there. Two of its passengers began slowly walking up to us. With all the people milling along the pavement, I didn't expect anything to happen.

The larger of the two, a youngish man in his mid-thirties, dark and well built, wearing jeans and a white shirt and very dark shades, as the modern man calls them, approached me.

'The boss wants a word with yer!'

'Pardon?'

'You 'erd, the boss wants a word with yer.'

The other passenger from the Cresta stepped forward. He was younger, a wanna-be gangster, but short. Again he was dark-haired with a definite tan from living at the seaside. He was wearing a suit, which in this weather seemed stupid.

'You 'erd,' he said in a broad Lancashire accent. He came round to the driver's side and began to open the door, which didn't go down very well with me.

'Touch that door again and you will be very very sorry,' I said, trying to sound tough.

The traffic had built up a little and one or two cars began hooting their horns.

'Come on!' the older man ordered. 'Get out the boss wants yer.'

'Look, fathead, this car weighs two tons. The bumper on this car could push your car against a wall and crush it . . . If you and your boss don't get out of the way, I'll do just that!' I started the engine, and shouted to some passers-by to call the police. Our assailants began to panic.

'Dennis, get in the fuckin' car!' the taller one said to the other.

'I can 'ave 'im easy,' he swaggered.

'Get in the fuckin' car now, ya stupid cunt.'

Reluctantly the 'wanna-be' gangster went back to the Cresta, whilst I began moving the car forward and went to within one foot of the Vauxhall and began revving, causing the two idiots to jump back in. I gently rolled forward, touching the Cresta's bumper and began to push. The driver deliberately held his foot on the brake to no avail as the weight of the Rolls began to push him. He took the hint and accelerated away.

'I want to go back home,' Francesca said almost in tears. 'It's ruined a lovely day.'

'Let's get lunch first and then decide. There's a lovely little restaurant in St Anne's. We could go there; it will be out of the way.'

We drove along the front, past the Pleasure Beach and into St Anne's, where we found the restaurant and parked in front. We sat down, ordered a crab salad and tried to relax for a few minutes. We could just see the corner of the car from where we were sitting and from time to time I went to check on her.

Just as our meal was served I saw the tall fellow from earlier looking into the restaurant. The reflection made it difficult, so he put his hands to his head to shield his eyes and then leant against the glass. This caused considerable discomfort to some diners who were sitting near the window, and the manager had to go out and move him on. Unfortunately, he saw us in the process and just hung around, waiting for us to come out.

'We'll call the police just before we are about to leave,' I said to Francesca. 'At least we can have our meal in peace.'

We deliberately took our time and what would normally have taken one hour took two. Just before paying the bill, I telephoned the police to explain the situation and they said they would send an officer round within a few minutes. We waited a short while, then paid the waitress. The moment we stepped outside, we were immediately accosted by the tall man, now accompanied by his little friend. 'The boss wants ter see ya.'

I snarled my reply. 'Tell your boss, if he wants to see me, I will only talk to the organ-grinder not his monkey!'

This made him take a sharp intake of breath and I could also see the other one brisling with anger. I knew that, if he had been given the opportunity, he would have flattened me. However, I knew the police would be here soon so I took full advantage.

'Do you understand what I have just said? If he wants to see me, bring him here; otherwise go and play somewhere else.'

He walked away and I heard our new friend phoning someone: 'He won't come wiv us.'

I didn't want to stand too long on the pavement and thought

it better to wait in the car. I unlocked the passenger door and held it open for Francesca to get in and walked round to the driver's side. I had just opened the car door when the pink Vauxhall Cresta raced towards us and braked sharply next to the car.

The rear nearside passenger window was wound down, sticking when it got to halfway. The passenger had to struggle to get it down the rest of the way. If he had wanted to play 'the big I am', it had backfired.

'A bit of butter in the mechanism would stop that,' I said sarcastically.

'I wanted to see you,' a voice said.

'Now you do!' I replied.

'I wanna buy yer car.'

'Don't be silly! You couldn't afford it. Now please go away and behave yourself.'

His young assistant, who had moved a little closer, took a swipe at me, hitting me full on the side of my face. I was knocked backwards and fell into the car, as the young man again lunged forward to strike again. He was called off by the boss, who added, 'You don't talk to me like that ... *That* was just a taster!'

In situations like this, Philip tells me that you should always bluff that you're the hard man by looking them in the eye and telling them so. That's just what I did. I got back up, with Francesca begging me not to do anything, but I couldn't stop. I leaned over toward the boss and snarled. 'You and your little friend ...' I was stopped in mid-sentence. The police had arrived.

Two officers sauntered over to the Vauxhall and one of them tapped on the roof. 'Come on out, Jason. What have you been doing this time?'

'I didn't hit him; it was Dennis over there. I just wanted to make an offer for the car.'

'Jason, Jason!' the policeman said patronisingly, 'How could you afford a car like that? Are you going to rob a bank?'

'No really, Mr Pedder, I was asked to make an offer for someone else.'

'Come on, all of you down to the station, and you, my lad, are under arrest for assault.'

The officer gave him a formal caution and put him in handcuffs; he wore them as though he was proud of the fact. The officer turned to me and said, 'We'll have no trouble with this lot. Just give your details to my colleague and as far as we are concerned you can go.'

We made our way back to the Midland Hotel, thoroughly dejected and wanting nothing more than to go home. We stayed in the hotel for the rest of the evening, with me nursing a big black eye and decided to check out the following day.

We arrived home about midday; I immediately telephoned David to tell him what had happened and he was as shocked as I felt. I told we had now made up our minds to sell II PY; we had had enough. I also phoned Morales and told him what had happened, how I had been struck in the face by this young lout and that they were trying to buy the car for someone.

'I do hope you had nothing to do with this. They almost caused an accident and I had to push them with the bumper of the car to force them to move . . .'

'It's not damaged, is it?' Morales asked interrupting me.

'No, not at all, perhaps a minor scratch on the bumper, but I haven't had time to check yet. Anyway I'll phone about selling the car the moment we get back from France.'

I rang off and spent the rest of the day in the garden just sitting with Francesca thinking on what might have been. I am sure you can imagine the reaction of our children when they saw my face. Philip would have killed them if he had seen them.

I put II PY in the garage and left it there until the journey to France. I had no desire to go out in it again. We spent the next few days preparing for the trip. The entire family was going: me, Francesca, Henry, Victoria, Philip, his wife Annabel and their daughter, Emily, who was just eight. We were taking II PY on the trailer while we travelled in Henry's Land-Rover Discovery. Naturally Emily was getting very excited and she would phone every day: 'Granny, only ten more days!' . . . 'Granny, only nine more days.' We hadn't told her about all the problems; no one wanted to dampen the enthusiasm of a young child.

However, we did come very close. A few days before we were due to leave we received a DHL parcel from an address in Blackpool. We were out when it arrived, but Henry took it in and signed for it. It was about the size of a shoebox, well wrapped and marked 'with care'. Henry telephoned us to say it had arrived. Francesca told him to open it and tell us what was in it.

'We've probably left something in the hotel,' I remarked.

'Of course, we always do!' Francesca agreed.

Henry began to open the parcel. We could hear him pulling on the paper to tear it open quickly . . .

'Jesus Christ!' he yelled. 'Dad! Stop the car and pick up the phone.'

I stopped the car and took the phone off loudspeaker. 'What the hell's going on?'

'Dad, it's a fucking hand. Christ, I feel sick!' Henry exclaimed, yelling down the phone.

'What did you say?' I asked.

'It's a fucking hand; someone's sent a fucking hand . . .'

'Don't swear. Please don't swear!'

'Dad, come home; I feel ill.'

'We're on our way.' I turned the car round and went straight back home. Francesca wanted to know what was going on.

'Darling, listen to this and you'll know everything.' I dialled the helpline at Keighley Police Station and asked for Inspector Walker. Thank God he was in. I told him what had happened, and he promised to send someone round immediately.

The police arrived a few minutes before we did, but Bill and Meg were almost back on form and wouldn't allow them to enter. I took them into the house where Henry was still in shock.

Fortunately he hadn't touched anything; he had simply opened the parcel. Inspector Walker put a surgical glove on and gently took out the hand, exposing a note underneath. It was the most horrible, macabre thing I have ever seen. The note was obviously written for my benefit and it read:

I am sorry for assaulting you. I can assure you it will not happen again,
   Dennis Smith

They had made him write this letter and then cut off his hand.

'Do you know this man?' Walker asked.

'No not really, but it must be the young man who assaulted me in Blackpool the other day. He was arrested for it, along with another man called Jason. I quickly filled the Inspector in on the events in Blackpool.

'This car of yours,' commented Walker, 'it must be made of gold, the amount of people who have been injured or killed over it.'

'You're right.' I replied. 'The sooner it goes the better. Only another ten weeks, I hope!'

It doesn't take long for bad news to travel and that day was no exception. By two o'clock we were besieged by the press, television and local radio. Unfortunately Annabel and Emily chose this time to pay a visit and were immediately set upon by the hordes. What do you think about the hand? What are you going to do? Is it anything to do with the car? Of course, at this moment neither Annabel nor Emily knew anything about the incident with the hand and were somewhat shocked at the ferocity of the questions. They avoided answering anything or making comment and dashed into the house.

'What's going on?' Annabel asked.

'It's a long story; I'll tell you in a minute,' Francesca replied, signalling with her eyes she didn't want to say anything in front of Emily.

Emily went to play with Bill, and while she was out Francesca told her the whole story.

'Oh my God! I just don't believe it. This is just getting worse and worse.' She was almost in tears.

Of course, Emily walked in just at that moment and seeing her mother upset, she too became distraught. It was becoming a nightmare.

The note put me in a difficult position. I was the one who had been assaulted and therefore had a motive to do it. I had to be interviewed at the police station, so naturally I asked my friend Keith Holden Fitzpatrick to come with me. Just for my own peace of mind.

We were met by Inspector Walker in the waiting room of the station, where he explained that he would not be conducting the interview and that a Chief Inspector Fothergill from Leeds would be taking care of it.

'Isn't that unusual?' Keith commented.

'Yes, but these are unusual circumstances, aren't they?' he replied.

Fothergill arrived. 'Robert Conway?' No pleasantries with him.

'Yes.'

'Follow me, please, and who is this gentleman?'

Keith introduced himself and followed us into an interview room, where we were introduced to Sergeant Wilkins, also from Leeds. We were then invited to sit down.

Fothergill kicked off straight away. 'May I ask why you have found it necessary to bring your solicitor?'

'I feel totally bewildered with all that's happened. I just felt I needed some moral support ... And then Inspector Walker pointed out that I could be in a difficult position.'

'Just tell us in your own words what happened in Blackpool,' Fothergill asked,

147

I looked at Keith, who just shrugged, and I went on to explain the entire escapade from start to finish. The two officers then asked a variety of questions, none of which could have incriminated me so Keith said it was OK to answer.

We had been in about an hour and matters were concluding when Fothergill asked, 'Did you tell anyone else about what happened?'

'Yes, of course, all the family. I had a black eye and they obviously wanted to know how I got it.'

'Anybody else?' he asked.

'No, I don't think so . . .' I paused for a moment. 'Just a minute, I did tell a lawyer named Morales. He has been trying to buy the car for his client in America. I asked him if he was responsible for the whole affair.'

'Why did you ask that?' Fothergill asked.

Of course, I had to explain the whole situation.

'Do you know where this Morales is?'

'No, but I do have a telephone number . . .'

Suddenly the questioning took a turn for the worse. 'Did you ask him to take care of Dennis Smith?'

Keith chipped in with 'That's not an appropriate question, is it?', but I was already answering with all the indignation I could muster.

'What on earth would I do that for? I and my family have been terrorized for weeks and I've not retaliated in any way. Why should I now?'

The interview drew to a sour close and I returned home feeling drained, hoping that would be the last of it.

Chapter 12

The day of departure had arrived. We had informed the police we were going away and what our likely destinations would be, and I actually sensed a relief in the voice of the officer dealing with it. We had decided that none of us would drive for more than an hour, with Henry taking the first and most difficult shift. It took us an hour to reach the motorway, when Victoria took over. The Land-Rover was struggling with the two-ton weight it was pulling and we were very lucky if we achieved anything approaching fifty miles per hour.

We pulled into Downtown Services at Grantham at ten thirty and for the first time I felt uneasy. I thought I kept seeing the same white BMW. Sometimes it was there when I looked round, sometimes not. I did mention it to the lads, asking them not to look and make it obvious; I didn't want to upset the party on the first day. We took no chances and phoned Keighley Police and spoke to Walker. Even he was beginning to be worn out by the whole affair, but said he would notify the police in the area. 'The sooner you're out of the country the better!' he joked.

We turned out of Grantham Downtown and found the white BMW parked on the slip road. Unfortunately Philip had taken over the driving seat and was not one to take the easy option. The Land-Rover and trailer slowly snaked out on to the slip road passing the BMW, just close enough to take a little white wing mirror off the parked car. The unhappy driver came thundering after us, pointing to Philip to pull over, but Philip would not; he just kept his position. Several times the BMW driver came level and indicated to us that we should pull over but each time was forced to retreat as he was holding up vehicles in the outside lane. Eventually Philip had had enough. Everyone in the party now realized that this was more trouble and we decided to meet it face on.

Philip pulled into a lay-by, which was deserted save for us and the BMW which followed us in. Philip and Henry, with me a little further behind, got out and raced over to them, before they had chance to get out of the car. The driver of the BMW began to open the door but found himself pulled out by Philip, who a moment late kneed him in the stomach. There were two other passengers in the car, but they were only young teenagers and wanted none of it.

'Why are you following us?' Philip yelled.

The teenage passengers were about to answer when the driver, who was still winded, managed to say, 'Shut up! Don't say anything.'

Philip landed another blow in the driver's stomach.

'Take no notice of him! Let's hear it from you,' he said, leaning over into the car.

'We were asked to follow you to the Dartford Tunnel and telephone several times to let them know where you were.'

'Henry, get their phones!'

They willingly handed over their phones while I searched the one on the floor and took his phone. We walked back to the Land-Rover and were just about to get in when Henry stopped, took out a screwdriver from the boot, returned to the BMW and, with two well-aimed blows, deflated two of their tyres.

We left what can only be described as a bunch of young lads, who couldn't even follow us without making it obvious, stuck in a lay-by miles from anywhere with a defunct car. You could have almost felt sorry for them.

Philip resumed driving and we continued on our way to the Dartford Crossing. The women admonished Philip for his aggressive behaviour; the holiday, they said, was spoilt before it had even begun. Philip couldn't conceal his annoyance.

'They were following us, for God's sake! What was I supposed to do?'

'He's right. Let's leave it at that!' I ordered, with my head-of-the-family hat on.

I had taken over for the last stint of driving for the day and as we passed the Channel Tunnel Station on the M20, Emily, our little observer in the back, shouted, 'Grandad, I think we have another spy.'

Henry, our resident expert on cars, asked, 'Which one, Emily? Is it that big black one just at the back of us?'

'Yes!' Emily said excitedly. She didn't seem at all disturbed by earlier events.

'It's a Dodge twin-cab. I haven't seen it before,' Henry confirmed.

'How long has it been there, Emily?' I asked

'I don't know.'

Victoria interrupted. 'I think about twenty minutes. I noticed it just after the Maidstone turn.'

We continued along, all of us looking around to get a better view. To no avail, as the Dodge was well tucked in behind the trailer. The Land-Rover struggled a little up the final hill, just before the Channel first comes into view, then down the steep slope into Dover and the docks. The Dodge was still with us, in spite of our speed at one point being less than twenty miles per hour. We pulled in by Customs for a brief chat, then made our way to the docks.

It was at this point that I decided to play a trick. I had booked with P&O but for a time pretended to join one of the queues for the Norfolk Line. Our Dodge driver took the line next to us, but fortunately for us arrived at the check-in a minute or two before us. Just as the Dodge was moving off to embarkation, clearly thinking we were following, we turned the full circle and joined the P&O check-in instead.

It was a moment of joy to see the look on the faces of the the two from the Dodge. They were trapped in a queue, waiting to embark. Annabel, the photographer of the group, even managed to take a photograph of them. On this occasion, though, they weren't the usual dumb brigade. One of them managed to get on our boat as a foot passenger. We now knew we were in for a difficult time and it would take all our resources to stay ahead.

Fortunately we had priority embarkation and were able to park the car and trailer at the front of the boat, knowing full well we would be first off the boat and, sure enough, an hour and a quarter later we were first off and went as quickly as possible to the Douane and immigration control point at the port entrance. As usual, it was empty and we sailed through, turning out of the port and into the centre of Calais.

I had, however, underestimated the intelligence of the man, a stupid mistake, which I never let happen again. I drove down the road only to find 'Billy Boy', as we had christened him, had ordered a taxi by phone and was following us. I had to get rid of him one way or another, if only to get a good night's sleep.

Philip suddenly said, 'I've got an idea! Pull up at the side.'

I did just that and the taxi pulled up behind us, almost hitting the back of the trailer. Without a word to anyone, Philip jumped out, ran to the taxi and got in next to the driver. Emily and Victoria – the only ones who could see what was going on – gave a running commentary. There was a little tussle inside the taxi, after which Philip got out holding the ignition keys and threw them as far as he could down the road, much to the chagrin of the taxi driver, who, of course, was protesting his innocence. As it was getting dark, he would have a little difficulty in finding them quickly.

Philip ran back to the Land-Rover and I set off as quickly as possible, hoping to get the car and trailer away out of sight before they could find us. Francesca telephoned the Metropol Hotel, where we were staying for the night, and asked them to open the garage ready for us, as I wanted to get the car out of sight. This all duly happened.

We had arranged a photo shoot the following morning at the Fin Palais restaurant in Calais. It was run by friends of ours, a young couple who had just had Jack, an addition to their family, and who also wanted me to take them to the church in the Rolls-Royce, for Jack's christening on the same day. We combined business with pleasure, enjoyed the meal and made the arrangements.

The following day we had a round of photo sessions. The car was a lovely sight and created a big stir. Me and the ladies were dressed in 1930s clothing, and of course, we too were photographed, not only by the official photographer and dozens of visitors, but also by the man from the boat. The black Dodge, too, had found us and was parked on the corner.

The final session in the north of France was in Le Touquet, at the Westminster Hotel. Le Touquet, of course was in its heyday when II PY was built and made the perfect backdrop. The shots here were simple. They just wanted several taken at the entrance, and of course Emily, who was in a lovely 30s frock, stole the show. Our friendly Dodge was still around, and I mentioned this to the photographer, Lionel Caderousse, also telling him a little of what had happened in the past. I thought no more about it, until I saw the men in the Dodge being questioned by the local police and eventually moved on. Within twenty minutes, however, they were back in the same spot.

'They're back!' Lionel shouted to us, becoming all excited as if he had been part of the adventure from the beginning. 'I'll phone the police again.' He continued shouting. He could not seem to concentrate on the job in hand, turning round at every opportunity to see what was happening.

The police came again and this time the driver was asked to get out of the car. We could hear the sound of raised voices, and shortly after four men were taken from the Dodge. It was difficult to get a good description, but they appeared to be all white, in their late twenties to mid-thirties. The driver was possibly in his forties. They were taken away in a police van and their car left where it was. The pièce de resistance was that within half an hour a tow truck came and took the car away for parking in a restricted area.

It was with some relief that later that day we set off southwards, taking the motorway past Paris and on to Reims, where we stopped for the night. Then it was on to Lyon and the south. We hadn't seen the black Dodge since Le Touquet, and we decided it would be safe enough for all of us to go in for a meal together; previously we had taken it in turns for one of us to remain with the car.

The St-Rambert-d'Albon Services is about twenty miles south of Lyon and was a welcome sight as we were all absolutely starving; the tensions and simply the length of the journey had taken its toll on us. Henry parked up in the lorry area, which was almost deserted, allowing plenty of room for us to manoeuvre out easily. In fact, we were lucky; we parked without a vehicle directly either side of us. After taking a good look round, we all left the car and went into the restaurant.

This was a disaster from the start. I couldn't believe how rude the staff were. I wanted the chicken casserole, without the couscous, which of course was impossible because, as the server pointed out, this would leave her with one portion of uneaten couscous and that wasn't allowed. We spent about half an hour complaining to each other about the food and the service before returning to the car, only to be met by our worst nightmare. The black Dodge, obviously accompanied by a maroon Renault 25, both with English registration plates, had parked either side of us and so close that we were unable to get in. Fortunately Henry was able to get in through the back door and reverse out, adroitly using the Land-Rover's front bumper to make a huge continuous dent along the flank of the Renault. Meanwhile, Philip did his usual trick with his screwdriver.

Daylight was disappearing quickly and we still had another two hundred and fifty miles to go. I was very concerned about being followed at this late stage as I didn't want the opposition to know where we were staying.

'Keep your eyes peeled for another car, even if it's just a pair of headlights that are keeping pace with us. That includes you, Emily. Your young eyes are better than ours in the dark,' I said.

We had been travelling for over two hours when, with me driving, I suggested that we were being followed. I couldn't see what by, but it had been there for well over an hour. I signalled to pull into the service area at Montélimar, driving extremely slowly for the last four hundred metres before eventually stopping on the hard shoulder just before the final entrance. I wanted to see what sort of car it was and whether it could have been following us. The whole area was covered by bright lighting, not only from the road but also from the service area itself. We could see everything. The headlights had slowed down but were unable to stop as we did and gradually the light became a car. It was an old blue Volvo.

'They're going to pass us,' I shouted. 'Don't look at them! They mustn't know we've flushed them out. Henry get out and pretend something's wrong. Quick! They're coming!'

Henry quickly jumped out of the car and began to inspect the trailer, only a moment or two before the old blue Volvo passed us. By its position in the road, it had no alternative but to turn into the service area.

'They're looking back at us,' Victoria said. 'They've stopped!'

'Philip, get out and start walking as though you're going to get help,' I commanded like some general making snap decisions.

Philip got out of the car and started to walk towards the service area and the Volvo gently drove away towards the restaurant area. Philip quickly returned to the Land-Rover, followed by

Henry, and we set off on our way, driving off the slip road and back onto the autoroute.

'Good thinking Dad!' Victoria said, lavishing me with praise.

We knew we would only have a few minutes before we had them on our backs again, but at least we had fooled them yet again. It was however still very important that we lost them or face the consequences of them finding out where we were staying and I couldn't contemplate the thought of that. The problem was, we were just too slow and that would always be the case.

We were approaching Aix en Provence towards the end of our journey, when we noticed the headlights back again and, just to make sure, we slowed down as we approached the next services and, sure enough, it was the blue Volvo. It was like an old U Boat trailing the convoy, keeping its distance just out of sight and range, waiting for darkness before attacking its prey. At least this convoy knew he was there and perhaps had the upper hand, for the moment.

For many years, I had taken advantage of using Telepéage on the Autoroutes in France. A gadget is placed on your windscreen which enables you to pass through the toll booths quickly, avoiding the queues and delays and the necessity of taking a ticket. Often at night a queue can be as long as during the daytime because the toll companies operate on a night shift, with a much reduced staff and I was counting on this. I wanted him to follow me closely through a Telepéage booth, hoping that he had not got the facility, and then it could take five to ten minutes before he could actually pay and go through.

I explained what I was going to do, but I wish I hadn't bothered; no one had confidence that it would work. The only abstainer on this point was Emily, who was still fast asleep, oblivious to everything that was going on.

I could see the bright lights in the distance and knew we had about two miles to go before the peage so I slowed down to about twenty miles an hour. He had to come closer, simply because for a car without a trailer it was difficult to drive slowly.

'Don't turn round,' I whispered loudly in order not to wake Emily. 'I don't want to give them an inkling of what I am up to.'

There were now only two thousand metres to go and my heart began to race, everything seemed quiet and I could only hear the Land-Rover's diesel engine struggling to keep at the snail's pace, but it was working – he had closed the gap between us.

The headlights then caught the next sign; it was now only 1000 metres to go and the gap closed even further. I began to see the shape of the car instead of just the headlights. I could now see the shapes of its passengers, as the light from the car behind shone through the Volvo's windows, also hitting my mirror.

'Come on, come on, a bit closer.' I said to myself, giving telepathic instructions to the driver of the Volvo.

'Dad – ' Henry began before I shouted impatiently, 'Shut up! Just leave it.'

Four hundred metres and I could now see the booths. I was in luck: there were two pay booths open, both with queues, and of course Telepéage open and free. I slowed down to ten mph and so did the Volvo. Two hundred metres left and I was slowly making my way to the right hand pay booth to join the queue, followed by the Volvo. Was he falling into my trap?

I was absolutely tingling with excitement and anticipation, gripping the steering wheel as though my life depended on it.

One hundred metres to go and I suddenly swung the Land-Rover over to the left, crossing all the traffic lanes, to pass through the far left Telepéage lane. The driver of the Volvo, seeing the erratic manoeuvre, must have thought I was trying another trick and followed suit.

I screamed out, 'He's fallen for it. We've got him!' waking poor Emily up.

I drove straight into the booth area followed by the Volvo driver and another two cars followed behind him! I just knew he would not have the Telepéage recorder and I was right. I passed directly through but the barrier came down and he was stuck. He now had to reverse out of the booth, moving two or even three other vehicles, and then go over to one of the other pay booths.

I had ten to fifteen minutes start at the most, to put my foot down and leave the motorway at Aix, then I knew he wouldn't find us. I could not stop laughing and at last the others knew what I had done.

'You crafty old man, you,' Philip sneered, reminiscent of Steptoe and Son.

'Less of the old,' I replied, still laughing. 'I just had a feeling they would walk into that one. Anyway, it's given us a head start. I'm going to leave the motorway at Aix; they won't think of that.'

I put my foot down, actually touching seventy at times, the Land-Rover simply purring along, despite the weight she was pulling. Fortunately the roads were quieter than normal. We flew past the Victory 'V' sign at the start of Aix, passing under the rather attractive Roman-style bridge before leaving the motorway just before the next toll area. All the time everyone's eyes were skinned on the road to see where the Volvo was. We were in luck! We had definitely lost him and I could relax.

We bypassed Aix, joining the Route Nationale 7, or the Route Napoléon as it's sometimes called. We passed through Trets, St-Maximin, Brignoles and then on over the mountains to Le Garde-Frenet, Grimaud and on to La Croix-Valmer, our destination.

Chapter 13

We had built the house at La Croix-Valmer ourselves many years before, when property was somewhat cheaper. La Croix-Valmer was a lovely little town between St-Tropez and Cavalaire, and the house had two beautiful sun-soaked terraces, one of which over-looked the sea.

Francesca and I got up about ten the following morning to a Continental breakfast already prepared; Henry had been into the village for baguettes and croissants, butter, fresh milk and cream. Who could wish for anything more? Particularly as it was a lovely fine day, still warm enough to eat alfresco. November could often be a rainy month, but for now it was beautiful, what we would call an Indian summer. The crowds had gone but there were still many hundreds of tourists around; but at least you could get into the shops without queuing.

Whilst some of us we were here for a holiday, others were here to do a bit of work and let II PY earn her keep. Immediately after breakfast I telephoned Ed Special to make the arrangements for our first photocall.

Ed was, as usual, full of himself. He told me to meet him at his temporary office, which was situated in a special compound at the top end of the main car park by the port of St-Tropez. I had arranged to be the driver, with Francesca and Emily accompanying me just for the ride. I was hoping to get Emily into the film, just for fun, so the three of us wore our period costumes to attract a little more attention. The rest of the family followed in the

Land-Rover. I felt so proud! I wanted to make sure everybody saw us and drove through the centre of St-Tropez, past the Senequier, the café where everyone sits to watch the world go by.

Ed came out to meet us. 'Wow! Hi there!' were his first words, as he walked towards the car. 'I'm impressed with the outfits,' he boomed, as he stretched out his hand to meet mine with that enormous smile only a producer could possibly have. 'And what a pretty little girl!' he continued, seeing Emily getting out of the car.

With that he signalled for my companions to come in and look round, whilst he and I discussed what was to happen. We left them to it, whilst I took Ed out in the car and he explained what he wanted me to do.

'I've got a surprise for you,' Ed exclaimed. 'I've got a 1929 tall ship arriving this afternoon and it's ours for twenty-four hours only. So everyone has to be here for six o'clock in the morning.'

'What?' I screamed jokingly. 'I've never heard of such an hour!'

'The boat's costing a fortune, so I want all the shots taken before 1500 hours.'

Back at the trailer, Francesca and the rest were enjoying a chat with Ed's number one, Marion Spacci, who was very American – full head of dark hair, the well-made up face, with the more-than-white smile and, of course, the big chest, held together by the tightest sweater she could have been poured into. She was very good at her job and controlled everything with a rod of iron. Henry, of course, was trying to create the right impression, though Philip summed it up by telling him: 'She would eat you for breakfast.'

Francesca and I arrived at the site bang on time the following morning and as expected I was actually driving in earnest at twenty past. Ed had actually asked me to keep wearing my boater, just in case I came into shot, though I never did. We had a sensational model working with the car and a swarthy Italian guy who acted as the chauffeur opening the doors of the car and helping her on to the ship. The young Italian never actually sat in the car, but when I saw the rushes, you would have thought he had done everything.

We broke early for lunch, which Francesca and I spent in the Senequier, enjoying *un sandwich au jambon blanc* and a pot of good tea. We were joined by Ed.

'I would like to use little Emily, if that's possible?' he asked. 'She's a pretty little thing and I think it would go down well with the theme. She's your granddaughter, isn't she?'

I phoned Philip and Annabel and put Ed's proposition to them and they promised to ring Ed back directly. Of course the moment Emily knew about it, there really was no going back. They telephoned Ed and within thirty minutes an excited Emily with two bewildered parents arrived on site to discuss what she would have to do.

We spent the next two days working very hard, and by the time the weekend came I was glad of the two days' rest. The only disappointed member of the family was Emily, who had enjoyed every moment and wanted it to continue. The consensus was we would take a picnic to the countryside and simply relax. We locked up II PY in the compound in the knowledge that it was under heavy security.

We packed our picnic hampers and cool bags, loaded with enough food and drink to feed a regiment and set off into the hills. It was a glorious day. There wasn't a cloud in the sky, leaving a completely blue ceiling apart from the sun which was determined to burn us if we didn't take care. We took advantage of the four-wheel drive and drove on unofficial tracks until we found an ideal spot between Plan-de-la-Tour and La Garde-Freinet. Unfortunately several others had found the same place, but it didn't matter too much as the place was big enough for all. We were virtually on the peak of the hill on a flat plain about as big as half a football pitch. We parked about two or three yards from the edge overlooking some wonderful scenery which included the Bay of St-Tropez. The hillside dropped away steeply but was covered with hundreds of oak and pine trees, including the distinctive *pin parasol.*

We played a few games with Emily and ran around a little, and finally settled down to our feast. It was at this point that we spotted the black Dodge appear and park to the rear of the area away from us.

Philip was incensed and immediately stood up, determined to go and confront them. It took all our efforts of persuasion to prevent him from doing so.

'How the bloody hell did they know we were here?' he asked.

'They followed us of course,' Annabel replied.

'No, they didn't,' both Henry and I said in unison.

'I was watching all the time, and I didn't see any sign of any vehicle following us,' I added.

'There's a tracker on it. It's the only answer,' Henry suggested.

'Oh my God, in that case they know where we live!' Francesca sighed.

'Come on, let's go! The day's bloody ruined,' I said begrudgingly, starting to pack up some of the things.

'I've had it with them! Please yourselves but I'm going to sort them one way or the other,' Philip said angrily and then turned and began to walk over to the Dodge.

We heard them start up the engine and saw it slowly move towards Philip. It was like a Hollywood Western: Philip stood his ground, but the Dodge didn't stop. Now there was only five metres, three, two, one, and still it didn't stop. Philip was forced to leap out of the way at the very last moment but the Dodge kept coming; it was going for the Land-Rover! Just a few more yards and we heard the driver slip into low-range gears and the revs increase.

'He's going for the Discovery!' Philip shouted.

It was too late. His bumper was at the back of the Discovery and the car was slipping inch by inch to the edge.

Philip tried to break into the Dodge without success, and

several other visitors came running across to help us but to no avail. The Discovery's front wheels were now over the edge, and Henry was making an insane attempt to get into it. We were all shouting for him to let go, but with the noise and the adrenalin rush, he couldn't hear.

Momentarily everyone stopped, looking on in sheer amazement as the Discovery slowly disappeared over the edge, with Henry still clinging on to it. For a second or two, no one knew exactly what to do.

Suddenly the Dodge slipped into reverse gear and with wheels spinning raced backwards, scattering everyone who had come to help. A moment later it had disappeared off down the track. We were in total shock. No one moved a muscle for what seemed like minutes and the silence was eerie, broken only by the occasional twitter of birdsong.

We were only brought to our senses by Henry shouting for help. Everyone ran to the edge to see him sitting on the side of the hill. He had jumped clear as the Discovery had started rolling down. He was level with the vehicle, which was about ten feet from the top; it had only been prevented from falling further down by the scrub and was resting precariously on a young oak tree in the middle of the front bumper.

Henry went over to the Discovery and steadied himself on the open door. There were a few worried screams from some of the onlookers as the Discovery jerked and slipped another inch down the slope.

'Leave it, Henry! The fire service will be here in a minute. They'll get it for us,' I yelled, hoping he would leave things alone.

'Philip!' Henry shouted. 'If we can get the winch on it we should be able to pull it up. Do you wanna give it a go?'

Philip slid down to Henry and stood by him whilst he undid the winch, causing the Land-Rover to slip another inch. It was obvious that any sudden movement could send the vehicle crashing down the hill sideward.

Emily began crying in absolute terror when she saw her dad down with the car.

'I've got to get the winch free,' shouted Henry, who was now in front of the car. 'We need to run the cable underneath the car and in the rear bracket.' The car slipped another inch or so as the tree bent a little more. 'We haven't got much time. Come on, Philip. Hold my arm; if it starts to go pull me out of the way.'

'What do you intend to do with your other arm?' Philip asked humorously.

'I'm going to pull the cable out of the winch, just enough to go under the Land-Rover to reach the end. Then I'm going to crawl under it and pull the cable with me and then fasten it to the end. We can pull the cable to that tree over there and with a bit of luck winch her up.'

'Over my dead body are you going to go under that car!' Philip shouted out.

'Look, if it goes, it will go past me. I'll be underneath. What would be helpful would be if Victoria and Annabel could stand either side of the back and gently keep the car straight whilst I do it. OK?'

Philip thought about it for a moment and agreed it could work. He shouted instructions to the two girls, who immediately came down, joined by two Frenchmen. They all rested lightly on either side of the Discovery, as Philip held on to Henry's arm whilst he released several yards of cable. There were screams from all the onlookers as the car lurched downwards and Philip had to yank Henry out of the way, nearly taking his arm off in the process.

'You needn't pull my bloody arm off, you stupid . . .' Henry shouted.

'It was your arm or your head,' came the reply.

Henry had now pulled out enough cable to feed under the car and went to the front. Francesca was pleading with him not to do it, but when she realized he was taking no notice she began begging him to be careful instead.

There was a deathly silence as we all watched Henry roll over

164

on to his back toward the centre of the vehicle and then slide slowly but surely under it, pulling the cable with him. Sure enough, the Discovery slipped again, much to the anguish of the crowd, several of whom turned away, too afraid to look.

Henry began the sixteen-feet crawl on his back to take the hook and cable to the rear. Inch by inch he crawled up the sandy hillside pulling the cable with him and inch by inch Philip was crawling at the side of it telling him how far he had left to go. The two girls and the Frenchmen were still pushing gently on either side to ensure the car didn't slide sideward whilst he was underneath.

At last he was there! He reached the tow bar and handed the hook to Philip, who then pulled him from underneath. There were relieved cheers from the onlookers.

'Phase one completed satisfactorily!' Henry said, pleased with himself. He seemed to be doing quite well at this point so I left it to him to give the orders. 'Gently pull the cable straight and walk with it over to that tree. There should be plenty to wrap round it.'

Philip did as he was told for a change, took the wire and tied it round the tree. The car was not out of danger yet, however. The winch lock still had to be put on to prevent more cable running out if the car started to fall. The lads repeated the movement, Philip holding on to Henry's arm whilst he reversed the winch.

The next manoeuvre was just as difficult and dangerous. Henry explained that he would have to turn the engine on and control the winch from *inside* the Discovery. Henry, who was acting more and more like an autocratic general as his confidence grew, told everyone to stay in their positions.

The first problem to be overcome was the whereabouts of the keys. Unfortunately they had been put in the only picnic basket to be placed back in the car, so Henry had the tricky movement of opening the rear door, removing the basket and closing the door again without disturbing the position of the Discovery. This turned out to be a most difficult task. The moment the door opened it shifted the balance of the car causing it to realign itself, terrifying the four who were still holding it as steady as possible. Then the car slipped again, six or seven inches along the tree, which was now leaning well over forty-five degrees and appeared to be cracking with the strain. Once again the relief of the crowd was palpable once Henry had retrieved the key. He now prepared to turn on the ignition.

A hundred questions raced through my head. What would happen to the vehicle when the engine started? Would the vibration move it and send it falling sidewards? Would the weight snap the cable if it started to fall? Would Henry be trapped by the open door if the vehicle did slip?

Holding on to the end of a blanket, with Francesca and Philip holding the other end in case it slipped, Henry slowly leaned into the vehicle. He couldn't quite reach and stopped, placing his other hand on the floor to gain balance and to gently push himself further inside. The car dipped a little but didn't slip. His hand was now on the ignition.

'Right, hold tight!' he shouted as he turned the key.

It fired first time, but the Land-Rover seemed to bounce forward. There were shouts of despair from the onlookers as they could see the vehicle very slowly slipping along the oak tree. It was as though the oak had now given up; the weight was too much and its branches were now only a few feet off the ground. It had slipped another two feet and both front wheels were off the ground as the car balanced on the oak tree. Almost everyone seemed to scream as the car slid yet again but then held.

Henry was braver now. He felt the cable would hold even if he had to get inside the vehicle to control the winch. Fortunately, however, he could reach the controls without risking it. Philip and I took over from the girls and together with the two French-men managed to hold the car in a straight position to facilitate an easier exit.

We were ready again. Henry started the winch. The cable tightened and the Discovery began to move, only a fraction at a time, back up the slope. We all moved inch by inch with the car back up the hill. The oak tree had also started to come up a little, straightening slowly with the car. It had now moved a yard. There was a deathly silence; even the birds appeared to have stopped singing. All we could hear was the low buzzing sound of the Land-Rover's winch straining to pull itself up the hill.

Another yard had been achieved. The oak tree had become a little more erect and suddenly there were shouts of 'We can see it!' from the ladies and the little French crowd began cheering and clapping – 'Allez, les anglais!' Philip and I were now at the top of the hill, together with the Land-Rover's rear wheels.

Then it was over; the Discovery was back at the top. The small crowd were roaring with delight. You would have thought Marseilles had scored a goal. Everyone hugged each other in total wonderment. I don't think I have had so many kisses from so many different people in my lifetime. It was a wonderful, exhilarating experience, but one which I would not want to repeat.

Chapter 14

Saturday was ruined, but at least we had the satisfaction of knowing that they hadn't beaten us and none of us had been hurt. I now felt sick of everything and quite frankly wanted to go back to England and get rid of the car. I had one more week of filming to do before I could escape and start for home.

On Sunday the weather turned. It had become very hot and humid and we were expecting a thunderstorm. We decided to go into St-Tropez to see if II PY was OK and to have a look at the town by night. Our visit was cut short, however, when it began to rain. We ran back to the car park, collected the Discovery and began to drive slowly out of town. The heavens opened and the storm came with a vengeance.

As we we drove slowly past the port, looking at the boats that were being lit up by the sudden flashes of light, Philip suddenly shouted to Henry to pull over. He had spotted the Dodge.

'Oh Philip, leave things alone! Your mother and I have had enough of this,' I said wearily.

'Not on your life, Dad, not after what they did yesterday. Those bastards could have killed one of us,' Philip answered, his anger beginning to burst out into the open.

Henry pulled over. There was no mistaking it was a black Dodge twin-cab pickup, but it was too far away to identify it positively. There were some men running backward and forward from the vehicle to a boat moored nearby, so it was impossible to get any closer.

'Go round again and pull into the car park. I'm going to take a closer look,' Philip demanded.

I tried to dissuade him but he was obstinate.

'I don't care. I'm going to look whatever anyone says,' Philip countered. 'Henry, just take them home and I'll wait here until you get back. I'll keep my eye on them.'

'No, Henry,' I insisted. 'I'm not leaving, knowing you're going to do something rash. So tell me, what are you proposing to do?'

'I don't know yet, but I want to take a closer look to see if it's them.'

Henry drove round the block and back into the car park, parking well away from the black Dodge. Having instructed the ladies to stay in the Land-Rover, the three of us ventured out into the rain to take a look. My involvement was supposedly to make sure the lads didn't start something they would regret. At least, that was the promise I made to Francesca as I left.

'I'll go and have a closer look, you two stay here,' Philip said, trying to take control of the situation.

He casually walked along the edge of the port, pretending to admire the boats, even though it would have been obvious to any-one that no one with half a brain would be doing that in this deluge. The Dodge was parked up close to the water's edge, with its rear end backed up close to a gangplank, where two men were unloading boxes and scurrying with them on to a motor cruiser. The boat itself was about ten metres in length, not very big, but ideal for a holiday cruiser.

Philip came back about ten minutes later, looking like a drowned rat, to report that is was impossible to get close enough. 'But it won't be too long,' he said gleefully. 'It looks like they have just unloaded several packs of '1664' on to the boat. They've left one at the top of the gangway.'

He paused for a minute and then said quite calmly, 'I'm going to give them a taste of their own medicine.'

'How's that then?' I asked.

'Dad, it's as easy as falling off a log.'

'Go on!' I said. Both Henry and I were all ears.

'I'm going to push the car into the water.' He paused and looked quizzically at us.

There was silence for a few seconds and then both Henry and I burst out laughing, much to Philip's annoyance and embarrassment.

'Listen!' he said angrily. 'Listen. His back wheels are on the smooth round concrete edge. His front wheels are on gravel. It would be like pushing something on ice. Easy!'

'Have you thought that you would be on the ice as well?' I asked.

'Yes and I wouldn't be. It's only when you have moved a metre or so that the front wheels would hit the gravel, but I still would have the back wheels on solid ground. I know it would work. Surprise would be the thing. They won't be coming out in this weather and if we give it a few minutes, we could quickly drive round, bumper to bumper, and push. No one would see and they would never hear a thing over the thunder.'

'You don't even know if it's the right car yet, do you?'

'Yes I do! It's them and I'm going to have 'em Dad.'

I quickly went back to the Land-Rover and told them what Philip was up to. I also suggested they take a taxi home. No one, however, wanted to leave. To my surprise, Francesca, more than anyone, wanted to stay and see it through.

Philip and Henry returned from a speedy reconnoitre of the area, with the news that they were now completely satisfied that the Dodge was the one on the mountain. They launched into an enthusiastic outline of their plan.

'Just a minute!' I said, interrupting Philip in full flight. 'Let me explain how I would do it and see what you think.'

'I'd like to do it how I said,' Philip interjected.

Victoria gainsaid him. 'It's not going to hurt us to hear what Dad has to say, is it?'

There were a few mutterings from the lads but they gave me 'the floor'. 'Philip's plan is a good one, so all I'm doing is refining it a bit. We take the Discovery down quietly some twenty to thirty yards away and line it up straight with the Dodge. One of us will go over to the boat and listen to see what state they're in and whether the coast is clear. If it is, we drive quietly in, drop it into low range and push like hell.

'The gangplank is in the middle of the boat. Either side there are two mooring ropes fixed to a cleat on either side of the boat's deck and then around the two capstans on the dockside. Philip, you were very lucky; the Dodge could have been parked in front of a capstan and it would all be for nothing. Had you thought of that?' I asked

'No. I hadn't,' Philip admitted, somewhat sheepishly.

'I think when fifty per cent of the Dodge is over the edge the gangplank will break – after all, it's only light aluminium – and the weight will be transferred to the mooring ropes, which will either snap or pull the cleats out of the boat. Whatever happens, because the front of the boat will be well out of the water, it will have the effect of bouncing away from the edge of the dock with such force that the passengers will be tossed around pretty severely, especially when the boat tries to get back to its normal position. This should give us time to get away. In the meantime, because the boat will have moved away from the edge, the Dodge should topple into the water. If and when the ropes break, the boat will be cut free of its moorings and float around a little. They won't be in danger but they shouldn't be able to get off either.'

For once there was silence in the family. They were all dumb-struck, not able to believe that their 'old man', as I have heard them refer to me could have thought out the plan in such detail and so quickly.

'Do you want to go ahead?' I asked. 'Because there's no turning back once we've started.'

They all agreed without exception and without reservation, which left me with one thing to do: organize our duties.

A little later Henry backed out of the parking place and slowly drove down toward the Dodge, stopping only to let Philip out to confirm that everything was in order and guide him into position. With Emily concealed in the back, the ladies were keeping a lookout. Henry got into place waiting for the signal to start.

Philip waved his arm and Henry slowly but surely drove across the car park and gently touched the bumper of the Dodge. Philip signalled OK but then stopped any further movement as he listened out for sounds. Despite the rain, we could all hear the laughter on the boat. It was obvious that they had all had a few by now and the advantage was with us for the moment. Philip held his hand in the air, waiting for the right opportunity to attack, rain falling away from his elbow like a tap that has been left on. The tension was unbelievable.

Philip's hand fell and the Land-Rover in low range and full throttle began to push. Suddenly Philip was waving frantically for Henry to stop. Henry cut the engine and the noise dropped. We could hear the silence on the boat; even the sound of the rain falling did not mask the quietness of the moment. We all looked on in fear as we saw the anxious face of Philip trying to see what was happening.

The laughter returned as suddenly as it had stopped, and Philip again directed Henry to push. The Land-Rover's engine roared into life again; as Henry began to push at the Dodge's bumper once more. You could now feel the weight of the Dodge baulk as it tried desperately to resist the power of the Land-Rover. It was in gear, which gave it more power to resist, but Philip was right; the surface was slippery and once the weight was on the move it was not too difficult.

The Dodge was soon over the edge, with the front resting on the gangplank as I had predicted. Philip signalled for more power, but the Land-Rover had little left to give. Henry, still pushing hard on the accelerator, was willing it to move faster. Inch by inch, with the Land-Rover wheels spinning, he managed to almost reach the fifty-per cent goal. The gangplank didn't break but simply bent in two. Still, it had the same effect.

We heard the screams of the men on board. 'You've left the

fucking brake off . . .' and then there was silence as the weight of the Dodge fell on to the last inch or two of the decking, causing the bow to rear up sharply. The boat slipped away from the moorings, as the the ropes snapped with the tension.

By now the weight of the Dodge had carried it over the edge. The boat freed itself from the vehicle, sending the bow crashing back on to the water. It began to dance violently like a rocking horse.

It was time for us to leave. Philip scuffed over our tyre tracks with his boots and jumped into the Land-Rover. We were on the way home. For some strange reason there was no euphoria, just silence. I think we were all worried as it dawned on us what we had done and what the consequences might be.

I turned to see the boat still bouncing around like a cork and the front end of the Dodge rising up out of the water, like some wartime hulk that had been scuppered in the shallows.

Monday morning soon arrived and, after the weekend from hell, starting work again seemed as good as a rest. Francesca, Emily and I decided to take a taxi to the set, leaving the Land-Rover for the rest of the family to use. Somehow I felt it would be better if the Land-Rover was not seen in St-Tropez for the next few days!

We arrived on the set to be greeted by Ed, who was anxious to get started the moment it was light enough. I drove the car to the Senequier, positioned it where I was told and waited. Francesca, wrapped up warm against the early-morning cold, watched from the comfort of the Senequier.

Eventually I plucked up the courage to ask Ed if he had heard about a car falling into the water.

'Drunken bums!' Ed replied. 'The police have got them in gaol for something else. They got the car out and impounded it. That's all I know. I think it might be drugs or something.'

I couldn't believe my ears. Not only did everyone think they did it themselves but they'd been arrested for something else. I couldn't wait to tell the others. To celebrate I telephoned the Cigale Restauarant in La Croix-Valmer and booked a table for seven; two ice-cold bottles of champagne were to be at the ready for our seven-thirty arrival.

What a wonderful evening it turned out to be! I cannot remember laughing as much about anything before in my life.

Chapter 15

The final week in St-Tropez passed without a hitch. It was sad to have to leave but we still had the inaugral Rolls-Royce and Bentley race to look foward to, taking the first bottles of Beaujolais Nouveau to the restaurants of London via Paris.

On Saturday, we left La Croix-Valmer at about ten o'clock, hoping to arrive at Charnay early in the afternoon. We made our way to St. Maxime, passing Port Grimaud, the Venice of the South of France, which like its counterpart in Italy is also very beautiful, but of course not in the same way.

We passed through Telepéage and made our way slowly to Aix and on towards Lyon. It was a slow, tortuous journey. The motorway signs were warning of violent winds, but there was no need. We were being buffeted by them, so much so it was impossible for Henry to drive any faster than 40 mph as the trailer and the two-ton weight of II PY were being blown from side to side. This was putting our target of reaching Charnay by early afternoon in jeopardy.

Soon after the Aix péage, Henry said, 'Look, I don't want to worry you, but I think we are being followed. We've had a black Cherokee Jeep on our tail for at least forty miles.'

Of course we all turned round to see the Jeep some two hundred yards behind us keeping at the same pace as ourselves. It was not easy to get a clear view because of the height and width of the Rolls. However, we could tell they were driving at the same steady 40 mph as we were doing. We were the slowest vehicle on the road and the Jeep was the only vehicle that stuck behind us.

Philip was the first one to become annoyed at the possibility that they were trouble and was all for nipping matters in the bud. He suggested Henry pull in at the next rest area, just a few miles after Aix. This he did, as we were all filled with apprehension and sensing trouble again. He stopped in a place which gave him ample opportunity to pull out cleanly if there was to be trouble. We all waited in absolute silence to see whether it would follow us in. It didn't take long; the Jeep also pulled in to the area and drove on to the other side, a little away from us.

It took all my powers of persuasion to stop Philip going out and confronting the people in the car as, at this moment, there was no proof of any thing untoward. For a few minutes we just sat in silence looking at the Cherokee.

A minute or so later a white BMW also pulled in, followed by an old blue Volvo estate, which we were sure was the one following us on the way down. They pulled in to the marked parking bays and the passengers and drivers got out, to either walk around a little or visit the toilet block. The cars all bore French number plates and, apart from the Volvo, we thought nothing of them. However, our eyes became fixed on the Jeep as neither the driver nor any of its passengers got out.

Henry suggested we have a break and stretch our legs, which was quite frankly the best idea, as we were all becoming so tense that I, for one, certainly couldn't think straight.

I asked Henry, 'What about those other two cars? Have you noticed them on the drive at all?'

'No, I haven't and I'm not sure yet whether the Volvo is the same one.'

That reply made me feel a little safer. With those other two cars around the people in the Jeep would not start anything.

Philip became concerned about Emily, who was playing on the grass near one of the cars.

'Come on, Emily, this is not the best of places, we are going to stop a bit further on. Come on, into the car, quick,' Philip demanded, trying not to upset the others, but also ushering them into the car. The ladies were being somewhat quizzical as to the rush.

Once Emily and the others were safely in, Philip took it on himself to walk over to the Jeep. Henry shouted to him, 'Leave them alone; it may be my imagination.'

'We'll see,' he shouted back, as he continued over to the car.

He didn't get the opportunity. The Jeep immediately sped off out of the rest area and back on to the autoroute. 'They bloody were, the bastards,' Philip roared. 'Come on, let's get out of here,' he continued, walking back to the Land-Rover.

I didn't notice what happened to the other cars, whether they remained in the car park or not. I was simply concerned about getting on our way. However, Victoria had been watching the people from the other cars and had noticed them looking intently at Philip's actions.

'It is possible it's my imagination playing tricks with me, but I think I did see them earlier,' she said, getting back in the car.

Henry had done his fair stint of driving, so I took over. Francesca sat with me in the front, the two lads with Annabel in the centre seats and Victoria and Emily in the back. I pulled back onto the autoroute and continued travelling towards Lyon at a steady 40 mph, again with every heavy goods vehicle passing us without much difficulty. We spent the first half hour or so discussing our situation; naturally we were all somewhat concerned about our safety and therefore decided to keep to the areas where we knew there would be many people around, just in case. I gave a running commentary that everything was OK behind, with Victoria confirming every move she could see.

We had all gone quiet, not a sound for mile after mile, not knowing but feeling something was going to happen. My mouth had become dry, with my lips beginning to stick to my teeth. Francesca began to grip my leg as she could see and feel the tension building up in my body.

A few miles further on, we all noticed in the distance the black Jeep on the hard shoulder. To my horror I could see it was indicating to return to the highway. We drew closer and closer and still it hadn't made its move.

'Oh, it's waiting for us,' I sighed.

My heart skipped a beat, as I could hear the others take sharp intakes of breath. We were now level, none of us knew whether to look at it or just ignore it. I stared inside; I wanted to see what our possible adversary looked like. Philip too stared menacingly at the Jeep.

As soon as we passed it, the Jeep pulled out and remained within fifty yards of II PY, maintaining our speed. We no longer thought we had problems, we knew we had, and it was just a question of when, not if, they would start on us.

We continued for another five minutes, when Victoria yelled, 'That white BMW is passing us.'

To my horror, it did overtake us and then dropped down to our speed, about one hundred yards in front of us. We seemed helpless, unable to counter any move they made. Everyone kept on turning round to see where the Jeep was.

Victoria thought she could also see the Volvo approaching fast. It was and I now saw it in my mirrors and it too dropped to our speed, just in front of the Jeep. We were all now very concerned and knew we were in trouble. It was obvious to us they were after II PY and for the first time I thought I would give them it.

'They can have the bloody car, if that's what they want,' I muttered to the others. The two lads, almost in unison, replied, 'Not on yer bloody life!'

Philip continued. 'Let these bastards win? I thought you were made of sterner stuff, Dad.'

'I am, but it's not just me and you this time. I've got a car full of my family and I don't want to risk anything for the sake of the car.'

'It's the principle, Dad, principle. That's what you've always said.'

I thought for a while, constantly watching in my mirrors and constantly having reports from everyone, including Emily, on what was happening.

'Well, what do you think?' I asked everyone.

I need not have bothered to ask. The 'Dunkirk' spirit came to the fore. Everyone, including myself, decided we would fight.

I was fired up. Francesca was gripping my leg again and smiling encouragingly. This, to put it simply, gave me more strength to fight whatever was to come. I was gripping the steering wheel so hard, I could hardly turn it. The lads were leaning forward giving me instructions, but there was nothing I could do as they, 'the villains', hadn't done anything yet. However we did not have long to wait,

We had just passed a sign showing 2000 metres to the next rest area when the Jeep came alongside and also maintained our speed. It was just slightly behind the Land-Rover; with the result that we could not see the people in it. The BMW then slowed down and remained about thirty yards in front of us. Everything seemed to be happening, the tension was almost overwhelming. I could also see the Volvo closing the gap between us. It was now so close I could not judge how far it was from the trailer. We were effectively trapped between the three cars. We carried on in this vein for about 1000 metres, when the Jeep pulled level with the Land-Rover. The front passenger signalled that we should turn into the next rest area.

'Don't look at him Francesca,' I yelled. 'None of you look at him, just stare in front. He's trying to get me to turn off and that's the last thing I'm going to do.'

'The Volvo's now only about ten feet away,' Victoria informed us. They were now pulling out and in erratically. 'I think they are trying to attract my attention.'

'Ignore them, love. You too Emily! One of you telephone the police,' I ordered. 'Just dial 17. Ask for the Gendarmerie.'

It was sod's law, or very careful planning by the 'villains', that the mobile telephone was out of service. We had no alternative but to sort this out ourselves.

The passenger of the Jeep became irate and began signalling like mad, to make us turn on to the fast-approaching slip road to the rest area; but still we were ignoring him. The driver also joined in and began blasting his horn to attract our attention. The Volvo in the rear kept speeding up, almost touching the trailer, then slowing down, only to repeat it time and time again. The driver of the BMW then reduced his speed dramatically and we were now only ten yards behind him. I just did not know which vehicle to watch as they were all acting aggressively.

'Bugger 'em, Dad, crash into the BMW. Don't turn off!' Philip was yelling at the top of his voice.

'Speed up, Dad, it's our only chance. We've got the height and weight to push the BMW off the road,' Henry urged.

We were all, without exception, worried and scared. We were miles from anywhere without any support, still unable to telephone and we had at least ten men in the three cars intent on robbing us. The odds were not attractive.

I took Henry's advice and put my foot down and in the remaining time before the turn off managed 45 mph. I had reduced the gap between us and the BMW to five or six yards and effectively issued a challenge. It was obvious to everyone, including the drivers of the three cars, that we would have an accident rather than turn off, despite their manoeuvrings.

Emily now was so upset and terrified she was sobbing her heart out, wanting her mother. Victoria was trying to comfort her in the back and at the same time trying to keep us informed of what was happening behind us. The lads and Annabel were holding on so tight to the front seats, in anticipation of a crash, you could see the whites of their knuckles.

Philip began shouting. 'Get those bastards, Dad.' He was totally fired up. He would, in his state, have been capable of taking the lot on, all by himself. There was now a mixture of fear and determination in all of us, with the latter gaining the upper hand.

The Jeep began to move closer to us in an effort to force me to enter the slip road. I responded by turning into the Jeep, forcing him to take evasive action. The trailer responded violently, swinging left to right, confusing the driver of the Volvo.

'Christ it's going to tip over,' I shouted, as the shaking began to affect the Land-Rover. I was now within six feet of the BMW and I could see the rear passenger mouthing some instructions to the driver. At three feet away he was beginning to panic. He was trying to hold his ground and was obviously under orders. I was not holding back. I was only one foot away, now six inches, three, two, one and the Land-Rover's bumper nudged the back of the BMW. We could all see the panic of the rear passenger as I was now pushing him, backed up by the load of a two-ton Rolls-Royce.

The trailer had calmed down and I had better control. I was almost at the slip road, still pushing him with my foot to the floor. He was trying to hold his position, with the result that we kept bouncing on to his boot. He had no chance, our combined weight hitting him made it impossible for the driver to control the car. His situation was made worse by the fact his passengers were not wearing seat belts and were being thrown about. The passenger of the Jeep just could not believe what he was seeing and looked on in absolute astonishment, unable to assist in any way.

We were now level with the slip road and there was no chance for them to force us off the road. The Jeep signalled to the BMW to move away, which it did complete with an almost written-off rear end. It moved about fifty yards in front of us and once again dropped to our speed.

'That's round one to us,' I shouted and we all cheered.

The Jeep also dropped back, remaining just in front of the Volvo. Both vehicles kept pace but it was obvious that they hadn't finished with us yet and therefore the tension soon returned.

It was extremely surprising that this behaviour on the autoroute had not at least attracted some attention, especially as the motorway was reasonably busy, but no, we were still on our own.

I was becoming more concerned, as I had noticed a large Giraud lorry approach quickly and maintain our speed not far behind us.

'Dad,' Victoria commented. 'A lorry has been following us for a long time now.'

'Yes, love, I've seen it. Keep your eye on it, we may have further problems.'

We kept in convoy for several miles. The pressure was still on us as all protagonists were still there. It was now only 10 kilometres to the next rest and parking area. Would they try again?

We were travelling in total silence, each one of us looking in any direction to see what the opposition was doing. We did not have long to wait. The same procedure had started. The Jeep came alongside, swinging in to be near, but not too near to allow me to turn into him. This time they were determined. The front passenger began waving a shotgun out of the window. He pointed it at Francesca, who tried to ignore it, but couldn't; she was terrified. To make his point on what he would do to us, he leaned out of the Jeep window and fired two warning shots over the Land-Rover. This was a very different situation we were now facing, as we continued towards the next parking place and possible battleground.

'There's a lorry coming up in the middle lane,' Victoria yelled. 'It's a Giraud and there's another one just behind. They're both going to pass.'

'Look Philip, they can have the bloody car, we can't fight them as well,' I said, desperation in my voice.

He had nothing to say. We were all beginning to despair.

'They're nearly here!' Victoria shouted again.

The first one was almost level with the trailer and began blasting his horn at the Jeep, which was cruising in his lane. It was obvious that the lorry wished to overtake. Strangely the other lorry had dropped back a little and was just behind the Volvo. The Jeep accelerated a little and then pulled in just behind the BMW, allowing the Giraud lorry to pass, which it did remonstrating with the driver of the Jeep.

'They're not with them,' Henry shouted

'They're not with us either,' Annabel commented, as the lorry was now passing the BMW. It was the first time she had made any comment since the whole incident began, having sat in a petrified silence for the whole terrifying episode.

The Jeep now resumed its position at our side and the passenger began to remind us of his previous threat, by showing us the shotgun.

'Get your camera,' Philip ordered Annabel. 'See if you can get a photo of that bastard with the gun. We might find it useful later on.'

Unbelievably, the man was so blasé, he actually posed for the picture with a smile, brandishing his shotgun.

'Victoria. How far behind is the other lorry?'

'It's just behind the Volvo,' she replied. 'I can't see very well, but I think it's now pulling out to pass it. It's about fifty or so yards back.'

I was the only one concentrating on the road ahead and the only one watching the lorry passing the BMW. The others were watching the Jeep and its antics, with its passengers showing off and having a good laugh at us, watching the fear in our faces, as the front passenger was waving the gun. They were so busy having a laugh at our expense, they didn't see the Giraud lorry had cut in front of the BMW a little sharply. I was the only one who had seen that and it was perhaps fortunate that the BMW's driver wasn't caused a major problem. However, the lorry had just completed its manoeuvre when all hell let loose.

The Giraud lorry slowed dramatically, the trailer almost jack-knifing, leaving the driver of the BMW with no chance. He ran straight into the back of the lorry. The car was finished and to my utter astonishment and that of Victoria and Emily, the other Giraud lorry, which had started to pass the Volvo, simply ran it off the road into the ditch.

The Jeep, just by sheer luck, missed the mêlée and took the least line of resistance, escaping through the only available gap between the crash barrier and the front Giraud lorry. I was in complete shock at what I had just seen. I braked very hard, almost standing up on the pedal, as the weight of the Rolls was still pushing us. We stopped inches before we did any damage.

The Jeep, with its armoury, was fast disappearing into the distance, leaving its poor henchmen to face the consequences. It was fortunate that none of us were travelling at excessive speeds, with the result there were no fatalities.

However, the driver of the BMW was trapped in his car. He was the only one wearing his seat belt and that, coupled with the driver's air bag inflating, gave him difficulty in releasing himself from the car. His three passengers had no trouble. They made good their escape by running across the adjacent fields.

The driver of the first Giraud turned out to be a woman. She had seen the three men escaping across the fields and the driver still struggling to get out, but she had none of it. She jumped down from the lorry, raced to the BMW armed with a metal bar and warned the driver what she would do if he tried to escape. He took the line of least resistance and gave up.

The Volvo had been tipped into the ditch and was almost on its side, making it very difficult to open the doors. Two of the men eventually managed to get out but quickly realised there was no place to go. They began remonstrating with the driver of the second Giraud lorry for causing the accident, making all sorts of accusations, and denying emphatically they were in any way involved with the other vehicles. Their protestations however were somewhat diluted as the third man from the car also managed to get out and ran off with those from the BMW. The other two sensibly remained with their car awaiting rescue and the police, or was it because the Giraud driver was muscle from head to toe?

'Are you all right?' the second driver asked as he walked over to us. I've been looking at you for many kilometres. It was bad,' he said in pidgin English, with a strong French accent.

'Thank you,' I said, almost in tears with the relief.

We were joined by the lady driver, who introduced herself as Simone. She was a wonderful woman, quite attractive, a little on the large side, but very feminine and she too spoke a little English, also with a most appealing French accent. I say she was wonderful because she had sensed we had a problem at the first incident and decided to follow at a discreet distance. When she noticed the same scenario happening on the second occasion, she felt she had to do something. She was driving in tandem with the other lorry and persuaded its driver to help us. Which I am thankful he did. No other driver had attempted to help us and there were many which passed.

It was also quite evident to her that we were all suffering from shock as we stepped out of the Land-Rover. Emily was still sobbing, but at last being comforted by Annabel. None of us had much to say, apart from Philip, who wanted to exact revenge on the remaining protagonists.

He walked over to the BMW driver, who had succeeded in getting out of the car, grabbed him by the pullover and pulled him almost into his own face. 'I'll fucking kill you, you bastard,' he shouted. The driver himself was almost like jelly, even before Philip had assaulted him. He simply collapsed into a heap as he let go of his pullover.

'Would you all like a drink? I have plenty in the cab,' Simone asked.

The other Giraud driver joined us, advising Simone that should move her wagon as it was partially blocking the motorway, which she duly did.

The other driver introduced himself simply as JP. When he had satisfied himself that we were alright, he began to explain from his point of view what had happened. He told us that Simone had seen what had been going on and asked for his help.

They had planned what they were going to do as they were driving along. He explained how excited she became with her running commentary, trying to emulate her voice, 'They are trying to push it off the road. No!No! He's waving a gun. Oh God, he's shooting it! Come on, JP, we've got to do something.' With that she put her foot down and charged at the Jeep. 'You take care of that Volvo, leave the others to me.'

'I just did as I was told,' he said, smiling.

Simone returned to us after moving the lorry, and we all thanked her from the bottom of our hearts for her bravery and for helping us.

Simone had telephoned the gendarmes the moment the action had stopped. You could hear the many police sirens approaching fast. They had even launched a helicopter which was hovering overhead and remained there until the main force of the gendarmerie arrived, many with automatic rifles.

Reality had struck the three remaining lads, who had somehow managed to get together and were obviously concocting their story. They were looking extremely contrite. They were not the brave young men of a few minutes ago, when they were trying to bully us. They were now very frightened, pathetic little men.

The gendarmes soon finished securing the area and announced that they would like to speak to Simone Gontard. They took her to one side and questioned her for many minutes, refusing to allow any other of the parties to converse with each other with the exception of ourselves. as we were all together in any case.

During the questioning of Simone, they called another officer over, who immediately went to JP and began questioning him. It was obvious after a while that they had confirmed each other's story. Instructions were immediately given to the helicopter, which was still circling overhead, to try and find the four men who had run away. It left straight away to begin the search.

They did not bother at this point to question the three remaining men, they were simply arrested. With all the previous aggression they had shown towards us when they were in their cars, they were now like minnows, cooperating with all the police demands without a murmur.

Police sirens were now heard again as they were escorting two breakdown lorries to the scene of the accident. The police were not taking any chances; the vehicles were taken away for investigation under heavy police escort.

It was now our turn to be questioned. Unfortunately it all had to be conducted in French as none of the officers could speak enough English. I acted as interpreter as well as I could. However, before they started questioning, they wanted to see the vehicle under the cover, on the trailer. Henry now had come into his own; he took the cover off, went into the Land-Rover for the 'flying lady' and placed her on the radiator. The gendarmes were impressed, even more so when he explained that we were going to Beaujolais and the car was to lead the procession for the Beaujolais race starting in Charnay.

Despite all the travelling and the work she had done, II PY was still looking good. Traffic, which had been allowed to continue after the breakdown lorries had left, had now slowed almost to a stop, as motorists began slowing down to look at the car, in spite of the gendarmes' efforts to move it on.

We were all questioned, with me as the driver taking the lion's share. We told them exactly what had happened, emphasising the bravery of the two Giraud drivers and in particular Simone. I told them about the Jeep, but that I hadn't been able to get any details of the number. I told them I could recognise the Jeep if I saw it again, as it had a distinct white scroll on the bonnet. The gendarmes advised me that Madame Gontard had supplied all the details they needed and that they were hoping to catch the Jeep at the péage just before Lyon.

Once we had given details of our passports and addresses, we were allowed to go on our way, but not before we had the pleasure of seeing the three men bundled in to a police van and driven away to await their fate. The final bit of luck for us was when we saw the excitement of the gendarmes, as the helicopter had notified them that they had spotted three men running away. The traffic was stopped and several gendarmes ran to their cars and set off in hot pursuit, naturally with all alarms sounding.

The whole process had taken about two hours and we were now a little tired and hungry. As a thank you to the Giraud drivers we invited Simone and JP to have a meal with us at Latitude 45, a services which was about 60 miles away, and to my astonishment they agreed to meet us there.

Henry took over the driving, the recent experience having worn me out somewhat, and we made our way steadily towards the services. Everything now seemed unimportant, we were so relieved that it was all over, time didn't matter.

We arrived about an hour and a half later, with the two Giraud lorries already waiting for us. Philip volunteered to stay with 11PY whilst we went into the restaurant with the drivers. It was a very pleasant experience and a good way to say thank you. We exchanged names and addresses and of course invited them back to England, and parted with the knowledge that we had two new friends.

The next stop was Limonest, just after Lyon. We pulled into the giant Auchan supermarket car park as we had done on the way south; it enabled us not only to fill the Land-Rover with cheap diesel, but also to fill the Rolls to the top with petrol and save any potential difficulty in Charnay later on. It also gave us all the opportunity to stretch our legs and pick up some local wines, beers and cheeses.

Half an hour later we were on our way to Charnay. Normally, the quickest way was to drive straight from Lyon up into the hills. But taking this route we would have had to travel on roads which were not only steep, but also very narrow and winding. It would be a tortuous route for the Land-Rover with a two-ton load on the trailer. I thought it would be easier to stick to the autoroute to Villefranche and then turn off to the villages of Beaujolais and finally to Charnay. At least this way, three quarters of the journey would be on wider roads, which would be better and safer for Henry to drive on.

We were already very late as it was now around seven o'clock. I had phoned Alain, our friend and host, and explained the situation, but like any good friend, he was more concerned about our health and welfare than the time.

We had probably travelled about ten miles along the auto-route, when I saw the Jeep travelling in the opposite direction.

'It's over there!' I shouted excitedly to the others. I could also see that the driver and passengers of the Jeep had seen us.

'What's where?' Henry responded.

'The bloody Jeep is. Look!' I turned round to see the Jeep accelerating away. 'Put your foot down now, as fast as you can. Let's get off the motorway quick. I'm sure they won't be expecting that,' I continued.

'Are you sure it was them, Dad?' Philip asked.

'Absolutely positive.'

Henry had also seen them looking at us as they drove past and noticed their acceleration away. He put his foot down and managed 55 mph, before the trailer started to snake, forcing us to slow down, so we continued at that. The talking stopped. We were once again filled with worry and anxiety. We were all wondering what was going to happen next and how we could get out of it long before it actually happened.

We seemed to be thundering along. The noise of the Land-Rover at full throttle gave a false impression of speed – we were almost crawling.

'Come on, come on,' I was saying to myself, as I could see the péage in the distance.

'I'm going as fast as I dare,' Henry protested.

The péage was now only four hundred metres away. 'It's just round the bend,' I yelled.

The barriers came into view. 'Take the one to Villefranche, quick!' I yelled again. I was desperate that we got through quickly.

There was an empty line at the turn off. Henry raced in to beat everyone else, forgetting we had a two-ton weight on the back and it would be difficult to stop. How he managed I do not know. Everyone was looking at us as the tyres squealed towards the barrier, stopping just in time to avoid a collision. We drove through the Telepéage and on to Villefranche and Charnay. Annabel and Emily were in the back this time, so I asked them to keep their eyes open. At the moment there was no sign of the Jeep, but we all knew it would be after us.

'How on earth did they get past the péage and not get caught?' Victoria asked.

'It's not difficult, if you are determined,' Henry told her; I reminded her of the time many years ago, when we had broken down at Nemours and were taken off at one of the many little private tracks which leave the autoroute.

I directed Henry out of Villefranche and on to the route fleury, through the villages of Beaujolais and finally to Charnay. He kept the speed up to try to put as much distance between us and them as he could.

We were all thinking the same question and suddenly I remembered the possibility that we had already thought of during our picnic up in the hills.

'The car's bugged!' I exclaimed.

Henry was more precise. 'It could be on the Rolls, the Land-Rover or the trailer. The important thing is to find it and find it quick.'

'But when would they have had the opportunity to put a bug on the car?' Annabel asked.

'It wouldn't be hard,' I answered. 'Just think of all the rallies and publicity stunts we've been to. Anyone could have done it. It would only take a second or two.

'I'll give Alain a ring, tell him where we are and ask what he suggests. OK?'

Alain was to be our host in Charnay and a close friend. He was now semi-retired but had been the director of his own company, which was involved in repairing IBM computers. He was not only a computer genius but also a master of all electronic technologies. If anyone could find the bug, he could, or at least he would know someone who would.

The phone rang; Alain was on the other end. 'Bonsoir, Alain, c'est Robert.'

'Oh hello, Robert, where are you?'

'We're still a few hours away, that's all, but we're going to need your help, *d'urgence*! I had already told him about our woes earlier in the week, so he wasn't surprised when I added, 'We're absolutely sure the car is bugged. Can you help us?'

Alain had a lovely way of making everything sound so simple and replied, 'Pas de problème, mon ami.'

By mid-afternoon we were winding up into the mountains, through some of the most beautiful countryside in France. The trees had now taken on the golden shades of autumn, but none of us had the inclination to admire them. We were all too intent on seeing if we were being followed.

We were about ten minutes away and the phone rang. It was Alain.

'Would you come straight to the town hall and not my house? It will be better if I take you to the garage. He's a friend of mine.'

'Yes, of course!' I replied. 'Naturally he's a friend of yours!'

Alain laughed.

Charnay was that sort of place; everyone knew everyone else.

We arrived at last at the town hall, which like everything else was built in beautiful golden-red brick. Alain was waiting for us. He was a big man, somewhat overweight but very fit nonetheless. We didn't have time for pleasantries and simply followed him through the winding streets to the garage, which stood almost at the end of the village.

The owner and mechanic was Henri Dupont, a slim, weather-beaten, grey-haired man in his eighties. He couldn't speak a word of English and it was therefore left to Alain to translate. Alain briefed him on what had happened and you could see him actually becoming more and more excited as he passed on the details.

We were ordered to take the car off the trailer and put it in the garage, leaving the trailer at the side. He opened the garage doors to reveal a time warp – we were back in the fifties. The garage from the outside looked as though it had been constructed in that period, but inside it was for definite. Naturally he was also up to date and proudly showed us his latest computer-controlled testing equipment.

Henry in the meantime had been taking the covers off to reveal II PY.

'Oh la la!' Monsieur Dupont exclaimed, pausing for a moment. 'C'est une Phantom 11 Sedanca de Ville. C'est superbe. C'est une Continental, n'est-ce pas?' He was absolutely delighted.

'Vous connaissez bien les Rolls-Royce donc?' I asked.

'Oui, absolument!'

He went on to tell us proudly how he had worked on Rolls-Royces when he was young, just after the war.

I drove II PY into the garage and over the inspection pit, as directed, just as Christophe Platini, Alain's friend, arrived.

'He will find the bug if there is one!' Alain exclaimed.

I am sure you can imagine an electronics whizz-kid. A high forehead accentuated by receding dark hair, thick glasses and the whole appearance a little unkempt. That was Christophe. He was, however, a genius with surveillance equipment and was very much involved with counter industrial espionage. He immediately started work. He checked the trailer first, with no result, and then the Land-Rover. To our utter astonishment, he found one.

'This is not a problem,' he said, speaking in English, as he took the bug from under the rear wheel arch. 'This is for short range. It has been on a long time.'

We just couldn't believe it. It had obviously been put on at home in England, but where?

'How short is the range?' I asked.

'A few hundred metres, depending on the terrain.' This made it sound even worse. Were they always so close at hand?

He then took out some other equipment and began to scan the car. Again to our amazement, he found another two. 'These have been put on, I think you say, very unprofessionally.'

'Amateurishly,' I interrupted.

'Yes, that's it, very amateurish, but the *matériel*, the equipment, is very professional and *très cher*,' he said, repeatedly lapsing into French. 'This one here has a range of several kilometres,' he added, removing it from the inside of the interior lining in the back of the car.

'How on earth have they had the time to get it into that position? We've been with the car all the time,' Francesca asked quizzically.

'Obviously not *all* the time,' I interjected.

Christophe took seconds to find the other. It was simply fitted to the inside of the front bumper. There appeared to have been no real attempt to hide it, but perhaps that's why it was so successful; we didn't notice it. 'I do not think there are any others. There is no indication of further radio frequency activity,' he said, packing up his equipment.

We were all very grateful for his help, offering to pay for his services, but he refused, saying he had enjoyed doing it and that Alain had helped him on many occasions.

Christophe then threw a spanner in the works and put fear back into our hearts. 'They will have got a fix on this place already. If they are controlling the two bugs from different area, they will be very accurate. I don't know too much about this second one. I think it is from Czechoslovakia, but we must assume it has the same range. There is a possibility that the hills will distort the reception but you cannot guarantee that. The best thing for you to do quickly is to put the two bugs, together, on another slow-moving vehicle and drive it around slowly to confuse them. You must not give the impression that you have found them because they will have a fix on this place and will come and this way they will think you have moved on. Do you understand what I mean?'

'Yes, of course,' I replied.

We could see M Dupont becoming very excited as Alain translated what Christophe was saying to us. He was keen to get involved.

Alain, speaking in French, said, 'We need time. We need to take the bugs somewhere else. It's no use going by car. They will see it and know it's a trick. Any ideas?' he asked.

At this point the excited M Dupont went over to the phone and called his friend in the next village. In five minutes he had arranged everything. His son would take the bugs over to his friend, who happened to be a haulage contractor. They would fix the bugs on a fifteen-ton lorry and drive it round slowly for the next few hours. This would give us time to sort things out.

Alain then explained that the car was being used in the *vendange* and again M Dupont became excited. 'We must protect the car whatever,' he said, sticking his chest out with pride.

Chapter 16

M Dupont spent a few minutes admiring the car explaining what this did and what that did and how it was made. Suddenly a puzzled look appeared on his face.

'Un moment!' he said. 'La voiture n'est pas originale.'

My heart skipped a beat. What did he mean? I called Alain over to help me translate in case I was misinterpreting. Francesca could hear the panic in my voice.

'What on earth's the matter?' Francesca asked.

Alain immediately asked M Dupont what the trouble was.

M Dupont explained with Alain translating.

'It's the wrong chassis. It's too big and it doesn't look right. The battery box is too deep and he feels there is a slight problem with the back seat; it doesn't look absolutely correct and even the boots on the end of the springs look too elongated. He says he has the workshop manuals for it and will go and get them.'

I didn't need the translation. I knew exactly what had been said and I felt sick. There was a deathly silence while he went to collect the manual.

M Dupont returned with a well-thumbed manual and took me into the pit, with Alain and Henry joining us to see what the problem was. He opened the manual, thumbed through the pages until he arrived at the right one, ran his finger down the page and announced the dimensions to us all.

'It should be about four inches on each side and I can see it's more than that even without measuring it,' I said with a very heavy heart.

M Dupont took out his measure and announced the actual measurements. It was six and a half to seven inches – almost three inches bigger than it should have been all the way along the car.

In a flash, everything became clear to me. 'Stop!' I shouted, suddenly full of adrenalin. 'That's why they're after the car. It's a false bottom. It's full of drugs.' I shouted excitedly. 'They've been after the car since it left America. The Drug Enforcement Agency didn't find them because who would think that a big chassis would conceal them? They just look like steel girders . . . I am absolutely sure the car is full of drugs.'

Alain was translating what I was saying word for word and M Dupont became more and more excited. There was no doubt that he was enthralled at the prospect of 'having a go' at the crooks who were trying to steal the car.

'We must phone the police,' Christophe said.

'No, I don't want to do that. Not at the moment. I would like to phone our friend in the States and tell him of our possible find first. It's only a possibility and I don't want the car interfered with until after the race. No matter how sure I think we are.'

I warned everyone of the possible consequences if the villains knew that *we* knew where the drugs were; it could be fatal. It was also very important that no one should attempt to search the car for fear of disturbing vital evidence. We would all have to behave as though nothing had happened.

Alain made arrangements for me to take the Rolls to the house of the *ancien maire*, the former mayor Étienne Simplan, where it could be concealed in his large garage. The trailer would be hidden in Monsieur Dupont's garage and the Land-Rover, as it would be needed to transport us about, was to be hidden at Alain's. Alain also arranged for an urgent meeting with the current mayor at the town hall. The community would work together, he told us, to foil the criminals. We felt as the world had been taken off our shoulders.

Alain agreed with the mayor that we should all meet at about eight-thirty, which gave us only half an hour to freshen up and have something to eat back at Alain's house. Built in the local stone – the *pierre d'or*, or 'golden stone' – it looked magnificent, standing proudly on the hillside. We were met at the door by Marie, Alain's wife. She was a lovely lady, very kind and thoughtful, and extremely elegant to boot. She ran the family property company with great success. Alain had obviously briefed her as to our situation, so the moment we arrived she had tea and sandwiches ready for us.

A few minutes later Alain, Francesca and I went back to the town hall for the meeting and were greeted on the steps by the mayor, who immediately whisked us into the meeting chamber. There were already about twenty people waiting for it to start – we were five minutes early – but the mayor insisted we wait until the appointed hour, as there were more people expected. He was right; thirty-three people turned up to discuss what we could do to foil the villains.

The mayor, a tall grey-haired man, wearing a light camel-coloured cashmere jacket, opened the meeting and invited me to brief everyone on the situation. I didn't feel I had enough knowledge of French to do it, so I left it to Alain to explain.

'Robert here . . .' he began, pointing to me, 'has brought his wonderful vintage Rolls-Royce to Charnay to take part in the inaugural Rolls-Royce and Bentley Rally . . .'

'A wonderful car it is too!' chirped M Dupont excitedly.

'Well yes,' said Alain, continuing. 'It is also very valuable and once belonged to an American gangster. It was the only thing he ever loved and now that he is out of prison, he wants it back. He will do anything to get it back. He has tried on several occasions to steal it back . . .'

'Tell the police!' a few in the group called out.

'They have already been involved and if we call them again we may not be able to use the car. They may suspect something else and it may be taken away. What we do know is there were three tracking devices on the car and one on the Land-Rover towing the car.'

There was a definite intake of breath from many in the audience. M Dupont chirped up again. 'Yes, and it was Alain and his friend who found them in *my* garage.'

'OK, Henri, we must get on,' the Mayor said, hinting that he wanted no further interruptions.

Alain continued. 'Robert believes he saw the crooks on the *autoroute*. Christophe. who found the bugs, believes they probably know where the car is. To fool them we have hidden the car and transferred the bugs somewhere else.'

'Not in Henri's garage, I hope!' Pierre Lescaut, the baker, interrupted. Everyone laughed at the thought.

'Oh no, no, no!' Dupont shouted over the laughter. 'It's at the house of the *ancien maire* . . .' Again there were roars of laughter. 'Sorry, Alain, it's the excitement. I haven't had so much since my wife found me with Eloise and chased me round the village naked . . .'

'Come on! Come on!' the mayor shouted, bringing everything back to order. 'We must get on. Time is of the essence. Alain,' he said, inviting him to continue.

'Well, now the world knows where the car is, but hopefully the crooks don't. It's agreed then: no police at this stage?'

'It wouldn't make any difference if they were! It's after six o'clock and they're probably having a drink with the *ancien maire*.' There were once again roars of laughter.

Alain began waving his arms at the meeting with the intention of calming them down, so that he could continue. 'Look! Look!' he shouted, the laughter subsiding. 'There's one more thing I must tell you before you decide.' He stopped and waited until there was absolute quiet in the room before he continued.

'They've tried to take the car several times in the past and we know they are likely to be armed.'

'I can stop them!' said a voice from the back of the room.

'What is it, Étienne?' the mayor asked kindly. Étienne was in his mid-twenties and was the town hall's concierge. He was a lovely lad and would help anyone, but he was a bit slow.

'Well, you know the road stingers the gendarmes left after M Chirac's visit. Well, I put them in the storage room.'

'Go on!' said the mayor, a little taken aback by the thought that the village had effectively nicked a couple of stingers from the gendarmerie.

'Well, I thought,' Étienne continued, 'if we put one on the road at the top of the village, we could stop anyone coming in.' The laughter started again.

The major interrupted sternly. 'I don't think that would appropriate, Étienne,' but then added a little more kindly, 'But thank you for the idea.'

Alain took the floor again. 'Can I take it we are all agreed, no police at this stage?' There was a mumble of assent in the room.

'The next thing we have to decide is how we are going to stop them stealing the car. We must assume that they will visit the garage.'

'I'll be ready for them!' shouted Dupont.

'No guns! We cannot use firearms. We don't want to get into any trouble . . .'

'We could use Brigitte. She'd stop anyone with her cleavage!' some wag shouted to more laughter.

'M le Maire!' Jacques Millou shouted to attract attention. Jacques had been the local policeman until he had retired more than twenty years before. He had been in the Resistance during the war and knew all about tactics without weapons. He was now ninety years of age, very unsteady on his feet and very short of breath.

'Yes, Jacques?' the mayor said, inviting him to speak.

'M le Maire, I once had a woman . . .' he began with a shaky voice.

'I don't think you can claim just once, Jacques!' the butcher shouted over the eruption of laughter, causing even more.

Jacques continued. 'Listen to me! I had this woman working

for me in the Resistance. She and I had been given the job of stopping a German column which travelled every night to avoid detection. It was delivering ammunition to the front.' He paused for breath. This time there was no noise, only respectful silence Jacques was a local hero and knew what he was talking about.

'You often see films showing natives making traps by digging deep holes and covering the top with soft material. Well, we did just that and fooled the Germans. The front vehicle of an armoured column fell into a deepish hole; it became totally stuck and enabled us to attack the vehicles at will. It held up the supply column for twenty-four hours and saved many lives at the front ... We can do the same again. We can put one of the bugs in Frédéric's barn and one at the beginning of the track. They will think it has fallen off and make their way to the barn ...'

'He's still the same old Jacques,' One of the group commented quietly as he continued.

'We could get Frédéric to dig out the hole, cover it with tarpaulin, stretched tightly and ...'

He was stopped in mid-sentence by the *ancien maire*, Étienne Simplon. 'Sorry, Jacques. M le Maire, if we are going to talk tactics, I think we should form a committee and go over to my place. We're not going to get very far with a group this size, are we?'

The mayor quickly agreed and after ten minutes of haggling and deciding who would be useful, the numbers were brought down to twelve.

We all quickly made our way across the road to the Étienne Simplon's cellar, which was notorious as a local drinking den.

The meeting was convened by opening several bottles of Beaujolais and by electing a chairman, which turned out to be Alain.

'Jacques, I want you to continue where you left off,' Alain announced.

The old Resistance leader took the floor, beginning by recalling the events of many years before. 'Once the tarpaulin had been stretched across the track and pulled tight over the area, we then covered it with the earth, ensuring of course that none of the cover was visible. We then ran a wheel lightly over it ensuring the print of the wheel could be seen and then similarly over the other side to ensure two tracks were visible.

'In the dark it gave the impression that a vehicle had been over it. The important thing to remember is that the tracks have to continue from the trap and of course in front of it. If it's windy, it's impossible; the earth will blow off.'

'It could work!' Alan commented. 'Frédéric, would you take as many men as you need to dig the hole out and prepare something they will never forget?'

'*Volontiers*, but one thing, Alain.' Frédéric responded. 'Even if they do fall into the trap, they'll still want to see inside the barn and try and take the car.'

'You're right,' Étienne Simplon interrupted. 'Perhaps we should set some other trap inside.'

'I'll organise that,' Lescaut offered. 'I know just the people to help. Leave it to me and Frédéric.'

'OK.' Alain replied. 'But remember: no firearms,' he shouted, as they left with three others.

It was now half past nine and I felt time was running out. Another bottle of Beaujolais had just been cracked open. Alain leaned over, seeing the worried look on my face, and whispered. 'Don't worry, my friend, all will be in order. We just need a little more of this and the best ideas will come!'

The barn was a fairly large old ramshackled building with large double doors, one of which did not appear to have been opened since the Second World War. As you entered, apart from trying to avoid the 'antiques' and the 'useful' materials, you could see a mezzanine gallery on three sides, also full of 'junk'. The building was already a death trap, even without the 'additions' added by Alain and his crew.

I had collected Philip and Henry from Alain's house, leaving the reluctant ladies to stay with Marie. Lescaut had telephoned Beraud, who had brought the bugs to the barn. One was placed at the junction of the drive to the barn and the main road and the other one inside the barn, where Alain's group had already set up a large trailer covered with plywood sheet and tarpaulin; from a quick glance in the dark, we hoped, you could be fooled into believing there was a car hidden inside. Frédéric left with the JCB to assist in the movement of the stingers; Étienne's idea had been found to be useful after all, as a backup if all else failed.

Philip, Henry, Lescaut and I hid behind a stone wall opposite the drive, just about in earshot of the entrance, while Alain and his team hid inside the barn. It can be very cold in the Beaujolais region at night and we were well and truly wrapped up. Lescaut had brought two bottles of delicious home-made fortified wines, which quickly gave a warm glow. You have to hand it to the French – they go to war in style.

From where we were we could see the lights of Charnay on the hillside and the route any vehicle would take should it come our way. One by one the lights went out in the houses until all that was left were the street lights. There was now an eerie feeling in the air. A chilly wind had sprung up giving an occasional icy blast. Clouds gathered and from time to time passed over the moon, leaving us in total darkness.

Alain and his group were becoming worse for wear as the alcohol began to take over. They began singing what sounded like French rugby songs and then several verses of the Marseillaise, followed by roars of laughter.

We had been in position for about an hour and a half, when Lescaut stood up to stretch his legs and walk round a little.

'I think they're coming!' he shouted in French.

We all stood up to see two pairs of headlights, slowly making their way down the hill. It was difficult at this stage to ascertain what sort of vehicle they were in, but one thing was certain we had to stop the raucous noise emanating from the barn.

'For God's sake, they're bloody pissed!' I said angrily. 'Is there anything we can do to shut them up?' I said, turning to Lescaut.

'Oui,' he replied 'I will telephone Alain and tell them they are coming,' he continued in broken English and proceeded to telephone Alain on his mobile.

'They're on the way. You must keep quiet,' I heard Lescaut pleading. 'They will hear you.'

But his pleas seemed to fall on deaf ears. He ended the call despondently.

'They're all drunk!' Lescaut said looking at me with some sadness. 'They are not taking things seriously.'

'What can we do?' I asked. 'They will be here in a minute.'

'Nothing; we can just ope for the best.'

I rang Alain myself and pleaded with him to keep quiet and to leave the phone open so that I could tell them what was happening. Fortunately Alain wasn't pissed, just enjoying himself, and he promised to shut his companions up. Sure enough things went quiet.

The two pairs of headlights were now about four hundred yards away. Philip was psyching himself up, punching his fist into his hand. We ducked down behind the wall, in case we were picked out by the headlights. I was terrified and was beginning to sweat. Lescaut, too, was beginning to realize things were getting serious.

'There are two cars; three passengers in the front one,' I whispered to Alain.

The cars were crawling along and were now only fifty yards away. We were now all tingling with excitement.

'No one move, until I give the word,' I whispered.

They had arrived. One car drove slightly past the entrance, coming toward us and then stopped; the other stopped across the entrance. All the occupants got out. We were right; there were three in the front car, but four in the back one. We were totally outnumbered. The boss got out of the front car; I presume he was the boss because he was controlling the radio equipment searching for the bug and all the others seemed to follow his lead. It was only seconds before they found the first bug, which had been placed at the entrance.

'I've found one,' he said quietly to the others in English. 'It must have fallen off.'

My heart was now pumping so loud I began to wonder if they could hear it. It was impossible to see who we were dealing with in the dark. It sounded as if whoever was in charge had decided the car was in the barn and began directing operations.

'You two!' the boss commanded. 'You go round the edge of the field that way and then across to that building, see if the car is in there.'

'Why can't I go down the road?' one of them asked.

'Shut the fuck up! Just do as I say. They might see you walking down the road,' he said angrily. Then, pointing to the other two from the front car, he added, 'You two go that way and do the same.'

Suddenly I noticed a further set of lights coming down the hillside toward us and silently pointed it out to the others. Our confidence began to evaporate. Were there another four on the way? Should we act now, whilst the odds were almost even? Our deliberations were halted by a loud crashing noise followed by howls of laughter and breaking glass.

The first two men had reached the barn; one had decided to go in, leaving the other outside to keep watch. Alain's brother-in-law, Fernand, had, we learnt later, decided to throw a bottle – an empty one of course – at the intruder. The balcony on which he was standing gave way and he fell with the debris to the floor. This was too much for the inebriated gang and they could not contain their laughter any more.

Alain began throwing the bottles at the intruder, followed by the others shouting and yelling and throwing anything they could get their hands on at the poor unfortunate, who, in backing away, fell against the large wooden door causing it to fall outwards and on top of his companion standing outside.

Fernand, seemingly unperturbed by his fall, stood up and charged after the intruder in full voice. The hapless villain under the door was just beginning to lift it away from him when he stopped, first by the weight of his escaping comrade, then by Fernand and finally by Alain and the remaining members of his group, all charging over the fallen door, also in full voice.

In the comparative darkness, four large yelling Frenchmen charging out of the barn must have been an awesome sight. The other two turned tail and ran, the first of them springing the trap in the road and falling into the hole with some force.

I was just about to signal for us to join the fray when the other pair of headlights arrived on the scene. I could not believe my eyes: it was Frédéric and his JCB. He was roaring at the car in the entrance, giving the men no chance to move it. The JCB was at full power, the bucket went down and then there was an almighty crash as it went into the offside corner of the car, lifting it into the air. Frédéric pushed the car into the exposed trap, just missing the man who had fallen in who scrambled out just in time.

The boss drew out a pistol and began firing at Frédéric and was soon joined by one of the others. Despite Alain's moratorium on using firearms, Frédéric responded with a hail of bullets from his pump-action shotgun. Suddenly it was like the Wild West.

The four of us still in hiding seized the opportunity to jump over the wall and make for the six men, who were now trying to get into the remaining car. Philip flung a handy stone through the windscreen and made a grab at the driver, but to no avail; he had already started the engine and was pulling away, as the men were still piling in. The nearside rear door was left wide open as the sixth man was being pulled in by his associates; unfortunately his legs were still hanging out as the door hit the wall, causing it to crash on to the man's shins. We all heard his scream. His companions managed to pull him in and made their escape.

We were all beginning to congratulate ourselves on a wonderful achievement when Lescaut suddenly remembered there were seven men and only six had got away in the car. For a moment we were all a little panicky, but then Henry spotted the missing villain under the door. He was so still I thought he was dead.

'He must have got squashed; it serves him right,' Lescaut commented.

We lifted the door off the hapless seventh man and for a few moments just stared. There were no visible signs of injury but he was clearly concussed. Alain phoned for an ambulance as well as for the police, while we covered him up and gently carried him into the barn out of the wind.

Chapter 17

It was the third Wednesday in November. The grapes had been picked, the wine made and we were all waiting for the start of the race the following day. Charnay was decked with bunting, and the the mayor, in full regalia with his red-white-and-blue sash, was rushing round to make sure every last detail was correct. In the town square The Hôtel de Ville looked absolutely magnificent in the early morning sunshine, while on one of its corners a wineshop was already open and doing a roaring trade.

On the lower slopes they had prepared temporary parking for the competitors as well as a space for manufacturers' and sponsors' tents, together with cafés, restaurants and play areas for children.

The police had believed our story about the attempted theft of the car and the secret of the hidden drugs had remained just that. The resultant arrests of the six remaining criminals also produced another desirable effect in the form of the large number of local municipal police that swarmed the village. There was no doubt they were not going to allow any trouble to spoil this grand occasion. What was even more satisfying was that no one, not even the owners, was allowed to touch the cars after ten o'clock

We had all been given our numbers for the race and mine was number one. In total, there were one hundred and twenty-three cars entered, with a possibility of eleven more on the day. Il PY also had *la place d'honneur* at the front of the Hôtel de Ville, ready to set off in the front of the parade. Much to my chagrin, some of the local children began to cover it in bunting and there was nothing I could do, except grin and bear it; but at least it was tasteful, befitting an old lady of her age and standing.

At 2 p.m. on the dot a cannon was fired and the mayor announced the start of the procession. I started II PY and, with the three men in the front and the four ladies in the back, I pulled slowly out from the parking bay to fall in line with a military brass band which was to lead the procession. It seemed as if the whole of the Beaujolais region had turned out to see us. The circular route took an hour to complete and back at the Hôtel de Ville each car was ceremoniously presented with two cases of Beaujolais Nouveau.

I had to deliver six bottles each to Le Grand Colbert and Le Crillon restaurants in Paris, and then six more each to the Robert Carrier and Belfrey restaurants in London.

That evening the village put on a splendid buffet at the Hôtel de Ville for all the competitors and dignitaries. To my surprise and pleasure, Blessington-Smith and his wife were among the guests. We greeted each other like old friends.

'What time are you off?' he asked, referring to the following day's race.

'I think I'm fifty-third away so about ten, I suppose. And you?' I asked.

'Fifty-ninth.'

'Well, we'll probably see each other en route. Best of luck anyway.' I couldn't make up my mind about Blessington-Smith; he was never far away and certainly wanted the car, but I could not tell if there was more behind his intense interest in II PY.

It was approaching midnight and, like New Year's Eve, we had a countdown and at one minute past twelve Beaujolais Nouveau legally went on sale. Of course, we had to taste just a few drops of the delicious young wine.

*

The following day the weather was glorious. It was ten o'clock and Francesca and I were now waiting in the line for my time of departure. The rest of the family, as the rules dictated, would be following with the Land-Rover and trailer, once all the competing cars had departed. We were now on the line with the seconds ticking away. Down went the flag and we were away.

'Bonne chance!' the starter yelled.

'Good luck, Mum and Dad,' we heard over the roar of the crowd, as Francesca waved madly to everyone.

We were now heading north, through the villages of Beaujolais with their winding, narrow streets and sharp hairpin corners. The first was Arcy, then Lachassagne, where saw our first competitor in front of us, giving me the spur to put my foot down a little. Soon we had passed Pommiers, then Limas with its beautiful houses and square, then into Villefranche and the first inevitable traffic jam, before joining the N6 to Macon.

Francesca was almost breathless with excitement. 'There's another of them,' she cried. It was Willy Thornbeck's Phantom, which already looked as though it was in trouble. I signalled to Willy as we passed, but he indicated he was all right.

I had said earlier that we had entered the race and were driving just for fun, but you get a strange feeling when you see a car in front of you. Your competitive spirit takes over and you just want to overtake it as quickly as you can. We were certainly kept on our toes.

On the N6 Francesca phoned Philip to see where he was and amazingly he was ahead of us. Alain had suggested he miss out the Beaujolais hills and villages and take the *autoroute*. Whilst the N6 gave us plenty of opportunity to put our foot down and make good time, it also put us in a very vulnerable position, in view of the distances between towns and villages. I had passed through Macon and Cluny, heading towards Beaune when I had noticed I was being followed by a motorcyclist. I also felt there was a white Mercedes involved, as it kept popping up at odd times. This went on for several miles until in the distance I noticed what looked like a furniture removal van broken down at the side of the road. Its tailgate was down and two men appeared to be inspecting the back wheel. Ironically I had suspected that something was going to happen sooner or later, as we had been on our guard, but I didn't think it would happen on a busy road like the N6.

We were now approaching the removal van somewhat quickly, driving on the inside lane. Suddenly the white Mercedes, which had been behind for several hundred yards, came alongside and slowed to my speed, making it impossible for us to pull out and avoid the van. I was forced to brake sharply and come to a stop just three or four metres from the back of the open van.

Within split seconds the two men had pulled a chain out from the back of the van and hooked it on the metal bar which held the front bumper on to the Rolls and immediately began to winch the Rolls toward the tailgate. I tried desperately to stop this happening by actually standing on the brake pedal, but to no avail. The Rolls continued to move towards the van, albeit very slowly. We could actually hear the winch straining under the pressure, particularly when I managed to put the handbrake on as well.

'Lock your door!' Francesca was the only calm one at this stage, immediately phoning Henry to tell them what was happening and to get him to contact the police. 'Get help, they're trying to kidnap us!' she shouted down the phone.

Our only chance was to stay in the car and try to prevent it moving. The winch was struggling. You could hear the low groan up and down, up and down, as it fought the resistance of the car. It was obvious they were having difficulties.

The one on the winch shouted in English: 'Don't jus' sit there gawpin'. Get in the Merc an' push!'

The driver of the Mercedes quickly reversed to the rear of the Rolls and did as he was told. The Rolls had now mounted the tailgate but its weight was making the tailgate bend. It would be virtually impossible to load the car without a great deal of support from a vehicle pushing. What was more, the bumper of the Mercedes began to buckle and its wheels started to spin uncontrollably. The winch groaned to a stop, and smoke poured out of the back of the van; it was finished,

'Get the bastard off the brake!' the winch man shouted.

The motorcyclist ran into the van, grabbed the wheel brace and ran to my door, smashing the window into pieces. I was covered in glass and began bleeding profusely from the splinters, but had the sense to grab the lad's arm as he put it inside to try and open the door. I bent it backwards with all my weight behind it, supported by Francesca, who had climbed over to assist me. She too attacked the young man, grabbing at his ear.

The Mercedes backed off a little and then banged back into the rear of the Rolls, tossing Francesca and me against the front windscreen. Francesca, however, didn't let go of the lad's ear. There was a terrifying scream as it was almost severed from the lad's head. She let go of the ear, only to attack the head, pushing it down on to the broken glass. The screams of the lad became unbearable as the glass began to cut deeply into his throat. Francesca let go and the lad fell to the floor, twitching and writhing in agony, like a worm with its head cut off. He would die unless he got help.

I gabbed the wheel brace, opened my door and went for the nearest of the men. I had no fear or even thought; I just went like a madman at him. He turned and ran, but not before I caught his back with a terrific blow from the brace. I then turned on the Mercedes and flung the brace into the windscreen, almost hitting the driver as he ducked to avoid it.

I was now temporarily disarmed, but with an equally determined wife running to my assistance, the Mercedes reversed quickly out and almost simultaneously the two men jumped into the back and left at full steam.

We stopped the first vehicles that came in either direction and asked them to phone the police and for an ambulance. Francesca became extremely worked up with the thought that he might die, but within minutes a police car arrived and a couple of gendarmes began giving him first aid, managing to stem the flow of blood. They were also administering to me but, despite the blood all over me, my wounds were superficial. The ambulance arrived and without much delay the young man was whisked away under escort to the hospital at Chalon.

Yet again I had to be questioned by the gendarmerie because someone had attempted to steal the car. The gendarmes, however, were very kind and sympathetic and amazingly knew all about the exploits of the car.

'Don't worry, Mr Conway. We have the young man in the hospital; he will, I am sure, tell us who the others were,' the officer in charge advised me in perfect English. 'Is the car fit to continue the race?' he asked.

'Yes, I'm sure it is, but I'm not!' I replied sadly. 'At least not at the moment.'

In the meantime, the Land-Rover had arrived, and once the questioning was over we were allowed to see the family. But now Francesca, who had been a tower of strength, suddenly broke down as the shock of what had happened hit her. She had had enough. I told the family about my plan to pull out of the race. Henry, of course, had other ideas.

'I'll take it! We can't drop out now. The car's all right; it's only the driver's window broken. We can't be that far behind. I counted eleven competitors in the queue and there must be several further back. Go on, Dad, let me take it.'

'Don't be so bloody daft!' Philip interrupted angrily. 'They've tried that many times, do you think they will ever give up? It's too bloody dangerous!'

Henry looked at me, his eyes begging me to agree.

'If the police say you can take the car, you can take it,' I eventually replied. Philip looked furious. 'It's only going to Paris, Philip, and the roads are very busy, not like here. The nearer he gets to Paris the safer it will be. And Victoria, if she agrees, can go with him to act as translator.'

'Yeah, I'd love to go,' Victoria rejoined. 'We've come this far; we might as well try,' she added with more than a hint of excitement in her voice.

The police allowed II PY to continue and gave instructions on how they should be contacted. With their blessing, and without another second's hesitation, Henry and Victoria set off with our best wishes and Philip's disgruntled wave.

Chapter 18

Despite Philips doubts, Henry did a fantastic job, crossing the finishing line in the Bois de Boulogne in twenty-eighth position. The press was there in force, of course, and naturally we all had our stories to tell. None of us, though, spoke about the episode at the port of St Tropez. 'It's a family secret,' Emily said delightedly.

It was almost nine o'clock before we were able to book in at the Hotel Mercure. We were extremely tired and very hungry and increasingly made irritable by the small number of journalists who had persisted in following us, hoping no doubt for that 'exclusive' story. We were too late for the evening meal and I, rather unfairly I admit, began giving the young receptionist a hard time. I was interrupted by a very attractive, middle-aged French lady called Françoise Petalin, who introduced herself as a reporter from *Le Monde*.

'Allow me to assist you,' she said in perfect English and then proceeded to speak to the receptionist, asking for the night manager, who duly arrived. She introduced herself to him and went discreetly into his office. Two or three minutes later, they were both delighted to tell us the chef was prepared to stay on and we were welcome to go into the restaurant. She asked if we would care to have a meal with her and that *La Monde* would foot the bill. I, of course, accepted.

Françoise, as she insisted we call her, had played her cards well. She had got us to ourselves for as long as it took to eat what turned out to be an excellent meal.

That night, in the privacy of our hotel room, Francesca and I had a long chat about the car and we decided there and then that the car had to go the moment we got back to England. It was not so much that we were afraid; we were purely and simply fed up with all the trouble. What we both wanted was peace and quiet.

There being no moment like the present, I phoned Morales. He seemed a little surprised by my call, as if he'd been caught on the hop.

'What can I do for you?' he asked.

'I'm afraid, Mr Morales, the Rolls-Royce has been damaged.'

I could hear his slight intake of breath. There was a long pause, before I asked, 'Are you still there?'

'Yes!' he said abruptly. 'Continue.' He seemed to sense his attitude was not going down very well and added. 'I'm sorry; it's just a shock to hear that. What happened?'

I explained briefly our adventures in France. 'I thought I had better tell you what's happened. I know you wanted the car and I promised you first refusal. But I will understand if you change your mind. I have had a very good offer from a gentleman in Paris for the car as it is,' I added, trying to stop myself from laughing as Francesca repeatedly whispered across the room, 'Liar, liar!'

Morales sounded concerned and confused. 'What sort of damage has been caused?'

'It's superficial: the front bumper is bent, the rear luggage box is dented and the driver's window is smashed. I don't think there's been any damage to the paintwork, but in fairness I haven't had the chance to look at it carefully.'

I waited for Morales to comment and for the first time his answer showed he might have had something to do with it.

'It won't happen again.'

'What won't happen again?'

Morales must have had plenty of practice of thinking on his feet as he came back at me quickly. 'I meant that I *hope* it won't happen again. My client wouldn't want the car damaged further.'

'You still want the car then?' I asked

'Yes!'

'I will phone you the moment we get back to Haworth and make the arrangements, assuming, that is, nothing else happens.'

Morales rang off, and I immediately telephoned David. For the first time I let him know of my suspicions about something being hidden in the car.

'I knew it! I knew it!' David almost shouted down the phone.

'What's the programme from now?' he asked.

I quickly described the next part of the journey. 'I'm surprised the car doesn't know its own way out of Paris; it's the same journey you described, just before John Maitland broke down . . .'

'I remember it well!' David replied, 'It will all be in the book.' He was, he'd already told me, halfway through writing an exposé of the whole Maitland affair.

'I want a signed copy when it's finished!' I said as a parting joke.

The following morning we swiftly made our deliveries of Beaujolais Nouveau to Le Grand Colbert and Crillon restaurants, then hurried back to the Bois de Boulogne for registration and the start of the second phase, Paris to Calais via the Arc de Triomphe and the Champs-Élysées. I was once again back at the wheel.

From the original number of starters, only fifteen had retired, one of those a Silver Spirit less than fifteen years old. It didn't break down, 'it failed to proceed', as it's known in Rolls-Royce parlance. Eventually we were away, this time twenty-eighth off the starting line. However, this was not important; it was the aggregate of the three journeys that mattered.

On the outskirts of Paris, the weather took a turn for the worse and I handed over the driving to Henry. Philip and the rest of the family – except for Francesca, of course – were travelling in the Land-Rover; we had agreed to meet them later, outside Amiens cathedral, and go for something to eat. It started to chuck it down. The plastic we had put over the window began letting in the rain, not only soaking Henry but the seats as well. All the same it proved a very easy journey, II PY simply whispering along at a steady sixty to seventy miles per hour, well within her capacity. Even before Amiens we had passed two of the other competitors and had several others in our sights.

In Amiens Philip took over the helm, much to Henry's chagrin. I could tell by the way Philip was driving and the fixed smile on his face that I had made his day. He was thrilled, particularly when on arriving in the station car park in Calais – the finishing point of the second stage – he realized we had made up fifteen places and were now lying in fifteenth place, less than one hour behind the leader.

As in Paris we were inundated with reporters. To my utter astonishment Clive White was amongst them and was trying to attract my attention.

'Robert!' he shouted. 'We need to talk urgently. Something's happened.'

I pushed my way through the bustling reporters. 'What the hell has happened to bring you over here?'

'I was coming anyway . . .' He paused for a moment. 'You haven't heard, have you?'

'Heard what, for God's sake?'

'One of your attackers has been murdered . . . a young man in his twenties . . . He was in hospital . . .'

We had been joined by Francesca, who almost wailed with horror.

'It was a particularly nasty murder apparently. The killer entered the hospital, posing as a consultant, he found out where the man was and went straight to his room. He dismissed the police officer on duty and then cut the man's throat. The murderer then washed his knife in the sink near the bed and walked out, making a point of thanking the officer, who was by then returning.'

'Did they get a description?' I asked.

'Yes, a tall thin man with dark hair, although the French police have no match in their records.'

Both Francesca and I were reeling – Francesca because she couldn't stop thinking about the young man she'd nearly killed and who had now been murdered. Me, because I remembered Morales's rather odd words about it not happening again. I put Clive fully in the picture and we all dolefully walked across to the Metropol Hotel to check in and relax. There was nothing more to do but eat and sleep until the start of the third and final stage of the race the next day.

We set the alarm for six o'clock and, I was pleased to say, a good night's sleep was had by all. The lads skipped breakfast and caught the early boat. The rest of the family, the three ladies and Emily, came with me. There were now only eighty-six cars left in the race and, to our surprise, on registration for the final stage, we found that, whilst not in the overall lead, we were ahead in the pre-war Phantom class. All the same, we still wanted the big one.

It was ten o'clock local time when we drove off the ferry in Dover. The road was clear enabling me to go flat out. It almost seemed that the Rolls had become used to travelling at speed and it wasn't long before we passed several of the our competitors who had left before us.

As we came closer to London, the traffic began to build up. It was at this point that we put our 'special' plan into action. Philip had very early on worked out that London's traffic would snarl everyone up and that the person who dealt with it best would have an advantage. With this in mind, he'd contacted one of his friends in the Metropolitan Police, who'd promised to do 'something'. What that 'something' was Philip wouldn't tell me. Perhaps he didn't know either, but at the time it seemed like a miracle.

We had been sitting in traffic for a few minutes, with me tapping the wheel in annoyance, when we heard a police siren. Nearer and nearer it sounded until it stopped right beside us.

'Follow me, sir!' the officer on the passenger side said. 'Come on, we'll get you there!'

And without more ado we followed the police car as it sped with blue light flashing and sirens blazing, though every traffic light, every roundabout and every obstruction.

I couldn't believe it; it was like a dream come true. And what a joy to see the faces of our fellow competitors as we passed them! I can still see the face of an American who was in one of the Derby Bentleys, open-mouthed and waving his hand out of his window in protest as I glanced back.

The first signs to Tower Bridge appeared.

Emily started to shout in the excitement: 'Come on, Grandad!' which caused us all to enter into the spirit of the occasion. The weather was cold and cloudy, but this didn't stop Victoria from opening the Sedanca roof and standing on the front seats, head and shoulders out of the car, cheering and waving. I could sense something fantastic was about to happen. I was tingling from head to toe with excitement; gripping the steering wheel as though my life depended on it.

One and a half miles to go . . . one mile to go and the first of the TV cameras appeared, capturing the police car as it escorted us towards the finishing line. Small groups of people gathered at the roadside.

Four hundred yards to go and we could see Tower Bridge. The police car slowed down and pulled over, allowing me to pass and sounding its horn in a victory salute as we glided past and, moments later, crossed the line. The first to do so, but had we won? It would all depend on the timing achieved by the current leader, who needed to cross the finishing line within forty-one minutes to beat us.

It was an agonizing wait. I was now pacing up and down like some caged animal, repeatedly asking Francesca what the time was.

'I told you one minute ago that there was ten minutes left. So now there's nine,' she said sarcastically.

Three minutes to go and still no sign of our rival. By now the five of us were all standing in a line, fingers crossed, simply staring along the road, willing him not to arrive.

Two minutes . . . one minute . . . thirty seconds . . . ten, nine, eight, seven, six, five, four, three, two, one . . . we had won!

We were jumping and whooping for joy. It was a wonderful achievement!

We were the first of the competitors to arrive at Battersea Park for the celebrations. It was as though we had returned to France. There was an open air market, dozens of French wine stalls with Beaujolais as the main attraction. There were also the usual sponsors' tents and the associated memorabilia on sale to the thousands of visitors who were flocking round the park.

We were unofficially told we had won but there had been several objections to the result because we had had police assistance. We were called to the Marshall's tent to explain our side of the situation, and finally the result was confirmed. The car was then put on the winner's stand in the centre of the presentation tent, cordoned off to prevent sticky fingers from having a piece of her. She looked absolutely filthy but still good.

The Lord Mayor of London made the appropriate presentations to the winners accompanied by the French Ambassador. II PY picked up the overall Winner's Cup and the fittest of the pre-war Phantoms. They made the usual promises of further mutual cooperation, but the real winners, I was pleased to see, were the vignerons of Beaujolais, who took many orders.

The American was surprisingly sporting. He came second only

four minutes behind us and promised to beat us next year. I didn't like to tell him we were going to sell the car.

II PY had been a wonderful car not only for its beauty but also for its engineering. It was seventy years old and it had been hammered along the French roads almost flat out for mile after mile and had never missed a beat. It was fitting that Henry and Philip arrived in time for the presentation so I asked them to collect the prize on behalf of the family as without them we would not be in the position we were in.

We were all in a state of exuberance when we were brought down to earth with a bump. Francesca and I were separated from the others simply because we had different things to see. It was on one of our walks around the market stalls that we were stopped by a youngish man in his mid to late thirties.

'Congratulations, Mr and Mrs Conway, on your excellent but unexpected win,' he said, smiling at us.

'Thank you,' I replied, 'but we were determined to do well and I knew we had a chance,' I said with a big satisfied smile on my face.

'Now I must insist,' he continued, 'I want you to look after my car and not get into any more scrapes. Remember – drive carefully.' The last few words spoken in the most supercilious manner you could imagine.

For a second or two we were both stunned, but then in unison we yelled at the top of our voices, 'Get the police, quick! Help! Police!'

For a moment he too was stunned at our response, but composed himself quickly and ran. He was soon lost in the crowd, but we both had a good description of the man and the moment we saw the police, his details were circulated to all areas of the park.

When we were reunited with the rest of the family, Philip and Henry insisted that we were not left alone for the rest of the evening.

The exhibition was to remain open until five o'clock on

Sunday afternoon and the winning car, II PY, was to remain on the stand until that time. As with every event of this nature, we were assured that the car would be under a security blanket that no one could breach.

Philip and Henry made a couple of phone calls to organize picking up the trailer, and set off to collect it. Francesca and I had the evening to ourselves, which was quite pleasant as we both knew London well, having met and married there many years before.

Sunday was a huge anti-climax, apart from the newspapers with their wonderful headlines and photographs, 'Police ensure prize comes to England', 'II PY conquers all the odds'. There were dozens, all of which were very flattering, but apart from these, we had to spend the entire day at the exhibition, as the winning car was required on the stand until the end.

We were dined by the sponsors and had a series of photographs taken with them on the stand, but that was that. Philip and Henry arrived with the trailer and took their turn answering visitors' questions about the car and the race.

We were allowed to remove the car at half past three, which quite frankly could not come soon enough. We thanked everyone for their efforts to make it a wonderful inaugural race and I genuinely hoped it would be the first of many. We then loaded II PY on to the trailer and immediately set off for home. The conversation was naturally about the trip to France, the race and the troubles; but already rose tinted glasses obscured the nasty side of the adventure.

It was here that we informed the family that we had definitely decided to sell the car, as we could not stand all the troubles and worries. We were also too old to take on whoever was behind the trouble. All but Henry voted for the sale and I must say I did with a very heavy heart; after all, we had won the best car in the show at Kelmarsh, several other smaller shows and now the inaugural Beaujolais race to Paris and London. It was a wonderful record and one which I didn't want to forget. In my heart I did not want to part with the car that gave me such pleasure, but all the troubles, and now the latest threat, really tipped the balance in favour of the sale and it was left at that.

We left London and made our way to the M1. Henry was at the wheel as I had had enough driving to last me a lifetime. I don't know whether we were still suffering with paranoia, but we were all convinced we were still being watched or followed. There had been two cars swapping places behind us and yet they were both still there. Henry had fluctuated his speed and so had they.

I telephoned the police to advise them what was happening. Here, when you are in trouble, it really can depend on who you speak to, whether you get any help or not. Today was a case of no help at all, from an officer who treated me with contempt and thought we had nothing to fear.

'Now do you see why we want to get rid of the car? It's a bloody nightmare to your mum and me,' I said angrily. 'We are sick to death of all this trouble.'

We decided to pull into Leicester Forest East to have a cup of tea and assess our position, and possibly to call the police from there and maybe get a better response.

Henry signalled he was turning off, giving plenty of notice to all those behind and slowing down well before the turn. I couldn't believe my eyes. The man who had spoken to us at Battersea Park was in the blue Vauxhall. I shouted, 'Philip! He's there!' The blue Vauxhall had come level with us on the offside and was also signalling to turn in. He saw me looking and grinned, teeth clenched, as if to try and intimidate me.

'Who?' Philip demanded.

'The man from Battersea, I told you about him. He's at the side of us. He's coming in with us.'

We all turned to see the Vauxhall quickly pull in front of the Discovery and make its way to the parking places, with us following some thirty yards behind. The other car we believed had been following us also pulled into the services and parked up. We remained in the Discovery for a few minutes waiting to see what reaction we would get, but it was too much for Philip. He got out of the car and walked quickly over to the Vauxhall and made grab for the door. It was locked.

'Roll yer fucking window down before I smash it open,' he yelled at the top of his voice, causing a few passers by to stop and listen. The driver did not appear to want a confrontation at this point and began to pull away. This was too much for Philip, who let fly with a massive punch at the window, smashing it to pieces and cutting his hand badly in the process. The driver got out of the car, to be joined by several bystanders, who came in support, not knowing the full facts.

'I saw him do it,' one shouted in support.

'He's a fucking lunatic,' another shouted. 'I've phoned the police, they'll be here in a minute.'

'Good job,' Philip replied. 'They'll be interested in this one.'

The driver was not going to be around when the police arrived and got back in his car to drive away, shouting at Philip as he did so, 'I'll fuckin' 'ave you for this, you bastard.'

Philip let fly with a kick at the driver's door, putting a large dent in the side. 'This is just a little memento, to remind you of me when you decide to return,' he yelled at the departing driver.

Henry had run across to support Philip, just as the police arrived to investigate the problem. They had only taken a couple of minutes as they were already parked at the services.

The man who had phoned them gave his story: 'I saw that young man deliberately punch a hole in the window of a blue Vauxhall car; the driver got out and the strange thing was, the moment I mentioned I had called the police, he upped and left and that young man kicked at his car. That's all I can tell you.'

'Thank you, sir,' the officer replied. 'Now, young man; what's all this about then?' he said, turning to Philip.

I had joined them by this time, mainly to give Philip support but also to ensure the police were fully aware of what had been going on. I pointed out the white Honda to the police, but the moment the driver saw us looking, he drove steadily out of the service area.

The officer immediately phoned his control and gave them the registration of the car and its description. 'We'll get him,' he said somewhat proudly. 'He won't get far on this motorway.'

With the formalities over we took the opportunity of having a break and refreshments, although once again, with all the stress and the trouble, neither Francesca nor I felt like anything. It now wasn't a case of 'If' – it was a case of how quickly we could get rid of the car.

'Come on, everyone. Let's get on home,' I said, trying to put a brave face on it. It didn't work; we left the cafeteria like dejected souls on the way to a funeral. The car was still there, a police car next to it.

'I thought we would keep our eye on it until you came back,' the officer said.

We couldn't believe it; it restored our faith in the police and human nature and in fact cheered us up a little. At least we began talking to each other.

We thanked the officers and made our way out of the services and back on to the M1 and there was no sign of our shadows. The police action must have scared them off. However, we had been driving no more than half an hour when Henry noticed a couple of young men leaning over the bridge we were approaching. He thought nothing of it, as many people watch motorway traffic from the bridges. We were almost there when he yelled to all of us, 'Get down quick!'

Before we had had the chance to duck down, there was an enormous bang on the roof of the Discovery and another bang on II PY behind. Henry quickly pulled onto the hard shoulder just past the bridge and Philip jumped out of the car and ran up the bank after the perpetrators. We were all once again in shock. Emily, who had screamed with terror, was crying uncontrollably, with Annabel trying desperately to comfort her. It was the first time she had actually been really directly affected by the troubles as the rock hit the Discovery just above her head. Victoria had the common sense to phone the police, who arrived within a few minutes.

I could not get out of the car; I began shaking like a leaf; it was all starting to be too much for me. The police officer came over to me to see if I was all right and also checked the others, who had managed to get out and were standing on the hard shoulder. I was thankful it was the same officers who spoke to us at the services. Their 'bedside manner' made me feel at least somewhat calmer.

Henry spoke to the officers first. 'There were two men; they appeared to be in their thirties. I am not sure, but when I close my eyes and try and recapture the moment before they threw the boulder, I thought I saw a white car parked up, at least the roof of it.'

Philip came running back. 'I can't see anyone around,' he shouted to us as he approached.

The police officer joined in. 'We know about the white car, but unfortunately it was displaying false plates; so unless we stop all small white cars we are in difficulty.'

He walked over to II PY to see what damage had been done, something that none of us had bothered to do. We were more interested in ourselves for the first time.

The rock turned out to be a large block of concrete, which had fortunately hit the roof of the Discovery and bounced on to the Rolls. It had gone straight through the protective cover, through the windscreen, smashing it and the mirror to pieces and then bounced on to the seat, cutting a large gouge out of the leather, causing many hundreds of pounds worth of damage. The roof of the Discovery was almost through, but even that would be a write-off with a nine to ten inch dent in it.

Two other police vehicles arrived, together with an ambulance, and they blocked the two nearside lanes off while they carried out a thorough check of the area. But it was to no avail; they found nothing. Once again we were questioned, made statements and after the medical staff had ascertained we were alright and didn't need an ambulance we were allowed to go on our way.

It was a tortuous journey as, apart from Philip and Henry, we were all still in shock. Emily in particular had many crying outbursts, not being able to fully understand what was going on. However, the rest of the journey was at least trouble-free, with no further attacks.

The house, the dogs and the front door were the most welcome sights I had seen for weeks. The French trip, the race were all for nothing. I never wanted to see the car again.

Chapter 19

Being at home in Haworth and doing something normal was just what the doctor ordered. Francesca and I simply walked around, looking at the village in a way we hadn't seen for a long time. The past was beginning to seem unreal but the future as far as we were concerned was certain. I would contact Morales and offer him the car.

It was fairly late one Sunday afternoon. Haworth had been busy with hundreds of visitors coming to see an old festival called Scroggling the Holly. It was now quite dark and there were only a few visitors promenading up and down the main street, looking at the quaint shops. Haworth is well known for its November mists and today was no exception. The outer reaches of the village can seem sinister as you wander down the lanes at twilight, with the street lamps surrounded by mist.

I had noticed one particular tourist standing alone outside the Brontë Parsonage Museum; he seemed to be looking at us with some interest. Perhaps, I wondered, he'd seen us on TV. I didn't tell Francesca and we continued to walk arm in arm along the lane, from the museum towards the church and the Sunday School. For some reason the street lamp was out and, with the tall stone walls either side, we were now in virtual darkness. The entrance to the Sunday School has a large open stone porch, and that too was in total darkness. I really didn't want to pass it, particularly as I heard the sound of steel toecaps slapping the cobbles coming nearer and nearer.

I felt Francesca tense and grip my arm.

'Come on, darling, let's go quickly,' I whispered. We set off briskly and then began to run as fast as we could past the porch. To our relief there was no one there. We raced to the church, through the wishing gate and into the churchyard, with all its old-fashioned gravestones in memory of Haworth's famous families – the Brontës, Whitakers and Shackletons.

We ran along the path, turning right and up into the main grave area, thanking God for the fog. We dropped to the floor behind one of the headstones. It was cold and very wet and within seconds we were soaked and filthy from the mud. Suddenly the gate clanged we heard the click of steel on the stone flags of the path. We looked at each other and realized the coldness of the evening was making our breath appear like the steam from power-station cooling towers; he would see it. Francesca put her hand across her mouth, her eyes wide open with fear. I signalled her to lie down as we heard the tapping stop.

We heard him make his way quickly round the path to the front of the church and then stop; he must have realized we couldn't have got that far and turned and slowly retraced his steps. I could hear him now coming toward us and we both held our breath, which was torture in itself as we had been running. I couldn't believe it – he chose the exact route we had taken.

We were now shivering both with fear and cold and could not see or hear where he was. We gripped each other's hand as if we were on some white-knuckle ride at the fair. He slipped or tripped on something and cursed. He had passed us and yet none of us had seen each other. He was now well behind us.

I whispered into Francesca's ear: 'Shall we make a run for it?'

We heard him slip again, cursing as he fell to the ground. Only this time he must have been holding a gun because it now accidentally went off with a tremendous bang, causing the large colony of rooks that live in the churchyard to start squawking. The din was unbelievable, the fog acting like a blanket not allowing the sound to disperse.

I took a chance and pulled Francesca to her feet and ran with her down the path and out towards the front of the church. A car which had been turning in the distance momentarily lit the area in its headlights; I saw the man running at the other side, also towards the front. We stopped in our tracks; we were going meet him. I again pulled Francesca, this time into the church entrance and off the path. The rooks had stopped their squawking and once again there was silence.

I tried the front door and, thank God, it was open! We quietly walked into pitch black, the only light the occasional distant headlight hitting the top of the stained-glass window near the altar.

'Go and hide by the altar, where the choir sit,' I whispered as we made our way quickly in that direction.

'No I can't! I want us to be together,' she replied, quivering with fear.

'Darling, we can't. There's not room for the two of us. I'll be at the front here. Please don't worry. We'll be all right,' I said, trying to give encouragement and comfort.

Reluctantly she stepped over the cord designed to prevent the thousands of tourists from walking to the altar and hid at the end of the choir pews. I ducked down just in time to hear our pursuer enter the church.

The click of his shoes echoed round the church. 'Come on, Mr Conway, I know you are in here.' His voice was eerily gentle, coaxing. He lit a match, holding it up to get his bearings. The whole place seemed to light up. How could we possibly not be seen? The match went out and once again we were back in the dark.

I kept perfectly still, almost under the pew seat, trying desperately to calculate where he was. He pushed open a door at the back of the church, only to find it was where the vicar kept her publicity. He walked slowly round the right-hand side of the church – click, click, click – occasionally striking a match which lasted mere seconds before the draught in the church blew it out. 'Come on!' His voice grew in menace.

Click . . . click . . . click. He was slowly edging nearer to me. The clicking stopped as he walked into a carpeted section of the church. He struck a match yet again and soon found it was empty. Click . . . click . . . click. He was slowly making his way towards the altar . . . and Francesca. He lit another match. I could see his feet; he was at the altar and once again on carpet. I saw him step over the rope before the match blew out. I couldn't stand it any longer.

I stood up quickly and shouted. 'It's me you want. I'm Conway.'

He lit another match and turned. 'Mr Conway, you have caused me no end of trouble.' The match went out. He lit another and went over to the lectern, where he tore several sheets out of the Bible. He lit the paper and continued his sermon by the light of this makeshift torch.

'Mr Conway, you have cost the lives of several people in my employ and you still have something I want.'

I could now see Francesca getting to her feet. She stepped over to the altar, quickly and quietly picked up the cross and tiptoed towards the back of the man. I tried desperately not to look at her and carried on with the conversation, saying anything which came into my head.

'You're not the boss, you work for Maitland or that sneaky lawyer Morales. You haven't got the brains to be a boss.'

The paper was burning down and he had no choice but to tear out more pages and set them alight, dropping the blackened papers on to the floor.

Francesca had stopped in her tracks for fear of being seen, but my jabbering maintained his concentration on me.

'You couldn't *afford* my car. Look at you! With those clothes you couldn't afford to fill the bloody car with petrol. What kind of a boss are you?' I sneered.

'*This* makes me the boss,' he answered, suddenly pointing the gun at me.

Francesca was now almost upon him. Just a few steps more.

But I couldn't stop myself looking at her, so fearful was I that he might see her. He turned round in time to see the crucifix coming down on his head. Francesca had swung the cross with all her force. He tried to turn his body to avoid it but was too late. The arm of the cross went into his neck and he fell to the floor. I snatched up his makeshift torch and ran out of the church, pulling Francesca along with me. I ran to the phone box and dialled 999.

The first police car arrived even before I finished telephoning – someone must already have rung after hearing the gunshot. We all ran back into the church and found the man still lying on the floor with the cross in his neck. He was still alive. His gun lay just a few feet from him where it had fallen.

Chapter 20

The following day the police called to confirm that there would be no charges pressed against us and that the man, Chester Fleet, would be remanded to the hospital wing at Armley Prison on a charge of attempted murder. After the latest episode, I felt even more strongly that we would never have any peace until the car had gone. I had promised I would contact Morales immediately on our return, but it was obvious that someone knew we were home and hadn't fulfilled our promise, so perhaps this was a reminder that I should contact him. I did, however, phone Clive just to put him in the picture.

I also phoned David to bring him up to speed, but it turned out to be the other way round, with him spending over an hour putting me in the picture.

Maitland, it seemed, had successfully argued that his accounts should be unfrozen and some soft judge had been persuaded to agree with him. Sweeney had also discovered that Maitland had started a new company called Plover as a new cover for his operations.

Sweeney, who was being fed information by Fink at the DEA, swiftly exposed the new company in the *Times*, headlining with 'Back in Business?' A few days later the president and the director of the company were 'unfortunately' killed in a car crash. It was, by all accounts, a clumsy affair: the investigation proved that the injuries sustained were not caused by the accident as their necks had been broken beforehand. But it closed another weak link as far as Maitland was concerned.

Maitland then closed the company down, but within a week a new company had been formed; this time Swallow. He did this several times and each time Sweeney found out via Fink that she thought Maitland was behind it he would write and publish a little story. The real advantage of this operation was that Maitland couldn't ship large amounts of money out of the country and it put pressure on his operation.

The work of an undercover agent had also begun to bear fruit. Every time there was a hint of illegality, either the NYPD or the DEA would suddenly appear on the scene. However, this had more of a nuisance value than anything else, but it kept the pressure on and must have been causing concern to someone. Then one day the agent informed Fink about a shipment of cocaine. However, it was only a small amount and was obviously used as a means of flushing out the grass. It's certain that the agent didn't say anything as his body was discovered along with five others hanging up in a cold-storage building, with their tongues cut out and stapled to their lips.

This certainly sent shivers down the spines of the *New York Times* readers, as Sweeney made a meal of it. 'Let's Run these Butchers out of Town', 'Gang War Erupts in New York', 'Not since the St Valentine's Day Massacre have so many Villains been Killed in One Day'. These were the storylines in all papers. Whilst it may have terrified his men into silence, it did once again focus the attention on Sweeney's theories about Maitland and further resources were made available to the DEA.

It seemed obvious to the DEA that the warehouse where the drugs had been found would not be used again, for logical reasons. Maitland, however, seemed to be one step ahead in the game and continued to use it, but here Fink struck lucky. The gang members were naturally concerned about the police activities in the area and posted men on watch and naturally were on the lookout for anything suspicious.

One day three of the gang had loaded about two hundred thousand dollars' worth of pure cocaine into a Renault Espace.

The authorities didn't know where it was going, but the driver, it seems, left the warehouse without concentrating on what he was doing and crashed into a van totally unconnected with the affair. The men panicked, thinking that the two men in the van were undercover police, opened fire, killing the two men and fleeing the scene on foot. In their haste they left the cocaine in the van. It was another nail in Maitland's coffin: they had lost another two hundred thousand dollars and no business legitimate or otherwise could afford to haemorrhage like that.

You can imagine what Sweeney printed the next day: 'Innocents Murdered: When is it going to stop?' He took the chance and linked Maitland's name to the story, and brought the expected call from his lawyers. Sweeney duly issued an apology on behalf of the *New York Times*, stating he was sorry that Maitland's name had been used and he regretted the confusion. He then went on to explain that Maitland was a convicted drug dealer, which was possibly the cause of the confusion.

Two of the three men involved in the accident were duly executed and hung up in an empty warehouse. They were minus their hands and feet. The coroner thought that they had been cut off when they were alive, but is was a little difficult to tell as the bodies had been badly damaged by flies. The third man was still in hiding. Everyone, on *every* side, was now looking for him; he would make a perfect stool pigeon.

At this point, David's tale came to a close. I was riveted and I promised to phone him back on a regular basis. Things were moving fast.

The following day, Sweeney for the first time rang me direct.

'Hallo, I'm Jason Sweeney. I'm the editor of . . .'

I interrupted him. 'Good morning, Mr Sweeney, I'm Robert Conway. I've heard so much about you; I feel I must have known you for years.'

'Well, Bob. May I call you Bob?'

'I prefer Robert, please.'

'OK, Robert, sorry! But as you appear to have known me for some time, it's Jason.'

We had a little chuckle at that and at least it broke the ice. Sweeney continued: 'David has put me in the picture about what's been happening to you and I think you are right. I also think that there are two sets of people after the car. Am I correct?' he asked without waiting for an answer. '. . . He also told me about the offer you're considering from Morales. Have you seen him yet?'

'Not yet,' I replied carefully.

'Would you let me know straight away when you do?'

'No, I'm afraid not.'

Sweeney was taken aback. 'Why not?'

'I don't know you, Jason. I've never even met you. I've only spoken to you for about two and a half minutes and you expect me to discuss my private affairs with you. You could be anybody! I have a contact and his name is David Mainwearing . . .'

'God, Robert, you're a cool customer! David said you were careful and he was right. Look, you are damn right and I can see I must be losing my touch. But I will contact David straight away and arrange a meeting with you. OK?'

'OK!' I replied. 'But over here. I don't want to go to New York again, if I can help it. I'll let David know immediately if and when Morales calls.' The phone call ended.

Francesca came in a little concerned. 'Have you had a row? I heard your raised voice and wondered.'

'No, it's just that chap Sweeney. You know, he's the one David goes on about. He just wanted to talk and now wants to come and see us.'

I phoned David and put him in the picture. He was a little surprised, but said that's how Sweeney was. He thanked me for my loyalty and promised to let me know if it was Sweeney on the phone.

Later that same day I also received a call from Morales. 'Good afternoon, Mr Conway, Federico Morales here,' he said somewhat condescendingly.

'Yes,' I answered, 'I recognize your voice. What can I do for you?'

'I wonder if it's time to talk about the car. My client is aware that the car has been damaged but would still like to buy it in its current condition.'

'Well, that's very fair of him, but I think you ought to know that whilst in Paris we had two genuine offers, one from an American businessman and another from a Belgian dealer. I did tell them both that I would give you first refusal and that, subject to the price, the car was yours.'

Morales breathed a sigh of relief before thanking me, but I did stick the knife in a little when I told him that the American had been on the phone several times, increasing his offer on each occasion.

'When can we meet?' he asked. 'It's important that we conclude this affair as soon as possible. My client is very anxious to have the car.'

We arranged to meet in ten days, that being a week on Friday. I hadn't had a definite offer, but business is business, I thought.

David rang the following day, first to confirm it had been Sweeney who'd telephoned, and second to make an appointment to see me, with Sweeney and Janice Fink of the DEA, sometime in the next two to three weeks.

'It's highly likely that we will be accompanied by a senior English police officer,' he said with a hint of self importance.

It was then I dropped the bombshell that Morales was coming to see me a week on Friday and that he had upped the price.

'Oh God! I'll have to ring you back. I know the DEA wanted to see you before you made any deals.'

'OK,' I replied and he hurriedly rang off. Only minutes later David rang again and made arrangements to meet us on Monday morning.

I had also promised Clive White I would keep him informed and invited him to come and see us. He arrived quicker than I expected and was enthralled at the story which was unfurling. He stayed about an hour making copious notes, but had had to promise he would not print anything until the DEA gave us clearance. In any event, I promised he would have the story from start to finish long before anyone else.

Monday came all too quickly. David rang to say they were ten minutes away and to warn us that there were also five police officers with them. The dogs gave the warning that they had arrived and, simply by the sheer numbers that were at the gate, everyone in the village would soon know something was going on. The dogs were called off and the party came down the drive to be welcomed by Francesca offering tea and biscuits. The lounge in a three-hundred-year-old cottage was not conducive to a meeting with ten people present, but we managed. The introductions were pleasant enough over tea and coffee, but it was obvious from the start it was going to be a police matter.

Janet Fink of the DEA outlined what the situation was, mainly for my benefit, as it was obvious that the police had already been fully briefed.

Finally she asked, 'Who are you selling the car to and when?'

'Actually we haven't made our minds up yet and we've only had one serious offer, despite what the papers say!' I replied.

Fink interrupted me. 'We would like you to sell the car to Mr Morales. Jason here thinks he might be associated with Maitland.'

'It may not be the best offer,' I said with a smile on my face.

Fink responded. 'We are going to make you an offer you can't refuse.'

Everyone's ears pricked up.

'Go on, I'm all ears,' I said, still smiling.

Fink continued: 'We would like to examine the car quickly, and this is where Commander Bacon comes in. He will take the car to an establishment where they can test to see whether or not something is hidden in the chassis . . .' Bacon nodded to us. '. . . This will be undertaken with maximum security and this is where the other officers will come into their own. They are specialists in security and protection. Inspector Stanton will be in charge and will brief you fully later. I need not remind you all that maximum security means just that and nothing must be said outside these four walls. I have no need to remind you of the dangers that you have already faced and what type of person Maitland is.

Now,' she continued, 'if drugs or other incriminating items *are* found in the car by Commander Bacon's team and we can, in time, pin this to Maitland, we would then confiscate the car again and be prepared to give it back to you.'

There was a shocked silence from everyone. I was standing open-mouthed for what seemed like minutes, until Francesca calmly whispered, making sure everyone heard.

'Darling, close it, you're catching flies.'

'What about the money I will have received?' I finally asked.

She interrupted me. 'What money? That will be yours. It's a legitimate sale made through a firm of American lawyers acting on behalf of an unknown client.'

'I have to admit that's a fantastic offer. What do you want me to do?'

Commander Bacon took over. 'We have already arranged to take the car today . . .'

'Where to?' I asked, interrupting him.

'The less you know the better it is. The car will be brought back tomorrow. It's not going to be touched in any way, just X-rayed, to put it simply. Can we take the car from the back of the house, without loading it in the street?' he asked.

'Yes, but we're pretty sure we're being watched all the time.'

'We'll take care of that,' Bacon replied. 'Where's the car now?'

'In the garage'

'Good. Inspector Stanton here will just go and check it over to see if we have any bugging equipment hidden on it. Would one of you take him there?'

I was very glad the car arrived back the following morning, but shocked at what the officer told us in confidence. The chassis was indeed hollow; there was also a small section at the base of the battery case, which appeared to have been given a false bottom, and these, together with a false section at the back of the rear seats, were where they all suspected large quantity of drugs were hidden. David was fascinated and he tried to glean further information, without success. The officer felt he had said too much already.

David was staying with Sweeney at the White Lion and now went back there to put him fully in the picture. They no doubt spent the evening plotting Maitland's downfall, but whatever they did, we were not able to see either of them again on this trip. Once the car was back in the garage, the police left us to it. They did, however, keep a discreet watch at all times on the house. The following morning we had a call from both David and Sweeney to say they had had to return to the States quickly and that they would be in touch. We were, I confess, a little surprised. No thank-yous or good-lucks. But that's life.

Friday couldn't come quick enough. The subterfuge was beginning to wear us down and I was again beginning to wish I had never seen the car. The stress for us in particular and the rest of the family was enormous. We were in fear when we went to the shop. We were in fear when we went for a walk. We were in fear when we were alone and most of all we were in fear in our own home.

Morales rang and told us he was at the gate and could we please move the dogs.

I ran out and called them in, leaving the path clear for him. He walked very carefully down to the house, fearing they might suddenly come out again. We took him into the lounge, where only four days before, eleven people sat plotting his client's downfall. 'Good morning,' I said, trying to put him at his ease. 'It's nice to see you again.' He looked decidedly uncomfortable. Francesca invited him to have a coffee, which he accepted and then began to relax.

'We saw some articles in the English press about you selling the car,' he said, starting the conversation.

'Yes, I don't know where they got that from, but we have been pestered by a chap from California, who desperately wants the car. But I told him that you have first option. He has actually offered me two hundred and twenty-five thousand pounds. Then we had a phone call from this man in Belgium. He wouldn't leave his name but is ringing this afternoon. He gave me the impression that he knows the car very well.' I paused for him to respond, but he didn't. 'I don't know what it is about this car. I know it's magnificent. Perhaps it's the publicity it has been given. Everyone wants to touch it; it's incredible. But we've had some grief.'

'What do you mean by grief?' Morales asked.

'Trouble!' I replied. 'We've been shot at. People have tried to steal the car and we've been followed everywhere. I will be glad to sell the car. That's grief!' Again I waited for some kind of response, but none came. I took the bull by the horns.

'Well, anyway how much have you been told to offer?'

'My client is prepared to pay two hundred and thirty thousand pounds.'

'Two fifty and it's yours.'

Without a murmur, he took out a cashier's cheque and handed it to me.

'Thank you. The car will be picked up this afternoon. Can you make sure all the papers are with it?'

'No, no!' I said quickly. 'I must cash the cheque first.'

'It's a cashier's cheque. There won't be any difficulties, I can assure you.'

'I know there won't. I won't let there be any. I will telephone my son and he, along with my wife, will take the cheque and cash it. Once the money is safely in my bank, then you can come and collect the car. I am sorry, but that's how it is.'

I don't think Morales was used to dealing with people like our family. He worked for a firm which obviously acted for crooks and gangsters and was used to everything being agreed in advance. 'I agree,' he said reluctantly.

'I'll telephone now to make the arrangements.'

Henry arrived about fifteen minutes later and both he and Francesca left with the cheque.

Morales was embarrassed at having to wait and shuffled from one side of the chair to the other, not knowing of what to talk about next. That he suddenly got up and announced. 'I think it would be better if I go now. if you could give the people collecting the car all the papers and, of course, the keys . . .' which was soon wiped off his face when I replied.

'But you haven't bought the keys!'

I could not believe the look on his face. It was one of sheer astonishment and shock. He had absolutely no sense of humour! I put him out of his misery.

'I was only joking. Telephone me in about two hours. That should give us plenty of time to sort things out. In the meantime you can make your arrangements to collect the car.'

Relief flooded back into his face. 'Oh, by the way, I have promised a reporter that I would let him know when the car is going. He wants to write a story about II PY leaving the country and going back to the States. I hope you don't mind. He'll be taking a few photographs as it goes on to the trailer.'

Morales thought for a moment. 'No, I don't see a problem with that . . .' He paused. 'No, I don't see a problem. What is II PY?'

I laughed. 'You've just parted with two hundred and fifty thousand pounds and you don't know what II PY is?'

'No!'

'It's the number given by Rolls-Royce for your car. It's the most important number of all. Goodness me!' I exclaimed. 'Don't you know anything about the car?'

This prompted me to ask him a question which not only surprised him but completely took the wind out of his sails.

'Why didn't your client simply increase his bid for the car at the auction?' I stopped for his answer, but it didn't come, so I continued: 'I couldn't have afforded to go this high. The money you've paid me is more than I've had at any one time in my life.'

Morales simply replied, 'I don't know,' and we parted company.

I walked him to the gate, holding both dogs; they could obviously sense he was a crook. He was making it worse by trying to dodge them and then running to the gate. Once outside, his ruffled composure disappeared. We said our goodbyes and he went away. I watched his car, a black Mercedes, turn out of the road and at the same time noticed he was accompanied by two men.

I duly phoned Commander Bacon the moment they had gone. I was beginning to feel paranoid, so I used my mobile phone out in the garden in case the house was bugged. Whilst discussing matters with him, I jokingly told him how I felt. Within the hour he had an officer checking over our house. We were clean, and our minds were now able to rest. No matter how sad I felt, we knew when the car had gone, all our troubles would be over.

Bacon was clearly anxious to move things quickly, apologising that he would have to curtail our conversation, with the promise he would ring back. 'Please let me know as and when the car is paid for,' he remarked as he put the phone down.

Shortly afterwards, Francesca phoned to say that the cheque was genuine and that it had been cashed. 'We now have two hundred and fifty thousand pounds in our account!' she almost screamed in excitement.

She detected a note of sadness in my voice. 'You can always buy another one,' she said, trying to give me some crumb of comfort for having to sell the one thing I had always wanted.

'Yes, I know, but not like that one,' I replied a little dolefully. The thought of the money, though, helped to soften the blow.

I telephoned Clive White and told him what was happening. He said he would be there within the hour with his photographer. They duly arrived, but waited in his car on the road, much to our surprise.

Everything from then on moved quickly. Morales phoned and I confirmed that the cash was in my account and all the papers were in the car. About an hour later a huge container lorry arrived. It was too big to turn round into our road, so I telephoned the police to ask if it would be all right to load the vehicle on the main road and to my surprise they confirmed it would and that they were sending officers straight away to assist with traffic control. The cavalry arrived, two cars, four officers, sirens blazing, and they took control. The container was offloaded on to the road and for the last time I drove II PY up our drive and out on to the road, then directly into the container. After stopping at various intervals for the appropriate photographs to be taken, the last one being the door closing on the rear of the car, it was locked away, hauled back on to the lorry and taken away.

It was a sad moment seeing the car drive away for what could be the last time. Francesca put her arm around my shoulder and we walked slowly back into the house, feeling very sorry for ourselves.

I phoned David in New York and told him the car had left for the States, though I didn't know how it was being transported. However, it looked like it would be by ship as it had been containerized.

'You can bet it will be travelling by air,' said David. 'That man never does the expected. I'll pass the news on to Sweeney and Fink.'

The next day I sent David a copy of the *Daily Mail*'s and *Mirror*'s stories on the sale. 'Farewell to a Great Lady' and a 'Champion is sold to the States' were the headlines. It almost made me weep.

Chapter 21

David kept us fully up to date on what happened over the following days and weeks. He was himself kept informed by Sweeney, who in turn was fed by Fink. All in all, it was a very smooth communications chain.

David was correct in his analysis; Maitland never did anything anyone expected. The car was transported via P&O Dover to Calais in France. The police were able to follow the lorry easily without being detected. The car, still in its container, left Calais via the *autoroute* out of the port, passed Dunkirk and was then taken over the border to Oostkamp, a small Belgian village, where it was off loaded and remained in a garage and out of sight for the next twenty-four hours.

The first real break for the investigating team, which now excluded the English police but included the Belgian and French gendarmeries, came about lunchtime the following day, when an old insignificant Renault 25 taxi pulled up outside the garage. Its passenger alighted and went straight into the garage, but not before his picture was taken and, thanks to modern technology, flashed to Interpol and back to the States for identification. Within a few minutes the results were sent back: it was none other than Gerry Rider, Maitland's trusted chauffeur.

At exactly six o'clock the garage doors opened and II PY, still looking as elegant as ever, was driven out and on to the road, with Gerry at the wheel. He drove out of Oostkamp and back on the *autoroute* towards France.

It was dark when Gerry left the *autoroute*, drove into the centre of Calais, and pulled up outside the front door of the Metropol Hotel. (This, you may remember, was run by my good friend Philippe, and was where we had stayed once before with II PY.) He then took his hand luggage inside and registered for the night. The receptionist, Catherine, tried to make polite conversation, but Gerry would have none of it, possibly because he did not speak too much French. However, Catherine spoke reasonable English and gave him instructions for the hotel's private garage and he immediately took the Rolls round the corner. The garage door was already open, and the minute the car was inside the roller shutter slid down.

The French police had taken over the surveillance of Gerry and the car and one has to say they were very professional. The hotel was completely covered from all angles and within seconds of Gerry going to his room an officer in plain clothes had entered to find out which room he was in and what his plans were. He introduced himself as Lieutenant Deschamps and advised Catherine that he and another officer would be staying the night. She was quite thrilled at being part of this little adventure.

The officer asked her to tell the man that she had reserved a place at the Fin Palais for him, as he was too late for a meal in the hotel. With that he quickly left the hotel and spoke to several colleagues in the adjacent car park. A male and female officer left the car park to go to the Fin Palais, whilst Deschamps encamped himself with another female colleague in the foyer with a cup of coffee.

The officers arrived at the Fin Palais and explained the situation to the proprietor, who was also the chef. They then went to address the diners, asking them to act as normally as possible during what he described as an important police operation. The two officers were to be given a table adjacent to Gerry's, which was kept empty pending his arrival.

Twenty minutes later they received a call from Deschamps –

Gerry was on his way. Two more officers arrived to pose as diners at a nearby table. Soon after, Gerry himself entered the restaurant and was directed to his allotted table. It was obvious from the moment he set foot in the place he couldn't speak French or read the menu. He must have considered he was safe, and unlikely to be understood, because when his phone rang he became engrossed in a conversation in which he explained where he was, where he was going and at what time he expected to be there. He confirmed that he was going to Orly and that he hoped to be there about lunchtime. The car was booked on a cargo flight around 2 p.m. He did not, however, give any clue to where the car would be going, though this would be a simple matter for the gendarmerie to find out.

Whilst Gerry was in the restaurant, Deschamps had searched Gerry's room. There was nothing, except two plane tickets, one at 19.50 hours for a Rolls-Royce Sedanca de Ville from Orly to New York, the other, obviously, for Gerry, a flight from Charles de Gaulle to New York at 20.20 hours. All this confirmed what had been said in the restaurant and was passed on to the DEA.

Towards ten o'clock Deschamps saw Gerry returning through the foyer windows. Deschamps rejoined his companion on the settee in the foyer bar just as Gerry walked in.

'Cent vingt-six!' he said as he approached the desk.

'Ah, vous parlez français, Monsieur,' Patrice, the night porter, replied. He had been forewarned and was desperately trying to calm his nerves.

Gerry obviously understood that much French. 'No! I've been practising that all night!'

They both laughed, which was the best thing that could have happened, as it put both men at their ease.

'Would you like something from the bar?' Patrice asked.

'No thanks. I'll just go and see if my car is OK. Oh and tell that young lady the restaurant was excellent,' Gerry replied, again in his strong accent.

'Is your car that Rolls-Royce?' Patrice asked. 'I've been looking at it,' he continued without waiting for an answer, which made Gerry look a little anxious.

Patrice, seeing this, pointed to the TV screen of the garage, which showed II PY in all her glory.

'No one is allowed in the garage, except the owners of course,' Patrice continued, putting Gerry further at ease.

'That's great. I'll just go and have a quick look. Thanks!'

Gerry wandered off to the garage and was soon picked up on the CCTV checking over the car. Gerry even looked up at the camera and waved, knowing that Patrice might be watching. A little later he came back into the foyer, took his room key and retired to bed.

Deschamps had put a very small bug into the room. It was simply to detect sound, the signal of which was relayed to a vehicle in the adjoining public car park. The gendarmerie wanted to know when Gerry was asleep so that the next part of the operation could commence: checking the car over.

It wasn't long before the signal was given. The gendarmes arrived in force, much to the consternation of Patrice, and six mobile trolley-type jacks were taken into the garage, via the foyer, in absolute silence. Next a battery of electronic testing gear and various other ingenious detection devices were carried across the room. Not a word was spoken. The total silence was broken only by the occasional footstep on the tiled floor.

The whole process took about an hour, during which they photographed and videoed every inch of the car. The equipment was then swiftly carried back and hustled into a waiting van. Janice Fink was very pleased with the outcome: the vehicle had not been tampered with in any way.

Gerry was up early and went to the reception desk to pay the bill. This time it was Philippe, the proprietor, on reception.

'A friend of mine used to own your car,' Philippe said somewhat proudly and proceeded to show Gerry some of the photographs that had been taken outside the hotel.

Gerry was clearly a little taken aback, as indeed was the undercover officer standing nearby.

'It's not my car. I'm just the driver. That's all,' Gerry said ruefully.

'Is it easy to drive?' Philippe asked.

'No. It weighs two tons and even with the specially fitted power steering, it's damned hard work.'

'It's a lovely car,' Philippe responded, handing him his account. 'Sixty euros please.'

Gerry took out a large wad of hundred-euro notes and peeled one off for Philip. 'Give the change to the young woman and the night porter. They were very helpful. Thanks again.'

With that he handed back the room key, picked up his case and went quickly to the garage. He superficially checked the car, waved to the camera and then backed II PY out on to the road. Philippe had watched every move he made, quietly relaying it to the gendarme.

Gerry took the simple route to Paris using the *autoroutes*. At Orly – the airport from which II PY was due to be transported – Gerry did all the necessary paperwork with the airline and then made his way by taxi back to Charles de Gaulle, where he took his late flight back to New York.

The surveillance operation had been flawless.

Chapter 22

Gerry arrived at Kennedy Airport at about 8 a.m. looking very tired and immediately took a taxi home, which of course was at the family home of John Maitland. There was nothing unusual in that. However, the car was a different matter. It arrived the following day much later than expected. There had been a mechanical problem with the aircraft. This had caused some concern but no one had been near the car during its enforced stay.

Gerry was duly notified the car had arrived and was ready for collection. Maitland had been careful; his name was not on the manifest. He was really playing hard to get and he left II PY with Customs for well over a week. He knew Customs would search the car, so he gave them ample opportunity to do so. He also knew that if they did find anything, they couldn't pin it on him. I don't think Gerry realized he would have been the fall guy at this stage.

Gerry eventually collected the car and it was duly driven straight to Maitland's home and directly into the garage in Greenwich Village, but not before Maitland was seen to give it the once-over. He was obviously proud of the car; simply by the way he ran his hand along the front wing, you could tell he was glad to have it back. The car remained in the garage for three weeks and even Gerry did not take it out to give it a clean and polish. Fink and the DEA knew, however, that sooner or later the action would start and they had to be prepared.

Sweeney had been briefed on what had taken place and immediately wanted to resume his campaign against Maitland. He had a series of punchy headlines ready to roll, but he was persuaded – perhaps that's too soft a word – was *told* to lay off until Maitland had been seen in the car and Fink gave the word. Sweeney naturally agreed, but from then on he was chomping at the bit. He did begin to prepare his campaign and instructed David to resume his investigations into Maitland's affairs. This David did with gusto.

It was another three weeks before we received David's next phone call. He was somewhat excited as things had begun to happen.

'I told you we would get him . . .' David said, opening the conversation, ' . . . and we will.' Then he added, 'Did you know Amelia and Eleanor are still friends?'

'Yes, I remember.'

'Well, she came over to see Eleanor the other day very distressed. She complained that John had been terrible in recent days, like a bear with a sore head. What's worse Aprilla's been taken to hospital very ill and Gerry just can't cope. You know how close they are.'

John and Gerry, David went on to explain, had fallen out, because Gerry wanted to go and see Aprilla and John wanted him to do this and that. For the first time ever, Amelia had overheard John swearing at Gerry. John apparently wanted Gerry to take the Rolls to the garage and Gerry had said he would do it later, as he had been called to the hospital urgently. John had said no and reminded Gerry that he worked for him and couldn't please himself. When Gerry protested, John lost his head. 'I couldn't care less about your fucking wife, you can find plenty where she came from.'

John then went on to say if he didn't get the car out and take him to the garage he would wish he hadn't been born. From that moment Gerry was in a daze. Gerry, too, was now in a terrible mental state. Everything he valued had suddenly been turned upside down. His boss whom he had given loyal service to for many years had suddenly turned on him and had made him make choices. But there was no choice to be made, as far as he was concerned. The only thing that was now important to him was Aprilla. Amelia even thought she saw John holding a gun and pointing it at Gerry; he made him get the car out and take him where he wanted to go.

The DEA had a permanent watch on all the activities of the Maitland household and followed everyone, discreetly of course, wherever they went and today was no exception. Fink's men watched the Rolls leave the house and went gliding through the traffic, which was quite heavy due to some emergency roadworks elsewhere. A little later they stopped at the traffic lights, and then suddenly Gerry quickly opened the door of II PY, slid his body over the handbrake and jumped out of the car. Maitland was stranded, too shocked to take any action, except shout out, 'Get back here, you fool.' But Gerry had disappeared into the crowd. Maitland struggled into the driver's seat, but the traffic was already building up behind and the police arrived to see what the delay was.

The officer recognized not only Maitland but also the car, and asked him to pull over.

'I'm in a hurry,' Maitland protested.

'So am I, Mr Maitland. Pull over there and turn the engine off,' the officer commanded impatiently.

Maitland had no alternative. Not used to driving the car, he found it somewhat difficult, which caused the officer to ask sarcastically, 'Have you got your driving permit, Mr Maitland?', much to the amusement of the crowd that was now gathering. Maitland certainly wasn't used to being treated this way.

'Look, Officer. Do you understood who I am? I've given more money to your police charity than you've ever earned,' he bawled.

'I understand perfectly well who you are, sir. You're John Maitland, the convicted drug dealer, and it would appear you can't drive an automobile either.'

Maitland's world fell apart for the second time in almost a year. The first time was in the face of all the might of the American judicial system; the second time it took only a simple New York cop to bring him down to earth with a bang. He was lost for words.

'Go on get out of here!' the cop ordered.' 'And take that old heap with you. It cuts no ice with me!'

Maitland sheepishly restarted the car and jerked it into gear several times, causing it to stall, much to the onlookers' amusement. Eventually he managed to drive the car out of the area and appeared to be going home rather than towards the garage. He had momentarily forgotten Gerry, who had left him in the lurch; he simply wanted to get away from all the embarrassment and home was the safest place.

The news of a possible falling-out between Maitland and Gerry delighted Janice Fink and she in turn had called the captain who was in command of a specially formed anti-drug squad. George Younger was totally committed to the destruction of all drug dealers. He was a young man to have achieved that position, only forty years of age, but had served a very good apprenticeship in the force, receiving many awards, and had achieved success in every position he had held.

Fink picked him up from the police headquarters and took him to the hospital, via a short detour, in order to discuss their plan of action with Gerry. Gerry, Fink realized, could make a first-class witness against Maitland, but there was the risk that, by approaching him, they could blow their cover. They decided to risk it. In the worst-case scenario, they would hold Gerry for as long as possible without charge in the hope that Maitland would make his move to the garage.

They entered the hospital and approached Aprilla's room, passing the 24-hour guard who had been discreetly placed on her room. They could see Gerry was distressed, pacing quietly up and down the room. He turned and saw them looking in. Younger took out his badge and showed it to Gerry and signalled for him to come outside. Gerry looked shocked. As if he hadn't got enough troubles, without the police adding to them! He kissed Aprilla's forehead and she opened her eyes.

'I won't be a moment,' he whispered softly in her ear and walked out to meet them.

'Yes?' Gerry said in an annoyed tone.

'My name's Younger of the NYPD and this is Janice Fink of the DEA, we would like to ask you a few questions.'

'I've got nothing to talk about; I've done nothing wrong,' Gerry replied, turning to go back into his wife.

'We could do this down at headquarters if you prefer,' Younger replied firmly.

Gerry continued towards Aprilla's room but stopped in his tracks when Younger said loudly, 'You're under arrest for the illegal importation of drugs.' Janice Fink was absolutely aghast at Younger's action. She felt he had overshot the mark and declared his hand too quickly.

Gerry walked back to them.

'No, no! I can't go anywhere at the moment. I can't leave her now. She needs me!' he pleaded.

'Well, we just want to talk to you. For a few minutes, that's all,' Younger responded.

Gerry followed them into a nearby waiting room, which they immediately commandeered. They sat down and Fink immediately explained Gerry's position, not trying to soften the blow. 'Look, Gerry . . . May I call you Gerry?'

'Yeah! Why not?'

'I want to explain your position – fully,' Fink began. 'We have been watching you and your employer John Maitland for the last twelve months. We know you and he are partners. You may not be equal partners, but partners nonetheless . . .'

'Oh no! No. No, no, no,' Gerry interrupted. 'I'm his driver, that's all. Nothing else, nothing at all!'

'I said we've been watching you for a long time. We know you put drugs into a false chassis on the car. We know that you knew the drugs were in the car when you picked it up in France. We know you had the underneath of the car checked out in Belgium, to see if the car had been tampered with, and we also know that John Maitland covered his back when you went to Europe in case you got caught. Your fingerprints were the only ones found on the car, so you would have been the one holding the baby.'

'I will spell it out,' she continued. 'What we know one hundred per cent is that you were to be the fall guy. You still *are* the fall guy, Gerry. When all this comes out Maitland will say you brought the car in and that he had nothing to do with it. You'll be the one going down, Gerry . . . Who will look after your wife then?'

Gerry looked shocked, but got up to go back to his wife.

'Before you leave here,' Younger said, 'I want you to realize that *everyone* involved in this crime will face at least twenty years . . .'

Gerry stopped in his tracks.

Younger continued: 'Go and see your wife for a few minutes and think about it. Don't think about escaping; all the corridors are guarded . . . Oh and one thing more, Gerry, if you do decide to see sense and give us a little bit of help, you may just avoid imprisonment . . .'

Gerry left the waiting room and returned to his wife. He was in tears. He stayed with her for about an hour before he was called back into the room. He was in a daze, holding his head in his hands, not knowing what day it was, let alone the time. Younger decided to take a softer approach, seeing Gerry's distress.

'She will be all right, you know. Janice has spoken to everyone about her and they all say she'll be OK.' He paused for a moment to let it all sink in. 'Before you left the room I said there was a "Get-out-of-gaol-free card" on the table and there is. If you are prepared to take it, that is.'

Gerry looked up and began listening. This time Fink continued. 'We only need one thing and you know what that is. We need you to testify against John Maitland. We will put you and your wife on the witness-protection programme, we'll give you new identities and . . .'

'If I testify,' Gerry interrupted, 'it will be because I want to, not for what I can get.'

Both Younger and Fink realized that Gerry was at a crossroads; Younger decided to take the plunge.

'Why did you suddenly get out of the car at the traffic lights and run away, Gerry?'

There was silence. Gerry simply put his head in his hands again and for a while there was an uneasy impasse. Gerry looked up, tears in his eyes, as he began telling his story, sobbing like a baby as he detailed all Maitland had said and done. He had turned the corner.

'Where were you going?' Fink asked.

'I was to take him to the garage near the docks,' Gerry replied.

'What for?' Younger asked.

'I think the car was to be checked over. I don't know'

It was obvious that Maitland had completely underestimated the love and closeness of Gerry and Aprilla and this was the Achilles heel of his entire operation.

'You do appreciate that Maitland knows where Aprilla is and you do appreciate that he'll know where you are,' Younger reminded him.

'Yeah!' Gerry murmured,

'You do realize he'll get at you through Aprilla.'

'He'll try!' Gerry murmured again.

'You know if you are made the fall guy, you'll probably never be able to get close to your wife again,' Younger interjected.

'Shut up! Shut the fuck up!' Gerry shouted.

'Gerry, we really don't have long. I know Maitland will come and find you. We need to hide you away quickly so that he doesn't know we've spoken to you.'

'But I haven't yet.'

'Of course not, but he won't know that, will he?' Fink responded.

'What about Aprilla? I can't leave her,' he asked.

'You won't have to. We'll put you up in a hotel tonight and we'll move your wife to a private clinic, where she will get the best treatment possible and tomorrow we will move you to a quiet town a long way away from here where you will both be safe and you can see your wife whenever you like.'

This was the moment the DEA had been waiting for, the moment Sweeney had been waiting for. If only he could have been there. Gerry Rider had agreed to testify against his old boss John Maitland. Janice Fink wanted to let out a scream, but protocol wouldn't let her. You could see why Younger had made it to the top so quickly.

'Look, Gerry,' Younger said, 'you go back to your wife and leave everything to us. You have to trust us as much as we've trusted you. Everything will happen quickly, don't worry.'

Gerry looked up and straight into Younger's eyes.

'I am not a traitor. I am not going to be paid for giving him to you. I am doing it because *he betrayed me.*'

Chapter 23

Maitland had arrived back home and spent the rest of the day pondering what to do. He had effectively lost another day. Another day when pressure was building up against him and every minute counted. He had to get the car into the garage and quickly. In some way he believed or hoped that Gerry would come back full of apologies, but by late evening, he realized that this would not be the case and started to call in a few favours.

For the first time ever he allowed 'undesirables' to visit the house – drug dealers, gangsters, thugs from the streets, even – in order to help him find a way out of his present situation and find Gerry. Amelia was not only horrified but frightened; these people were invading her world and she wanted no part of it.

She called for Gerry, but of course there was no answer.

'Where is he?' she asked John

'I don't know!' he snapped back.

'You don't have to talk to me like that.'

'I said I don't know! Now get the hell out of here! Can't you see I'm busy.'

Amelia didn't get the chance to speak to John again until late evening, but he was just as nasty.

'If you won't tell me where Gerry is, I'll ask at the hospital,' she snapped back.

But the hospital told her that neither Gerry nor Aprilla was there.

She stormed in to John. 'What have you done. She's not at the hospital.'

'Who's not?'

'Who do you think? Aprilla!'

Maitland was shocked. 'Where the hell are they then?'

'What on earth's the matter? You look as though you have seen a ghost. What have you done, John? Tell me!'

'Fucking leave me ALONE!'

Amelia burst into tears. She knew he was in trouble.

Younger and Fink arrived at the very smart hotel where Gerry had been given a refuge. It was early but both of them wanted results ... fast. Gerry was just returning to his room, when he bumped into them walking along the corridor.

'I feel like a condemned man. That's the best breakfast I have had since Aprilla was taken ill,' he said patting his stomach.

'How's Aprilla?' Younger asked.

'The clinic says she's progressing well. She'll be sitting up tomorrow, they say,' Gerry said, smiling for the first time.

'Aah, that's good,' Younger responded.' 'Did you sleep well?'

'OK, considering all things.'

They entered the room. Gerry ordered coffees and the revelations began.

Janice Fink started by asking what his involvement was in Maitland's businesses and straight away Gerry explained that he had no dealings whatsoever in his affairs. He was just his driver and on occasion acted as his bodyguard. Aprilla was simply the housekeeper for Maitland's wife and seldom had anything to do with him.

'Why did he want to risk getting the car back?' Fink asked.

'It had the cocaine in it and you lot missed it when you checked the car the last time. He hasn't paid for the stuff in the car and still owes his suppliers. You hit him again a few weeks ago and he hasn't paid for that either. By getting the car back he knew he would be financially in the clear.' He paused for a little while before asking, 'How did you find out the stuff was in there?'

'We didn't and we still didn't know until you just confirmed it. As you probably know, the previous owner was coming under a lot of pressure to sell – pressure of an unpleasant kind – and he quickly came to suspect there was something fishy about the car. He thought it might be Maitland, but we were all beginning to think there was some other interested party involved. Was there?'

'No one,' Gerry said. 'Only a few trusted friends knew what was hidden in the car. Maitland wanted to make sure that that man in England sold him the car. He arranged for a crooked lawyer named Morello or something like that to organize all the activities. He wanted to make sure they would be frightened into selling the car and wouldn't change their minds. He didn't care who got hurt in the process.

'He had the car followed all through France when the Englishman went on holiday with his family. When he agreed to sell the car, Maitland put more pressure on him to make sure he didn't back out. No one was allowed to touch the car. People didn't matter, but with the car, it was different. Not one scratch was put on the car during the whole time it was away. He even had photographs taken everywhere the car went and had the pictures wired back. I've seen them; they're on his computer at home.

'Everything in Europe was arranged by the lawyer. I was beginning to see a side of him I hadn't seen before. Normally he was cool and made decisions rationally but now . . .' He paused.

'Do you realize that several people have been killed doing just what you have described and an innocent family have been tormented by his actions and his silly little games?' Fink said a little angrily.

'It was nothing to do with me. The only thing I did in Europe was to bring the car back.'

'And the drugs,' Younger commented.

'What about the little garage in Belgium? Where does that fit in?' Fink asked.

'Maitland would hide some of the cocaine in his car, and ship it to Europe on the pretext of going on a rally. The car would supposedly break down and we would take it to the garage where the drugs would be offloaded.'

'Why didn't he offload the drugs in Belgium this time, before you brought the car back?' Younger asked.

'He really didn't know if the cocaine was still in the car, and he had a big cash customer desperate for stock here in the States.'

'Who's that?' Younger asked hurriedly.

'I don't know. I told you, I wasn't told anything about the distribution of the drugs, or his business. It's just what I have found out over the years.'

Fink called a break to the proceeding and suggested that Gerry go to see his wife; they would resume after lunch. In any case it gave Fink and Younger time to think about Maitland. They had no doubt that he would come after Gerry, if only for revenge. He would also want to take the Rolls to the garage at the docks, so he could retrieve the cocaine.

It was therefore urgent to set up more surveillance around the garage area. Younger telephoned one of his trusted lieutenants and told him to organize the men.

'We've just ordered lunch,' Younger said to Gerry on his return. 'Would you like some?'

'Yeah, I sure would,' Gerry replied. It was the first time he'd felt like eating anything for three days.

They continued to question him over lunch and he became a willing participant, determined to help them. It was his way of getting back at his old employer.

Early on, Fink received a call from one of her officers. The Rolls was on the move, but it was on the back of a breakdown truck.

'Keep your eye on it,' Fink commanded. 'We'll be there in ten minutes.'

Suddenly Fink heard a yell. 'He's gone. Where's the mother-fucker gone?'

'For God's sake, will someone tell me what's happening?' Fink demanded. There was silence. She shouted the order again. The officer replied. 'Rolls-Royces don't just disappear,' Fink replied. 'Find the damn thing before I get there.'

All this time Gerry was smirking. Much as he hated Maitland, you had to give him his dues.

He gave his companions some advice. 'I told you he'd do everything you least expect. He's obviously not taking a chance with the garage near the docks. But he does need Willy Pressburger to take the cocaine out of the car. I don't think he will trust anyone else. I don't mean with the merchandise, but with the car. It's a skilful job to make the car look as if it's not been tampered with. I suggest you keep your eye on him ... Pressburger.'

'What does he look like?' Younger asked

'He's very tall and thin. Really skinny. He's the cleverest body repairer of them all.'

'Any other features . . . We need to move quickly?'

'Yep, fair-skinned with red-blond hair. Nearly forty years old. That's about it really. I don't think he has anything to do with the drugs. He may be under some pressure. Another thing: watch the garage, follow the tools. Willy would need to take the specialist tools with him or for someone else to take them for him.'

'Thanks, Gerry, we'll have to go. Wait here. If you think of anything that could help us, call me.'

Chapter 24

It was an agonising ninety minutes. Reports came in every few minutes but always the same: no sightings. Younger paced up and down like a man possessed.

'A Rolls-Royce and a red-and-white breakdown lorry cannot just disappear!' he kept murmuring to himself time and time again.

The first break came about midday when CCTV confirmed that a truck carrying what looked like a large old automobile had been headed for Bronx. Within the hour a lorry matching the description was stopped in the Bronx; the car, though, was gone. The driver seemed reluctant to talk to the officers.

Younger spoke directly to the officers detaining the driver. 'Look, we don't have time to mess about. We want to know where he left the car. Surely you know how to question a suspect,' he added angrily.

It was only a few seconds before the officer came back on the phone.

Younger listened impatiently. 'He *will* answer. Put your phone on loudspeaker and let him hear what I've got to say,' Younger yelled.

'Put the bracelets on him and charge him with assisting in the importation of twenty million dollars' worth of cocaine. Don't mess about! Just lock him up, we've got enough proof to put him away for ten to twenty.'

This seemed to work a treat. The lorry driver began to bleat. He'd passed the car on to another lorry driver, a Latino. It was a large articulated truck with rigid sides and belonged to a company called Wiseman.

'Where was it going?' he was asked.

'To a scrapyard south of the city,' came the reply. 'I thought it was funny that a lovely car like that was going to a scrap-yard.'

Younger brought the phone call to an abrupt end.

'I heard everything. Lock him up. Don't let him talk to anyone, not even a lawyer, until I say so. OK?'

Younger and Fink, driving in Fink's Chrysler, made their way southward. just in case there were developments. Younger's phone rang again. It was the surveillance team at Maitland's house. Maitland was leaving and was driving a grey Cadillac, California plate 6429, and heading for the city.

Fink continued to drive southwards but they still had no news of the Wiseman truck's whereabouts.

'Ring Gerry, see if he knows of any demolition yards; it might just help,' she suggested.

Younger rang the hotel, but to no avail, and his heart sank for the moment. He tried the hospital and, thank God, Gerry was at Aprilla's bedside. Gerry told him about the Wiseman Company, which belonged to Maitland's holding company. Willie Wiseman, the owner, was very weak, easily bullied. The mention of the scrapyard, though, at first drew a blank. However, half an hour later Gerry phoned back.

On his way back to the hotel he'd remembered a man called Ace Berridge who had a business on the South Side, though he didn't know what.

'Every little helps!' Younger said.

The moment he put the phone down, Younger was on to his office for them to trace any business with a person named Ace Berridge involved. 'Concentrate on any involving scrap or demolition.'

Another report came in. Maitland was heading south towards Brooklyn, stopping off at various offices en route.

'Don't be fooled! He could be testing us out, checking to see if he's being followed. You've got to be more careful from now on. Try and change the cars. Don't leave anything to chance.'

The worst news of the day now hit them. The Wiseman truck seemed to have vanished.

'Check the out-of-state roads, though I don't think you'll find anything. I think the truck is still in the state. But check anyway. Call me back as quick as possible.'

Younger then called Phil Brookes, the officer assigned to watch Wiseman, the one-time owner of the truck company now part of the Maitland empire. 'Phil, I've got a difficult job for you to do. I want you to call on Wiseman. Get past his secretary and whoever else. Don't tell him you're a cop. Take him out with a gun if necessary. But tell him to tell his secretary he will be about ten minutes. We should be there in about fifteen. His workforce must believe he'll only be a few minutes. I want him off that site as quick and as quietly as possible. Have you got it?'

Phil Brookes, Younger knew, would be prepared to bend the rules to get what he wanted.

A while later, Phil phoned back. Younger could hear pleading in the background and someone else swearing, talking aggressively.

'OK Phil, have you got anything for me?'

'Yeah! Wiseman's squealing. The truck's gone to Ace Breakers downtown . . .'

Younger stopped him mid-sentence. 'Phil, stay on hold. Don't go away, we might have something.' He immediately called up the bureau to get an address for Ace Breakers.' It came back within seconds.

'Right I want full surveillance on this yard. Find the truck and don't try and enter until I give the word. Is there any news on Maitland or Pressburger?'

'Maitland was crossing Brooklyn. Pressburger was still inside the garage, but a Hertz Ford Transit had entered the building about half an hour before.'

'Good work, everyone! We're going to get the bastard this time, I can feel it! . . . Back to you, Phil. Put Wiseman in the car, arrest him for assisting in the importation of narcotics. Keep him out of view. Don't let him have any contact with the outside world until I say so. Clear?'

Younger received another message. The Hertz van had left the garage, with two unidentified Caucasian males in the front.

Younger and Fink had now arrived in the vicinity of Ace Breakers but, like the rest of the team, kept well concealed. Things began to happen quickly. News came through that Maitland was within about two miles of the breaker's yard. He didn't seem to realize he was being followed.

The Hertz van, too, was on its way and they now had a positive ID on Willie Pressburger. The Wiseman truck already stood in the middle of the yard. The Rolls was probably inside.

Maitland arrived and pulled up alongside the truck. He got out of the car and was greeted by another white male, which was presumed to be Ace Berridge. No section had any description of him and there were no recorded details against his name, not even a parking ticket.

'He sounds too good to be true, particularly in the game he's in,' Fink commented.

'Well, he's into something now, big time,' Younger snapped. The pressure was beginning to tell on him.

Younger then spelled out the next part of the operation. 'When the Hertz van is in the yard, we have got to give them a chance to start work on the car and get some of the drugs out of the chassis. I am hoping the DEA can get a better view of the operation. In fact, I think it's essential that someone gets into the yard and tries to tip us off when the operation is taking place . . . Janice, can your man get into the yard?'

Fink used her own phone to give some orders.

Younger continued his instructions: two teams were to cover the rear, fully armed with shotguns and automatic weapons;

others were sent to the sides while twenty officers were to take part in the frontal attack.

'When the van goes in, I'll give you the word and you take up positions. Any person leaving the yard before the attack starts must be stopped and taken out and away until it's over. I don't want anyone giving warning to those on the inside. I want to avoid shooting if possible. We want Maitland alive . . .' He was interrupted.

'The van's going in . . . it's in,' an officer yelled in the background.

'Can we see it? Anyone? Can anyone see it?' Younger was demanding.

Someone reported it was now parked behind Maitland's Cadillac.

'Take up your positions!' Younger instructed in full military fashion.

The team were fully primed and ready for action. For a few moments there was absolute silence.

'Where's the Rolls?' Younger demanded.

'It's just being brought out now, boss,' came the reply.

'Give me a running commentary!'

'The car is gradually coming down the slope. Maitland is in it driving. It's now off the truck. Hell! There's four men leaving . . . all getting into one car . . . the car's pulling out . . . they're heading for the entrance. I can't see them any more!'

'Let them get out of sight and take 'em out now,' Younger yelled.

The four men in an old Buick didn't know what hit them. The car was stopped, three seriously armed officers suddenly attacked the car, and within two minutes they were handcuffed and driven in their car out of the way.

'Well done, men!' Younger exalted.

The officer continued his running commentary: '. . . The truck is pulling out of the way. I think it might be coming out . . . Yes, it is.'

'Stop it out of sight and arrest him for the transportation of narcotics. Again no contact,' Younger repeated.

'The Rolls-Royce is on the move. They're taking it to what looks like a hydraulic ramp. We're OK, I can see everything. The Hertz is moving. It's parked up next to the ramp. The Rolls is in the air, but I can't see what's happening.'

'Try and get nearer!' Fink ordered.

The officer ordered up some wire cutters and cut his way in. Then on his stomach, he crawled through oil and filth to find a better place to see the car. He had to lie in a pool of almost solidified oil, which clung to everything that touched it. He was covered head to toe in thick black oil.

'I can see it again. The tall guy has got what appears to be a lance, but it's nothing like an acetylene burner. He's cutting at something under the car. It seems to be going very slowly and Maitland is getting very agitated. He's still working on it . . .'

The tension mounted. Their nerves were trembling. It was almost impossible for them to keep still.

Then Younger received the news they had been waiting for.

'I think he's finished. He's removing a piece of metal. He's pulling out brown packs. He's given one to Maitland. He's pulling out others . . .'

Suddenly there was silence, then dogs barking. Two shots. Silence again. The officer must have given his position away. Younger had to act quickly.

'Attack! Attack! Go get 'em lads!' Younger ordered.

Within seconds the well-planned operation came into action. Five cars screamed into the yard, four officers to each car. The entrance was blocked and so was every conceivable exit. Warning shots were fired and the loudspeaker, this time with Fink in control, gave the warning: 'Move a muscle and you're dead. We have one hundred officers and there is no escape. You are completely surrounded and we are heavily armed.'

There was no escape, but even so several of Berridge's employees took up arms against the police. They could see Maitland scurrying into the office area out of the way or trying to find a way out of the situation. Younger was now directing a fighting platoon, signalling to several officers to make their way round the back of the office, while several others were told to draw fire whilst he and Phil tried to break in from the front. 'Let me know when you have got into position,' he asked the group attacking the rear.

Younger received the signal.

'Heavy fire and break in,' he ordered.

The law-and-order mob far outweighed the employees of Ace, but the latter put up a hell of a fight. They knew the yard like the back of their hands; all the little gaps between the old cars and trucks awaiting demolition and the piles of old washing machines and refrigerators. They knew where they could crawl and hide, and for several minutes the law officers did not know how many they were dealing with. It was easy for Ace's men to shoot and move quickly to another vantage point.

Younger led from the front, as any good general would. He was only after one prize – Maitland. The latter was seen with Ace and his 'bodyguard' running away toward the office block. Younger was not put off; he and two others, ignoring the crossfire, simply charged across the yard and followed Maitland into the building.

They had managed to run up the stairs before Younger had entered, which made matters more difficult as they had to check the downstairs rooms before moving on. One by one they tried each door, bursting in with guns at the ready. They were now operating by pre-arranged signals and were operating in total silence. They moved toward the stairs, the front man leaning against the wall as he started up the stairway. Step by step he slowly made his way upwards followed by Younger and the other officer; all three pointing their firearms toward the next floor. There was a huge crack as the bodyguard fired at the leading man, but missed, the bullet ricocheting from wall to wall.

They did not return fire; they simply stood still, assessing the situation, before Younger signalled to advance further up. Again they moved and the front man could now see the next floor. There was no one there, but he could see a slightly open door. There was another loud crack and this time the officer was hit in the arm, momentarily falling backwards into the path of Younger. The bodyguard seized his chance and broke cover in his attempt to finish the two officers, but he had not anticipated the third man waiting for him. There was another loud crack as the bullet went straight through the heart of the bodyguard. He fell backwards, dead.

Once again there was silence. Younger told the injured officer to keep still – they would be back for him in a minute or two – and then went on to search for Maitland. Once again they used the same technique, searching each room, each cupboard, kicking open every door as they passed. To Younger's surprise, who should they find but both Ace and the king of drugs, Maitland, both sitting on the toilet.

'Well, well,' Younger said to Ace, half laughing? 'Is it catching?'

'What?' replied Ace.

'The shits! It would appear you and your friend have caught the same bug. It must have been something you ate.'

Maitland came out, trying to put a brave face on matters.

'What's all this about then?'

'You know very well!' Younger replied, 'You're under arrest.'

'You'll be sorry for this,' Maitland responded.

'I don't think so! Particularly when a jury sees what's in the packages you were handling.'

'What packages?'

'Don't waste my time. Put your arms behind your back. NOW!' Younger ordered.

Younger walked out of the office building with Maitland in handcuffs like a trophy. Younger called for a police van and Maitland was unceremoniously thrust into the back of it.

Chapter 25

David and Eleanor arrived at Manchester Airport looking relaxed and glad to be back in the UK. They were full of smiles as they walked along the arrivals gangway and even more so when they saw us waiting at the end. It was almost a year since they had last made this trip together in completely different circumstances.

'Hello, Robert,' he said, hugging me. 'It's good to see you again. I'm sorry, Francesca, that was very rude of me.'

'Don't worry! I suppose it's a man thing,' Francesca replied, as she went to kiss Eleanor.

'We can relax this time. No more adventures, eh?' I said, laughing. I noted a knowing look pass between David and Eleanor. Come on, I'll get you home.'

'Before we do or say anything else, I want to tell you that your car will arrive here on Thursday around three o'clock. She looks as good as ever,' David announced. I obviously didn't respond as enthusiastically as I should have done. 'Are you pleased?'

'Of course I am, but we're still very nervous.'

'There's no need to be. I'll tell you all about things when we are in the car,' David continued.

We left the airport with both of us itching to know the rest of the story; I really believed he was stalling to deliberately whet our appetite. 'Come on, cut to the chase!' I demanded using a phoney American accent.

David laughed and then began his story. It was as though we were sitting in the café at Grant & Bulldozer's all over again.

'I sent you a copy of the *New York Times* with a picture of Maitland stepping out of the police van in handcuffs. You got it of course?'

'Yes, we did.'

'That's when I got more involved. I had no feelings for the man whatsoever, even though he had been my friend. The things we were hearing before the trial, and then during it, made you utterly despise the man.

'Fink had kept her promise and the very moment Maitland was in handcuffs she phoned Sweeney and told him to be at New York Central Police Station in half an hour, with a photographer as she had a big surprise for him. Sweeney knew what it was; it was the moment he had been waiting for well over two years. He immediately phoned me and asked me to be there with him.

'I duly arrived and waited outside the station. It was dark but there was a element of excitement about the place, as several officers kept going in and out as if they were waiting for someone. Sweeney arrived, with Dave Shaw, the best photographer in the business, and I knew then we were in for a treat. Sweeney didn't say a word; he just waited in silence for over an hour until the cavalcade arrived: two police outriders, the first of five police cars, all blue lights flashing, and then the police van. Captain Younger and Janice Fink got out of one of the cars and they both went to the rear doors of the van. It could all have been stage-managed.

'They opened the door and told the person inside to step out. It was John Maitland, of course. He momentarily looked up before he stepped down the steps and that was the first photograph. Perhaps it was the flash of the camera which caused him to stumble as he stepped down, or was it because he unable to hold on as he was cuffed? Whichever it was, he fell on the floor and looked every bit the broken man.

"Don't feel sorry for him!" Sweeney yelled. "He's made more kids fall than any other person I know."

'This made Maitland look up again, hence the next photograph. But he then saw me and I know he was embarrassed because he never looked up again. He was taken into the station where he called for his lawyers and of course within thirty minutes Wendlesmit turned up with a couple of new faces I hadn't seen before.

'Sweeney went over to Janice took her head in both hands and kissed her on her forehead. She gave him the rough details of the arrest and told him to be at he office at nine o'clock the following day.

'Sweeney stopped everything at the paper and the Maitland story was plastered all over the front page: "Drugs Baron caught with Twenty Million Dollars worth of Cocaine". Sweeney made the most of it, as he only had thirty-six hours before the rest of the press and the other media would have the same story.

'Maitland was questioned for twenty-four hours before he was brought before a judge to apply for bail. The court was already packed before he arrived, so someone had not been discreet. He was well-dressed and clean but he looked anxious and . . . yes . . . scared.

'The assistant district attorney gave details of what Maitland stood accused of and objected strongly to bail. Then Wendlesmit gave his reasons why he should be granted his temporary freedom. Sweeney and I were lucky to have seats in the courtroom and heard Wendlesmit speak on Maitland's behalf. He was magnificent; there's no other word for it. He spoke about how his client's beautiful car had been used and abused by others. How the DEA have given it a clean bill of health when it left the States, and how his driver, who had now disappeared, had brought it back full of drugs. He didn't know anything about it until he had to drive it. It had seemed out of kilter so he took it to be checked. Did anyone think a person who had given so much to New York and its people would be involved in something like this, Wendlesmit asked rhetorically.

'It was a wonderful speech which, believe it or not, won applause at the end of it, much to the judge's annoyance. But I think the speech and the applause influenced him, and he granted bail for ten million dollars.

'There was shock and uproar in the court, which took Judge Parker a good five minutes to control. When the noise subsided, the assistant DA said he wished to appeal and at the same time, after being prompted by Fink, asked for the Rolls to be confiscated again. This was granted

'Wendlesmit however, had one point to argue. His client could not possibly afford the required ten million dollars. This, thank God, was rejected, although Wendlesmit told the judge he would appeal.

'We left the courtroom dazed: how on earth a man facing such charges could get bail was incomprehensible. We all knew within a few hours he would have put up the money and we were right. Within five hours, he was back on the streets. All the same, he wasn't smiling when he was taken from the court; we could all see he had a mountain to climb.

'We were all relieved the DEA were ready to present their case against him quickly and that they were able to fast-track it into the court. It was a shock for Maitland and his team, as they were expecting it would take a couple of years for the case against them to be presented, but the day of judgement arrived just five months after his arrest and Maitland found himself fighting for his freedom and the rest of his life.

'The courtroom was packed again and the judge, Winston Spencer Seymour, presiding was well respected in legal circles and a great disciplinarian. Wendlesmit, of course, was representing Maitland, who looked decidedly uncomfortable. The State was represented by none other than George Belshaw, the wily old district attorney, a formidable opponent.

'The State's first witness was Janice Fink. Her evidence was that the DEA had made a mistake in not taking the Rolls-Royce apart; if they had done so they would have found the drugs in the first place. She also explained how Maitland knew the drugs were still hidden in the car and in order to get the car back, he terrorized you and your family into selling the car back. She outlined everything that happened to you and all the people killed and injured as a result. How the Frenchman noticed something was wrong, how they X-rayed the car and saw a substance which they now knew was pure cocaine with a value of twenty-nine million dollars. Her evidence took three days to deliver and the cross-examination took two, but she was flawless in her presentations.

'Next to give evidence was Willie Pressburger, the body-shop man. Pressburger didn't care whether he lived or died and told a tragic tale that wracked the court. One of Maitland's men had got his thirteen-year-old daughter hooked on drugs. You know the usual promises given to young girls of love and riches; once they get them hooked they are into prostitution and that's just what happened. Willie was without doubt the best body repairer in the business and Maitland wanted him. His daughter was effectively kidnapped; she was actually living with a man at thirteen. Maitland promised she would come back as and when he did the work for him.

'Pressburger had lived for months in the hope she would be returned, but he found out on his arrest that she had been murdered several months before. He told the court how he himself had designed the place for the drugs and that it was undetectable unless you knew the car, which the Frenchman did. He was an honest man who had been totally used and abused by Maitland. On cross-examination he admitted he would like to see Maitland dead.

'The next witness was the biggest surprise to the court – it was Gerry Rider. He had made a statement to the police, but no one had expected him to turn up. He stood in the witness box and took the oath and not once did he take his eyes off Maitland. Belshaw began the questions and soon it was clear who he was and what he was doing and why.

' "Mr Rider, is it true you were offered witness protection?"

' "Yes," Gerry replied, looking directly at Maitland, who, however, was unable to look Gerry in the face.

' "Why did you not accept it?"

'Gerry then poured his heart out in court. He was almost in tears. "Why should I need protection from someone like that? If people want to kill me for standing for my only bit of family, then they will kill me, but I am not hiding in fear for the rest of my life." There were a few ripples of applause from the courtroom, which again Seymour soon put a stop to.

'Belshaw then got Gerry to outline what he had done on his trip to Europe and his importation of the car.

' "Did you know there were drugs in the car?"

' "Truthfully? No. The DEA had searched the car and even the boss wasn't sure. I had to take the car to Belgium and have it checked over and even then we didn't know. But in fairness we had a good idea they hadn't been found."

' "Did you know how much they were worth?" Belshaw asked.

' "No!"

' "When did you find out?"

' "When the NYPD told me. I was amazed."

' "What do you know about what happened, when the car was in England?"

'Gerry then outlined what he had overheard and what he had been told by Maitland and it painted a horrible picture of what Maitland and his enforcer had done with the help of the lawyer Morales.

' "You mentioned John Maitland had an enforcer. Tell the court about this man."

' "I can't say much as I was never allowed to meet him and I wasn't sure if he worked for Morales or John Maitland himself. What I can say is, I saw them together very often and I know he was sent to Europe to control the activities there. He had to keep his eyes on the car at all times and prevent it getting damaged."

' "Describe this man to the court."

' "He was a very tall man with dark hair, always wore a suit and shades and was very thin. He was ruthless. He manipulated various gangs to attack and terrorize the Englishman. People were

276

maimed and killed in his efforts to get the car back for Maitland. Even after the Englishman had agreed to sell, Maitland ordered him to put more pressure on to make sure he didn't back out. On one occasion I heard him say to Morales he had spent over three million dollars on this little adventure." He paused and added, "I believe it was just to make the man's life a misery."

'Judge Seymour stamped on that point! "What you believe is irrelevant," he said sternly. "Only what you *know* is acceptable. Strike any of those references from your minds," he instructed the jury.

'Gerry turned to the judge. "It isn't what I believe, Judge; it's what I know. That was how it happened. I could always sense his anger when he spoke about someone else having his car. He even considered having the family bumped off, but Morales told him it could hold the car up for years in legal argument."

'"I presume by 'bumped off' you mean killed?" Seymour interrupted.

'"Yes."

'"He then made sure no harm came to them just in case," Gerry continued. "But every week he would receive reports about what they had done to intimidate the family and he would brag about his successes. However, he became very angry when he found out they were hitting back and that people had been arrested."

'"You love your wife, don't you, Mr Rider?"

'"With all my heart. Nothing else matters."

'"No further questions!" Belshaw said loudly.

'It was now Wendlesmit's turn to ask the questions and cross-examine Gerry. He clearly relished the task.

'"Well, Mr Rider," he began, "You're a very lucky man, aren't you?"

'Gerry didn't answer.

'"Well, I will answer for you. You are the only one in this room who has a guarantee that he will not be prosecuted for his crimes. Is that right?"

' "I don't know if there are any more people."

' "Come on, Mr Rider, you know what I mean. You can say what you like, call your ex-employer a crook and get away with, can't you?"

'Gerry didn't answer again.

'Judge Seymour intervened: "You will have to answer some of the questions. Let's start now."

' "Judge, I can't say what I like, I can say he was disloyal to me, I can say he called my . . ."

'Seymour stopped him. "Just answer the questions properly . . . Jury, strike out what he has just said."

' "I have got immunity, but I will only tell the truth."

'Wendlesmit began in earnest. "Were you asked by your employer to collect the Rolls-Royce from France?"

' "No." There were loud surprised murmurings in the courtroom.

' "Who asked you?"

' "His lawyer, Morales, asked me to go."

' "Would it surprise you to know that John Maitland does not have a lawyer named Morales. Furthermore, there is no Federico Morales registered on the American Bar Association.'

'There were more surprised murmurings in the court, somewhat louder than before. Things were going better for Maitland. The star witness was crumbling.

'The judge silenced the court which allowed Gerry to answer. "Yes it would, because I have seen him with Mr Maitland for years."

' "Yes, of course you have seen him for years because he was seeing you. Isn't that the truth?"

' "No, it's rubbish," Gerry replied firmly.

'Belshaw called out, "May we approach the Bench?"

'Seymour signalled for the advocates to come forward. "What is it?"

' "If Mr Wendlesmit insists on asking about Morales, I would like to call an extra witness; a person who has met this man Morales, in New York, England and France, and who paid for the car by cashier's cheque."

'Wendlesmit turned away from the subject, but he had already put some doubt into the jury's mind. We could all see the way his case was being played. They were trying to pin everything on Gerry as he had immunity. If it hadn't been for Gerry fighting back and some extra evidence the DEA brought almost at the eleventh hour the case might have been lost.

'Wendlesmit started on Gerry again. "You admit you brought the drugs into the country from Europe."

' "No I don't. I wasn't sure what it was, but I knew it was important to him."

' "To whom?" Wendlesmit interrupted.

' "To him," Gerry replied, pointing to Maitland, before continuing. "He was like a cat on hot bricks before I went. He was desperate to get the car back. He even had photographs taken of the car and sent back to him. Hundreds of pictures were taken in England and all over Europe. Wherever the car went, someone took pictures. I've seen them, they're on his computer. He had pictures taken of the inside of the car and all the underneath. Why would he have photographs of the underneath . . ."

'Wendlesmit tried to interrupt and stop Gerry saying more, but couldn't; Gerry was in full flight.

'Gerry repeated himself: "Why would he have photographs of the underneath of the car if there wasn't something hidden there?"

'Again Wendlesmit tried to stop him and looked at the judge for support.

' "Just answer the question. Don't add other thoughts and remember you are not here to ask the questions," Seymour said.

'Wendlesmit repeated his initial question: "Did you know you were bringing drugs into the country?"

' "No I didn't. In any case, where would I get the money to

buy twenty million dollars' worth of drugs. I could only just afford to pay my wife's hospital bill."

'Wendlesmit had him or so he thought. "Now that's a lie, isn't it, Mr Rider? An out-and-out lie! We know from the records that the DEA put your wife in the clinic as part of the deal, to get John Maitland.' There was uproar in the court. You could now feel the court was on Maitland's side.

'Wendlesmit turned to Gerry and said loudly, "Go on now admit it you lied in court."

' "No, I didn't!" he replied.

' "Didn't what?" Wendlesmit asked, looking at the jury.

' "Lie," Gerry replied.

'Wendlesmit looked puzzled and then shocked as Gerry continued. "I accepted immunity for the sake of my wife, but I wouldn't accept anything else. I wouldn't allow the DEA to hide me and I certainly wouldn't let them pay for my hotel. I, and I alone, will pay for my wife's health bill. I have the receipt here . . . He felt in his pocket, took out his wallet and handed the receipt to the judge. "I have said all along: Mr Maitland was totally disloyal to me and there was no reason in the world to pull a gun on a person who has given years of good service. Other than that I would have willingly gone to prison with him."

'Gerry looked to the back of the court where Aprilla was sitting. She smiled. She was there to give him one hundred and ten per cent support. I even detected a little smile from him.

'There was pandemonium in the courtroom. Seymour had to stop proceedings and retire until the hubbub died down. Maitland was shamefaced and he knew he was done for. The final nail in the coffin came when the district attorney called another DEA witness.

'David Murphy had worked for the DEA for a number of years. You remember me telling you about the chap who crawled through all the oil, when they raided Ace Breakers?' David asked.

'Yes I remember,' I replied.

'Well, he had been trying to take pictures with a small digital camera, but it got severely damaged in the mud and oil. Believe it or not, though, he had the presence of mind to take one with his phone. Only one was possible because he was soon fending off the dogs, but one was enough: it showed Maitland holding one of the bags taken out of the car. The best was yet to come. He was wearing surgical gloves. Why would anyone wear surgical gloves if he had nothing to hide?

'Belshaw couldn't wait to get Maitland in the box, but he had to wait a few days as Wendlesmit was taken ill and the trial was adjourned for a week. We all thought it was convenient, especially as he came back with renewed vigour.

'Sweeney, too, was now like a cat on hot bricks. He felt the end of the "Drug Baron" as he now called him, was near.

'Maitland took the stand. He was like General Custer fighting to the end with nowhere to go.

'"Mr Maitland," Wendlesmit said, "I want to deal with the last point made by David Murphy first, just to clear the matter up while it's fresh in the jury's mind. You remember the point: when the prosecution were concerned about you wearing surgical gloves and holding a brown package. Why would you do that? Was it to hide your fingerprints, as they implied?"

'"No, of course not!" Maitland replied. "They were not surgical gloves either. I got them free when I filled up with gasoline at the Star Station; I have another pair here."

'There was hubbub again in the court until the gavel of the judge calmed things down again. It was a real piece of theatre.

'"Why did you use them?"

'"It's obvious. You heard what the man from the DEA said. It was filthy with oil everywhere."

'Sweeney leaned over to me and whispered, "The bastard! He might get away with it yet."

'"What about the brown-paper parcel? Why were you holding it?"

'"I knew I had a problem with the balance of the car. It had been damaged in France by the previous owner. The driver's window got broken. The balance of the car seemed to be upset. That's why I couldn't drive it properly. A picture of me having problems with the car appeared in all the newspapers."

' "He's a clever little bastard!" Sweeney whispered angrily.

' "I couldn't take my car to the normal garage because I had a dispute over the last work they did for me and I hadn't paid them. I asked a friend to look at it for me, which he did, and of course you know the rest. He found there was a false bottom on the car and we all found packages hidden there."

' "This friend, was it Willie Pressburger?"

' "Yes. I did promise to try and help to get his daughter back. I asked one of my charities dedicated to helping kids in trouble to search for her. Sadly to no avail. I would add I have given this charity eight million dollars over the last fifteen years to help them."

' "I wanna be sick!" Sweeney said loudly enough for the judge to hear.

' "If the gentleman is feeling unwell, he should leave the court. Otherwise he should be silent," Judge Seymour said angrily, looking directly at us.

' "What was your intention when you found the drugs?" Wendlesmit asked, prompting another sickly reply.

' "Look, I could say anything. I didn't have the chance to do anything. We were charged by the DEA. There was confusion everywhere. Several of the workforce retaliated, as we all simply thought we were being robbed. There was obviously a lot of money in the office; it's normal for that type of business." Maitland's confidence was returning.

'Sweeney grunted.

' "I shan't warn you again!" the judge said directly to Sweeney.

' "How long have you owned the car?" Wendlesmit asked.

' "A long time. I can't remember exactly when I bought it."

' "So you would know all about the car?"

' "Of course!"

' "How do you explain the false bottom on the car?"

' "How can I? The DEA took the car off me. I think it was unfair, but they sold it at auction and there was nothing I could do about it. There was nothing on the car when it left them. They searched it thoroughly, no doubt using all the modern techniques at their disposal, and didn't find anything. So how would anyone expect to be more knowledgeable than a major scientific department of the United States? I didn't see it again until it came back to me. I bought the car back from a dealer in Mexico; my lawyer has the receipt. I had heard on the grapevine it had been bought from the Englishman."

'We were now in the fourth week of the trial and the probable verdict was now running very much in favour of the defendant. The judge called time at the end of the last answer and adjourned for lunch. Maitland stepped down more confident than ever and walked out of court as though he had already won, smiling at reporters and waving to imaginary supporters.

'Sweeney and I met up with Fink to drown our sorrows. We walked over to our normal little restaurant and began by ordering a couple of bottles of wine which were soon downed in an effort to curb a growing depression brought on by the thought of Maitland getting off.

' "He's a clever bastard!" Sweeney commented. "You would have thought with all the photographs he's supposed to have had taken, something would have shown up." He paused for a moment. "Janice, what did you think of all the pictures Rider mentioned?" Janice looked puzzled. "You haven't seen them, have you?"

' "No, why?"

' "Why? Isn't it obvious?" Sweeney asked a little sarcastically. "They may have shown pictures of the car in specific places. They may identify the false bottom ... anything! They may show various people who have been involved. If you can prove he knew about the false chassis when it was in Europe it would make a difference."

' "It certainly would," Fink replied. She was silent for a few moments, thinking out the problem, leaving Sweeney and me just looking at each other.

' "Did you take pictures when you searched the car on the first occasion?" Sweeney asked. Fink, however, was still lost in thought.

' "I've got it!" she suddenly remarked and picked up the phone to ring Younger. He was unavailable.

' "Get hold of him now! Tell him it's Janice Fink and I want to talk urgently. I don't care where he is, just get him. Now!"

'Five minutes later the phone rang with Captain Younger on the other end. She told him how badly the case was going, then added, "We need to lift his computer quickly; it may help us. How soon could you get a warrant to search the place and get hold of it?"

'Younger agreed to do his best.

'The questions and answers went on for another day, before Belshaw was to begin his cross-examination, and it was then we all had our first bit of luck. Maitland did not go home at the end of the day. There was no need to as Amelia had moved out whilst the trial was on and he had stayed in town at a local hotel befitting his position. He had no idea Younger had been successful in obtaining a warrant and no idea that his computers had been taken.

'Belcher started taking Maitland's evidence apart bit by bit, but Maitland seemed to be on the up, countering every line of questioning. Then, suddenly, a chink began to appear in his armour.

' "Mr Maitland, Gerry Rider claimed you had photographs taken of the car throughout its time in Europe and that they're on your computer. Is that true?"

'Maitland paused for a moment, which caused Belshaw to step in.

' "Come on, we are waiting. You shouldn't need time to think."

'There was no doubt he was caught on the hop. Eventually he

said, "Every person in the household uses my computer. Gerry Rider did and so did I, but I honestly can't remember what's on it."

'This caused an outburst from Gerry at the back. "I don't even know how to use a computer," he shouted, to which the judge riposted, "Mr Rider! If you make another comment like that I will have you locked up and I personally will throw the key away. Jury, you must put that comment by Mr Rider out of your minds as it has not been proved or disproved."

'Belshaw wanted to keep Maitland on the run. "I would like to see that computer of yours."

'Maitland shrugged.

' "You would have no objections then?"

'Maitland looked to his lawyer for guidance, but Wendlesmit, too, looked a little confused.

' "Good I'm pleased about that because the New York Police Department have successfully sought a warrant to seize the computer . . ."

'Wendlesmit was on his feet again. "I object. May we approach the Bench?"

'The judge nodded and invited him to approach him. "What is it, Mr Wendlesmit?" he asked.

' "This is totally out of order. We have had no prior warning that this evidence would be used and no time to consider it."

' "Mr Belshaw?" the judge said, inviting him to respond.

' "I haven't asked for it to be included. All I said was that a warrant had been applied for and the computer had been seized. Judge, the mention of Mr Maitland's computer came up when Mr Wendlesmit was cross-examining Gerry Rider's evidence. There was ample opportunity to refute what was said and he didn't. He brought it up, not me," Belshaw said firmly.

' "Mr Wendlesmit?"

' "If it is to be used, we would like to see the evidence before it is presented."

' "That is your right," the judge responded.

It was almost four o'clock and the judge decided he had had enough and ended the last session of the day.

'That night, at two o'clock in the morning, the phone rang. I told Eleanor I wasn't going to answer it, but it rang and rang, giving me no alternative. I picked up the phone somewhat angrily, but before I could answer I heard the voice of Sweeney shouting down the phone.

' "David, David. There's a car waiting outside. Get here as quick as you can. I've got a surprise for you, or I should say, Janice has."

'I arrived at the office at almost three o'clock. It was an ungodly hour. The night patrol let me in and gave me a warning. "The boss must be on something; he's dancing round like a young virgin."

'I went up to the office. He and Janice Fink were drinking champagne . . . *at three o'clock in the morning.*

' "Come and look at these!" Sweeney shouted. "It will make your day, or should I say night?"

' "It better be good, to get me away from a warm bed and a good wife," I said.

'I started looking at the pictures. They were taken all over the place. Remember Kelmarsh?' David asked me.

'Yes, of course,' I replied, 'How could I ever forget?'

I was somewhat tired and hungry at this point. Although the story had been fascinating, the driving and hunger were beginning to take their toll, so I suggested we stop at the services for a drink and something to eat. I duly stopped at the first available.

I pulled off the road into the Little Chef at Rawtenstall. 'You can finish the story inside the café,' I continued, anxious for David to carry on. We were shown to our table, but before we could sit down, I almost shouted, 'Come on, what happened next?' I was like some small child being read to at bedtime, wanting to know the end before he went to sleep.

'Where was I?' David asked.

'You were looking at the photographs on the computer,' I replied.

'Oh yes! They had wonderful pictures of the car winning the Kelmarsh Rally; none of mine of course. Then everywhere you went you were followed. There were pictures of your house, your drive, your dogs, your house in France, all over. Well, one of the pictures . . .' he hesitated, glancing at his wife and Francesca.

'Remember you told me how you were attacked in Blackpool and that you nearly crashed the car.'

I nodded. How could we forget.

'You remember, too, what happened after that?' David asked. He didn't wait for a reply. 'You received someone's hand through the post, didn't you?'

Francesca became upset. 'Stop it, please. It was terrible.'

'Well, that poor kid is on the computer with his hand on and his hand off. It made me absolutely sick. He was involved with that as well.'

'You remember the attack during the Beaujolais race?'

'Very much so. We'll never forget it,' I replied.

'And you will no doubt remember the young motorcyclist who nearly cut his throat on your side window?'

'Yes, of course I do.'

'Well, there's a picture of him lying in his hospital bed with his throat cut.'

'Oh my God, I don't believe this. It's just terrifying that things like this can go on,' Francesca said sadly.

'It was a warning to all those involved: what would happen to them if they damaged the car or took things into their own hands. He seemed to have photographs of everyone who had been involved . . .'

We were fortunately interrupted by the waitress, who came to take our order, though by this time my appetite had almost vanished because of what I had heard.

'Keep going! We're getting to the interesting bit,' I urged.

David continued. 'I didn't go back home that night in Sweeney's office. I was too excited. We were desperate to return to court and face Maitland with what we had found, so I stayed at work and fell asleep in Sweeney's chair only to be woken up by the normal hustle and bustle of the office at eight o'clock.

'We arrived at the court early. Fink had already briefed the district attorney on the new discoveries and he was as anxious to start as we were. There was a real buzz in the court. Maitland was still looking confident, but I saw his expression turn to concern when he saw all the prosecution team smiling. Belshaw made the most of it.

'"Can we approach the Bench?"

'Seymour nodded.

'"I have a big problem," Belshaw said, opening the discussion. "I think it better if we discuss the matter in your office."

'"Are you aware of what's to be discussed, Mr Wendlesmit?"

'"No I am not, but if the district attorney thinks it's important, then who am I to argue?"

'Two hours later the court returned to session, with Maitland still on the stand and Belshaw in full flight. Maitland looked strained. Belshaw piled on the questions regarding the pictures, but each answer was basically the same: it was all down to Gerry Rider; he knew nothing. Belshaw began to put the pressure on and play the jury.

'"Mr Maitland, three of those pictures show a young man first with his right hand on, then with his hand cut off. The next one shows the hand in a box ready for posting to Mr Conway, the Englishman who bought the car."

'Pandemonium broke out in the courtroom. Judge Seymour temporary lost control and called in the court police to help restore order.

'Belshaw made his point again. This time you could hear a pin drop; no one seemed to be breathing. Maitland reiterated what he had said earlier: everyone used his computer; he believed Rider was responsible for the photographs.

' "I suppose this was done by Mr Rider as well?" Belshaw said, holding up another picture. "Look at this poor boy with his throat cut in hospital."

'There was uproar again, with Seymour banging his gavel as hard as he could to maintain order. He shouted over the noise. "The district attorney knows better than that. I will not have my courtroom turned into a circus. Silence, silence or I will abandon proceedings for the day."

'The questioning went on for hour after hour and you could see Maitland was bothered by the cross-examination, but he was still evasive and I must say he stood the pressure very well.

' "Now I want to start looking at another little problem I have," Belshaw said. "It's quite clear that there are many photographs of the car showing the underneath. Furthermore, looking at the dates of the photographs, there's one that is especially interesting. It was taken just one week after the car arrived in England, when it would have been impossible to have fitted a false chassis on a vintage Rolls-Royce in that time. Wouldn't you agree, Mr Maitland?"

' "I'm not an engineer, I couldn't say."

' "Would you then accept a statement from one engineer we consulted who said that it would take at least two to three weeks to fix it?"

'Wendlesmit jumped to his feet. "Objection! I don't see where this line of questioning is getting us and I can't possibly let my client accept such a statement. We could produce a statement stating it could be done in two days, or even one, if we wanted."

' "I agree," Seymour said. "Sustained. The district attorney should make every effort to get to the point quickly."

' "I'm coming to the point, your Honour. It will only take a minute or so."

' "I hope so," Seymour commented.

' "Do you agree it would take about two weeks?" he repeated, returning to Maitland.

' "No, I don't. I'm not an engineer," Maitland repeated.

' "Good. In view of this, would you say you were an ordinary man in the street and you would be able to make comparisons as an ordinary man would?"

' "I suppose so," Maitland answered warily.

' "Now, I want to give you a little test," Belshaw said, handing him four photographs. "Take a good look, as much time as you want, and then I want you to spot the difference."

'Maitland studied the pictures, or at least pretended to.

' "Well?" Belshaw asked. "Tell me if you can see any differences?"

' "Nothing!" Maitland replied.

' "Note that, members of the jury; the defendant could see no difference. Would Mr Wendlesmit or the judge like to see if they could see any difference?"

' "Objection!" Wendlesmit roared.

' "Over-ruled. But I will point out to the district attorney that this sort of theatrical nonsense will not be tolerated and that neither I nor Mr Wendlesmitt can give any evidence to support either side. He should know better."

' "Mr Maitland," Belshaw continued, "you have already said you owned the car for several years before it was confiscated and it was your pride and joy, didn't you?"

' "Yes"

' "The photographs you have just seen were all taken at different times. The first by the DEA before the car was confiscated; the second was found on your computer, and was taken whilst the car was in Europe; the third by the British Army before they began the scientific examination of the car and the last by the French police whilst the car was in France under constant surveillance. Of course, we have many others all showing the same thing but these clearly show there has been no alteration to the car since it was in your possession.

' "In view of this, I would like you to explain to the court how, having owned the car for that length of time, you could not have noticed what you claim to have been large alterations. Let us be honest for one moment: you yourself had them built into the car to conceal drugs. It couldn't have been Gerry Rider, could it? You would have known as it would have taken weeks to fit them, wouldn't it? Are we lost for words, Mr Maitland?" Belshaw asked.

'Belshaw continued, now almost shouting at the jury. "I will repeat: these photographs prove conclusively that the false chassis and the false battery box were on your car when it was in your possession. And I repeat: you also said in your evidence that you had owned the car for a long time. Then if what you say is true, Mr Maitland, this false chassis and this false battery box and the secret place behind the passengers' seats must have been on the car for a long time without you knowing and you so fanatical about Rolls-Royce cars!"

'There were loud murmurings in the court; the onlookers were beginning to sense another change in the way the case was going. It took a minute or two before Maitland could answer.

'"How many times do I have to tell you?" Maitland shouted back, beginning to lose his cool. "It fooled the DEA with all their fancy technology; how would you expect me to find it with just my eyes? I don't go grovelling under cars, I get a mechanic to do it for me."

'"Are you aware that there is a new scientific test that can prove conclusively when certain welding work was last undertaken?"

'"No!" Maitland replied.

'"Well, there is and I put it to you, that you were without doubt the owner of the Rolls-Royce when the work was undertaken."

'Maitland remained silent.

'"You will admit, of course, that you now know that there were false compartments in the car and that twenty-seven million dollars' worth of drugs was found."

' "Yes, I now know that."

' "Then, as the photographs show conclusively that the car had not been altered for several months, in fact since you owned the car, then the drugs must have been there when the car was in your ownership."

' "If you say so," Maitland said, shuffling uncomfortably in the box.

' "The important point is, Mr Maitland, the twenty-seven million dollars' worth of drugs were hidden in your car when *you* were the owner."

The murmurings in court were becoming louder and louder, as Belshaw increasingly gained the upper hand.

' "I'm now coming to the end, the court will be pleased to hear, but I just have a few minor questions I need to clear up. You stated on oath, Mr Maitland, that you believed Gerry Rider was probably responsible for these crimes."

'Maitland interrupted: "The more I hear, the more I am convinced."

' "Well, we'll see. Let us for one moment assume that Rider *is* responsible and that, however inconceivable we think it may be, you lent him the car for three weeks, sometime during your ownership of the car to have the false chassis, the false battery box and the false back seat support fitted . . ." He was stopped mid-sentence.

' "Objection, objection! He's not giving my client the opportunity to answer the questions. He's simply listing facts," Wendlesmit shouted.

' "Sustained! The district attorney knows better than that. The jury will erase this from their minds."

' "Too late!" Sweeney whispered. "They've heard it. The wily old bird!"

' "I'm glad you call them facts, Mr Wendlesmitt." Wendlesmitt blushed with embarrassment for the little slip he'd made.

' "Now we're back to Gerry Rider being the crook. You believe that whilst the car was in your ownership, Gerry Rider borrowed

292

it and had the false chassis fitted, a false battery box and a false seat support. You also believe that he did all these things from your office in your house and you didn't know about it. You also believe that Gerry may have kept all these pictures on your computer?"

' "I said he *may* have. I said many people use the computer," Maitland interrupted, becoming a little unsure of himself.

' "But you believe it may have been him?"

' "Yes."

' "I'm a bit of an amateur when it comes to computers, a bit old-fashioned, probably like some of the jurors, so would you explain? Do they have to be put on the computer manually or via the Internet?"

' "Either."

' "I see. So if it was Gerry Rider, how do you explain the date and the time of the last group of photographs? Mr Rider couldn't have put these onto the computer; it was the same day he returned from collecting the car."

' "He did it when he returned. I certainly remember him coming home," Maitland replied.

' "Yes, you're right, but when these were loaded onto your computer, Mr Rider was on the plane. His wife was too ill; she couldn't have done it. This leaves you and your wife. Are you going to blame Mrs Maitland next? No further questions," Belshaw yelled over the crescendo of noise.

'The district attorney had done a fantastic job and convinced both Sweeney and me that Maitland would be convicted, but the way this trial had ebbed and flowed, nothing was certain any more. After all the trial still wasn't over and over the next few days we heard a series of character witnesses on the stand praising what Maitland had done for the community and the amount of money he poured into charity. In fairness, all this impressed me, until you thought about where all the money came from. But what impressed me most of all was the way Belshaw crucified each witness with a couple of simple questions.

' "Well, Mr or Mrs Witness," he'd say, "Would you be a character witness for a convicted drug dealer?" The answer was always "No of course not." "Then why," Belshaw would counter, "are you standing for John Maitland, a convicted drug dealer." They were all devastated by the question and had nothing to say for themselves.

'Belshaw's summing up was equally as good; he never referred to a single note or document; he simply said what he had to say from the heart and looked at the jury all the time.'

Chapter 26

'The jury had been out for almost five days when we were all summoned back to the court as the verdict was to be given in thirty minutes. When we arrived the whole world seemed to be either in court or outside it. You could have heard a pin drop as the judge ordered the jury to take their seats. The air of expectation was almost overpowering. Maitland stood erect and unflinching, as if he was in no way contemplating defeat. Quite frankly, we ourselves were still unsure of the verdict.

'Judge Seymour addressed the foreman: "Have you reached your verdict?"

'All eyes turned to the foreman, who swallowed, his Adam's apple sticking out as though he was finding it difficult to breathe. We all waited, unable to take our eyes off him.

' "Yessss," he stuttered.

' "To the charge of the illegal importation of narcotics, do you find him guilty or not guilty?" Seymour asked.

'Still the silence, no one blinked; everyone was staring at the foreman. It seemed he had been struck dumb; the words would not come out and then suddenly –

' "Guilty!"

'The court was split between cheers of relief and cries of dismay. Maitland, in total shock, had fallen backwards and was slumped in his chair. He pushed Wendlesmitt away from him, arms flailing wildly.

'Judge Seymour hammered the gavel on to the bench and

shouted for silence. It took about ten minutes for the police and the ushers to regain control. The court had almost to be cleared before the sentence could be announced and the various applications made.

'Wendlesmitt and his junior assisted Maitland to his feet.

'Seymour pulled no punches. "You have been found guilty of illegally importing narcotics into the USA and in doing so you betrayed your friends and colleagues and used your charities to cover your tracks to hide the grubby little trade you ply. Your actions will have caused misery to thousands of people and their families as they became immersed into the addiction which you facilitated . . ."

'Seymour was interrupted as Wendlesmitt, no longer able to support his client's weight, allowed Maitland to slump back into his chair. He shrugged at the judge, not knowing what to do, but Seymour simply signalled to him to leave Maitland where he was.

' "You were without doubt the boss of the business and we have heard of the many people who have fallen foul of you. Whilst there is no proof of your direct involvement with their deaths, there is proof that you knew what was going on. Your intimidation of the Conway family in England, who innocently bought your car at auction, not knowing of its contents, was particularly cruel. All the good works you have done do not come near to paying for the damage you have done to the lives of the children you purport to help. That in my opinion was a sham to conceal your shame."

'Seymour paused and poured himself a drink of water. Once again the court was wrapped in silence. Every drop of water falling into the glass sounded like a waterfall cascading; every swallow like the last water leaving the bath.

'He began again. "There is no alternative but to give you an exemplary sentence and I order that you serve at least twenty years in the state penitentiary of which ten should be hard labour. Furthermore, I recommend that the police should carry out

296

further investigations into the deaths that have occurred during this terrible case."

'Seymour paused to allow the sentence to sink in and then continued in the same vein. "There have been other people involved in these matters, one of whom is the lawyer Federico Morales. I feel he should be called to explain his involvement and therefore I am issuing a Bench Warrant for his arrest, so that he may be brought before me."

'Maitland was still slumped in his chair, seemingly unaware of what had been said about him and the sentence he had received. Two police officers came over to take him away. He was hand-cuffed, lifted to his feet, and almost dragged across the floor. I felt terrible and I could see Wendlesmitt was visibly upset at his client's demeanour. The proud confident man had disappeared and the last thing I ever saw of him was the soles of his shoes as he was hauled out of court.

'Sweeney had no such feelings. He was glad to see the back of him and was disappointed he only got twenty years.'

I made a meal of it in the papers over the next few days: claiming the *Times* had brought a drug baron to justice and insisted that the police carry out the investigations into the death of Ed and the others, implying that they would not rest until the culprits were caught.

'I had permission to take the Rolls on your behalf from Fink, and I know you are angry about my having it repaired, but honestly, I have made a great deal of money out of this and if you hadn't agreed to sell the car back I would not have done. Therefore it was the least I could do. I have a book coming out as and when the appeal has been heard and I know advance sales are not bad.'

'What's it about?' I asked

'Obvious really, it's about a vintage Rolls-Royce used for smuggling drugs and, before you ask, it's called something like 'II PY – The Phantom Drug Trafficker' and it's about all the events that have happened, with you and your family as characters.

That's why I felt I would like to restore the car for you. I took photographs of the false bit coming off and got rid of them quickly, too many bad memories. But at least it's now back to the original. Sweeney wanted to take pictures of the before and after, to record a closure to the story, so if you want copies I'll get him to send them to you.'

'Who did it for you? Willie Pressburger?'

David laughed. 'No I took all the bits off myself and then had a restorer look at it,' he replied, with an occasional knowing look at Eleanor. 'You will be pleased to know that we are all sure you will never have another problem with drugs – before it left the country and after I had finished the repairs, the DEA did a full laser search just to make sure. It has a clean bill of health, as you would say.'

'It was very good of you to repair the car, but not necessary. I don't really think we wanted the car back, I know Francesca didn't; but no one looks a gift horse in the mouth like that, do they?' I replied. 'Perhaps when we see her again we might feel differently about things. Now come on, don't keep us in suspense any longer; what did he get?' I asked impatiently.

'This is not the happiest bit of the story,' said David. 'The judge deferred his sentence for one month, to enable him to get each and every body to give him support, which amazingly they did. I suppose he called in a few favours. As a result he got fifteen years.'

'Good God, that's a lifetime for him. He may not see the light of day again,' I remarked.

'Don't feel like that; think of the lives he and his gang have ruined. Think of Willie Pressburger and of what happened to his daughter. Think of the boy who had his hand cut off and think of the nine months of torture you had because of him. Think of the people he had murdered or who lost their lives in his service – and then there were my friends who he had killed. He should have got twenty five years of hard labour. Not fifteen,' David said angrily.

298

'Yes, I forgot there was Ed.'

'Well, to make it worse, he is out on bail pending an appeal hearing and it is likely his sentence will be reduced. He hasn't appealed against the confiscation of II PY, so he will never be back to get the car. Anyway he was going to scrap it when the drugs had been taken out, so there was not a trace of it left. That's how much he really loved that car. It was all lies.'

'How did Amelia take it?' Francesca asked.

'We still keep in touch,' said Eleanor. 'In fact, when we get back to the States we have arranged to go and visit her. She is a very wealthy woman now; her father died and left billions and she is the only one. She was very sad at what happened, quite naturally, and didn't want to stay around to see all her dirty linen washed in public. She's moved to Hawaii, to a beautiful place, and she can run all her affairs out there. She's not selling the house at the moment; half of it is John's anyway. I think she'll divorce him, but then, who knows.'

'What about Gerry and Aprilla? I presume they honoured his immunity from prosecution?'

'Oh yes, they did, he kept his word and didn't demand anything from the state and went to work for a former employer. They are both very content; Aprilla acts as housekeeper, Gerry the chauffeur and gardener.'

David stayed with us for just one week, long enough to receive II PY at the airport and to deliver it back to us. She was as beautiful as ever as she drove out of the airport gates into a waiting crowd which Clive and the *Mail* had whipped up. He had already printed the full exposé of Maitland and the car and this was just a follow-up to draw a line under the story. We signed autographs for various people, God only knows why; we were only known because of the car.

I drove it home, accompanied by Francesca, David and Eleanor, to be greeted by another little reception party, and that was the last time anyone bothered about the car.

It wasn't the end of the story however. One day, some time after David and Eleanor had returned to the States, we received a parcel via DHL posted in France. It was from a Roger Parent, rue de Grande Turenne in Paris. Its contents were listed as six DVDs of vintage cars. We opened the parcel with a great deal of curiosity as we did not know anyone of that name. We opened the outer brown paper and found further wrappings; one was none other than the *New York Times*, with the picture of the arrested Maitland getting out of the back of the police van. In the middle of the parcel we found six hollowed-out DVDs which concealed a large quantity of diamonds, with a value we later found out of over one hundred and fifty thousand pounds. There was a note with it, unsigned and simply stating: 'What diamonds? I don't know anything about diamonds.'

I telephoned David immediately and told him what we had received. Of course he knew nothing of it, but suggested it was probably a gift from someone who was grateful that Maitland had been brought down and that I should sell them as and when I needed cash. We put them in a safe deposit box at the bank and forgot about them, until one day, several months after the trial and sentence of Maitland, we had been shopping in nearby Leeds.

We returned home to find the dogs had been drugged and we could see II PY had been taken out of the garage on its trailer and almost smashed to pieces. I immediately telephoned the police, but was told they had already been called by our neighbour, Brian Uttley, and were on the way. I ran down the path into a war zone and saw the car had fallen off the trailer; I stood looking at it in shocked silence, unable to move. Every panel and window seemed to have been damaged; the sledgehammers, which were the tools of their trade, were lying on the floor with the exception of one which had been thrown through the window. I walked slowly round the side of the car and to my horror I saw Brian lying severely injured on the floor – he had been shot. There was also a man lying trapped under the back wheels of the car; his chest had been crushed and he was barely alive. I telephoned 999 again and called for an ambulance and the fire brigade, but now I could hear the sirens of the police vehicles approaching at speed.

Francesca phoned the boys and she and I tried to keep both injured, unconscious men warm until the ambulance arrived. The shock of what I was seeing was made worse when I took a longer look at the other man. It was the tall thin man; I could not believe my eyes.

The police too were shocked at the injuries and devastation and immediately cordoned off our road, house, garden and the railway yard which abuts our land. It looked as though the men had been disturbed by Brian and made their way out that way. The fire service arrived within a couple of minutes and quickly released the man under the car. He was rushed into the ambulance, but we all got the impression he would not survive and in fact he learned later that he died on the way to hospital. Brian was taken straight into intensive care as he had lost a lot of blood.

Inspector Walker was put in charge of the investigation, so at least we were kept informed of progress. I told him that we had seen the tall thin man on several occasions before the trial and that he had been present when we actually bought the car.

Walker informed us that they found a gun in his hand and it looked likely it was the one which had been used to shoot Uttley.

'I didn't see a gun when I covered him up,' I remarked.

'It was there. When the car fell on him, his body twisted and it was hidden under him. It was as though the car had taken its revenge on him,' Walker continued.

'It would appear they could not inflict much damage on the car while it was in the garage; there was not enough room, so they pushed it out on the trailer. The hand brake was not applied on the Rolls and they must have smashed the winch on the trailer, releasing the car. The tall thin man you describe is believed to be a professional – an enforcer, if you like. The gun he was carrying was fitted with a silencer, which is always the mark of an experienced villain. We will be following up some leads in the

States, but I think we know who the others were and therefore it shouldn't be long before we have them in custody. In the meantime let me know if you can think of anything else and I will keep you informed.'

Clive made the most of it, with photographs before and after and a storyline that befitted the circumstances, but it was the end. Strangely enough, neither Francesca nor I felt any sadness. We knew something like this would happen and we knew it would be the end of the troubles when it did. We put it down to Maitland's final act. But II PY had had the last laugh, she had finished Maitland and the enforcer was dead.

'At least we have something to spend the diamonds on now,' Francesca said cheerfully.

'Not on this car,' I replied with relief as we watched Glengarry Motors load the car onto their lorry to be sold for restorration. At least it was fitting that II PY should go to one of the best for the work, but it would not be for us.